"COME."

He pulled her to her feet. For a moment, his close proximity overwhelmed her. She looked up at his mouth, into his eyes— and then at his other hand holding a sprig of heather between them. Her heart boomed in her ears, and her kneecaps tingled. He'd told her he'd never picked heather for anyone.

No one had ever picked a flower for her.

She smiled, accepting his offering. He leaned in, as if he meant to kiss her mouth. She wasn't sure she would stop him if he did. He brushed his lips over the side of her jaw, softly, sweetly, making her toes curl in his spread-out plaid. She wouldn't stop him, she told herself as his hair fell across her face like scattering wings.

He didn't kiss her but withdrew with a sensual crook of his mouth. "Careful aboot lettin' me have my way, lass," he said on a husky whisper. "I might begin to think ye like me."

talent for providing the unexpected. This tale of revenge and redemption is sensual and poignant, powerful and meaningful. The nonstop action propels the plot as much as the twists and turns. Highland romance readers rejoice!"

—*RT Book Reviews*

"Top Pick. Ms. Quinn weaves a powerful story of redemption, responsibility, betrayal, and finally love between Temperance and Cailean."

—NightOwlReviews.com

The Taming of Malcolm Grant

"The gradual development of romance between the hard-hearted fighter and the resilient healer illuminates the fast-paced story."

—*Publishers Weekly*

"4 stars! Quinn and her Highlanders are a perfect match, and Malcolm Grant is the ideal Scotsman for a tale that's humorous, poignant, and highly romantic. Quinn understands and motivates her characters carefully. She delves into their deepest thoughts and makes readers truly care about their lives."

—*RT Book Reviews*

The Scandalous Secret of Abigail MacGregor

"4½ stars! With its quick-moving plot, engaging characters, and historic backdrop, the latest installment of The MacGregors: Highland Heirs is a page-turner. Quinn twists and turns the tale, drawing readers in and holding them with her unforgettable characters' love story."

—RT Book Reviews

"A wonderful book...Paula Quinn has raised the bar even higher with this newest novel in the MacGregor saga."

—NightOwlReviews.com

"I loved the enemy turned lovers theme that this story follows...the drama never stops!"

—HistoricalRomanceLover.blogspot.com

The Wicked Ways of Alexander Kidd

"Paula Quinn has done it again!...If there ever was a book that deserved more than five stars then this one is it. I was absolutely captivated from start to finish."

—NightOwlReviews.com

"The Scottish highlands and a pirate ship provide the colorful setting for this well-written, exciting, and action-packed romance."

—RT Book Reviews

"Vivid...Quinn's steamy and well-constructed romance will appeal to fans and newcomers alike."

—Publishers Weekly

The Seduction of Miss Amelia Bell

"Plenty of passion, romance, and adventure...one of the

best books I've read in a long time…a captivating story from beginning to end."

—NightOwlReviews.com

"Delicious…highly entertaining…a witty, sensual historical tale that will keep you glued to the pages…This beautifully written, fast-paced tale is a true delight."

—RomanceJunkies.com

Conquered by a Highlander

"Rich, evocative historical detail and enthralling characters fill the pages of this fast-paced tale."

—*Publishers Weekly* (starred review)

"What a conclusion to this fast-paced, adventure-filled story with characters that jump off the page and will capture your heart."

—MyBookAddictionReviews.com

Tamed by a Highlander

"Top Pick! Quinn's talents for weaving history with a sexy and seductive romance are showcased in her latest Highlander series book. This fast-paced tale of political intrigue populated by sensual characters with deeply rooted senses of honor and loyalty is spellbinding…Top-notch Highland romance!"

—*RT Book Reviews*

"A winning mix of fascinating history and lush romance…Readers will be captivated by the meticulously accurate historical detail."

—*Publishers Weekly* (starred review)

Seduced by a Highlander

Ravished by a Highlander

Also by Paula Quinn

Highlander
Ever After

PAULA QUINN

FOREVER
New York Boston

12/18

Copyright © 2018 by Paula Quinn
Excerpt from *A Highlander's Christmas Kiss* copyright © 2016 by Paula Quinn

Cover design by Claire Brown
Cover illustration by Alan Ayers
Cover copyright © 2018 by Hachette Book Group, Inc.

Forever
Hachette Book Group
1290 Avenue of the Americas, New York, NY 10104
forever-romance.com
twitter.com/foreverromance

First Edition: December 2018

Forever is an imprint of Grand Central Publishing. The Forever name and logo are trademarks of Hachette Book Group, Inc.

The publisher is not responsible for websites (or their content) that are not owned by the publisher.

The Hachette Speakers Bureau provides a wide range of authors for speaking events. To find out more, go to www.hachettespeakersbureau.com or call (866) 376-6591.

ISBN: 978-1-4555-3538-5 (mass market), 978-1-4555-3539-2 (ebook)

Printed in the United States of America

OPM

10 9 8 7 6 5 4 3 2 1

Acknowledgments

My MacGregor writing journey would have been less of a glorious adventure without the people who have celebrated the journey with me and supported me from the very beginning, loving the MacGregors as much as I do. Thank you from the bottom of my heart. Here's to the next one!

Christy Allred, Terree Lyman, Sharon Frizzel, Donna Killian, Ellen Ziegler, Cario Lamb, Leigh Hilson, Kay Duddie, Dana Constance, Debra Allen, Barb Batlan-Massabrook

MacGregor/Grant
Family Tree

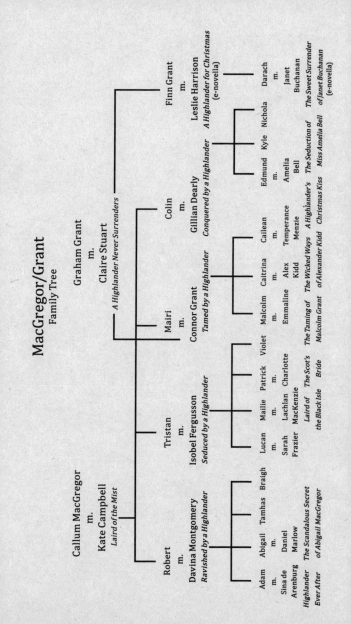

What do you think of a prince who does not want to be king? Is he a fool or is he wise?
Queen Anne

Highlander Ever After

Chapter One

Melusina de Arenburg ground her jaw, closed her eyes, and prayed. She hoped that since she was in a chapel, God would hear her request and grant it, even if she was a bastard. A royal bastard, but a bastard nonetheless.

She prayed this wasn't truly happening. That she hadn't been taken from her bed in Kensington Palace and brought to the Highlands. And oh, Lord, please that she wasn't about to be forced into a marriage with an outlaw.

Where was her father when the queen's men had carted her off to marry Adam MacGregor, son of a proscribed chief?

She opened her eyes and looked around the chapel at the faces of people she didn't know. People she didn't want to know. Barbaric in appearance. Nothing like the men at court, who dressed appropriately, tied back their hair, and covered their knees.

She knew she didn't look much better with her long blond tresses messily plaited over her shoulder, her ears and neck unadorned, and her body covered in a wrinkled gown.

"I wish to speak to my father!" she demanded, though it sounded more like a plea echoing throughout the chapel. "He is the prince elector, George of Hanover, heir to the throne. He would not agree to this! 'Tis a mistake," she called out, hoping, praying someone would listen. "I cannot wed this man. I am already betrothed to Lord Standish."

Someone behind her gave her a gentle shove to get her moving along. Her throat closed up. Her heart rang in her chest like an alarm, dire and urgent. *Run!* her head screamed. *Run the other way!* Where would she go? She didn't know where she was. She wiped her tears but they continued.

Why? Why her? She thought the queen loved her. Why would Anne wed her to a Highlander? They were savages who frightened the blazes out of her. Why had she been sent so far away from everything she knew?

She heard the sounds of women weeping and men swearing under their breath. Everything sounded louder. Everyone seemed bigger, including several enormous, deadly-looking hounds at the feet of their masters. She crossed herself and wondered if it was too late to pray because she was already in hell. She stopped and was shoved again, a bit more forcibly this time. She couldn't move. She refused to move. "I . . . I will not wed this man."

Her eyes swept to the man to whom she had to promise her life on the whim of a queen.

"'Tis the queen's order," a man behind her, the one who'd prodded her onward, whispered. "MacGregors are loyal to the queen."

The queen's order. Sina's eyes filled with more tears, blurring her vision of the groom. When she reached the end of the aisle, she was supposed to kneel beside him, but her knees locked together.

A deep, low growl drew her eyes to a black hellhound bent at his side, twice the size of the others, its lips curled over its white fangs, its dark eyes fixed on her.

Sina gathered every last ounce of courage she possessed not to faint at the sight of the beast. Oh! How could Anne have done this to her? Her anger at the betrayal kept her on her feet.

"No." Its master's command was low and deep, resonating through her. He said something else, and the hellhound lifted its haunches and moved to the other side of him.

He commanded devils. She closed her eyes and bit her lip to keep from crying. When the man behind her rested his hand on her shoulder, gently urging her to her knees, she went, dipping her head to weep into her hands.

Through her sobs she heard her soon-to-be groom mutter something angrily. Her heart skipped. Was he ill-tempered? She wiped her eyes and dared a glance at him up close. The first thing level with her eyes was his mouth. She caught her breath at the full, relaxed decadence of it. He was draped in darkness and light, with lightning in his storm-filled eyes. His coal-black hair fell to his shoulders and was swept away from high, chiseled cheekbones and a strong jaw shadowed by a dusting of dark hair. His ivory complexion was almost flawless—a strong contrast against his raven hair. His beauty was captivating, bewitching.

She followed his angry stare to an older man standing to her left.

Sina turned to look at him. She knew who the man was—the chief of these people. He was as huge and deadly looking as the rest of them. The one who'd read the letter she'd delivered from the queen. The groom's father.

She offered him her angriest glare. How did a man like him even know the queen? And who was he to give her to his son? She was already promised to Lord Standish, son of the Earl of Chesterfield.

The priest began speaking. God help her. A woman she loved and trusted had ordered this. Sina had no choice but to obey.

After a long benediction that gave her time to consider how horrible her life was going to be from here on in, here in this wilderness with these mountain men rumored to be so savage that they had to be proscribed. Her heart hammered in her chest, her throat. There was nowhere to run. What would poor William do without her? Would she ever see her dear friend Poppy again?

The benediction stopped, and silence descended for what seemed an eternity before the man beside her finally spoke. He looked as miserable as she while he promised to be her husband.

Would her father dissolve this marriage when he became king? Did he even give a damn? William did. Hadn't he told her every day since they were eight and eleven that he needed her? Hadn't he just told her what she meant to him when he returned from the grand tour? But what could he do when the queen had ordered this?

The priest set his stern gaze on her next.

She glared at him, refusing to wipe her eyes again. "I would like to know—"

"Just yer consent will do," the priest said, cutting her off.

"Well, you don't have it!" She swallowed and looked around at the brooding faces watching her. "I don't love him." It was all she could manage.

"Adam's being forced into this too," a woman called out.

"She defies the queen," a man grumbled.

Did she? Would she defy the queen for the life she'd always dreamed of? One with a family of her own, to a man she loved?

"Your consent," the priest prodded.

"Yes," she managed, hating herself for it.

A few more words and a blessing, and it was over.

Her husband pushed off his knees with an angry growl—or the sound could have come from his hound. Sina couldn't be sure. He rose to his feet, at least two heads taller than her when she rose. She tilted her neck to take in the full sight of him. She crossed herself.

Tightly leashed muscles stretched his léine across his chest. His large hands were balled into fists at his sides. Her gaze traveled upward to his face, dark and angry, beautiful.

She wouldn't consummate this marriage. She'd find a way to hold him off until someone came to help. Her father would come...or William...someone. The marriage could be annulled.

If any of these Highlanders thought her meek and mild, they would soon discover that they had misjudged.

She pulled a bit of her fortitude up now and girded it around her.

"I demand to know why this terrible thing has happened to me," she said in a soft voice on the verge of shattering.

Refusing to tremble, she raised her brow at her husband when anger flashed across his silvery-blue eyes. She was angry too! She met his gaze head-on, waiting for his reply.

"It has happened to me as well, woman." His voice burned across her ears. "I'll leave it to my faither to explain why."

She thought she was prepared to meet his anger straight on, but his deep, growling baritone and the bite of reply made it hard to stand.

She did, however, and turned to the chief, who was a tad less daunting than his son, and waited for an answer.

Adam MacGregor leaned back in a chair in Camlochlin's great hall. He ignored the servers scurrying about to prepare for the last-minute celebration.

He thought of the life he'd left behind a few moments ago. He'd stepped into the chapel a free man and came out bound to a woman he didn't know, for reasons for which he didn't want to be responsible.

He thought of his bride—rather than the implications of this marriage. She was quite lovely with her enormous, sparkling green eyes and small, pert nose swollen and red from crying. And hell, she could cry! He understood her misery, for he felt it too.

"Och, Adam, it canna be true!"

He turned to a group of at least a half dozen maids, and nodded. "Alas, fair ladies, 'tis."

Neither of them had a choice, he thought somberly, even as the lasses gathered around him. He shooed them away. "I am no adulterer," he muttered as they scattered. Hell, but he was giving up much for duty.

According to his father, whom he'd argued with moments before the ceremony, this union between the MacGregors and the House of Hanover meant much for his kin. The queen had wanted it done as soon as the lass arrived, which meant either her poor health had deteriorated further or there were some against the union. Most likely Sina's betrothed, Lord Standish.

Adam sure as hell didn't want to wed someone else's betrothed. He didn't give a damn about the throne either. He'd never been to England, nor did he want to go. He cared about the queen but not the power she brought with her during her visits to Camlochlin to see her sister Davina, Adam's mother. He felt the heavy weight his aunt bore that finally crippled her.

He didn't want to carry that kind of burden. He did his best to forget that side of his heritage, which made him, a Catholic, a direct heir to the throne. He was determined to stay in Skye, free from England and the danger of its power. He was even willing to give up his birthright as next clan chief to his sister to remain free.

But the arrival of Miss Melusina de Arenburg and the sealed letter she carried changed everything.

The burden of marriage fell to him as eldest son of the chief. He agreed to it—not because of loyalty to the future throne—but because it would ensure the continued utmost leniency where MacGregors and the laws against them were concerned once the queen was gone.

Adam had never wanted to be forced to make choices like the one tonight. Choices for the good of others and not himself. Even more, he hated being pushed around by power. It made him want to defy it, take it to the field, and battle it to the death.

He wasn't ready for a wife. She wasn't even Scottish. He liked his life, with nothing on his mind but a bit of mayhem and mischief. He was a raider of cattle and a master of deception. It had taken him years to convince his clan that he was a careless rogue, unfit to be chief.

And now this.

He wasn't ready for his life to change—and his father agreeing to this marriage meant that he had made his decision about who would be chief.

Adam guzzled his ale, then looked up for the server. He saw his bride entering the hall with some of the women of Camlochlin at her sides, trying to soothe her. He rolled his gaze heavenward when she looked at him and made the sign of the cross.

A man with auburn hair and a short beard to match stepped in front of him and blocked Adam's view. He grimaced and cast a brooding glance at the cup.

"I'll admit that was painful," said Daniel Marlow, retired general of the queen's army, straddling a chair beside him. "But she isn't hideous."

Adam hadn't time to grow especially close to any of his cousins when they were all younger. By the time some of them had gone off to stop the union with England act, Adam had already established himself as the pampered heir who couldn't be bothered with the affairs of England. In truth, he couldn't.

He attached himself to few, those without tails anyway. Daniel was one of the few.

"Ye had to physically push her, Daniel. She wept the entire time as if I were some beast and she'd rather God strike her dead than marry me."

"So prove her wrong," Daniel challenged, rising from his seat to greet the women.

"Who says she is?" Adam muttered, staying in his seat.

"I do," Marlow said, taking him by the arm and pulling him to his feet. "Show her the thoughtful, intelligent man behind your roguish smiles. Make her happy. 'Tis your duty now."

Aye, that's what he was afraid of. How tiring it must be to constantly try to make someone else happy. He wasn't looking forward to it.

His gaze fell to his reluctant bride. Her frame, in a gown that matched the emerald of her eyes, seemed too small to hold such a courageous heart. She'd done her best to refuse—or stall their marriage. Though it made him feel like hell, he liked her determination not to go down so easily—despite the fear that radiated off her.

Her hair fell like a golden flame over her milky cleavage. A slight smile, coaxed by something his sister said, brought a delicate dimple to light in her left cheek. She lifted her gaze and set it on him. His breath stalled a wee bit. Hell, she was beautiful, like a sparrow, small and shaking—

"Is it true?" she asked, reaching him. "Are you terrified?"

He narrowed his eyes at his sister and then returned them to the wide, waiting eyes of his bride. "I—"

"Because *you* are *home*, no? You reign over me now, no? Why should you be terrified?"

"I'm home but—"

"But?" She spoke on a whispered breath, yet the word came down on him like a hammer. She wasn't finished. His sister and the others stepped away.

A sparrow with the heart of a lion. Adam liked it.

"How has your life changed today save that there will be a woman in your bed tonight—though by the number of women crying over you in that chapel, I must assume that the end of this day will be no different. So please, tell me, what do you have to be terrified about?"

Did she not understand the weight of who she was? Aye, he was home, surrounded by people who loved him—and she wasn't. He understood. But his kin were the ones who would expect the most from him. Already, Daniel had reminded him how important it was to make her happy. He knew perfectly well how wives were treated in Camlochlin. He didn't have the time or the inclination to devote so much to one.

"The woman in my bed," he told her, his gaze falling to her hands wringing her already wrinkled skirts, "will be my wife, one to whom I pledged much, includin' my body."

"I can assure you, you've no need to pledge your body to me."

"And yet"—he stretched out his arms and smiled at her—"'tis yers now."

She looked at him with wide, frightened eyes. She said nothing, and lifting her skirts, she hurried away.

He didn't speak to her again until she arrived at their marriage chamber a short while later, looking as if the last of her strength had abandoned her and being gently urged along by some of his female relatives. They deposited her in front of him and his dog, Goliath, and hurried off.

She bit her lip, squeezed her eyes shut, and began praying.

He frowned, listening to her plead to God to deliver her from this savage. One thing Adam wasn't was a savage. He didn't like that she saw him as one. He might be rebellious to the life he'd been trained for, but he wasn't uncivilized. He could be gentle with her, make her first night in his bed a pleasurable one. In fact, he looked forward to undressing her, kissing her prayers from her succulent, pouty lips, and proving himself worthy of her most heated, secret desires.

He pulled off his léine and felt a wave of disappointment at her strangled gasp. Proving anything to her was going to be difficult. He cursed the queen for doing this to them. "I willna force myself upon ye."

He got into bed, turned his back on her, and closed his eyes. He felt her climb in a few moments later and poke him in the arm. He opened his eyes and turned to look at her.

"I love someone else," she declared as if somehow it would be enough to toss her out of his bed and out of Camlochlin.

"Thank ye fer tellin' me," he said and then closed his eyes again.

He lay awake for hours, lamenting while she slept. He didn't want a wife as much as he didn't want to be chief. There were enough married men in Camlochlin for him to know what would now be expected of him: giving in to her every whim, picking flowers for her, making certain she was happy. What would he get in return in a loveless marriage? He groaned thinking how terrible life would be. How could he make her happy if she was pining over another man? He felt a pang of something...jealousy because she was his wife? Or hopelessness for the same reason?

After another hour of restlessness and regret, he rose from bed, pulled on his boots, and grabbed his cloak. He called softly to Goliath, and left the chamber.

Chapter Two

Sina opened her eyes when she heard the click of the door closing. He was gone, thankfully taking his hellhound with him.

She hadn't dared move for the last four hours, terrified that the beast or the barbarian would turn on her in the dark. She'd prayed for courage and strength while the Highlander tossed and turned beside her. Every time he moved, she thought he would touch her. He hadn't. How would she ever fight him off? He was bigger and broader than any man she knew. But he hadn't touched her. He'd left her alone.

When he'd removed his léine, the sculpted cut of his arms, his chest, and his hard belly snatched her breath from her body—for more reasons than she'd admit.

Highlanders certainly did wear less clothes than the men in London.

She'd listened, still and silent, to his soft, anguished groans and sighs for four long hours, wishing he would sleep so she could weep without drawing his attention. But he hadn't slept, just as she hadn't. He didn't want this either. He didn't want her.

Oh, how could the queen sentence her to a life empty of everything Sina wanted? She was Anne's companion, and they'd spoken of it many times. Sina wanted a man who loved her, who would live or die for her. She wanted William. Anne had claimed to understand the fancies of a romantic heart, for she had loved her dearest George.

How could she do this to her? What were her motives behind it? Why did she care so much about some faraway warriors that she would use Sina to ensure binding them to the future throne? Who were they?

The MacGregor chief had claimed they were Anne's friends and that her father had been involved in the arrangement. MacGregor warriors were loyal and mighty. This union guaranteed their allegiance to her father while securing their safety against the laws of proscription.

Sina didn't believe any of it. Her father would not sell her for a handful of Highland fighters, no matter how skilled they claimed to be. Nor would he give her up to help a clan of outlaws. Would he? He had given her up once before to be raised by her relatives. Was this his way of getting rid of his bastard once and for all?

She rose from the bed shaking and went to one of the surrounding windows. She stretched her solemn gaze beyond the moonlit, heather-lined vale, to the cliffs in the distance. Everywhere else she looked was mountains and water. Were they at the edge of the world? Her heart sank deeper. She'd traveled for days, six perhaps, in a closed carriage. She knew they'd gone north, but how *far* north?

She prayed she was wrong about her father and that he would come.

Still, hopelessness covered her. Whatever would she do

here? What would she wear? Oh, her gowns. She would never forgive Anne for not giving her time to take her gowns. Who would she talk to every day? What would they talk about? Cattle? And poor William. He could have done better than agreeing to marry the bastard child of the prince elector. She loved him for it. William was refined and courtly. She—

She blinked at the mist settling over the landscape as light from the sun in the east spread a soft, golden haze before her...and on a lone man draped in a gray hooded mantle. Or mayhap it was a wolf she saw perched at the crest of a mountain. The black hound at his heels proved it was Adam MacGregor. What was he doing out there alone? Contemplating running, as she was? At least he knew which way to go.

She hoped he ran—very, very far away and never returned. Perhaps then she'd be sent back.

She watched him climb sure-footedly down the steep braes and walk toward the shore of a small beach. He moved with natural strength and grace, like something mythical come to life.

Why in blazes did he have to be so alluring? So... civilized? It would be easier to hate him despite his appearance if he behaved more like a barbarian. Even while she'd wept over their marriage and just barely gave her consent, he hadn't been harsh with her.

She thought of all the weeping ladies in the chapel. He was no doubt a rake, careless of the hearts he broke. None of them seemed to mind that so many others were crying, which only proved that he was a snake beneath all that beauty. He'd bewitched them all, but whatever these people considered charm wouldn't work on her.

She sprang back from the window when he turned and

looked up. Had he seen her? Her heart thumped in her head, making it pound. He was coming back inside!

She leaped for the bed and tried to remember in which position she'd been pretending to sleep.

She didn't have to wait long before he pushed open the door and then closed it softly. She peeped her eyes open and watched him from beneath her lashes. His back was turned to her.

He swept his cloak from his broad, bare shoulders. His loose hair fell like a dark cloud around him.

She wanted to close her eyes and not see the beauty of this Highlander and, heaven forbid, ever desire him. But she kept looking, drawn by the corded flare of his back tapering to his bare hips. She was certain none of the men at court were crafted so masterfully beneath their coats and garters and hose, or Poppy and Eloise would have told her. She swallowed, thankful he hadn't removed his pants earlier.

Still, the top half of him was enough to stall her breath, addle her good judgment for a moment, and tempt her to look.

He began to turn toward her. She snapped her eyes shut.

A low, guttural growl coming from behind her turned her blood cold. The hellhound! Why was the beast growling? Her pulse raced, and try as she might, she could not keep her eyes closed another instant waiting for the hound's fangs to sink into her back.

Her eyes settled on the half-naked stranger watching her. She had no time to be afraid of both him *and* his beast—or to admire him in the soft wash of dawn streaming in through the windows.

She felt something settle on the mattress behind her back.

With a cry of terror, she leaped up and hurled herself at the hound's master.

He caught her in his arms, against his hard chest.

"Goliath!" he admonished the beast while Sina buried her face in the folds of his silky hair at his neck.

The hound whimpered, emboldening Sina to look up— and to become aware of her body pressed so intimately to this man who was now her husband, held in the strength of his arms.

He smelled like the fresh mist outside. His eyes, up close, were like turbulent seas, roiling from someplace deep and hidden.

He tried to move her off him. She closed her arms tighter around his neck and cast a worried look over her shoulder.

"What is that thing?"

"'Tis a dog." His voice was like the low rumble of thunder across her ear.

"'Tisn't a dog," she insisted. "'Tis something born of nightmares."

He offered the drooling creature a pitying look and her an angry one. Then, using a bit more strength, he pulled her off him and set her back in bed.

"Goliath, come on," he ordered, moving toward the door.

Sina was hopeful they were both leaving again. She especially didn't want to be alone with her reluctant groom after she'd clung to him like scum on a pond. Heaven help her, but his body was as hard as armor. Still, she was certain she could feel his heartbeat through it, as accelerated as hers, as if he was also affected.

He opened the door when the "dog" reached it. They both stopped and looked at each other for a moment. The hound's eyes were large and repentant.

Sina felt a moment of guilt.

The Highlander bent and took the hound's large head in

his hands. "I canna let ye go aroond actin' like a vicious mongrel, now can I?" He pointed to the door.

With its long, furry tail between its legs, the beast hunkered out.

Straightening to his full, glorious height, MacGregor flicked his icy gaze to her, then looked away.

"Am I to blame for its wanting to rip out my throat?" she asked on her knees from the middle of the bed, where he'd left her.

When he didn't answer her, she left the bed. Let the hellhound back in, then. She'd rather sleep in the hall than in his bed anyway.

She passed him without a word, but when she put her hand to the door, he grasped her wrist and spun her back. She landed with her back up against the door, her wrist held above her head and his hard body pressed to hers.

"I willna have ye confusin' my dog," he said in a deep whisper.

"Let me go or I'll scratch out your eyes."

He reached down, snatched up her other wrist, and held that one over her head too.

He gave her a challenging smirk that set her heart thrashing in her chest. What was he going to do? Had she pushed him too far? She looked up into his eyes, afraid of what she would see.

What she saw surprised her. Regret, shame...just traces of it, but enough to make him let her go and walk away. He didn't go to the bed but fell into a nearby chair, stretched his long, powerful legs out before him, and rested his entwined hands on his bare, hard belly.

Still shaken, Sina stood in her spot for a moment not knowing what to do. He'd just proven he could dominate her in an instant...and that he wouldn't.

She tilted her chin and returned to the bed. She didn't really want to sleep in the hall. "What are we to do about this marriage?"

"There's nothin' we can do aboot it," he answered behind a cool veneer of detachment. "'Tis done. We must accept it."

"You don't want this."

"Nae," he said in a somber tone. He set his eyes toward the window as if something he loved and lost were out there. "But fate catches up with us."

She scowled at him. "This is not my fate!"

"Apparently, 'tis," he said, closing his eyes. "Ye'll settle in," he assured her quietly. "Goliath will get used to ye."

She didn't want to settle in! She didn't want his hellhound to get used to her! She wanted to go home to William, and her friends Poppy and Eloise. She wanted back the plans she'd made for her life. How was she expected to let it all go? What would she do here all day? Every day? Not knowing a living soul?

Longing and loneliness overwhelmed her and she began to cry.

"Do ye want comfort, lass?" His voice came soft and deep, stirring something deeper than her anguish and settling on her like a warm blanket.

She kicked it off.

"No. I want nothing from any of you. I will not settle in."

He ground his jaw but he didn't open his eyes. "Verra well, then."

A little while later she heard him snore in his chair, sprawled out like a spoiled prince. She got up and looked around the chambers for where they put the other gown she was able to grab after she'd been torn from her bed. There were several chests and wardrobes lining the walls. Was her gown in one of them? She didn't want to have to go through his things to find hers. She found the only pair of earrings she had taken. They were her favorites, gold with three dangling pearls. A gift from William.

Her husband stirred in his chair. She would have to remain in what she was wearing. Either that or wake him in her search. What would the others whisper about her wearing the same dress for two days? She tied her long hair into a thick, gold crown atop her head and adorned her lobes with her earrings. She missed her rings, her brooches, her wardrobes...

No, cease, she admonished herself while she crept toward the door. She would have them all back again.

But in the meantime, she would try to find something to eat before the second worst day of her life began.

She padded down the hall, fitting her feet into her silk slippers as she approached the stairs.

A set of doors opened to her right, and a man whom she'd heard about many times at the foot of the queen's bed stepped into the hall.

He stopped when he saw her, and a streak of panic flashed across his sea-green eyes before he remembered she had nowhere to go. She wasn't trying to escape.

"Good morn." He offered her a wide, pleasant smile. "You're awake early."

"General Marlow," she greeted. "Is this where all friends of the queen end up?"

His smile didn't falter at the sting toward the queen in her voice. "'Tis not such a bad place to end up."

What could ever tempt a man of his renown to spend his life away from everything he knew?

As if in response to her question, the general's wife

appeared at the doors next and stepped into the hall with
their three children at her full plaid skirts.

Abigail MacGregor was the most beautiful woman Sina
had ever met. Firelight infused her hair with shades of gold
and strands of pearly silver. She wore it braided intricately
at the temples, like the warriors of the old north, and the
rest cascading down the shawl draping her shoulders. She
smiled at her husband and then at Sina.

"Did ye sleep at all?" she asked Sina, moving to her side
and reaching for her hand.

Sina took a step out of reach. Adam's sister seemed nice
enough, and had been a bit brutally honest about her brother
yesterday on their walk to the great hall, but Sina didn't
want to get close to any of them. She wasn't staying, and
letting any of them in felt as though she was giving up. She
wasn't. She couldn't. Somehow, she would get home.

"No, I didn't sleep. I decided to start the day and get it
over with."

"I understand."

No one understood, Sina thought as she turned for the
stairs. She wanted to ask if Abigail would have slept her
first night torn from her family and dumped into the bed of
a stranger. But she curbed her tongue, not wanting to incite
anger. She had to live here for a while.

She would have preferred to eat alone, but she didn't
know where in blazes to go for food.

The general and his family led her below stairs to a large
dining hall paneled in rich warm walnut and hand-sewn
tapestries. A grand hearth carved in stone provided heat and
light, along with tall candle stands and beams of sunlight
breaking through the windows.

A long, polished table sat in the center with sixteen ornately carved chairs set around it and place settings before

each one. Painted clay vases were set about, bursting with pink and purple heather. It was rather cozy despite it being so big, though smaller than the great hall.

"Ye can have a seat opposite Daniel, there." Abigail pointed to a chair close to the head, next to a chair where Adam would have sat if he were not asleep.

"I think I'll just take my plate back to—"

"Och, please stay," Adam's sister begged. "Ye're kin now. Ye'll have an important place here."

Sina didn't want a place here, important or otherwise. She knew Abigail was being kind and she was thankful for it, but it wouldn't help her.

A few moments later, with the noisy arrival of Adam's brothers and the chief and his wife, the hope of eating alone grew bleak. With another gray hound and the main hell-hound itself entering and standing guard at the exit, it went dark.

She took her seat and dipped her chin to her chest, not knowing what to do or say to the strangers around her.

"Good morn to ye, Melusina," his father greeted politely, waiting for his wife to take her seat on his left.

Sina was still angry with the chief for obeying the queen. She could understand General Marlow pushing her toward her groom, but the MacGregors were outlaws. Since when did they do as they were told?

Robert MacGregor was an imposing man, bigger than any man at court, with shoulders as wide as a sunrise. He could snap her in two or order someone else to do it and they would obey him.

Sina cast him a dark look just the same when he turned to her.

"Where's Adam?"

"He's sleeping," she told him, keeping her voice soft and

neutral, a talent she'd learned while growing up. She wasn't one for outbursts. They were unladylike and unseemly. She was ashamed for crying out and making such a commotion in church, but she believed God understood. She didn't care if others thought her meek; she didn't have to shout to let her feelings be known. "He was awake most of the night, aggrieved, as I was. As I still am."

She could feel all their eyes on her, their ears straining to hear what she said in her small, soft voice that caused the chief to lower his jewel-like gaze.

"I'm sorry ye were no' given a choice in this," he said with sincerity. "None of us were. I dinna force my bairns to wed strangers."

"But this time you did," she pointed out boldly since he hadn't ordered her to be taken away yet.

"'Twas the queen's order," he defended. "'Tis a good union and will keep the clan safe."

"I know," she conceded, sparing him one last look before she veiled her gaze again. There was nothing else to say. For now, at least.

Chapter Three

Adam opened his eyes with a groan and kinked his neck. He was a fool for not sleeping in his bed. A fool for not taking what was his. Hell, he'd wanted to kiss her, feel her soft curves against him again, but he wouldn't do it while she hated him. He wasn't a complete rogue.

He reached for Goliath and touched the empty space around the chair. He frowned, remembering his wife's terror at his beloved friend. Goliath didn't like her. Not a good sign.

He sat up and stretched and looked at the bed. She wasn't in it. He hadn't slept long. Where was she?

Had she dared venture out without him, into the midst of the savages? If she only knew how women were cherished here.

It would likely make her more unhappy to know she would never be cherished so. He wouldn't open himself to her when she loved another. It wouldn't be difficult to remain unaffected by her. In fact, he hadn't met a lass yet who had had any impact on him.

He hadn't been married to any of them.

Hell. Did he want to be miserable until death did them part?

He rubbed his grumbling belly and rose from his chair to dress in fresh clothes. He'd think about it all later. He hurried, hoping his brothers Braigh and Tamhas hadn't eaten all the food.

Was Sina with them? Did he want her to be? The lads were rowdy, especially Braigh, who, if he wasn't feeding his six-foot-four frame, was likely wrestling Goliath and Bronwyn on the floor. They'd convince her that what she thought about Highlanders was correct.

It was, mostly. But there had always been extenuating circumstances to his clan's merciless reputation. He doubted she'd ever be interested in hearing them.

Donning doeskin breeches, boots, and a dark green tunic pleated at the waist with a belt, he left his chambers. He knew where everyone would be. He ran his fingers through his obsidian locks and then headed for the dining hall.

Goliath pounded up the stairs and met him halfway.

"I hope ye werena causin' chaos fer my wife," Adam told him, petting his head on the way down. "Hell, I know those words sound ridiculous. I know ye're likely jealous, but ye canna bite her. Understand?"

Goliath barked and, with his tongue lolling out of his mouth, followed Adam to the dining hall.

Before Adam stepped over the threshold, Bronwyn, his mother's loyal hound and one of Goliath's sisters, hurried out to him.

Adam stopped to give her a proper greeting, leaving the others inside waiting for him just a moment longer.

"Nip him in the arse if he does anything foolish," he told her about her brother and then stepped inside.

His eyes settled on Sina immediately. He took in the sight of her in her wrinkled gown and tousled bun, sitting beside his empty chair. She looked like a princess, regal and fragile...and alone in a hall filled with people.

She looked up from her cup, her large, luminous eyes lit by the flames and fear when she saw him.

He frowned, thinking that she was afraid of him and that last night he'd given her reason to be. But he'd been patient on their wedding night, hadn't he? He'd understood how all of this was affecting her, and he hadn't touched her.

She caught his scowl and lowered her cup, and her lashes. She was beauty incarnate, like a fine painting, halting his breath.

Drawn to her by the sudden desire to comfort her, he moved closer.

But she didn't want his comfort. She didn't want anything, and he didn't want to *have* to give it. But now that he was a husband, he could no longer behave like a careless rogue. He took his seat beside her and apologized for being late.

"Yer wife explained ye were up most of the night," his father allowed and offered the server a smile for hurrying to his son's plate.

She'd spoken up for him? How did she know he was up most of the night? Had she been awake as well—all those hours still and quiet? He slipped his gaze to her and raised his brows. Poor, determined lass.

She continued eating.

He liked the adornments dangling from her ears. The pearls added brightness to her cheeks and softened her already delicate profile.

"Adam," Braigh said, thankfully *sitting* at the table. "Ye still comin' raidin' with us?"

He wanted to. What would she do here while he was away? What did he care? She'd be doing the same thing whether he was here or not. Was she going to change his life the first day of their marriage? No. He wouldn't let this change anything.

"Aye, I'm comin'."

"What is it exactly that you'll be raiding?" his wife asked, looking a bit pale.

"Cattle," he replied. "'Tis a common and honorable practice in the Highlands."

"Among outlaws," she murmured.

"Among Highlanders," he corrected, cutting her a hard look. He didn't usually take offense to his clan's past. He knew the proscription was still in full effect. But no one was actively hunting them with dogs. In the Highlands, MacGregors gathered in numbers larger than four, and his kin defied the law and always carried weapons. Thanks to their kinship with the queen, as long as MacGregors obeyed the laws below the Highlands, they'd be left alone.

By tying him to the future king's daughter, illegitimate or not, Anne was ensuring his clan's continued safety.

Adam understood the importance of it for his kin. That was the only reason he'd agreed to it. But after a day and night of listening to her cries and prayers for deliverance from him, he was beginning to regret his decision—no matter the beauty of her frame.

She offered him a forced, overly sweet smile.

Sincere or not, the appearance of her dimple captivated him.

"I don't know anything about your way of life," she said, sounding meek to his ears. He knew better. "How could I?" she continued. "I was given no time to prepare for it. You will have to forgive my ignorance."

"I will," he agreed, lifting his cup to his mouth. "We'll remedy it, of course, and teach ye our ways. Will we no'?" he put to his kin sitting around them.

They all agreed, as he knew they would.

"I..."

He slipped his gaze back to Sina and her wide, reluctant eyes when she spoke. He waited for the rest.

Her breath grew short, revealed in the rapid rise and fall of her chest and the slight cleavage of her breasts. Her eyes weren't haughty or angry, but determined. "I don't want to learn."

He pressed his lips together and quirked his mouth to one side, more amused than angry. "Then this will be the only time I fergive yer ignorance."

She stared at him for a moment. Adam couldn't read her. He was too busy trying not to pity her too much...not to feel anything for her.

"I don't care," she told him on a soft whisper, helping him find victory. "I want to go home."

"This is yer home now," he said with a note of frustration tainting his voice.

"My home...and everything else was taken from me."

Adam spread his gaze over his kin. He knew them all well, knew the subtlest nuances of their facial expressions, the language of their bodies. They weren't enjoying breakfast. Even the twins fidgeted in their seats before leaving the table.

"Sina," Abby said after tossing him a sympathetic smile. "Please understand that this wasna Adam's choice either."

"I do," his wife replied.

Adam found his gaze fastened on her lips while she

spoke. They were narrow and plump, shaped like a heart...

"Do you think that makes it easier, or even more difficult?" she continued, breaking the spell her mouth had over him. "It gives no comfort to know he was forced, as I was."

"I'm glad to hear such a compassionate response from the woman who just became my daughter."

All eyes turned to Davina, wife of the chief, seated opposite her son. Adam smiled at her. He was happy his mother had been raised in an abbey, hidden from the world, free of her name and the weight that came with it. Everything about her was genuine, sincere, all bared in her wide, blue eyes.

"I know ye're unhappy, Sina," she told her. "Ye have every reason to be angry and unsure. We will do everything we can to help make this easier fer ye. But this is yer fate, daughter. By the queen's decree and yer father's consent. Nothing can be done. I'm sorry."

"As am I," Sina sighed mournfully, then rose from her seat. "If you will excuse me, I could use some air."

She didn't wait for any consent but left the table. When she moved toward the entrance, Goliath perked up his ears. It was enough to cause her to squeak and hold her hands to her throat.

She looked back at the faces watching her, then straightened her dainty shoulders and took a step toward the dogs.

Knowing she was terrified of his canine friend, Adam wanted to smile at her courage but kept his warning gaze on Goliath as Sina tiptoed around him.

She disappeared beyond the doors with Adam looking after her. He should go to her. There were likely to be more dogs outside by now—and more of his *savage* kin milling about.

With a heavy sigh and a dark scowl, he rose, grabbed a handful of figs, and followed her out.

So, he thought with disgust, this was what his life was going to be like from now on—always having to tend to someone else's feelings. He hated it already.

He pulled a plaid from a hook by the doors and left the castle with Goliath at his heel.

There was no moat, bailey, or wall around the castle his grandfather had built long ago, save the wall of mountain behind it. Everything was spread out before him. Houses great and small were scattered throughout the vale, with most of the larger manor houses belonging to his uncles and their families.

He greeted many of them as they set about their tasks for the morning.

Chickens pecked at the ground around his boots. Sheep and cattle grazed on the heather-lined hills beyond. The sound of the rushing waves danced across his ears. He looked out at Trina and Alex's ship docked in the bay. Camlochlin's children always returned. He smiled, wondering what his new wife would think about having pirates in the family.

His eyes found her trudging her way up to the crest of the vale, toward the cliffs. She didn't know where she was going. Was she going to try to escape? Or jump?

He spotted his uncle Tristan leaving his house with Ettarre, his loyal hound.

"Did the night bring any knife wounds?" his uncle called out as Ettarre raced to greet her brother.

"If it had, I would have let myself bleed to death," Adam called back, hurrying by him.

Aye, bleeding out on the floor of his chambers would be better than chasing down a stubborn, defiant lass with no other option than to surrender to her fate. As he must.

He ground his jaw and let his long legs bring him swiftly up the hill.

He watched her reach the crest and look toward Elgol while the wind beat against her.

She looked so slight that he feared the wind might carry her away, closer to the cliffs. He came up behind her and rested his hand on her wrist. "Ye wouldna make it across alive, lass."

He thought she would pull away. She didn't.

"'Tis beautiful in a terrifyingly lonely sort of way."

He didn't like the way her words pierced him. He didn't want her to see Camlochlin as lonely—or him as a savage. She wouldn't be lonely here, whether or not she ever claimed back her heart from Lord Standish in England. She wouldn't be lonely with his kin.

He nodded and handed her the plaid, then bit into a fig and bent his knees to sit in the grass. "Where did ye live before this?"

"At the palace with the queen," she replied numbly and let the plaid hang from her fingers. "I visited Kensington often as a child and finally resided there for the last two years as one of the queen's ladies-in-waiting."

"What do ladies-in-waitin' do?"

She glanced down at him with suspicious eyes and shook her head when he invited her to sit beside him. "We wait on the queen. I was one of her personal friends. Her companion. I thought I was important to her."

"And now ye think ye werena because she sent ye here?" He ate another fig and offered one to her.

She accepted and finally sat down next to him. He tried not to think about how lovely she was so close. Her skin looked as soft as velvet. He was tempted to touch it.

"What else am I to think?" she asked, setting her wide, wounded eyes on his. "I was traded away for your clan's guaranteed protection." She frowned as something occurred to her. "Just how do the MacGregors know the queen? Why does she protect your clan? Is it because of General Marlow? I know they were dear friends. Anne spoke of him often."

The queen hadn't told her that Adam's mother was the true firstborn daughter of James II. He breathed a sigh of relief. "Aye, their bond is strong."

He set his eyes toward the castle and all the houses nestled around it. "Ye could do worse."

"I suppose that's true. But I *hadn't* done worse. I was betrothed to a good man, a man I love."

He tossed his head back and groaned at the heavens. Truly, he didn't want this. Why was he fighting it? He'd done what was asked of him and took her as his wife. That was enough. He had better things to do, and nothing ever stopped him from doing them before. Nothing would stop him now.

She shivered beside him and wrestled with the tangled plaid in her lap.

Muttering an oath, he sprang to his feet and took the wool from her inept fingers. He flapped it open in the wind and folded it like a shawl. "If ye're foolish enough to try to cross the cliffs," he told her while he covered her head and shoulders with the plaid and placed the edges in her hands between her breasts, "stay close to the wall, face to the stone, arse to the wind. Keep yer eyes open if ye can, and look fer crevices to hold on to. Weight on yer feet though, aye?" He patted her shoulders and stepped back. "If ye return, ye're free to do as ye wish. This *is* yer home now." He smiled and turned back for the hill. "I'm goin' raidin'."

Chapter Four

"Y e dinna eat meat, d'ye?"

Sina turned and took a startled step back at the small, slightly hunched-over old woman who suddenly appeared at her side behind an old barn. Her hair was gray and swirled into a braided bun at her nape. She looked up at Sina with narrowed eyes.

"Well?"

What kind of question was that? Why wasn't she asking Sina what she was doing hiding behind the barn? Was this the village madwoman? A witch hunkering down, breathing out odd questions that mixed with the howling wind?

"What kind of meat?" Sina asked, afraid of the answer. Just how savage were Highlanders?

"What does *that* matter?" the old woman demanded, stepping around to face her. Her tanned face was weathered with age and distinction. She was still quite pretty, with a small nose and a fierce spark in her large blue eyes. "Meat is meat!"

"Not if 'tis..." Oh, it was too unbearable to think about,

but who knew what these people were capable of in winter months when food was low? William had told her once about some people eating— "Human meat."

The woman gasped and snatched Sina's arm. "Do yer people eat human meat?" she asked, horrified.

"No!" Sina quickly told her. "Do yours?"

"Nae!" The woman slapped Sina's hand away, though she was the one who'd grabbed it in the first place. "Of course we dinna. We're no' altogether savage."

"Altogether?" Sina's heart pounded in her ears.

"Well," the woman confessed, bristling in her plaid shawl. "The folks here do eat animals."

"Oh." Sina breathed a little sigh of relief and set her gaze back on the group of mounted men…and a few women, preparing to leave to go steal someone else's cattle.

From her hiding place, where she had been watching Adam MacGregor without his knowledge, her eyes found him again. He wasn't difficult to miss among the riders. He sat tall in the saddle, controlling his great black steed with the same command he held over his shadowy hellhound beside him. To keep his obsidian locks out of his eyes, he'd tied them back from his forehead and let the rest fall freely to his shoulders. He looked dangerous—masculine and barbaric with his long sword dangling from his hip. Beneath his dark brows, his eyes, the same color as the clouds, found and settled on her.

His full, bow-shaped mouth may have curled up at the corners. She couldn't be sure.

"Is he treatin' ye kindly?"

Sina had forgotten the woman was still there with her. She'd been caught watching him, admiring him. She wouldn't back down now.

"He hasn't been unkind," she replied truthfully. "Save

for when he gave me instructions on how to get across the cliffs." She looked toward him again as he rode off with the others. "I don't think he cared at all if I stayed or left."

"If ye want him to care, then give him something to care aboot."

"I don't want him to care," Sina was quick to assure her. What good would it do once she was back home? But there was a part of her that doubted anyone would come and she would live out the rest of her days here. What if she did? Could Adam come to care for her, then? Could she care for him?

"Well, then," the woman called out as she walked away. "Yer dilemma is solved."

"But I'm still here!" Sina shouted back at her. Oh, dear God, what was she going to do? She looked around. There were many people around, coming and going, from house to house or to the castle.

There were children everywhere, laughing, running through the spring flowers with dogs at their feet. Women hung clothes up to dry and stopped to gather and share gossip.

Probably about her, if their gazes on her were any indication. Was talking scandal as popular here as it was at court?

She straightened her shoulders and made her way toward the castle in her wrinkled gown. She'd go to her room and pen her father and poor William a letter. God only knew how she'd deliver them—or if the MacGregors had any quills or parchment. She had to do something. She had to speak to Anne, or have someone speak to Anne for her. She would do anything for the queen. Anything but live among the uncultured and wild. Men who raided cattle and called it honorable. She was afraid of never going back home. Afraid of spending the rest of her life here hidden from society in the mist-covered mountains of nowhere, denied what she'd always hoped for. She thought she might go mad thinking about it.

"I see ye met Maggie."

Sina turned to Adam's mother coming up behind her and tossed the gray hound from the dining hall a hesitant look.

"Oh, dinna worry about Bronwyn," the chief's wife sang. "She wouldn't hurt a mouse."

Sina looked into the hound's honey-colored eyes and then at its white fangs when the beast licked its chops.

"Dinna ye have dogs at court?" Davina asked.

Sina nodded, pulling her gaze from the dog to the lady. Heavens, but she was lovely, with the same pale blond hair as her daughter, hanging in a long braid over her shoulder. Everything about her though was smaller than Abigail, save her enormous silvery-blue eyes. "They are smaller, and I know them."

"Our gels will protect ye," Davina assured and set her elegant hand on Bronwyn's fur. "Ye have nothing to fear from them."

"And the male?" Sina asked. "Goliath?"

Her mother-in-law quirked her mouth and looked away. "He is verra protective of my son, but if he knows Adam disapproves of something, Goliath will never do it."

Well, that was a relief to hear, at least. Sina didn't want the chief's wife to think her too delicate to be around dogs, so she decided to stop worrying about them.

"So, who is Maggie?"

"Adam's great-aunt, Margaret MacGregor," Davina told her. "She was one of the first people to find refuge here."

"Refuge from what?" Sina asked her. There was something about the chief's wife that drew Sina to her. Her wide eyes were like fathomless pools of compassion and grace. Her smile was gentle and kind.

"From persecution because of her name. From life in a dungeon."

Sina's eyes opened wide, and she looked in the direction Maggie had taken. "She spent time in a dungeon?"

"Aye. When she was a child, she was locked in a small cage fer many years until her brother, Callum, who was imprisoned with her, killed the earl's entire garrison on his own and rescued her. 'Twas many years past. He built Camlochlin and brought her and any other persecuted Mac-Gregors here."

Sina's dry mouth made it difficult to swallow. Who would do such a vile thing to a child? And who was this Callum MacGregor that he could take down an entire garrison alone?

"Where is he now?" she asked, unsure if she wanted to meet such a fearsome man.

"He and his wife are visiting his grandson Patrick and his family in Pinwherry. They'll all return in the fall. Maggie adores him and all his bairns. Dinna feel sorry fer her," the chief's wife confided with a playful smile. "She's no meek little flower and eats most of these big, brawny men fer breakfast. Be thankful she is almost always on the women's side."

Sina found herself smiling genuinely for the first time since she'd arrived. She thought she might get along well with Maggie under different conditions, and with Davina too.

But the queen's betrayal hurt too much to trust again. So many people in her life had abandoned her. First her parents, and even William when he went off on the tour. Anne had known how she felt and still sent her here. How could she ever learn to trust people she didn't know, when people she did know let her down?

The MacGregors might not be responsible for all this, but right now, they were all she had to blame. She did her best to keep her voice soft and nonthreatening when any of them spoke to her, but she wasn't sure how long that would last. She suspected that the more days she spent here, cast out of court, the more difficult it was going to be to hold back her tears.

"Come." Adam's mother looped her arm through Sina's and walked with her. The top of her head reached Sina's shoulder, but she walked with the regal elegance of a queen. When she spoke again, her voice, along with her gaze, was warm and inviting. "Let's go share a cup of wine in the solar. Ye can rest. I'm sure ye're weary, aye?"

"Yes," Sina confessed. "I didn't sleep at all last eve."

"Come, then." Davina's serene voice seeped through her. "I will tend to ye myself."

"No, you're the—"

"Please, ye've been through enough. I dinna mind at all."

Sina wasn't sure what to say. Davina MacGregor was a thoughtful, humble woman, unlike most of the ladies at court. She was refined and different than the other women here, who laughed and called out to one another with more vigor.

"You're very kind," Sina allowed.

"We all are," Davina assured. "Some of the men may bluster about from time to time, but they are harmless. More often than not ye'll find them picking heather."

Sina eyed her as they entered the castle. Picking heather?

Her mother-in-law continued speaking while she led Sina upstairs to the solar, a cavernous chamber bathed in golden light from the tall arched windows and the roaring flames of the great hearth. Despite its size, it invoked a feeling of comfort and warmth with colorful tapestries hung amid paintings and bookshelves. Bookshelves? Sina thought with surprise and a bit of delight. Did the chief's wife read? She couldn't help herself and moved toward the lined volumes. Some titles she knew, some she did not.

"You have many books."

"Och, that's nothing compared to my mother-in-law's grand library. From the great hall, 'tis two lefts and a right."

They read. She hadn't expected it. Had she judged them solely on their appearance? On gossip?

Ornately carved tables sat amid a dozen oversized, over-stuffed chairs upholstered in different dyed linens. Each table hosted an array of things, from books and flagons of beaten bronze to chess sets.

"Who plays chess?" she asked curiously.

"Everyone," Davina answered lightly and moved forward to pour their drinks. She passed a beautiful settee and a large fur rug beside it.

Everyone played chess. Who were they? How did they live without the luxury of cobblestone streets, where one could actually stroll? Without shops and theaters, universities or coffeehouses?

Two particularly large chairs sat close to the hearth. Davina pointed to one and handed Sina her cup.

"What else can I get ye?" she offered. "Are ye hungry? A blanket?"

"No, nothing else. Thank you," Sina told her and sipped her drink. It was warm going down.

Davina fell into the matching enormous chair and tucked her feet under her while Bronwyn curled up before the fire. "Would ye like to speak about yer family? Yer father—"

"My father is not a part of my family."

The door opened and Adam's father stepped inside. He certainly was handsome, like his son, with inky black hair that was gray at the temples. He was tall and as broad as a mountain—certainly able to fill these chairs.

"Och, Robbie, darling, would ye mind coming back later?" his wife called out from her chair.

Sina watched him murmur something under his breath. But he smiled at her and left without quarrel.

"Do ye read?" Davina asked when they were alone.

"Yes. Do you?" Sina asked hopefully.

"Of course."

"You weren't raised here, were you?" Sina asked, taking another sip of her wine.

"Nae, I was raised in an abbey."

That explained her grace and poise—

The door opened again. Sina looked up at another handsome, dark-haired man about the same age as the chief. His silver gaze skipped over her, and his mouth hooked into a smile.

"Robbie isna here, Will," Davina informed him with a charming smile. "My daughter and I are having some wine." She lifted her cup and waited for him to leave.

When they were alone again, Davina sat back in her big chair and pulled a nearby woolen blanket over her. "That was Will."

Sina thought she might be a little light-headed from the wine, for she covered her mouth with her hand and giggled. She didn't know why she found it humorous that her host would tell her the man's name when she'd just called him Will.

"He's our cousin," her host continued. "He lives here with Aileas, his wife, and their sons. Dinna worry, I'll make certain to introduce ye to everyone tonight at the gathering."

Sina coughed on the sip of wine she was taking and looked up. "Gathering?"

"Aye." Davina's huge eyes opened wider with excitement. "In the great hall. I thought it would be a good way for us all to get acquainted. This was a small raiding trip, so Adam should be back in time."

Sina liked Adam's mother. The last thing she wanted to do was hurt her feelings, but she didn't want to attend any gathering. She didn't want to be welcomed into the fold. She wanted them to help her get home.

She put down her cup and tried to gather her resolve around her. She leaned forward in her chair and clutched the folds of her skirts. "My lady, after all your kindness, it pains me greatly to say this, but I think this is all some kind of terrible mistake." She paused but then continued. She'd started. She might as well tell her everything. "I am promised to someone else. Someone I love. My wish is to go back to him."

As Sina suspected, Adam's mother didn't take it well. She pulled off her blanket and freed her legs from under her. "Does my son know?" she asked softly. Her eyes glistened in the hearth light.

Sina wanted to weep at how unfortunate this was for all of them, how cruel her words must sound to her groom's mother. But she wouldn't cry. Not again. "Yes, he knows."

Chapter Five

𝒜dam looked across Camlochlin's vast great hall and watched his wife mingling with his kin. He scowled into his cup thinking about having to go to her and stand at her side while his endless list of kin introduced themselves to her. This "gathering" was his mother's idea. She'd cornered him the instant he'd returned from the raid and told him about the celebration she'd planned without his consent—or Sina's—and that he had but a short while to make himself presentable.

It was what his mother hadn't told him that pricked at him. His bride had told her she loved another man. Adam could read it in his mother's softer, kinder expressions. She felt sorry for him.

She should.

But he didn't want her to.

"If ye want to stow away on the ship, just let me know."

Adam turned to look into the vivid blue eyes of his cousin Caitrina. She winked and offered him a deeply dimpled smile.

But it wasn't such a poor idea. *Poseidon's Adventure* was a big enough ship and he wouldn't have to stow away, since it belonged to his cousin.

"Can we leave now? Ye know how I hate these things."

"Ye mean havin' to spend a little time with everyone? Aye, I know."

"Ye did good on the raid today, Trina," he told her, changing the topic before the temptation to flee became too great to resist. "'Tis good to have ye and Risa home." He smiled at the blond hound baring her fangs at her brother, Goliath. "Alex too."

"'Tis good to be home." His cousin looped her arm through his and reached up to plant a kiss on his cheek.

"I never thought I'd see the day ye were wed."

"Nor did I," he murmured. "Keep the ship close by."

"Come, introduce me to her. She looks a bit overwhelmed."

"Aye," he said. Sina looked weary and her gaze went distant often, as if she was wishing she were someplace else. "She was taken from her home and family," he said, not knowing why he felt compelled to defend her.

"Ye should go to her."

He nodded. It was his duty to see to her comfort whether she wanted it or not—according to his uncles Connor Grant and Tristan, whose advice he'd asked on the way home from the raid in Torrin.

Damn it all to hell. Usually, after a raid, he liked to go off on his own and find comfort in a warm, willing body. He met his wife's gaze across the hall as he approached with Trina on his arm. She cast him a scornful look and then looked at him no more.

He wasn't going to find warm and willing tonight.

He let go of his cousin and reached Sina an instant before

Trina did. "I'm glad ye didna choose the cliffs," he murmured, bending to her ear.

"Don't think I wasn't tempted," she whispered back, then set her eyes on Trina.

"May I present my cousin Caitrina, daughter of Connor and Mairi Grant." He paused to motion with his cup to the couple sharing words with his mother. "Granddaughter of Graham and Claire, whom ye met a few moments ago."

"Cousin?" his wife echoed, looking, much to Adam's trained eye, relieved. Why would she be?

"Aye," he told her with a slight smile, watching to see how her delicate sensibilities would handle it when he told her, "and wife of the notorious pirate Captain Alexander Kidd." He pointed his cup in the other direction.

"Pirates," she said, reaching her slender fingers to her earrings. She looked down at the cutlass dangling from Trina's belts, her beringed fingers, her breeches and boots—and Risa snapping and growling at Goliath.

"And you also have a hound."

Adam knew she was afraid of his kin, but he wasn't pleased by her aversion to the dogs.

He waited with her while more of his kin introduced themselves to her. She greeted everyone with polite, mild manners that Adam was sure she'd learned at court. Her obvious—to him, at least—disinterest forced him to be more friendly and open to keep conversations flowing smoothly.

He spotted Will MacGregor and his family coming forward. Will's dog, Ula, the biggest of Goliath's sisters, spotted her brother and galloped forward.

Startled, Sina took a step back and bumped into Adam's chest.

Ula looked up, noticing her and, sensing her fear, grew calm and wagged her tail.

Adam smiled. Ula was the sweetest gel of the brood.

He leaned down and said close to Sina's ear, "She wants ye to give her a pat."

"I couldn't," she answered, moving closer to him.

"She's verra bonny, nae?" he said at Sina's ear, but he wasn't speaking to her. Ula wagged her tail harder.

Adam reached around and took Sina's hand. She resisted slightly when he pulled her hand to the dog. "She willna bite," he promised in a low voice, setting her fingers atop Ula's silky chocolate-blond fur. "Will ye let her smell ye?"

She nodded, stiffening against him as the dog moved forward to smell her.

After a moment of sniffing Sina's skirts, Ula rubbed her big head against Sina's side.

His wife smiled. Adam let go of her hand and watched her stroke Ula's head.

"She likes you," Adam's cousin Duff MacGregor said.

Sina looked up, casting her softest smile on his cousin. It didn't last longer than an instant before she withdrew her hand from Ula, her body from Adam, and her smile from them all.

Adam's smile faded as well. As much as he didn't want to be attending a gathering after a day of raiding, he would have liked her to try to enjoy herself.

"It has been a long day," she said and hurried through meeting Will's family.

Adam watched everyone closely and soon realized that most weren't overly fond of his new bride. They whispered and watched her every expression. It was clear that she didn't want to be here meeting them. Her smiles were stiff and her greetings were short.

Adam wasn't sure how fond of her he was either. He thought he'd made some progress with her, with the dogs at least. But the moment she thought something from her most wretched nightmare might like her—and she might like it in return—she backed away. He thought of Caitrina's ship. Hell, if there was any way out of this without jeopardizing his kin, he would take it.

"Ye could pretend to enjoy yerself," he murmured.

"I did that two hours ago," she replied icily. "You weren't here."

Hell. She'd been keeping this up for two hours? Alone? He felt like a barbarian for being harsh with her when she hadn't even complained. "Did ye sleep today?" When she shook her head, he muttered an oath and took her by the hand. "Come," he said, leading her to a chair. "Sit doun."

"I don't want—"

He looked at his hand holding hers. He felt something stir in his guts, something unfamiliar and risky. He didn't want to ponder it now. He let her go and put his hand on her shoulder to push her down into the chair. He didn't need to use much strength. She was exhausted. He felt his heart softening for her. He resisted. His heart was his to command. He'd never given it over to the whims of women. He wouldn't begin now. Wife or not. Besides, she loved another.

"Are ye tryin' to make yerself ill?" he asked, straddling the chair next to hers. "Mayhap if we pen yer faither that ye're ill, he'll come fer ye? Is that what ye think?"

She spared him an incredulous glare before she set her eyes straight ahead...on nothing. "Yes, Adam, I'm trying to make myself ill in the hopes that one of you will pen my father and I won't be dead before he gets here.

If he comes." She slid her gaze back to his for an instant before she slipped it back to what she'd been staring at before.

But it was enough time for Adam to see the mist across the green expanse of her eyes. Her jaw tightened. She was trying not to cry again. He wanted to reach out and run his fingertips over her cheek. Damn it, he wanted to comfort her.

"Does it even occur to you how my life has been turned upside down?" she asked. "Taken right out of my hands before I could stop it? I'm sorry I cannot pretend to be happy when I am not!"

First, he liked how his name sounded on her lips. She spoke with a slightly Germanic accent. He knew she was angry, and he understood why, but hell, the sound of her voice was like music on the moors.

Second, how did she manage to shout at him without raising her voice? Without even sounding truly angry? He didn't like it. It wasn't real. Her shouting in the church was real. It wasn't beneficial for anger to simmer and stew beneath a mask of etiquette. Still, the power and control she possessed to maintain it astounded him.

Several wisps of her hair fell around her face and caught the light in the dips of its curls. He wondered what would happen if she weren't so proper.

He did understand, in part, what she was going through. If anyone understood, it was him.

"I've been thoughtless," he admitted, softening his gaze. "I should have known my mother would do something like this. She likes merriment."

"I like her," his wife said softly and closed her eyes.

Everyone who met Davina liked her. Still, Adam was surprised to hear Sina confess it.

"Have ye been on yer feet the entire time, as well?" he asked her.

She smiled without opening her eyes. "Yes, 'twas another of my plans for my knees to lock up so that I couldn't sit down unless I was forced." She squinted her eyes open and let her smile remain. "It worked."

She closed her eyes again and he watched her try to stay awake, but despite the clamor on every side, she nearly slipped from her chair and into his arms.

He gathered her up and left his seat.

"No!" she cried out briefly.

Was that wine he smelled on her breath? He lifted her closer and decided she weighed nothing at all. Had she been drinking all day?

"Shhh, 'tis all right, lass." He carried her to the entrance, then turned to his kin. "She hasna slept since she arrived— probably before that. She's afraid and powerless. Let's no' judge her too harshly, aye?"

Satisfied with everyone's agreement, though many appeared shocked at his thoughtfulness, he turned and headed for their chamber above stairs.

His eyes kept a constant vigil on her lowered lids and the lush spray of her deep gold lashes. Her plump, parted lips beckoned him to bring her closer, smell her, taste her. The sweet coral blush of her cheeks tempted him to rub his face against her skin and feel its velvet softness.

He was mad to let himself be taken in by her sublime beauty, her saucy, sweet mouth. He didn't want to be with her to fulfill some required duty. He didn't want to be married, tied down, a slave to a lass's desires. But damn it, he was and there was no changing it. Either he won her heart, or he'd be the only one in Camlochlin whose marriage was miserable. He looked down at her. He couldn't run from this. He couldn't run from any of it anymore. But still...he wanted to.

He continued on toward the bedchamber door with a groan. How was he expected to remain faithful to a heart that would never be his? The weight of it already felt crushing.

He brought her to their marriage bed and refused to look down at her again. He looked at his dear bed instead. How he missed it. The few hours of sleep in his chair had done him little good. After a long day in the saddle and a celebration to top it off, he was ready for sleep.

He set her down on the bed and didn't try to remove any of her clothing. He wouldn't force himself on her. He stepped over Goliath on his way to the other side, pulling off his léine as he went and tossing it over his chair. He missed. He kicked off his boots next and then whatever else was clinging to him and got into bed beside her.

When he closed his eyes, he saw her face. And then he saw nothing else.

Sina opened her eyes in the morning and pulled her earring away from her nose. Remaining still, she looked around, forgetting for a blissful moment where she was. Then she remembered and her heart faltered in her chest. At the edge of the world. In his bed.

How had she arrived here? Had Adam carried her, put her to bed, left her fully dressed? The last thing she remembered was smiling at him. Too much wine and not enough sleep. It was the only reason she would turn traitor on herself...but he hadn't mistreated her. He'd apologized for being thoughtless, and seemed concerned for her well-being. To make it all worse, the sight of him drew the breath from her body, sparked fires in her belly. But none of it meant she should smile at him. If he thought she was weakening—or if she began to weaken—and they consummated the marriage, there would be no hope of getting out of it.

She could hear his breath close to her. He was in bed with her. Why hadn't he slept in the chair? She remembered that he'd barely gotten any sleep the night before. She sat up with a sigh. Let him sleep, then. She wouldn't wake—

Was that his arse? Her eyes opened wider as they adjusted to the soft morning light. "You're naked!" she blurted. He'd had enough sleep for one night. "Adam! Wake up!"

"What the hell is it?" he asked, lifting his head off his pillow and coming awake.

"You're naked!" She pulled the blanket up to her chin for some ridiculous reason. It was he who needed covering. Thank God he was lying on his belly!

He looked at her through hooded eyes, felt his bare parts, and then closed his eyes again. "I dinna remember removin' my breeches."

His hand slipping down his body had drawn her eyes to follow. Her gaze had fallen over the carved contours of his back, the alluring curve of his hip, and then over his bare buttocks.

She remembered being pressed against all that muscle and then tried to breathe and averted her gaze.

"'Tis how I sleep," he said into his pillow.

He sounded more like a groggy bear than a man.

"Well, you must stop sleeping this way immediately!"

He grumbled something that sounded like marriage being a curse and rose from the bed before she had time to look away.

"Do you mind!" she gasped and closed her eyes. But it was too late. She'd seen his buttocks and the backs of his strong thighs. She knew immediately that the image was forever emblazoned on her. How was it that a man could look just as alluring from the back?

"Ye've never seen a man's body before?" he asked from somewhere off to the side, sounding amused. "No' even yer William?"

She didn't answer. Of course she hadn't seen William. What did he think she was?

"You can open yer eyes now, lass."

She didn't know why she obeyed, save that his voice pounded in her ears like ancient drums.

He stood in the light of a candle, wearing hose that reached just below his knees, and nothing else. The image that she thought emblazoned on her thoughts earlier was doused in the glory of this one. William could never look so pleasing in such scandalous attire.

"No," she managed and pulled up the blankets when he returned to the bed.

His strength and the warmth of his body drew her for a moment before she snapped the blankets back and rose from the bed.

And looked into Goliath's dark, dreadful eyes.

"Please," she said, closing her eyes and trying to keep her teeth from chattering. "Do something about this beast."

She heard him mutter a word, and the hellhound retreated to its master's side of the bed.

"He's called Goliath," the bear growled.

She heard him moving about on the bed, snapping the blanket—around him, hopefully.

"I don't care what it's called," she let him know, rubbing her fingers over a scar on her arm and remembering the last run-in she had with a dog. "It frightens me," she told him over her shoulder, chancing a glance at him.

He was sitting up with the blanket gathered low at his waist. His black hair tumbled over his strong, shadowy jaw. His gaze glinted like cool steel in the growing light.

"Well, ye had best care." His tone was smoother than the rarest silk, deep and musical, resonating through her. "He's my friend. He goes where I go."

"That doesn't mean he will be near *me*."

He smiled, giving her the win, and folded his arms behind his head.

He looked like a languid lover waiting for her to come back to bed. She certainly wasn't about to do that.

"Can you not look at me while I dress?"

"Ye're my wife." His husky baritone made her toes burn.

"I don't care."

He gave her a frustrated look, and she thought he might start shouting. He didn't. "D'ye care aboot anything?"

"Aye." She went closer. She didn't want to hurt his feelings, but she wanted him to know the truth. "I care about many things, but they are in other places. Poor William. He—"

He started to turn away from her, but she sat at the edge of the bed, stopping him. "I know you're against this. I know you are. Tell me why. What is this marriage taking from you that makes you as gloomy as I?"

"Same as ye," he said, staring out the window. "My choices."

She touched his foot and softened her gaze on him when he looked at her. "Then let's try to win them back."

Chapter Six

Adam was in the solar with Sina and his father. He didn't know what the hell he was doing here. She'd asked him to come, so he had.

He would have helped her dissolve this farce and to hell with the queen's order, aunt or not. It would be to his benefit to send her home. Plans to make him chief would change and he could have his freedom back. But he wasn't here to support her. He wasn't sure anymore if he wanted her to go. He didn't ever want to go through getting married again. It was done in the sight of God. Their fate together was sealed. There was nothing to be done.

"You must let me write to my father," she told the chief.

"No one said ye couldna write to him," his father replied. He leaned back in his big chair and folded his arms across his chest. "But the queen will no' change her mind."

"The queen will not live forever," she countered in a low voice.

Adam fell into the chair beside her and rested his face

in his hands. She didn't know the queen was the chief's beloved wife's sister.

"Yer father consented," the chief said stiffly. "If he does no' go back on his word and ye're forced to live here—"

She lifted her chin. "The marriage cannot be consummated. You must order that it be so."

Adam's father looked suitably horrified. "Are ye mad, lass?"

"I'd like to pen a letter too." Adam smiled and tossed his legs over the arm of his chair. "To the queen. I'd like to thank her fer this."

"You're free to pursue your passions elsewhere," his wife said shortly, realizing finally that he was here for entertainment purposes only.

"My mother was raised in a Catholic abbey," he told her, his smile still intact, his voice wooden. "As if that weren't enough, my grandmother has made it her life's purpose to make Camelot oot of this place. My sins are already piled up. I willna add adultery to them—though ye sorely tempt me."

"Then you will have to be strong," she muttered.

"What?" He laughed. "I can tell ye right now no' to count on that."

She stared at him. Her breath came short, flaring her nostrils. "You would force yourself on me?"

"Dinna be a fool. I've never had to ferce myself on any woman. Ye willna be the first."

She clutched the arms of her chair until her knuckles turned white. But she kept her damned cool. He was used to fighting lasses with tempers forged in hellfire. But this woman exasperated him by hiding behind her calm façade.

Adam wanted to unravel her.

"I will never consent," she promised tightly.

"Nae?" he challenged, even as his father rose from his chair. "How aboot I write to the queen and tell her that ye refuse? What will the bishop think? What will yer faither think when the crown no longer has the loyalty of the Highlands?"

Her large eyes narrowed on him. She turned them to the chief, who nodded at Adam and left the solar without another word.

Adam loved his father for standing with him and not opposing anything Adam had said—and for leaving.

He didn't like threatening Sina, but if she thought he was going to remain celibate for a year, she needed to be set straight. "Ye dinna have to love me," he told her coolly, feeling more like his usual self than he had since before his wedding.

"Love you?" she said, turning away from him. "I don't even like you."

Adam straightened his legs and sat forward in his chair. "What was that ye said? Hell, woman, speak up. Were ye taught to be a mouse at court?" A dark thought suddenly skipped across his thoughts. "I will never strike ye fer yer boldness. Is that why ye're afraid of me? Hell, ye've met my sister and my cousins. I can take yer worst."

"Of course you won't strike me," she told him quietly. "I will kill you if you do."

He smiled. She was no mouse. She was only disguised as one.

"As for my demeanor," she continued, "I was raised to behave as a lady, sober and well-mannered. I will speak my mind. I chose not to shout it."

"Good." He moved in a little closer. "Because this matter between us needs to be discussed."

"Which one? There are many."

"The one where ye think I'll be content to sleep in bed with ye fer a year and no' have ye. Yer Lord Standoff—"

"Standish," she corrected. "William Standish."

"—might be better able to resist ye, but I'm no'. If I must work so hard at keepin' ye happy, I'll have somethin' fer my effort."

"Your *effort*?"

"Aye, my effort. This works both ways," he told her, shifting his hand between them.

"What is this?" she demanded, aping him. "This marriage? This farce? It means nothing to me! Or to you, but you're too afraid to do anything about it."

"Ye dinna understand what's at stake."

"I know what's at stake for me!" she told him. "The end of everything I know and love."

"And it could be the end of everything I know and love if I send ye back."

"Then we will go on just like this," she warned through tight lips.

"That's fine with me," he said with a smirk. "I like lasses with some spirit. But ye will obey the queen and consummate this marriage or cause trooble to yer faither."

"My father will dissolve this marriage the moment he's king," she insisted on a shallow breath while she wrung her hands in her lap.

Adam noted the shadow of doubt that crossed her features. "What if he lets it stand?" he asked her, softening his tone. "How long am I supposed to wait?"

She closed her eyes and took a deep breath, clearly trying to keep her composure. "Until you rot, for all I care."

He laughed. He liked her fire, gently issued though it was. "Trust me, lass, I'll have ye long before that."

"You're a savage!" she finally erupted, springing to her feet.

"Ye're an overindulged princess," he responded calmly.

She gasped as if he had struck her, then she leaned over the table closest to her chair, picked up a chess piece, and flung it at him.

He ducked, narrowly avoiding a queen to the eye. He bounded to his feet, glaring at her.

Unfazed by his towering anger, she reached for a knight.

"That is my faither's favorite set," he warned. "Put it doun."

She looked at the knight, dropped it, and picked up a cup instead.

"Sina," he warned.

She pulled back her arm and let the cup fly.

Adam had had enough. "I dinna know what ye're used to." He swooped down on her before she had time to pick up anything else. He pressed his shoulder to her waist and hefted her up over his shoulder like a sack of grain. "But I know things are goin' to be different."

She could rant and rage all she wanted, but not in his father's solar.

Hell, she was ranting and raving now! Her punches to his back felt like sharp little needles. She kicked her heeled shoes, exposing her knees in front of him.

As was usual in the morning, there were many folks coming and going throughout the castle. For the most part, he kept his eyes on the stairs, though he did spot his mother and his aunt Isobel watching him, along with others with pitying smiles.

He sighed. The support didn't help. The madwoman over his shoulder was his problem.

But at least she'd finally shed that meek façade. She was

fiery and she would be happier if she didn't always try to control herself.

She cursed him in German and in English and pounded on his back.

Everyone else around her might be miserable, but she'd be happier—and that, according to Camlochlin's unspoken laws, was how it was supposed to be, wasn't it?

Thank God. The stairs. Goliath beat him up them. Adam wasn't far behind and pushed open the door to their bedchamber. He brought her to the bed and dumped her in it. He returned to the door, kicked it shut, and then ducked when he saw the small clay basin by his bed coming at him.

It crashed into pieces against the door.

She looked around for something else to throw.

"I could command Goliath to stop ye," he warned.

At the mention of his name, Goliath perked his ears and licked his chops.

She lowered her arm and her left shoe, which she was ready to hurl at him next.

He liked how she looked in his bed, on her knees in his blankets, her neat bun in ruins around her small, round face. He wanted to go to her and take her, as was his right. But she wasn't going back to England. They were about to begin their lives together, and she sparked a desire in him to be more than just her husband.

"The moment that hellhound is out of your sight," she promised, back to her usually quiet voice, "I'm going to make you wish you'd never met me."

Hellhound? Adam cast his friend an understanding look. "I'm never oot of my dog's sight," he told her, leaning his shoulder against the doorframe. "And I already wish I'd never met ye."

She flung her shoe at him and hit him in the chest with the heel.

He watched the shoe hit the floor, then spread his arms at his sides. "So ye care suddenly what I think of ye?"

She tossed back her head and laughed a little. His gaze raked over the delicate column of her neck. She was his. He stepped closer to the bed.

"I would have to care for you," she charged, still smiling when she looked at him.

Adam could do many things well, but reading people was his best skill. He'd spent most of his childhood around adults. They were often quiet around him, so he practiced watching for the subtlest nuances of changes in expressions, mostly the eyes, body movements, and a host of other things.

Her smile was forced. She was trying to conceal something else.

"And I could never care for a savage."

Her words pierced through his flesh like fire-tipped darts. He wasn't sure which part of her declaration bothered him the most, true or not, that she could never care for him or that she still thought him a savage, or why it bothered him at all. "Ye keep callin' me that, and I'll behave like one."

Her eyes blazed. Her mouth rounded like a cherry, dragging his gaze there.

"You don't think flinging me over your shoulder and parading my arse in the air in front of your family and friends was not savage?"

"Ye left me no other choice," he reminded her. Every part of him wanted to move toward her. How long would he go along with her mad request for abstinence in their marriage? "Yell and screech at me all ye want," he said, keeping his voice light and unaffected by her, "but there's no need fer violence. Aye?"

"Screech?" Her eyes hardened. His gaze fell to her other shoe now gripped in her hand. "You don't know how to speak to a woman. 'Tis obvious you don't know how to listen to one either."

She was a viper, Adam thought, lifting his amused gaze to hers. "Mayhap if she had something of interest to say rather than constantly remindin' me of her displeasure, I would speak differently."

"And perhaps if you didn't—what are you doing?" she asked, her eyes wide when he sat on the edge of the bed.

"I'm sittin' in my bed."

"Well, go sit in your chair."

He should. He should get away from her. He wanted to touch her, taste her, kiss her insults off her lips.

He didn't leave the bed, but lay back in it and looked up at her. "D'ye think me yer servant?"

She turned away from him, looking uneasy. She lifted her hand to her throat and expelled a short breath. "I—can you sit up while you speak to me?"

He shook his head. "I'm more comfortable like this."

"Barbarian." At least this time she didn't mutter it.

"If no' jumpin' at the whim of a spoiled brat makes me a barbarian, then so be it."

She leaped at him, her heeled shoe ready to swing. He caught her wrist and pulled her closer. When she tried to slap him with her other hand, he caught that one too and held her aloft above him.

So he discovered that she didn't like being called spoiled. Why?

"I said no more weapons," he said patiently while he stared into her glacial eyes.

"And I said I want to go home."

He could have her right now, wild and passionate in his arms, but he didn't want her passion to be hatred. She wanted abstinence, so abstinence she would get.

Even if it killed him.

Still holding her wrists, he pulled her arms above his shoulders, bringing her down on top of him. He held her there for a moment, her mouth so close to his that he could feel her breath mingling with his.

He leaned his head up and brushed his lips against her cheek...her ear. "Ye are home, lass."

He pushed her up and off him, then rose from the bed and walked toward the door.

"The sooner ye accept that, the happier ye'll be."

He stepped out into the hall and closed the door behind him. His shoulders bunched around his ears when another clay item smashed to bits on the other side.

Chapter Seven

Adam leaned back in a chair in his cousin Will's tavern on the outskirts of Camlochlin. He lifted his cup to his lips and downed the warm whisky inside.

He caught the eye of bonny Mary MacDonald serving at one of the larger tables and lifted his empty cup to her.

She sauntered over, her milky bosom pushing up from her tight stays.

He clenched his jaw and looked away.

"Why so somber today, Adam?" she asked, filling his cup. "Ye look like ye're in need of m' warm body to help bring back yer joy."

"Alas, lovely Mary," he lamented, stretching his long legs beneath the table, wanting to run. "I am wed. Yer warm body will be sorely missed."

"Wed?" she asked, looking and sounding as incredulous as he had after his father read the queen's letter out loud. "Why would ye do such a thing as wed a poor lass?"

He smiled into his cup despite this being the second most miserable day of his life.

"'Twas arranged," he told her quietly, hating once again the price of power he didn't want.

"Why did ye no' just refuse?" poor, ignorant Mary asked.

"If only 'twere so easy," he said after a long sigh.

He watched Mary leave. No matter what he had been before, that part of his life was over.

He looked into the cup he wanted to drown himself in and then peered up when Goliath leaped to his four paws and Daniel Marlow slipped into a chair across the table.

"Ye havena told me yet what ye think of this marriage," he said while Daniel lifted his hand to Mary for another set.

"I pity you."

Adam lifted his brow and one corner of his mouth.

"I'm completely sincere," Marlow insisted. "No one in the castle is happy about this."

"But nothin' can be done aboot it?" Adam asked. If anyone knew the law, it was the queen's general.

"No, nothing. If she decreed it and you don't do it—"

"I know," Adam stopped him. He didn't want to think about being pushed around by his aunt, who had done nothing to repeal his clan's proscription. He owed her nothing, not even his allegiance. Still, Sina's father, who would be king, had given his consent, so he wanted this too. It meant continued safety for his clan, and it meant Sina was staying, despite what they both hoped. The future king wasn't binding her to the future chief's brother—if that chief were Abby.

Hell, Adam hadn't planned on discussing this with anyone, especially not with his brother-in-law.

"This union canna be pleasin' to ye since yer wife believes she will be chief. Ye and I both know that now that I'm wed to a Hanover, there is no way I willna be chosen."

Daniel took his cup from Mary and took a swig of his

ale. "Abby knows. She also knows what's best for the clan."

"Aye, and she believes what's best is her. What if she's correct?"

"What if she's not?"

Adam listened, wondering if he'd had too much to drink and he wasn't hearing right.

"Adam." The general moved in a little closer. "I know what you want everyone here to believe. That all you care about is raiding, women, and whisky, but I know better. On the Black Isle," he confessed, "and I'll admit, before that, I saw a man who used mercy and fairness over judgment. That's why I asked for Lachlan's life to be placed in your hands. I knew you would make the correct decision."

"Abby would have made the same decision," Adam said into his cup before he drank from it.

"Abby would have done what her uncle commanded her to do. You put an individual before the whole. Hear me, I believe my wife would make an excellent chief, but so would you. 'Tis all I'm saying."

Adam laughed, but Marlow was serious. What the hell was he supposed to think about this? He was the second person, Lachlan MacKenzie being the first, to tell him he'd be a good chief. What did they know? "I dinna know whether I should thank ye, or strangle ye."

"I know the next chief will have huge boots to fill," his friend went on, proving he understood the enormity of this. His vivid green gaze softened. "Whether 'tis you or Abby who must fill them, I've no doubt the correct choice will be made. You are like them, brother."

"Like who?" Adam asked, tossing him a curious glance while he reached down and sank his fingers into Goliath's fur.

"Like your grandsire and your father, the great chiefs before you."

Adam laughed. Marlow must have been drinking before he came in. "D'ye jest? I'm nothin' like them. Ye're correct to say I care aboot things, but I'm no' passionate aboot the things they are passionate aboot. Ye speak of fillin' their boots. Tell me how Abby or I can ever do what they have done. My grandfaither fought a war against the Campbells *alone*. My faither—hell, Rob MacGregor is the best of men in my eyes and in my heart."

"In the heart of every person in Camlochlin," Daniel added, further proving Adam's point. "But so what? Everyone has their own destiny, brother. It seems Melusina de Arenburg is to be a part of yours. By marrying her you've shown the clan that their safety comes before your happiness. They all understand it now, even Abby. Believe me."

Yesterday, when he still had a choice about his future, this would have been a bad thing. But not now. His fate had been sealed in a chapel. He'd always defied it, doing everything he could to convince his clan that he would make a poor leader. Now that the choice was no longer in his hands, things felt different. He didn't have to be the person he'd become anymore. There was no point, but he wasn't sure he knew how to be anyone else. He was glad this marriage gave his kin the chance to see something new in him.

"'Tis one thing I've done. Is it enough to change their minds aboot what kind of leader I will be?" Hell, just the thought of it made Adam want to bolt. But he couldn't run from it anymore.

"You could have done a thousand things, but the one you did yesterday would still be the most important. Adam," his brother-in-law said when they put down their cups, "you must stop running from who you are. You want your freedom from the bonds of duty, but there's honor in duty. There's honor in Camlochlin and 'tis engrained in you."

"I know," Adam agreed, surprised that Daniel knew it too. Surprised that he'd looked deeper. No wonder Marlow had seven different titles, including general of Her Majesty the Queen's Royal Army and knight of the Most Noble Order of the Garter.

"I've never run from honor," Adam told him. "It may seem as if I dinna practice it all the time." He paused to curl his lips into an unrepentant smile. "But I'm no' ignorant to the teachin's of home. I just dinna know if I'm ready to be chief."

"You won't be alone," Daniel assured him.

For a moment Adam had to take it in again that this was his sister's husband sitting here encouraging him to accept his father's seat.

"Or to be a husband," Adam added.

"Again, you won't be alone. There are plenty of husbands in Camlochlin who will advise you."

"There's a difference," Adam told him. "You all loved yer wives before ye wed them."

"So," Daniel laughed and swigged the remainder of his drink, "there's a romantic beneath all that I-don't-give-a-damn veneer?"

Adam was almost certain he didn't possess a romantic bone in his body. But he *was* scared out of his damned head that he and Sina would never love each other and would grow old and miserable. But he'd save that confession for another day.

They both turned to the raucous voices of Adam's brothers as they entered the tavern.

"I dinna care. I'm sayin' something," Braigh insisted, leading the charge.

Judging by the deep scowl of determination his brother wore, Adam guessed he had complaints. Who didn't?

Behind Braigh, Tam, the quieter, slightly thinner of the two, poked him in the ribs and pointed to Adam and the general sitting at the small table.

Adam narrowed his eyes at them as they approached the table and pulled two more chairs closer. "We thought we'd find ye here bleedin' into yer cup."

Adam loved the twins, and sometimes when he looked at them, like now, he couldn't fathom where a score and four years had gone. They were as big as he was, but he still enjoyed playing and fighting with them, and mayhap, if he were fortunate, cause a wee bit of mayhem in their lives.

"Do I look like I'm bleedin', Braigh?" he asked, leaning back in his seat. "I was enjoyin' a drink with Daniel before ye two came in."

"Ye see?" Braigh turned to Tam with concern marring his golden brow. "Even his wit has gone sour."

Adam cast him a stony look.

"Aye, ye're correct," Tam agreed, studying Adam closely. "I see."

Adam hooked one corner of his mouth and met Tam's careful assessment with a smile and a tone laced with challenge. "What d'ye see, Tam? Tell me."

Tam, the youngest by a few moments, blew out a sigh and lifted his hands, giving in easily. Unlike his almost identical brother, Tam had little interest in combat and more in wooing bonny lasses.

Adam's victorious grin was instantaneous and brief. At least this one knew not to go up against him.

"I dinna even want to be here," Tam complained, unhappy and brooding now that he'd been singled out.

Adam slipped a furtive glance to Daniel, who chuckled softly while he listened.

"I left Marybeth MacKinnon on the braes of Bla Bheinn because Braigh told me there was something peculiar aboot ye."

Frowning, Adam kicked Tamhas under the table. "Why did ye leave her? My bein' peculiar is nothin' new." He then shifted his gaze to Braigh and shook his head. "And ye, never interrupt a man when he's in the arms of a bonny lass. What the hell is wrong with ye?"

Braigh took offense immediately and bristled in his plaid. "What's wrong with *ye*? Ye're the one who hasna smiled in two days. I'll admit ye seem more yerself presently—an arrogant, irritatin' pain in our arses."

With his hand over his heart, Adam turned to the general, pretending to be choked up.

"We dinna like yer wife," Braigh went on, as Adam knew he would. "We dinna like that she's makin' ye so unhappy."

Hell, the monsters weren't all that bad. Adam gave them both a long look, long enough to make them squirm. He'd had enough of teasing them. He was sincerely moved by why they didn't like his wife. But his wife would never be happy here if his kin didn't like her. And if she wasn't happy, she'd make certain he wasn't either. Life would be hard enough for him as chief without Sina and his kin not getting along. He had to mend things.

"She isna makin' me unhappy, lads," he told them in a gentler tone. They should be out kissing lasses and running from angry fathers, not worrying about him. "We were both thrown into this. Think of what 'tis like fer her. She doesna know any of us. She was taken from her home and those she loves." He paused as a faceless man invaded his thoughts. He pushed him away and swigged the rest of his drink. "She willna ever see them again since we dinna travel to England. Have patience with her."

He caught the general grinning and ignored him. "I'll tell ye what would make me unhappy, lads," he told them. "If my brothers didna even try to like her."

The twins exchanged a look and a nod. "Are ye goin' to try to like her?" Braigh asked.

What choice did he have? She was his wife. "Aye," he assured with a smile they were waiting to see. "Of course. Now let's get back. I should see to her."

They left their coin on the table for Mary and headed for the door.

Adam left with them, but when he looked into the sunlit vale with its dark castle rising from the mountain behind it, its meticulously built manor houses and well-kept cottages sprinkled about its vast expanse, his legs wouldn't take him where he wanted to go. Soon, everything would be on his shoulders. It already was. He had to go see to his unhappy wife and figure out a way to help his clan like her. Hell, he didn't want any of this. He wasn't sure he could do it.

"I'll be along in a bit," he told the others and turned back toward the hill with his hand on Goliath's head.

Chapter Eight

My dearest William,
'Tis with the heaviest of hearts that I pen this
letter. Though I know you will never read it, I can
pretend that I'm speaking to you. It might help me get
through this most terrible mockery forced upon me by
the queen! I am heartsick that I am bound to a man I
do not know. A man of whom I can find little to ad-
mire. He's arrogant and infuriating.

She paused as she remembered her outburst two days
ago. She'd never reacted so poorly in the past. Adam Mac-
Gregor brought out the worst in her. She had to admit,
though only to herself, that it felt rather good to kick and
scream and lose her temper.

To help you understand the barbarian I've been
sworn to, his closest friend is a black hound from the
piths of hell he calls Goliath.

Oh, William, the hounds. They are everywhere! They are as big as ponies. They frighten me. You remember Lord Sunderland's mastiff... I can still see its fangs sinking into my flesh.

Sina put down her quill and rubbed her fingers over a scar on her left forearm. She sat at a small table beside the window in Adam's chambers. She had barely seen or spoken to him in two days. He avoided her during the day and slept in his chair at night, gone in the morning before she woke up. She didn't mind his absence. The less she looked at him or spoke to him, the less she wanted to.

But she couldn't help but wonder where he was. Who he was with. Had his claim to remain faithful been sincere? What did she care?

I vow to you, my dear William, that I will never love him. If I am not released from this marriage and must stay here for the remainder of my days, I will never let him have my heart, for it belongs only to you, my beloved, dearest friend. I wish it were you I had wed. But alas, I am payment for MacGregor fealty to my father.

I can certainly understand why anyone would want the MacGregors on their side. They are great stalwart men and, to my astonishment, even the women practice swordplay! I can see them from my bedchamber window. They are at it day and night. They are fierce, and 'tis a shocking sight to behold. One of them is a pirate!

I could never be like any of them. I don't belong here.

As each moment passed, it hit her harder. What if no help came? As long as Anne lived, there was nothing anyone could do. No one could defy the queen's order without terrible consequences, from which Sina wanted none to suffer.

There was nothing she could do for now. It made her want to scream and go grab a sword and start swinging.

She turned to look out the window. She didn't want Anne to die. Anne had been more like a mother to her than her own. That's why this betrayal cut so deeply.

She wiped her eyes. She was done weeping. She was fighting the wrong people. If she had to live with the Mac-Gregors temporarily, she would try to get along with them. They didn't seem so bad, really. The women had all been kind, so far, despite her hesitancy to open up to them. The men, though frightening in size, all seemed unusually gentle and attentive. Save for raiding, they hadn't done anything savage yet.

She folded her parchment and went to the wardrobe where she'd finally found her other wrinkled dress. She slipped William's letter in the pocket of her skirts.

If they could read and one of them opened it...

No. She'd see William again one day soon and give him everything she'd written. Then he would know she had no part in this.

Pinching her cheeks to give herself some color, she stepped out of the chamber. She was tired of moping in Adam's room. She thought about going outdoors to watch the women practice. Should she? Watching them from the window had made her heart pound. They appeared so fearsome and beautiful with their braids and their swords swinging, going against even the men.

She spotted Adam's mother leaving the solar with her hound at her side, and called out to her. "May I have a word, my lady?"

"Of course," Lady Davina replied with an immediate smile when she turned to her. "Are ye feeling better?"

Sina paused, feeling her cheeks go up in flames. The last time Davina had seen her, she was flung over Adam's shoulder, kicking and shouting. It was shameful behavior for a lady of the court, especially witnessed by a woman of such natural grace as Lady Davina MacGregor.

Sina lowered her lashes to veil her humiliation. Best to get it over with and quit hiding. "Forgive me for my outburst. I'm not usually fiery tempered. I've been angry with all of you, when 'tis the queen and my father with whom I should be angry."

Davina bent her chin and looked away. "My hope is that one day ye will no longer be angry at all."

She finally lifted her tender gaze and reached for Sina's arm.

Sina let her take it. She didn't back away when Adam's mother twined their elbows together. In fact, she couldn't help but smile.

She appreciated that the chief's wife let the matter go while they walked together side by side toward the stairs.

"I was wondering about something," Sina said, remembering what she'd wanted to ask Davina in the first place. "Why do the women here practice fighting?"

"Everyone in Camlochlin knows how to defend their lives," the chief's wife told her, "whether it be with bow and arrow, or sword, fists, or pistol. Though we live a peaceful life here, the name MacGregor is still proscribed."

"Why are you proscribed?"

They reached the top of the stairs, and Sina looked down to see Adam taking the last two steps up to reach them.

Sina hated herself for looking at him with anything but

opposition and resistance. She didn't want to admire his striking good looks, his beguiling, plump lips.

He wore his hair pulled away from his forehead and temples and set free around his shoulders like shadows against the light. She didn't want to notice that he'd been scowling an instant before he looked up and saw her and his expression softened.

"The queen never spoke of us?" he asked curiously, reaching the second landing. His silver-tinted eyes settled for a moment on his mother, and then to her arm coiled with Sina's.

"Adam," the chief's wife said with a thread of admonishment in her voice.

Sina wondered why Davina would be bothered by such a question.

His gaze flicked to his mother. His smile softened as he acquiesced to her silent demand.

How precisely did the queen know the MacGregors? Had she met them through her dearest friend, General Marlow? Why did she allow Sina to leave her side and go live with people she didn't know?

"The queen may have mentioned the MacGregors when speaking of General Marlow," Sina told him, averting her gaze from his. "We never spoke of the proscription. I know of it only through kitchen gossip. I—"

"Ah, gossip," he said, as if the meaning of life had just become clear.

"Why are you taking that tone?" she asked.

He dipped his chin and, with a cock of his lips, fastened his eyes on her. "What tone is that?"

He knew exactly what tone she meant. Why was he speaking to her now and not running the other way? Perhaps a push would help him get moving and wipe that infuriating, bone-melting half smile off his face. The stairs were directly behind him. It was one way to get out of the marriage.

"It's true," she said calmly, not willing to lose her temper again in front of the chief's wife. "All I know of your people, I know from gossip. I...I may have judged *some* too hastily."

His smile turned into an achingly tantalizing pout. "Some?"

He was dangerous if she let him be.

"Aye." Holding on to his mother, she pushed past him. "Some."

He laughed behind her. She ground her teeth and kept going. She hadn't judged *him* too hastily. How many hearts had he broken besides the ones in the chapel? Did he think he could break hers? Was he trying to beguile her or irritate her already raw nerves? She had to stop him from doing both.

She turned to the chief's wife, her pleasant smile intact. "So, my lady, you were telling me about the proscription."

He stayed close while Davina told her of the ancient MacGregor-Campbell feud filled with violence and sorrow.

Sina was so caught up in the tale of Callum MacGregor and Kate Campbell finding each other amid the hatred that she was barely aware of Adam somewhere behind them or the two hounds trotting close by.

"Kate had heard terrible tales of the Devil MacGregor," Davina told her. "She considered the MacGregors the scourge of Scotland: uncivilized barbarians with no regard for honor or a man's family."

"When she first met him," Adam finally spoke as he came around them and swept his gaze over hers, "she discovered she was mostly correct."

Sina was certain she was. Poor woman. "And then what happened?" she asked while they approached the front doors. She was sure he was going to tell her that once she came to know the laird, she quickly fell in love with him. She would then ask him if his grandmother was betrothed to another man at the time.

"And then," he told her, spreading his gaze around the halls as if he too were caught up in his grandparents' tale, "she helped him build his kingdom. She looked deeper and taught him and his kin what they didna know."

Sina felt her heart go a little soft toward the MacGregors, especially Adam's grandmother. Sina couldn't begin to imagine taming a man who had inherited the title of the Devil and turning his isolated fortress into Camelot.

"Adam." They turned at Maggie's voice to find her hurrying toward them. "I was lookin' fer yer faither, but ye're just as good."

Sina watched him grace his great-aunt with a smile so tender that she almost doubted her first impression of him after all.

"Come tell the cook not to slaughter Sadie." Maggie took his hand and tugged.

"Who's Sadie?" Adam asked, taking a step to follow her.

Maggie stopped and turned her large blue eyes to him. "The brown cow with the white eye? Ye brought her in last night from the Dunbars' herd."

While she waited for him to remember, she turned to Sina. "I'm glad to see ye on yer own two feet, gel."

Sina lowered her gaze, sorry that Maggie had seen her fall apart.

"Next time," Maggie continued, pointing her finger at her, "dinna let this one cart ye around as if ye were his child. Make yer fight on yer feet." Her gaze slipped back to her nephew. "Adam, my love, what are ye still doin' here?"

"Let me go." Davina detached herself from Sina and

stepped away. She let out a little laugh. "I was on my way to the kitchen anyway."

Maggie tossed her a worried look. "Will ye be firm, Davina?"

"I may need yer help, Aunt Maggie," Davina answered and winked at her.

For a moment, Maggie looked a bit confused, but then, as if a bell went off in her head, she grinned and glanced at Adam and Sina before hurrying off.

"Verra subtle, ladies," Adam called out after them with a thread of low laughter tangled in his voice.

Sina felt ill. The two women in Camlochlin whom she liked the most were playing matchmaker to her and Adam. Everyone was trying to push her into his arms. She didn't want to go. Did she? She remembered being in them on her wedding night when Goliath frightened her. No arms had ever been stronger.

Keeping William clear in her head, she hurried away, leaving Adam alone in the hall.

Chapter Nine

Sina found her way to the training field and watched the women she'd seen from her window. She refused to let Adam MacGregor invade her thoughts while she enjoyed the afternoon.

She thought she'd be opposed to women warriors. She'd never seen any at court in England or Germany. But against the backdrop of rugged mountain ranges and a vast gray sky, they looked powerful and deadly, more wildly untamed and beautiful than any woman she'd seen in her lifetime.

She recognized Adam's cousin Caitrina slamming her cutlass against her pirate husband's blade. Both wore kerchiefs around their heads and gold loops in their lobes.

Captain Kidd held nothing back while he struck and parried. His wife took every blow and matched them with lethal ones of her own.

Sina couldn't look away. She could never fight like them. But, then, she wouldn't want to live a pirate's life either.

There were other couples practicing. Abby and General Marlow lifted their blades to each other, as well. Their swings were less treacherous and more precise, but no less terrifying.

Adam's brothers, Braigh and Tam, practiced with their cousins Nichola and Violet.

Everywhere she looked in the training fields, women fought with the men and with each other. They laughed and they argued, but none struck in anger.

"I could teach ye to fight."

She controlled her startled reaction to hearing Adam's deep voice behind her. She kept her eyes on the training and didn't move, despite the lure of his warmth and the urge to turn around and look at him.

"No, you would too often tempt me to kill you."

His soft, slow chuckle at her ear sent a lick of heat down her spine. She stepped forward.

"I can protect myself," he promised, coming around to stand beside her.

If he possessed the same skill as the rest of them, she didn't doubt it.

"Thank you, but I won't be here long enough to learn anything significant."

She was glad when yet another one of his cousins appeared and challenged him to the field.

This one, Luke MacGregor, was even bigger than the rest. He carried no weapon but his husky arms.

It looked as if they were going to fight with fists. Barbaric. She should leave.

Instead, she watched Adam meander to the field and roll up his sleeves. They exchanged a few words and laughed together before Luke threw a powerful blow. Sina squinted her eyes and felt just a tad relieved when Adam easily avoided the huge fist to his face.

Sina didn't know why she cared if Adam were hurt.

She'd wanted to hurt him herself on a few occasions. But other than irritate her, he hadn't done anything deserving of a beating.

And it didn't seem as if he would get one. He barely threw a punch and hadn't been hit by one yet. He side-stepped most strikes and blocked the rest with his forearms, frustrating his opponent.

In fact, he was quick enough to lean back from a right hook to the chin and take a moment to turn and cast her a brief smile.

Her belly coiled into a tight little knot. What was happening to her? Was she truly attracted to him? What about William? So what if Adam was pleasing to the eye and quick on his feet and with his mind? Any woman would find the dashing tilt of his lips and his playful gaze a bit irresistible.

She was too busy admonishing herself for admiring him and didn't notice Will MacGregor's hound Ula running toward her until the beast was almost upon her.

But Adam saw. Sina watched him lose his focus and get caught with a left jab just as Ula reached her.

Sina turned and held up her hands to ward off the beast. Her eyes opened wide with horror as Ula bounded up on her hind legs, standing as tall as Sina was, and brought her front paws down on Sina's shoulders. Her weight nearly brought Sina to her knees.

Death would have been better than staring, paralyzed with fear, at the fangs about to sink into her face. She couldn't scream. She couldn't make a sound or close her eyes. Memories of being bitten as a child overwhelmed her.

But Ula didn't bite her. She slopped her wet tongue on Sina's face from chin to cheek and then fell back to all fours.

Once the dog was no longer blocking her view, she saw Adam standing an arm's distance away. He quirked his damned sensual mouth when she wiped her face with her sleeve. Then he turned a much harder look on the dog.

"Ye know better, Ula. Go home."

With the edge of her sleeve still pressed to her cheek and her heart finally slowing down, Sina watched the dog turn away with a lowered head and tail. She almost called Ula back. The hound hadn't done anything but lick her...and frighten her half to death. Sina didn't want her to get into trouble over it though.

But she didn't want to care about these people—or their dogs.

"Are ye injured at all?" Adam asked her.

"No."

"She seems taken with ye." He set his luminous blue eyes on the dog in the distance and shook his head. "'Tis no' a good sign."

"Why not?" She looked toward the dog as well.

"Because ye might no' be able to rid yerself of her. The hounds grow to love certain people, and sometimes they choose to stay with them."

Love? Stay? Sina didn't feel comfortable hearing words like those. She couldn't give up hope that someone would rescue her, that the queen would change her mind, something.

"Your lip is bleeding," she said, not realizing that her eyes had dipped to his mouth.

He touched his fingers to his lower lip, then pulled them back to see the bit of blood there. He shrugged his shoulders. "I was distracted."

By her. He'd seen Ula and was struck just before the dog jumped. He'd been hit because of her.

"Did it hurt very badly?" she asked, trying not to sound overly concerned or guilty.

His eyes seemed to pierce right through her—like steel-tipped arrows—seeing what she tried to conceal. It made him smile and her look away.

"No' too badly," he told her softly. "He'll never let me ferget it though."

"Adam," his cousin called out from the field, as if on cue, "are ye quittin' because I hit ye?"

"Ye see?" Adam pointed out with an extra dash of amusement coloring his eyes before he turned to Luke.

"Ye struck me while I was distracted. How noble is that, knight?"

"In a real fight," Luke countered, "d'ye stop and wait until yer opponent pays attention?"

"'Twasn't a real fight, and my wife was aboot to be mauled."

"By Ula?" His cousin laughed. "Come back and prove it canna happen again."

Adam laughed and shook his head, then turned back to Sina. "D'ye want to take a walk?"

She blinked and realized she was smiling at him like some lackwit. "A walk?"

"Aye." His smile remained as he bent to meet her gaze. "Or d'ye have somethin' else to do?"

"No." She sighed inwardly. She had nothing else to do and the day was long. "But after avoiding me for a pair of days, I'm surprised you're not running off."

"Runnin' just keeps leadin' me back to the same place," he said with the slightest of smiles.

With an arch of her brow, she turned to go. She would be careful around him—careful not to fall under the spells he wove so effortlessly with his voice, his expressions shifting from amused to even more amused, his words. She would be careful not to pick up a rock and smash it over his head.

"Are ye hungry?" he asked, keeping step beside her. "'Tis close to supper. We're goin' to be invited to eat in every house we pass."

He went a little paler than usual and tugged at his léine as if it were suddenly too tight. "'Tis important fer ye to get to know my kin."

"Why?" she asked on a soft breath. "To make it harder on us all when I leave?"

He looked at her, all emotion gone from his face. He seemed as if there was something he wanted to say to refute her. Finally, he lowered his gaze to the ground and continued walking in silence.

"Do you want to go back, then?" She paused and touched his arm. The sensation of wanting to touch more of him washed over her before she could stop it. She felt her face go up in flames and severed their touch.

"Nae," he said, watching her hand. His voice sent a cool shiver up her back. "'Tis still important to get to know my kin."

They were right back where they started. He hadn't budged in his unspoken conviction that she wasn't going anywhere.

She didn't want to argue with him on such a lovely day. What could it hurt to spend a little time with the others?

She wasn't sure she was ready for such open arms, but after sharing tea with Camlochlin's bard, Finn Grant, whose lilting voice made him sound as if he was singing when he wasn't, and his wife, Leslie, she decided she liked how easily she was being taken into the fold. Perhaps it was because they truly had found a haven from the laws against them, but there was a feeling of safety here, of lives well lived.

Every soul they greeted on their stroll wore content smiles and had kind things to say.

"The people here are quite nice," she remarked on their way to the next house.

"Aye," he agreed, bending to pet Goliath at his side. "What's life like at court?"

"Quiet and a bit stuffy," she told him, "with plenty of backbiting going on in the shadows. Scandals and gossip are fashionable presently. Everyone's eyes are on everyone else. I try not to involve myself in it too much…being unkind to others is cowardly. But living in the palace, I have succumbed to it at times."

"Mayhap Anne wanted a better future fer ye."

She raised her brow and smiled with him. She'd never considered that possibility. "Oh? Is Camlochlin better?"

"Aye, 'tis," he answered with pride he looked surprised at feeling. "We're all kin here. There's a scandal now and then, but no one is unkind aboot it."

"Kin?"

"Family."

"Oh, I see," she managed on the slightest of breaths. She was attracted to Adam MacGregor, but was this temptation too much? Family. It was something she'd never had, something she'd always wanted.

"What aboot yer kin?" he asked as if reading her thoughts.

"I was raised by my uncle and aunt, denied by my true parents. William and my dear friend Poppy became my family."

"Denied and separated," he muttered, shaking his head. "Fergive me fer callin' ye overindulged."

"We both made rash judgments."

He smiled down at her but it faded before he asked, "Ye've known William long, then?"

"Since I was eight."

They walked for a bit longer, and Sina felt sorry for ending their talk unpleasantly.

"'Twasn't always terrible," she assured him. "The queen often threw grand balls. I enjoyed the dancing and merriment." She smiled, remembering, and then dipped her gaze when she found Adam watching her.

"Did ye dance with yer William at these grand balls?"

"Before he left," she said, her smile going soft. "But"— her smile faded—"he has been away for the last three years on the grand tour. He only returned a sennight before I was taken."

"Ye havena seen him in three years?" he asked, looking incredulous and utterly irresistible. "And yer heart remains loyal to him?"

"Of course."

He pursed his lips and narrowed his eyes, looking through her for the truth of what she claimed.

"What kept him from ye fer so long?"

"A tour of Europe taken by some men and women of sufficient means to complete their education. William went so that he could be exposed to different cultural legacies and to become acquainted with polite society."

"Polite society?" he asked, grimacing, as any savage would. "He sounds painfully dull."

"He isn't," she retorted. She wouldn't let him speak ill of William. "He's gentle and sensitive and quite intelligent."

He chuckled and looked straight ahead but said nothing else.

She wanted to tell him about William, but she knew he

wouldn't want to listen. Hadn't he ever loved a woman and feared losing her in his life?

She decided to ask him.

"I've never been in love," he replied, shocking her.

"Never?"

He shook his head.

"Why not?" she asked. "Was your sister correct? Are you afraid of love the way you're afraid of being chief?"

He slid his cool gaze to her and pressed his lips together. "Abby said I was afraid of bein' chief?"

She nodded, lifting her gaze from his mouth. "Are you?"

He looked as if he might deny it, but then he answered honestly. "Aye. I am. My faither is the greatest man I know. He loves these people as a faither loves his bairns. He's dedicated his life to protectin' them, to keepin' order and seein' them all fed. They're all here because my grandsire defied the kingdom and its laws and would no' give up his name, despite the punishment."

She walked with him in silence a few more feet and then turned to him. "You don't strike me as a man without confidence."

He grinned at her and she almost grinned back. He was easy to talk to and nice to watch as different expressions frolicked across his features. She thought about kissing him and chastised herself for it. She didn't think about kissing William—even before he left for the tour.

"'Tis no' a lack of confidence," he corrected. "'Tis a lack of the passion fer the things that mean so much to them. I've never had to fight to bear my name—or strive to make certain everyone was happy." His eyes flicked to the side as if he were looking for the right words. "I havena earned their respect, but handed it over to my sister."

Sina listened, wondering if he was this open to everyone

and about everything. What more would he tell her? What more did she want to know? "You said you lacked passion for those things. What are you passionate about, then?"

She was almost certain he was going to answer that he was passionate about bedding women.

"This way of life," he replied, surprising her. "In freedom with my kin. Away from the rest of the world and its cripplin' sorrows. Away from the kind of power that forces faithers to abandon their daughters."

Aye, she parted her lips and breathed out a shaky sigh. God help her, she didn't think she would find him this likable. Every time they were together, he sparked a different desire in her. She wanted to run from him, hit him, touch him, kiss him...get to know him. Each moment with him made those desires stronger. But if she let him near—if they consummated this marriage, there would be no hope of rescue.

They reached the large home of Graham Grant, the Earl of Huntley and grandfather of the Grants of Camlochlin, and were invited inside.

The stone house rose two stories high, with mullioned windows made of clear glass letting in the sunlight and a chimney piercing the gossamer mist.

"Who builds these manor houses?" Sina asked, following Adam through a grand entrance while their host called up the stairs to his wife. The Earl of Huntley led them to a warmly lit parlor with carved wooden bookshelves and paintings lining the walls and rich, upholstered furniture set before an enormous hearth fire. As in Finn and Leslie's house, there were several vases of heather scattered about on different tables and ledges.

"I helped Callum build the castle," Graham told her, offering her a seat. "M' sons have become master builders."

Goodness, but the men here aged well. His dancing green eyes and wide, warm, dimpled smile must have broken the hearts of many in his younger days. When his gaze fell upon the woman entering the parlor, Sina was certain this was the only one who could break his.

"M' wife, Claire."

Sina had met her briefly at Davina's gathering and had seen her in the training field earlier, not fighting, but watching and instructing.

She was lovely, tall, with snowy-white hair braided down her shoulder. She wore no skirts but breeches and a billowing léine tied at her slim waist by a leather belt. Though her face was lined with age, her eyes were clear and vivid when they rested on her husband.

She joined them in a chair opposite Sina's and settled her eyes on her. "What do ye think of Camlochlin so far?"

"'Tis different."

Claire slanted a corner of her mouth and gave her a slight nod. "'Tis not what ye imagined, then."

"No," Sina told her truthfully. "'Tis filled with many surprises and curiosities."

Two maids entered carrying trays of fresh black bread with butter and cheese, and a tankard of whisky with four flagons to match. They set the trays down on the small table between the hosts and their guests and stepped back.

"Such as?" Lady Huntley asked, reaching for a slice of bread.

"Such as the queen's dearest friend, General Marlow, living here," Sina told her. "And Colin MacGregor, who, according to your son Finn, was once a close friend of King James and a general in his army. I'm also curious about how your husband, who has been a longtime MacGregor supporter, gained the title of Earl of Huntley."

She brought her cup to her lips and sipped the whisky. Immediately, she coughed and shook to her toes.

"Just breathe," Adam said, leaning in a bit closer. "It takes gettin' used to."

"After it burns your insides out," she managed to say.

His lips, closer than they should be, lifted in a wide, glorious smile that made her heart skip a beat or two and her belly burn hotter than the whisky had. He was too close. His gaze was too warm.

She didn't want to like him. She couldn't. She wouldn't betray William. He deserved someone as loyal to him as he had been to her. She could feel Adam chipping away at her defenses. She had to hold on for as long as she could. Anne wasn't well. She wouldn't live forever, and then William would find a way to help her.

"The MacGregors seem to have many different ties to the crown," she continued, doing everything she could to keep her mind off Adam's dominant presence next to her.

Graham told her about his part in restoring Charles to the throne, and the titles he was given for it. "Also, Claire is a Stuart. A distant cousin to Charles, James, Anne, all of them."

"Cousins?" Sina asked, feeling ill. If Claire was a Stuart, then all the Grants were related to the queen! Well, that explained why Anne had sent her here—*to her family*! Did her father know? "The queen never mentioned it."

"We're outlaws and pirates," Adam reminded her. "She doesna want to be linked to us more than she needs to be."

But she would bind Sina to them without a care. Sina didn't think she would ever forgive her.

"Och, Satan's balls," Claire muttered, setting down her cup. "We didn't mean to make ye so sad."

Sina realized she was frowning and lifted her eyes to her

hostess. "You haven't done anything but treat me kindly. 'Tis the queen's decision that saddens me."

"Mayhap," Graham said, finishing his whisky and rising from his chair, "she saved ye from a political life. Some of us lived there," he told her, moving toward the window. "'Tis better to raise yer bairns in Camlochlin."

Children? She couldn't help her gaze from slipping to Adam next to her, or her thoughts from imagining him carrying her to his bed.

She felt her face go red before she could do anything about it. She saw the trace of delight and the promise of decadence flash across his smile and wanted to kick him under the table—or crawl under it.

Or smile back.

Chapter Ten

"So d'ye still think us savages?" Adam asked Sina as they walked back to the castle. Though she seemed to enjoy their afternoon together, the darker it grew outside, the more anxious she became. No lass had ever feared him before. He didn't know how to convince her that he and his kin didn't go around slaughtering people. He was glad she spent the day with them, getting to know them beyond a simple greeting. He didn't want to think about why he cared. Thinking too much had kept him away for two days.

She looked up and smiled at him in the moonlight, and for a moment none of his misgivings about being married made sense.

"There were a few," she said, her dimple flickering, "of whom I still haven't made up my mind."

"Uncle Colin."

"Yes." She laughed, then sobered as she took his arm. "I thought he was going to hack off your arm when you practiced with him."

"He has the utmost control over his blade," he said, moving a bit closer. "But I like that ye worried aboot me."

She swung her teasing gaze away. "I don't like the sight of blood. It has nothing to do with you."

He wanted to stop and drag her into his arms. He'd stayed away, doing everything, save bedding lasses, to put her out of his thoughts. But she remained, haunting him.

He thought he might try to seduce her tonight. She seemed more at ease with him. If they sealed this union, mayhap she would cease insisting she was leaving. But he wanted to lie with her for so many more reasons than that. She was his and he wanted no man to question it. The more time he spent in her company, the more he enjoyed it. He wanted to break through William and claim her heart—not only because, if he didn't, he would live a miserable life— but because it was a heart he was coming to admire, fighting to the very end.

But it had to end soon. Whether she liked it here or not no longer mattered. This was her home now. He was her husband. He wasn't supposed to ache for his wife. He was supposed to—

She yawned. "I'm very sleepy."

—respect her wishes. But for how long?

"Of course," he said, entering the castle with her and stopping at the stairs. He didn't think he could spend another night with her without touching her. "Go on ahead. I'll be up later."

She didn't argue but hurried away to the room, leaving him looking after her, cursing under his breath when he finally turned away.

He didn't see her peek back out a few moments later, look around, and then hurry for the kitchen.

Adam drank with Daniel in the solar for over an hour, but Sina plagued his thoughts. On his way to his room, he thought about moving to another, but he was her husband.

He belonged with her. Whether he made love to her or just slept beside her, it was his place. And every man in Camlochlin would tell him so the moment they found out he left his bed.

He opened the door to his chambers as slowly as he could to stop it from creaking. It didn't help. Goliath slipped around his boots and sniffed the air, then took his place on the blanket on the floor.

Adam inhaled the faint scent of…garlic? Whatever it was, it faded and he didn't think on it again.

She'd kept two candles lit for him. He saw her asleep under his blanket, her back toward his side of the bed. Was she asleep? Was she dreaming of her William?

He crept inside and undressed. He was about to climb into bed, when her sweet voice touched his ears.

"Are you naked, Adam?"

He sighed and trod back to his chest of drawers. After rifling through it, he found a pair of thin knee breeches and put them on. He'd slept naked for years. He found it more comfortable. How much more was he expected to give up to make her happy? He'd already become celibate. More, he hadn't even thought of another woman since he first laid eyes on his weeping bride. He'd stayed away from her. He'd sat visiting with his kin—something he'd rarely done—for her. He'd thrown his dog out of his room!

He pulled the blanket aside and got into bed. He found her hand, grasped it, and then rested it on his thigh. "Happy now?"

She pulled her hand away and sat up. Her golden tresses tumbled free around her shoulders. She turned to aim a murderous stare at him, but Adam barely noticed. What the hell was she wearing? Her nightdress looked as if fairies that sought to make her appear even more delicate had spun it. He wanted to touch it, touch her.

He sniffed the air. "What the hell is that odor?"

"Garlic," she informed him. "I think we should—"

He sat up next to her. "Did ye bathe in it, fer hell's sake?"

"I went to the kitchen and rubbed some on me."

His eyes widened. "Why?"

She didn't answer. She didn't have to. Her eyes said more than her lips. She wasn't difficult to read. She didn't try to be. Even when she was reviling him with her mouth, her eyes remained sad. She was afraid of him, here in his bed. He felt a twinge of compassion but then almost choked when he inhaled again.

"So ye think I canna keep my hands off ye and rubbed garlic on yerself to keep me away?"

"You just made me touch you," she reminded him through tight lips.

"Aye, to prove I wasna naked," he countered, moving away from her. "Wash it off. I canna sleep with the smell of ye stingin' my nostrils."

She shook her head, but indecision clouded her eyes. "I would rather not."

"Sina," he warned, rubbing his nose. "Wash it off or I will."

"If you touch me," she said with a challenging stare, "I can assure you I will—"

She snapped her mouth shut when he bounded from the bed, and watched him as he padded around it. She tried to scoot back when he pulled her by the hand out of it. He tugged her toward the small basin and jug on a nearby table and pointed to it.

She laughed until he poured the water, dipped a cloth into

the basin, and lifted it, dripping, to her face. "Where should I begin?"

Her mirth faded, and she snatched the cloth from his hand and began wiping while he returned to the bed and pulled at the linens.

"I didn't think 'twould smell this bad," she finally admitted, sounding thoroughly repentant and looking a little sick to her stomach. She slipped her hand and the wet cloth down her shift and shivered. "I only thought to deter you because before we parted tonight, you seemed to want to..."

"I did." He scowled at her. "But I dinna now."

He wanted to be angry, offended, something, but how could he be? How was she supposed to know what to expect from a stranger? She had done her best to maintain her aloof resolve since she'd arrived. But things were beginning to sink in for her. He could see the panic in her eyes. She was afraid of staying here with him. He didn't want her to be. He didn't want to care how she felt, but he did.

"Ye need no' have gone to the trooble," he assured her and carried the linens to the door. He opened it, laid the linens to the side, and returned, shutting the door behind him. "I willna force myself on ye."

"But"—her lashes fluttered and she looked away on a series of short, quick breaths—"you said you would have me."

"Aye, but no' by force, lass. Hell."

"Do you vow it?"

"Aye." He sat on the stripped bed. "I vow it." It wasn't difficult to make such a promise. He knew there were men outside of Camlochlin who would do such a thing. But he never had, and he never would. He hoped, since he was bound to Sina, that she would come to want him. He had no choice but to try to win her heart.

"You think lying together every night will be safe?" she asked doubtfully.

"'Twill be temptin', nae doubt." He lay back on his pillow. "But 'twill be safe. Contrary to what ye think, I'm no' always a savage."

She cast him the slightest of smiles—one of a handful he'd pulled from her today. Mayhap winning her wouldn't be impossible. It was best for both of them. They didn't need to love each other. They only needed to not hate each other.

"That remains to be seen," she told him, turning the soft blush of her cheeks away when he smiled at her. "For now, I will trust your word."

"So no more garlic?"

"No more garlic." Her smile deepened and her dimple beguiled him senseless.

"Don't we have more linens?" she asked, returning to the bed.

"We do, but I dinna know where they are kept."

She looked down at him and shook her head. Then the rest of her shook as well. "Did you toss the blanket out as well?"

Aye, he had. It smelled foul. She was wet and there were drafts. He got out of bed for the third time and retrieved his great plaid from where he'd tossed it over his chair when last he wore it.

"This'll warm ye." He handed it to her and stepped around Goliath again while she spread it over the bed.

He waited while she climbed in next to him and pulled the plaid over herself before he blew the nearest candle out.

"Adam?"

He liked how his name sounded on her lips. "Aye?"

"What's the significance of all the heather? It was in

every home we entered. It fills every room in this castle, save for this one. Your mother said the men pick it."

"Aye, they do." He was glad she was curious about something, but the heather was a topic he preferred to avoid with a lass.

"Why do they pick it?" she prodded, her whispery voice saturating his flesh and bones. "Do they think it has magical properties?"

"Nae." He smirked and turned to look at her head poking out of his plaid. "My kin believe 'tis a symbol of love. My grandsire started pickin' it fer my grandmother many years ago. Now it has become a contest to see which man can pick the most heather withoot losin' any blossoms. The winner is the man who loves his wife the most."

They would soon expect him to start picking it. Hell.

Her smile brightened her eyes and tempted him to reach out and touch the gold tendrils falling over her cheek and forget everything but the softness of her skin. He hated admitting it, and he wouldn't, but he longed for her.

"My kin are ridiculously romantic," he warned playfully.

Her breath faltered on her lips. "Are they?"

When he nodded, her smile nearly stopped his breath. "I never would have imagined it."

He turned his body atop his plaid to face her and nodded. "Aye, we are savage in battle, but at home we are taught from the literary works of Monmouth, Malory, and de Troyes, to name a few. D'ye know the tales of Arthur Pendragon and his Roond Table knights?"

"I've read some works here and there. Such tales are out of fashion now." Her eyes and her smile widened; she was curious to hear more. "Do you know them?"

Of course he knew them. Everyone in Camlochlin did. She would come to learn them as well.

He told her the story of Sir Gawain and the Green Knight who went to Camelot to test Gawain's adherence to the code of chivalry.

She appeared suitably horrified when the Green Knight's head spoke after Gawain had cut it off.

She listened, watching Adam while he told her about Sir Gawain's exploits and the choices the brave knight was forced to make, and how he failed to keep his word.

"But he did it for a noble purpose!" she defended, prompting Adam's most tender smile. He liked that she looked deeper. He hadn't expected it of her.

"Ye shake the foundations of my first impressions, lass."

Dear God, she rattled him further with a grin that revealed not one, but two, dimples and made her beautiful eyes sparkle like faceted jewels in the candlelight.

"And you have shaken mine as well."

His smile washed over her, and he thought that being bound to her might not be so terrible after all.

"What is the code of chivalry?" she asked, her heavy-lidded gaze drifting over his features.

"Honor," he whispered, letting his gaze rove over her in return, "honesty, loyalty, and valor. But honor is the only one affected by the other three. Gawain lied to his generous host and he felt dishonorable because of it, even after he was forgiven."

"Do you follow those codes, Adam?"

He blew out a short sigh, then looked off to the side while he thought about his answer. "I try to be true to myself. I'm loyal to my kin and I'll be loyal to ye. I lack no courage. If an enemy came to Camlochlin, I would join my kin in battle and fight to the death if I had to. But if I must be dishonest to spare someone's feelin's, I can live with it."

"Have you been honorable toward women?"

He quirked his mouth at her. He wouldn't lie now. She wasn't fool enough to believe anything contrary anyway. "No' always. But I've always been honest with how I felt."

She closed her eyes, and he thought she might have fallen asleep. But then her soft, satiny voice filled his ears...and some other dusty, old part of him. "And have you ever picked heather for anyone?"

He stared at her in the flickering light. He wanted to slip under the plaid with her and pull her into his arms. Her small, plump mouth tempted him beyond reason.

"Nae, Sina. I never have."

And he thought he never would.

Mayhap he was wrong.

Chapter Eleven

Sina came awake to the faint scent of heather and mist filling her nostrils. She opened her eyes, finding her bed empty and herself clutching Adam's pillow to her face.

Where was he? Had he left the bed in the night because of her foul smell?

Someone knocked on and then opened the door. Sina sat up when she saw one of the maids. She was an older woman, with cheeks as round as her hips. Her wool skirts swished across the floor as she stepped inside. Her gray hair was tied neatly beneath cap. "Good God, I dinna understand," she cried, waving her arms about in front of her as if she were fighting off an unseen opponent. "Why does everything reek of garlic?"

Sina fought to keep from smiling. She had a feeling Adam would have laughed had he been here. He seemed to find humor in many things. Most of the time it was at her expense. But she would rather he smile than shout. And she knew she'd given him reasons to rant and treat her poorly. Save for tossing her over his shoulder, he'd been tender and patient. She didn't want to go through this marriage for however long it was kicking and screaming against him. She wasn't sure how long she could keep it up.

She wasn't sure she wanted to. She still didn't belong here. She still missed Poppy and William. But her hope of a rescue was dwindling. These people were Anne's cousins! Minds weren't going to be changed. At least not now. Was it true? Were the people she'd called savages relatives of the queen?

"Does madam need to bathe?" the maid asked, throwing open the shutters. "I'll bring ye some fresh rags and some warmed water, aye?"

Sina would love to bathe, and some of her gowns back at court would be nice too.

"I'll have yer linens changed."

"Thank you...?" Sina waited for her name.

"Teresa, madam."

"Thank you, Teresa." Sina smiled, drawing one from the maid to match. "Is there, by chance, a way to have breakfast brought up, as well?"

Teresa crinkled her nose at her. "Breakfast was hours ago. Midday meal is aboot to be served."

Oh no! Sina took a step back and looked toward the windows. She'd slept until midday? What would the women here think of her? They would think she was lazy and...spoiled.

"I'll have something brought to ye," Teresa promised with a wink of her chestnut eye as she headed for the door. "D'ye have a change of clothes?"

Sina shook her head. "I have another gown, but I cannot find it."

"Oh dear," Teresa said, turning to give her one more looking-over. "Well I'm sure 'tis bein' seen to. Leave yer nightdress on the floor ootside the door and I'll come back fer it and have it washed." She brushed her hand across her nose again, lifted a curious brow at Sina, and then left.

A little while later two more maids arrived. One carried fresh cloths for washing and a jug of warmed water to her basin. The other brought a bowl of rabbit stew and fresh bread.

"Would ye like help oot of yer gown, madam?" asked the ginger-haired maid setting down her bowl on the table. She sized up Sina's body with resentful eyes.

Sina remembered her from the chapel as one of the women weeping.

Sina's eyes slipped to the bed. She didn't know why she felt a stab of jealousy that this woman had likely spent time there. She quickly composed herself. She didn't care about his past—or about him, she reminded herself, and looked at the door. What if he came barreling in while she was washing? "Why are there no bolts on the door?"

"In Camlochlin," the redhead told her, "only marriage chambers have bolts on the doors. No one is rushing to add yers."

"Edith!" the second maid with the water jug admonished.

Sina wasn't angry that no one was hurrying to add locks to her bedchamber door. But she was surprised that the women in the castle didn't use better discretion. "Weren't you afraid someone would walk in and see you?"

"See me what?" Edith's eyes widened and her cheeks flushed. "I have never been invited to this bed or any other bed in the castle belonging to the chief's sons. No one has."

"Frolickin' in the future marriage beds of the chief's handsome sons is highly frowned upon," the second maid informed her. "What the lads do ootside of these walls is their own business."

Sina glanced once more at the bare bed. This time, a warm trickle heated her belly. No other woman had been in it but her. It made the bed, the chamber, and the vows said before the priest more sacred. She didn't want to think of any of it as such. If she did, she'd have to admit that consummating the union was now her duty.

She dismissed the idea and the maids with it, ate her stew, and then slipped out of her nightdress. Naked, she reached for Adam's plaid on the bed to wrap around herself while she washed.

The door opened while she was stretched over the bed. When she saw Adam standing there, she gasped and straightened, pulling the plaid to her.

His gaze, though he looked as stunned as she, heated her flesh as he took in the full sight of her.

"Get out!" she commanded on a panic-stricken breath.

He went without quarrel, disappearing in an instant behind the door.

Dear God, he'd seen her naked! How would she face him? He was going to look at her differently now, wasn't he? She felt ill…and a little warm.

Her blood raced through her veins while she thought about the way his eyes traced over her bare flesh, her bottom. Her face would never stop burning. She quickened her washing. He didn't *have* to leave. It was his right as her husband to stay. She was thankful for his consideration, for giving up what was rightfully his.

She thought about all the things he told her last eve about honor and heather, and how he looked while he did it.

She thought about what would have happened if he refused to leave. If he'd come inside and taken her where she stood.

She cast a worried glance to the door. Her heart banged

in her chest as if it were trying to escape. What was happening here? She couldn't be feeling something for him. It was impossible! She loved someone else. Lust. That's what it was. He was virile and handsome and thoughtful. Of course she was attracted to him. So was every woman who wasn't his relative! She wouldn't be hard on herself about it. She wasn't made of stone. His playful smiles and his eyes laced in mystery and mischief affected her. She admired his dedication to his family in agreeing to bind himself to her. So what? It meant nothing.

She blinked to clear her head. The problem was that she was beginning to think of him more than she thought of William. She bit her lip and pinned her hair up off her neck.

He saw her naked and he left the room at her request. She could tell by the way his eyes took her in that her body didn't displease him. He'd wanted to kiss her last night while they walked home, so she spread garlic all over herself to keep him away. She'd been afraid. Afraid of wanting him and giving up everything. But he stayed, and he wasn't angry. Oh, damn it all. She did like him. A part of her even thought it quite romantic that he wanted her and fought his desire. He was completely different from the men at court. She couldn't even imagine him there, towering over everyone else, dressed in garters and heels! She smiled, thinking how he would frighten everyone if they saw him in his plaid.

At first she thought him nothing more than a careless rogue, taking her as a wife just to have her in his bed. But she was discovering someone entirely different—someone who was beginning to tempt her toward a different life.

No! She was stronger than this! She wouldn't be compelled so easily by another man's charms. Even if those charms felt completely genuine.

But how long could she keep him from having her? How

long did she want him to stay away? Was she willing to give up everything for a Highlander?

Sina stood at the entrance of Camlochlin's great hall and looked around at the men inside. Where were all the women? The solar perhaps?

She turned to leave but spotted Adam amid the brawny, boisterous men of his clan.

Bathed in firelight, her groom stood out among the others. Light and shadow flickered across his features as his sober gaze drifted over the faces in the crowd. He declined a cup shoved at him by one of his relatives and rubbed his forehead.

Was he thinking about her naked body? Was he trying not to? She should run. But where would she go—to the cliffs? Was she mad? Of course she shouldn't run. She'd never make it across, and even if she did, what then? She didn't know which way to go, or where she was.

No, best to get this over now. She was stuck here, in his castle, in his bed. It was best to face what happened and carry on through it and never think of it again.

She waited while he opened his eyes and dipped them to the three hounds watching her.

The instant Sina's eyes met Ula's, the dog bounded to her feet, tongue dangling from her open jaws, and cantered toward her.

Seeing her, Adam met her gaze and also moved forward.

She could do it. She could look him in the eye. She could ask him never to enter their bedchamber without knocking first. He would do it—for her.

"Ula," he warned now before the dog reached her. Ula immediately slowed. She closed her mouth and pinned back her fluffy ears, making her eyes appear even bigger.

Sina was tempted to smile at her.

"Fergive me fer bargin' in earlier."

And just like that, she did. His apology was so unexpected that she lifted her eyes from Ula and let her dimple flash at him. "Thank you for leaving so quickly. I was quite embarrassed."

A hint of admiration—and something teasing and intimate—sparked his eyes. "Bolts will be put on the door before we retire."

Her belly flipped at unbidden thoughts of him bolting the door and stripping off her clothes—carrying her to his bed—the bolts were to keep him out, weren't they? Perhaps she should use them tonight. How could she desire him? Was her heart that traitorous?

He let his gaze rove over her face and the crown of golden waves atop her head. "Ye look rested and...bonny."

"What is 'bonny'?" she asked, trying not to sound too affected by his warm, deep tone.

"Beautiful," he told her, regarding her as if he meant it.

Careful, she reminded herself as her mouth went dry. *He's done this before. Remember the crying women in the chapel, the maid in your room. Remember William and how he needs you.*

"Thank you," she said, feigning detachment. "But you have seen me in a wrinkled dress for days now."

He smiled and leaned in slightly, clouding her thoughts. "'Tis no' the dress, woman. 'Tis ye."

Her defenses faltered as his warm breath fragranced in mint, not whisky or ale, fell across her face, as his words and the rich, husky cadence of his voice stole over her ears.

"There ye are, Sina!" his sister called out as she approached from the south wing, saving Sina from having to respond and breathe at the same time.

Abigail's resplendent smile lit the halls. Despite her heavy woolen Highland skirts and boots, she carried herself with regal elegance. Sina could easily imagine her holding court with the queen. "Mother sent me to find ye."

"Oh, I'm sorry to have put you to trouble," Sina said. At the same time, she realized Ula had slipped her huge head under her palm. She thought to move her hand, but she left it there, her heart beating hard and fast. She didn't want a dog—or a man—to win her heart. She must remain loyal to her other life.

"'Tis no trooble at all," Abby assured her. "I was worried ye might have awakened and gotten lost in the castle. But I see ye found my brother."

Before she could stop herself, Sina's gaze skipped to him. He was smiling at her as if seeing her for the first time. When she realized why he was smiling, she moved her hand away from Ula. She couldn't let him think she was giving in, accepting this life.

"The ladies are in the sewing hall," Abby said, taking her hand. "We'd love fer ye to join us. But if ye'd prefer to stay with Adam—"

"Nae," he said, looking inside the great hall. Someone threw a cup into the hearth. "I think," he said, turning his light gaze on Sina again, "ye will enjoy yer afternoon more with the women. They've been at work all morn."

Sina felt completely stunned and disgusted with herself at the twinge of disappointment she felt that he didn't want to spend time with her. They didn't have to stay in the great hall. They could take a walk—oh, what was she doing? She needed to spend less time with him, not more.

She didn't mind sewing with the other ladies. In fact, her embroidery was often considered among the best at court.

"Are the ladies working on a tapestry?" she asked Abby

with piqued interest. Why would she prefer spending another day with Adam when she could be sewing?

Sina let Abby take her arm and lead her away.

She turned one last time to look at Adam over her shoulder. She didn't want to do it. Her mind didn't listen.

He was watching her leave, his gaze on her backside, sweeping up to look into her eyes when he caught her turning. He winked, patted Ula on the head, and returned with her to the great hall.

"He's really no' so bad," Abby told her, smiling in a way that made Sina want to deny whatever the possible future chief might be thinking.

"I'm beginning to see that," Sina told her honestly. "He's been kind and thoughtful, but I don't—"

"Aye," his sister agreed. "He's been known to be those things on occasion. Daniel thinks verra highly of him. He believes Adam takes things more seriously than he lets on."

Sina agreed with General Marlow's assessment. "And you?" she asked softly. "What do you think of him? Do you think he could be chief?"

"I dinna know," Abby told her honestly as they turned the corridor that led to the sewing room. "He has never proven to me that he even *wants* to be chief. I care too much to let someone who doesna care aboot the clan lead it."

But Adam did care about the clan. He cared enough to marry her for *their* good. He cared about its values enough to memorize their origins.

She thought about why she was willing to defend him when he didn't even want to be chief.

They reached the sewing room, and Abby pushed open the door. Light from the high windows and two enormous hearth fires drenched the room and the women looking up from their needles.

Heavens, they were all here. Sina felt as if she was on display as she stepped inside. Lady Davina's smile was warm and familiar. Adam's great-aunt Maggie hurried to her side with a strip of olive-green fabric. She held it along the length of Sina's arm, around her waist, from her neck to her torso. "Just as I thought, gels. My measurements were correct."

"No one doubted ye," Adam's aunt Isobel assured her, exchanging a smile with her daughter Violet.

Did Maggie just measure her? Sina looked around at the patterns of dyed wool the women were each working on.

"What are you all sewing?"

Maggie looked up at her and blinked her wide eyes. "Why, they're dresses fer ye, dear. Ye're a MacGregor now, and wearin' the same dress fer days is a bit…" She paused and offered Sina a little quirk of her mouth. "…savage."

Chapter Twelve

$\mathcal{L}$ord William Standish shoved his finger under his large, high-parted wig and scratched his itchy head. He wanted to tear the heavy wig off him, rip out his sword, and slice open George of Hanover's belly.

"Tell me this is a cruel trick," he demanded, refusing the chair he was offered in George's private chambers. "You did not send your daughter to the MacGregors."

The prince elector raised his gaze from the flames in the hearth. The fire continued to burn in his dark eyes when he set them on William. Very few knew Sina was his daughter, and even fewer were bold enough to speak of it.

"Use caution, pup, and think about who would love you next if you didn't have a tongue. Now, you will use it to tell me who spoke to you of the MacGregors."

"'Twas the queen." William tried not to reveal the pleasure he felt at seeing Sina's father squirm. The prince elector never liked him. George had agreed to bind his daughter to the powerful Standish family for his own good. He looked down on William, always seeing a scrawny boy with a bloody nose or a bruised face.

"Through Sina, the queen and I became friends," he said with a slight upward tilt of his chin. "I went to her before I came to you. Knowing of my love for Sina, she finally gave me the name."

It wasn't exactly what had happened. Anne had been barely coherent. She had no idea who William was while he kneeled at her bedside. She babbled words, some unintelligible, some meaningless to him. A few words she repeated. The others he kept to himself.

"Sina was sent to the MacGregors," he continued boldly, proving he was no mouse. "Probably in the care of Anne's beloved General Marlow."

Rather than give William the satisfaction of seeing the soon-to-be-king flounder, George rose to his feet. "Wherever she is, 'tis done."

William almost shook with rage. He held it at bay, having learned the art as a child. "Do you know what you handed her over to?" He didn't care what George did to him. If he'd truly traded his daughter over to these people, he deserved to know who they were. "I'd wondered about the outlawed clan since I learned General Marlow wed himself to one of them. It didn't take long to discover that a band of MacGregors were responsible for kidnapping the Duke of Queensberry's niece. They held her for ransom to force the duke not to sign the union with England act.

"There are others who are said to have killed Andrew Winther the Baron of Newcastle in cold blood. 'Tis not surprising since one of them was James I's private assassin. If all that weren't enough, I've discovered that some of them are known pirates!"

Her father finally spoke, concern marring his voice. "Pirates?"

"They sail with Captain Kidd, son of the more infamous William Kidd, who was hanged right here in England."

George wiped his brow and moved away from the hearth. "Is there more?"

"They are Jacobites, in favor of a Stuart crown. Lady Claire Stuart, a distant cousin of Anne's, is married to one of them."

George's expression dissolved into horror. "Anne tried to keep the Stuarts connected to the new crown."

"So 'twould seem. There might be more. I'm looking into it."

William would do anything to get Sina back. If any savage had touched her, he would find a way to kill him. No matter what it took.

Her father nodded his head and waved his hand to dismiss William.

"And if you decide to have her returned to the palace," William pressed, "will you honor the promise you made with my family?"

"We shall see." George faced him and took a few steps closer. "In the meantime, enjoy the masquerade ball tonight. I'm certain 'twill be as rife with decadence and gluttony as the many scandalous nights of anonymity you enjoyed while you toured Venice."

William's blood went cold. Someone had told George of his lustful appetite while he was away. "I was gone for three years," he ground out in his defense. "Would you have me be celibate?"

George's smile did not reach his eyes. "I would have you not disgrace my name. Based on what I've been told about your behavior, my decision on where Melusina might be better off will not be an easy one."

William's muscles twitched beneath his long, flared coat and hose. Everything—everything he'd worked for, his betrothed, his aristocratic life among the gentles. He wouldn't lose it all. He wouldn't lose her. "What you heard is not true, my lord," he promised, his chin now dipped to his chest. "I give you my word as a gentleman. I had a few dalliances, but my behavior remained impeccable. I ask you to allow me to face my accuser."

"I just might," George assured him. "You may go."

William left the chamber and leaned against the door when he shut it, trying to control his temper. He'd learned much on his adventure across Europe, fencing and dancing in France; he'd endured crossing the Alps, tested his mettle, and studied the ruins of ancient Rome, but nothing had prepared him for losing Melusina.

He couldn't fathom never seeing her again. He'd thought of her often on the tour. Her sweet laughter and large innocent eyes haunted him on many nights. Of course he'd found ways to get her out of his dreams.

He was a virgin when he'd started his adventure. But oh, the decadence of Venice especially had lured him into a different life than the one of polite society he'd sought. After his first taste of a woman, his desire became an obsession. He never thought Sina's father would hear of it—that he would rip her from William and put her in the arms of another.

He'd gone on the grand tour for her, for his future with her, and for the things her father promised him. Was it too late to get her back?

He walked the hall on the way back to his chamber. At least there was the ball tonight. He would drink and dance, but he would keep his lance in his breeches. He'd prove his loyalty to George's daughter and find out more about the MacGregors.

His eye caught sight of a pretty servant girl heading in the other direction.

He would begin tomorrow.

His blood still boiled over being so poorly treated by George.

He called out to her, halting her departure. "You! Come here!"

He smiled slightly at her breathless response, her pretty brown eyes wide with fear. It made his blood rush to his groin. It was so much better than him being afraid. Still, she wasn't moving quickly enough.

He stepped forward and grasped her wrist. He yanked her close and growled against her ear, all courtesy gone. "Do as you're told."

Davina reached for a small, handled mirror, much like the one Sina had seen in the queen's chamber.

All the women—fifteen in number—crowded around Sina in the sewing room. They had fixed her pleats and dusted unseen motes off her skirts. Fingers belonging to more than half a dozen women had pulled at the soft wool at her shoulders, her waist, her hips, and her bosom. Now most stepped back, waiting while Davina held up the mirror for her reaction to all their hard work. Abby and Nichola finished weaving the last of the tiny sprigs of heather into her thick blond plait and joined the others.

Sina stared at her reflection, her breath stalled at her lips. She brushed her hands over her belly and the snug stays holding her together beneath a white arisaid with stripes of crimson, black, and blue. The wool was finer, softer than anything she owned or that she had seen at court. It reached from her neck to her heels and was fastened at the breast with a lovely silver buckle and tied at the waist with a belt.

Her rich, deep blue petticoats beneath were full, falling to her ankles, swaying with the hems of her arisaid as she moved.

"How did you produce such a vivid blue?" she asked breathlessly.

"Some woad and blueberry," Maggie told her proudly. "Does it please ye?"

Sina swallowed. She looked as if she belonged here with them, dressed like a Highland lass. Her home and the people she loved pulled at her heart, but these women had toiled all day, perhaps even days, making these garments for her. "I don't own anything this fine in England," she told them truthfully.

The women smiled, pleased with themselves—and pleased with her for the first time.

"We made ye two dresses," Maggie said, pointing to Gillian and her daughter-in-law, Amelia, who was heavy with child, while they held up another dress stitched in tartan similar to what the others wore.

"And," Davina added, springing to her feet and reaching for a bundle of brightly colored gowns. "These were mine. Dearest Aunt Maggie made them for me when I first came here." She exchanged a warm smile with Adam's great-aunt as they shared fond memories. It struck Sina suddenly what a happy life Davina seemed to live, taken in by this clan. They all seemed happy. No wonder Adam laughed so often.

"We adjusted the size and added a lovely hem fer length," Davina continued, returning her attention to Sina. "But I'm afraid they are long out of fashion. Ye'll let us know if there are other alterations ye would like us to make. I know ye must miss yer own gowns. Ye're welcome to sew with us and design whatever ye like."

Sina eyed one of Davina's gowns, dyed lavender in a

wool and linen blend. It looked elegant, yet simple, without the wide hoops popular at the palace. She would have loved to try it on now. She didn't know what to say. A simple thank-you didn't seem enough. "You are all so kind and I have been so dreadful."

More than half of the women refuted her charge. A few of them agreed. Violet spoke up. "We thought ye hated us."

"No," Sina promised regretfully. "I was dealt a deep wound by the queen. I was angry. I fear I still am, but not with any of you. Forgive me if I was rude."

She caught Davina's eye and the furtive smile the chief's wife offered her. Davina was pleased with her apology. Maggie and the others appeared pleased as well, forgiving her generously.

"Which will ye wear today?" Maggie asked her with a curious slant of her brow.

Again, they all waited to hear her choice. Sina wasn't ready to integrate so quickly, but what could she do without insulting them? And the wool was so fine. What was dressing like them for a day going to hurt?

"I think I'll remain in this."

A collective sigh rang out at her decision. At the same time there came a knock at the door.

It opened and the women parted in front of her, creating a path and an open view of Adam standing at the door, staring at her.

She felt flames burn across her face as he took in the sight of her, pausing to smile at the heather in her hair, and then at her. He liked how she looked. Why shouldn't he? She looked like she belonged to him, *with* him, here in the mountains. Here, with his family.

Oh, she cursed her traitorous heart for allowing herself to be so bewitched and beguiled.

"The ladies have been busy," he said softly, tracing his gaze over the length of her until his eyes came to rest on hers. "Are ye pleased with yer new clothes, Sina?"

"Very pleased," she replied. Only when she tried to smile did she realize she was scowling.

He quirked his lips and arched his brow, then smiled at the women. He thanked them for their thoughtfulness, scooped up the rest of the garments, and announced that he'd promised some of the men he'd bring Sina by their homes for a more personal visit with their wives, most of whom were in the sewing hall.

"Why are you brooding, Adam?" she asked after they climbed the stairs. "Don't you like the dress?"

"I do. Ye're the one who doesna like it."

"What?" she demanded, pulling on his sleeve to stop him before they reached their bedchamber. "What do you mean? Why would you say that? I'm wearing it, am I not?"

"Aye," he allowed, "but ye dinna like it."

Her eyes opened wider. She tightened her lips. She could have slapped him where he stood.

He didn't back away but stepped closer, tempting her to breathe more deeply and wash herself in the scent of clean air and mountain mist.

"When I asked ye if ye were pleased with yer new clothes," he continued, lowering his voice and his gaze to her lips, "yer reply wasna truthful. 'Twas clear in yer eyes." He lifted his gaze to hers. "In the subtle nuances of yer expression. Ye are *no'* pleased."

She felt defeated. How could she keep her true feelings about being here from him if he could read her so easily? Since he could, she wouldn't make a fool of herself by continuing to lie. Besides, for some mad reason, she liked that he forced her to be truthful, mostly because for some even madder reason, she trusted her truths with him. Possibly because he'd been forced into this life with her. He understood how she felt better than anyone else because he felt it too.

"I'm trying to make things a little easier, Adam. What more do you want?"

His gaze on her cooled and then softened before he stepped away and reached for the door. "Ye're right. I should be praisin' ye fer puttin' my kin's feelin's above yer own. Ye have my sincerest apologies."

She paused behind him and couldn't help but smile. She knew he wouldn't remain angry. She liked his lackadaisical nature, but she understood that such a trait wouldn't benefit a clan leader.

She hurried in after him, noticing, with an odd quiver over her spine, that a bolt had been nailed to the door.

"'Tisn't that the dresses don't please me," she tried to explain when he reached the bed and dropped the clothes onto it. "They are beautiful and well crafted. I'm just not—"

"Aye, I know," he assured quietly.

"Thank you."

They stared at each other across the bed. "Thank ye fer tryin'."

"As long as I'm here, I may as well try to get along with everyone."

He nodded, his gaze going hard. "Use whatever part of the wardrobe ye want, or the trunks to store them, as long as ye're here." He moved toward the door, averting his gaze from hers. "I'll go tell the lads we'll be by another time."

She turned to look at him. She thought he wasn't angry. She wished he were as easy to read as she was. "Why are we not going?"

He stopped and turned and held up his palms. "To what end, lass? Are we to pretend this is workin'... that there could be somethin' between us? Is that what ye want to do?"

Pretend that there could be something between them. Could there be? Why did his words feel like little darts? Why did she care what he thought of her? She pressed her closed hand to her chest and shook her head. "What else can we do?"

He regarded her with a mix of determination and pity in his eyes. "No' pretend . . . and stay away from each other. I'll sleep somewhere else tonight."

He turned to leave again.

"Adam." Her voice stopped him. Why was she calling him back? This was what she wanted. This was in her best interest if she ever returned to England. An annulment. Her marriage to Adam dissolved in the eyes of the church.

It was best if he stayed away. She thought of him too often. She enjoyed his company. She didn't want to lose it and be here on her own.

"You proved last night that you could be trusted in this bed." She was mad. She was lonely. That was why the words left her mouth.

He turned to capture her gaze with his. She felt a charge, like lightning going through her. "I hadna seen ye naked last night, lass."

She swallowed and lifted her fingers to her throat. So, then, his leaving was about *that*. "Very well," she said softly, utterly disappointed in him. She turned away now. "If you cannot control your urges, then 'tis best you go."

She thought of the many times William had controlled his over the years. The savage between Adam and William was obvious. Her flesh burned with thoughts of Adam pulling off her nightdress and burying himself in her.

The door slamming behind her snatched her from her

madness and then made her angry. She was dressed in layers of wool to sit alone in her room. Her arisaid had taken precise work to get the pleats just right under her belt. She'd denied herself the lavender gown. And for what? To be left behind while he made apologies for her?

What was she supposed to do now? Chase him? She glanced at the table by the window. She went to it and threw herself into the chair. She snapped up a piece of parchment and the quill and began writing.

Dear William,

I fear I may be losing this terrible battle to keep from... Oh, he makes me so angry...

She ran a line through it and crumpled up the parchment.

Her gaze slipped back to the door. She didn't want to write a letter that might not ever be read. And she didn't want to sit here alone all night.

Did he think she wouldn't leave the castle without him? He was wrong. She straightened her shoulders and stormed toward the door with her unfinished letter in her hand.

Chapter Thirteen

"What am I to do aboot her?" Adam looked down at Goliath while they walked together up the heather-lined hill toward the crest above Camlochlin. He didn't feel like explaining to his kin why he and his wife were postponing their visit. Hell, he'd spent more time with his relatives in the last few days than he had in a year.

His life was changing quickly. Too quickly. He needed to sit and ponder things for a bit. What were his choices? What did he want to happen? The first answer was simple. He had no choices. If he didn't consummate the marriage and sent Sina back to her father, what would it mean for his outlawed clan? The queen was trying to protect them by having them bound to the future crown with this alliance. Sending her back could be a disgrace to her father—which wouldn't be good for his clan. As much as he didn't want to care about such things, he did. This wasn't about some English law that would affect Scotland and most likely not the Highlands. This was about Camlochlin. He had to keep her here with him and either live apart from her or with her, and in both cases, remain celibate.

"Hell," he muttered miserably when he reached the top of the hill. A refreshing, cool wind blew his hair away from his face as he turned to look down on the vale.

He wouldn't force her, but he couldn't seem to win her. She still hoped she'd be rescued.

"She isna goin' to change her mind aboot Camlochlin and just settle in," he said, sitting on the ground beside his dog. "I dinna blame her. If I were taken from my home and my kin and forced to remain at the queen's court, I'd be just as resistant. How do I get her to like it here? Is it even possible?"

Goliath growled and lay down with his nose between his black paws.

Adam spread his gaze over the castle and caught sight of his wife's striped arisaid as she hurried out the doors. He watched while she made her way to a fire barrel and tossed something into it. She looked around at the houses and then went still when she saw Ula standing a few feet away from her. Adam smiled. Ula was perceptive. All the hounds were. They looked deeper than the flesh.

Sina wasn't difficult to like, not since Adam had gotten to know her. He wanted to be compassionate about her desires, but images of her naked body bent over his bed were driving him mad. All day she haunted him. Why had he walked in when he had? Who had opened the damned shutters on the windows so that the sun could bathe her in its golden light as she reached for his plaid on the bed? Her thighs were smooth and creamy white. Her arse, firm and round, tempted him to prove that he could indeed be a savage.

He'd done what any other married fool would have done when his wife ordered him out. He went.

He wasn't sure how long he'd obey *that* command if he continued to sleep with her though.

He kept his eyes on her now as she took a step closer to Ula—and Ula took a step closer to her.

"Easy, gel," he murmured, though the hound was too far away to hear him, "dinna frighten her."

His smile deepened as Sina lifted her hand and Ula slowly fit her head under it.

Adam had no idea why the sight of her petting Ula on her own made him happy. He glanced at Goliath. "Ye could stand to be a bit nicer to her."

Goliath closed his eyes.

Adam shook his head, then stuck a blade of grass in his mouth and returned his gaze to his wife. He sat up straighter. What was she doing bending her face to Ula's? Whatever she did...or said, caused the hound to wag her tail and turn her huge head in Adam's direction.

It was too late to hide. Besides, he wouldn't do such a cowardly thing. She was looking for him. He wondered why. He'd been tortured enough for one day. He didn't want to invite her to sit with him while the sun set, especially when she looked so damned bonny in her Highland skirts and arisaid. Why didn't she just leave him in peace?

Sina looked toward the hill and, spotting him at the top, gave Ula an extra pet behind the ears.

When she started up the hill, Adam let out a deep exhalation and bent his knee to rest his elbow on it. He was surprised to see she hadn't changed her clothes. He was happy about it too.

Rising to his feet, he brushed off his breeches and started down.

He hadn't yet answered the second thing he'd come to ponder. What did he want to happen? Did he want to let himself fall in love with her? How difficult would it be? How would it change his life?

Hell, he needed a drink.

He looked back up the crest at Will's tavern and stopped to wait for Sina to reach him. Mayhap she could use a drink as well.

He was surprised and pleased to see Ula keeping close to Sina's side. He liked knowing that if he was away, there would be a pair of eyes…and a nose on his wife to help keep her safe.

"Adam," she said when she reached him.

He still liked the way his name sounded on her lips. He liked it more every time she said it.

"I would like a word with you, please."

"Over a drink?" he offered, pointing to the tavern. "We could bring Ula back to Will."

"Oh." It was a slight sound, ushered in on a reluctant breath as she exchanged a solemn look with Ula.

There was a bond already. Adam was glad that his wife didn't hate dogs, but Ula belonged to someone else. He looked around for Goliath and found him hanging back, not even greeting his sister.

What the hell was wrong with him? "Goliath, come on."

When the dog finally moved his arse, Adam led the way to the tavern.

He stepped inside after Sina and before the hounds. He looked around. There were two large tables and three small ones. At one of the larger tables, a few of Camlochlin's bards reclined with their lutes and listened to the pirates sitting with them and telling them tales of the sea.

Will was not among them, but his son Duff was there, adding wood to the cool hearth.

Adam watched with Sina as Ula returned to her hearth.

"She'll be back at yer side before too long," he said, leaning down to his wife's ear.

She didn't answer but looked a bit flushed and stepped away from him.

He knew immediately that it would soon grow too warm for Sina's arisaid. "Ye'll need to take that off." He motioned to her arisaid and led her to a small vacant table near an unshuttered window.

She shook her head. "I could never get all the layers right again, and the pleats—"

"I'll do it," he promised. He didn't tell her *why* he knew how to drape a lass's arisaid. She didn't ask. "But if ye drink and ye're hot, ye'll likely pass oot, and I canna carry ye home from here."

She nodded, and he was thankful that she hadn't been difficult about it. Before taking her seat, she unclasped the silver buckle at her breast and the belt around her waist.

He watched, unable to do anything else while she pulled herself free of the heavy layers and exposed a tightly clad body in sapphire-blue stays and a thin, long-sleeved linen shift beneath. Her skin already glistened in the warm glow of candlelight. She breathed a sigh of relief and brushed her thick braid over the front of her shoulder.

He blinked as she sat, then raked his gaze over some of the men also watching her. He'd go a round or two with any one of them if he had to remind them whose wife she was.

"Do women come here often?" she asked, looking around just as the men averted their eyes.

"Trina's here," he told her across the candlelight. "They have all been here, even Aunt Maggie. We're kin. We drink together."

"Greetin's, Adam."

He looked up into Mary MacDonald's warm brown eyes, smiled, and introduced her to Sina.

"Yer wife—" Mary looked her over with narrowed, critical eyes, then tossed him a smile. "Ye did well in marrying Adam MacGregor. He's a fish many of us wish we had caught."

"Ale," Adam told her, trying to stop her before she said anything else.

Were those Sina's teeth he just saw?

"And that will be all, Mary." The past was over. He wasn't the kind of man who looked back. He had other things to think about, such as if his reluctant wife was jealous.

"You don't seem the type who can remain celibate."

Whether she was jealous or not, Sina's insult stung a little. "Ye would be surprised at what I can do." Wait. He didn't want to be celibate. "But what ye ask is . . ." His eyes slanted to the side in search of the right word. "'Tis unholy. Ye agreed to take me as yer husband in the sight of God."

"I was forced," she defended, struggling to keep her voice soft and steady.

"Ye could have refused," he insisted just as gently. "We have Mass on Sundays if ye want to ask the priest."

She wriggled a bit in her tightly laced stays. They were god-awful things designed to squeeze the life and size out of a lass.

"You would have a woman who hates you?"

He smiled but his eyes did more than that. "Ye dinna hate me, Sina."

She didn't bother denying it. How could she? She'd sought him out with Ula. She enjoyed his company . . . as he enjoyed hers.

"You're really quite arrogant," she tossed at him.

"Just observant," he countered with an easy smile.

"Oh?" she asked, arching a golden brow. "What have you observed about me?"

He leaned forward in his chair and rested his elbows on the table. "Ye wield great control over yer emotions." His eyes danced over her features. "Most of the time. Yer heart is steadfast and true, and though I wish it weren't, I admire it. And, ye're growin' less afraid of me."

She flashed her dimple at him and opened her mouth, then closed it again when Mary returned with their ale.

"I wasn't afraid of you," she corrected him when they were alone again. "Well, perhaps just a little."

"And now?" he asked.

"Now," she told him, pushing up her sleeves and lifting her cup to her lips, "I'm not. I cannot say the same for your dog though."

He laughed. "Goliath will come around. He's no' used to there bein' someone else important in my life."

Her smile softened on him, making his guts hurt. He wanted to sit with her alone for the next five nights.

He noticed a jagged scar along her slender left forearm and pulled it in for closer inspection. "What is this?"

She looked as if she didn't want to tell him, but then, with a quick glance at Goliath, she sighed and began. "When I was a child, William and I were running from some boys, and we ran straight into Lord Sunderland's mastiff. It came at my face. I covered it with my arm."

Adam breathed in. "A mastiff? That's a deadly dog. How did ye escape with just this?"

"Lord Sunderland showed up and called it off. Thankfully the beast obeyed."

Adam looked at Goliath. That was it. No more frightening her. He wanted to know more about her, despite William being a big part of her past. "Why were ye runnin' from boys?"

"They often picked on William."

He didn't want to sit here scowling like a fool, but it was difficult not to. "So he ran? Why did he no' fight them?"

"There were too many," she defended.

"He had no brothers, no kin to help him?"

She shook her head. "Only me."

Only her? What the hell did that mean? A wee lass with no kin of her own to protect her? Adam wanted to wring his cowardly little neck—and he might if he ever met him, which thankfully he wouldn't.

"How could ye protect him?" he asked with anger lacing his voice.

"Most of the time I couldn't, but I still fought at his side. That was really what he needed. Someone in his life who cared."

How could he be angry with that? She had a compassionate heart and the courage of a hundred men.

"That's how I became friends with Poppy."

"How?" How could he help but smile at her?

"Poppy was friends with William's enemies at the time. The boys had been picking on him unmercifully once again. She joined in the laughter and I punched her."

Adam smiled, thinking of Sina kicking and screaming as he hauled her up Camlochlin's stairs. What had happened to that part of her? Had fitting into polite society cost so much?

"We knew we would be punished for fighting," she continued. "But I was especially terrified. My uncle's home was in Hanover. I was only visiting the palace. I feared I would be sent home and not allowed to return. William begged Poppy not to tell. She went to my grandmother and told her that she started the brawl. We became friends after that."

Adam was beginning to understand a bit of what Sina and William's relationship was about. He wanted to hear more, but soon his cousin Duff joined them at the table and the conversation turned to Ula, which pleased Sina well. She even laughed with Trina and Alex when the pirates joined them, bringing their rum.

It wasn't long before several villagers arrived and they moved to the largest table.

Adam was a wee bit uncomfortable with so many in such an intimate setting and felt his defenses rising. Walls made with stones of detachment and carelessness. But soon, Sina's laughter put him at ease.

"Amelia and I were expectin' ye both earlier," Edmund MacGregor complained the moment after he sat.

"As were Sarah and I," Luke grumbled, straddling a chair to the right.

"Och, hell!" Adam blurted, feigning absentmindedness. "Fergive me fer fergettin', lads. It has been a harried few days fer Sina and I."

"That's true," Sina validated, sipping from her second cup of rum. "He's not pretending." She didn't look or sound drunk, but when she smiled and winked at him, he knew she was. She seemed to be handling it well, even putting aside her cup.

"Tell us, Sina." Adam's brother Braigh dropped into a chair close by. "How terrible is it bein' wed to this rogue?"

"No' as bad as 'tis goin' to be if ye're his brother," Adam warned him with a tight smirk.

"Worse than bein' yer brother is now?" Braigh asked, then shrugged his strapping shoulders. "I doubt it."

Adam laughed. "I know 'tis hard to measure up to me…and even to Tam, but jealousy is only poisonin' ye, lad."

"Ha!" Braigh tossed back his head and howled with

laughter. "What have I to be jealous of besides yer bonny wife?"

"Ah, good"—Adam held up his cup—"ye like her now."

Sina gasped and hiccupped, then turned to Braigh with large, teary eyes. "You don't like me, Braigh?"

"What?" Braigh choked out. He stammered for a moment, as inept with his words as Tam was with his fists. He glared at Adam, who knew his weakness, and then aimed an ill-practiced smile at Sina. "Of course I like ye, lass. Adam's just bein' an arse."

Adam knew Sina wasn't likely to remember much of this tomorrow. Her eyelids were heavy, and she was sitting to the left just a bit. He smiled, taking in the shape of her nose, the alluring curve of her jaw, the way her soft golden tendrils captured the candlelight.

She caught his gaze, and for a moment she looked content enough to fall asleep. He needed to get her home while she could still travel on her feet.

"Sina." He stood up and reached for her arisaid. "Come, lass. Let's go home."

"So soon?" she asked, looking up into his eyes as she reached for his hand and rose from her chair. "I was...I..." Her gaze was glassy and distant. She reached for him with both hands and stumbled into his arms.

She remained conscious, which earned her a round of applause from the others. Adam wasn't sure how long her admirable condition would last and hurried her out of the tavern. He stopped with her outside the door and arranged her arisaid around her as best he could, trying to be quick. He was strong, but he'd never carried a lass home from the tavern before.

"Keep a clear head, aye?" He kept his voice low and soft while he covered her head with the fine wool.

He smiled at her chin, her throat as she lifted her head to the sky. "So many stars." She began to tip backward. He moved to her side and fit his arm around her waist to hold her up. "I liked tonight. I like your kin."

"That's good, love. They like ye too."

Did he just call her *love* or *lass*?

"Ula?" she called out and tried to turn to look around her, taking no notice of his previous reply.

"She's with Duff."

He caught the distaste in her gaze when she set it on Goliath.

Adam winked at his dog and held up his wife as they walked carefully toward the vale. There was only moonlight and torchlight from the castle to see the way. But Adam didn't need either.

"I haven't forgotten why I came looking for you earlier," she said, pressing herself to him for support and possibly warmth. It wasn't to seduce him, but that's exactly what it was doing. Seducing his muscles, his mind.

"I will not be kept cooped up in the castle!"

He laughed softly in the silvery light and stared at her. "I marvel at the control ye wield over yer tongue, even as yer strength is slippin'."

"My strength is not slipping."

"Good. And I promise no' to keep ye cooped up anywhere."

She sighed and snuggled a little closer.

"It smells good here." She tipped her nose to the heather-scented breeze and then rested her head against his chest.

Adam didn't hate this. In fact, he liked her leaning on him. He wished she didn't need to be drunk on two cups of rum to do it. Damned pirates. The ale at Will's was watered down to keep folks from stumbling home, but the rum was pure fire.

He felt her go heavy in his arms and reached around to catch her just before she wilted to the ground.

They were less than halfway home. "Sina," he whispered close to her face. "Try to stand, lass. A wee bit longer."

She looped her arms around his neck and hung there instead.

He had to carry her the rest of the way. Likely the first of many duties he'd have to see to now that he was wed.

"I'll no' have ye drinkin' rum again, wife," he said, cradling her in his arms for the second time in days.

"No rum," she agreed, resting her cheek against his chest.

Hell, he didn't mind this. He liked how she felt against him, her heart beating close to his. She didn't weigh much, and even if she did, he felt strong enough to carry her to Portree. Mayhap taking care of her wouldn't be so terrible. Keeping his hands off her would be more difficult.

When he reached the castle, he carried her up the stairs to their chamber and set her on the bed.

He sat at the edge, knowing he had to untie her stays. The damned things were likely stopping her air. His fingers paused at the laces at her breasts. He should have called one of the maids to see to her.

His breath sounded in his ears, hard and slow while he pulled each lace, freeing her and then lifting her slightly to pull her arms through the loops. Her body was limp against him, her head thrown back over his arm. He lowered his face to her neck and closed his eyes, inhaling her. She smelled like heather and peat. He smiled, thinking it was likely the first time she ever smelled like such things.

He looked down into her face and felt his most resistant

resolve falter. No. How could he give his full heart to a lass who loved another?

Even though William wasn't here, Adam still had to win Sina from him. He'd never tried to win a lass before. The only way he knew came from books. So when he had her out of her skirts, he fought the desire to keep undressing her. It wasn't overly difficult. He wasn't a dishonorable rake.

Finally, with his legs and back aching, he fell into his chair and watched her for a little while.

He wanted to go to his bed. He wanted to lie beside her, take her in his arms... He closed his eyes, heard something in his back crack, muttered a curse, and fell asleep.

Chapter Fourteen

Sina woke in the stillness of dawn and to the sound of screeching gulls in the distance. She sat up and reached for her head. Rum. Oh, never again. She squinted and fixed her gaze on Adam sprawled out asleep in the chair. Save for his plaid, he was fully dressed. Had he carried her back from the tavern? Had she dreamed of being cradled in his arms? He'd said he was going to find another room, and surely there were many in the castle, but he'd stayed with her. In a chair again.

She looked down at her shift. Where were her stays and skirts? Had he removed them?

She remembered their conversation in this room before she met him on the hill last night. He didn't want to pretend there was something between them, or that there could ever be. She'd agreed. Yet she'd foolishly spent more time with him and enjoyed it—what she remembered of it at least. Damnation! A thread of panic coursed through her. What had she forgotten?

She remembered Ula and the hound's large, bright eyes.

She hadn't expected the dog to gain her trust so quickly. She hadn't wanted to let herself care for anyone or anything here, but she felt her walls crumbling.

She also remembered Mary and how she'd held up Sina for inspection. And Adam, doing his best to make a quick end of the busty serving wench.

Sina knew her husband was no angel. But he was no longer a fish for the net. She hated that she was a bit possessive of him. She had no right to be. But flashes of the quirk of his mouth, the arch of his raven brow while she shared pieces of her life with him, the way he exhilarated in the playful banter with his brother dashed her logic to pieces.

Was withholding her physical affections truly unholy? She had, after all, agreed to take him before God's priest. She was most assuredly attracted to him, and she would admit that thoughts of kissing him had invaded her mind more than once. She tried to fight them. She wanted to love the man to whom she gave her body. She always believed that man would be William.

How could she just give up the life she had planned to have with him? The life she had been planning since she was a child? How? How does one do such a thing?

"Ah, ye're well."

Adam's deep, smoky voice wound itself around her, pulling her gaze to his.

He stretched like a languorous prince, frowned at his boots still on his feet, and then smiled at her.

Her gaze on him softened. "Did you carry me back last eve?"

"Aboot halfway."

She knew it was a long walk and that he hadn't wanted to have to carry her back. She hadn't meant to cause him such trouble. "'Twill never happen again," she promised softly, dipping her chin. "I should not have drunk so much."

"There are some winter nights"—his lilting voice beckoned her to lift her gaze; she didn't want to look at him and be tempted by his beauty—"when the cold gets doun in yer bones. Those nights we drink until our blood drips fire."

She finally looked up. He must have recognized her horror at the thought of living someplace where it was possible to freeze to death, because he quickly disregarded his words with a wave of his hand. "Ye and I dinna have to stay here. Most of my kin spend the winters in Perth or Ayrshire."

She liked sitting with him as if they were friends, the way she and William had before he'd gone on his three-year tour. Though she couldn't remember ever longing to be kissed by him.

She'd missed William when he left, but after the first year, her time without him grew easier. She hadn't felt lonely then the way she did now. She didn't want to fight. She wanted someone to talk to. Someone who could empathize with her.

"As chief, my faither must stay with the villagers," he went on, finally kicking off his boots and making her forget William. "If I'm made chief, I will have to stay as well."

She met his gaze across a shaft of sunlight spilling in from the nearest window. Regret painted his eyes blue, but his determination was chiseled in silver. He had no plans of ever helping her get back. He was telling her what her future would be like because she was his now.

Well, she was just as determined. Yet…she swept her gaze to the other side of the chambers, afraid he would see the uncertainty in her eyes when she spoke.

"I won't be here."

"Perth, then?" His tone was laced with humor.

"London," she answered, slipping her gaze back to him and adding a challenging smirk. "Or Hanover."

He smiled, but she noted the slight hardening of his gaze. "What would ye have me do, lass? Put everyone here in danger? Ye heard me tell ye my kin visit the south. The only reason they can—withoot fear of bein' arrested because of their name—is because of the queen."

"I would speak to my father on your clan's behalf, of course," she hastened to tell him while he stood from the chair. But she knew what she was asking of him, and she wasn't taken aback by his response.

"Marriage is the only way to secure an alliance."

She knew he spoke true. It had happened for centuries in royal families or families with high peerage. Daughters were promised off for one thing or another, but it didn't make her feel any better.

Madly, watching him cut across the room with Goliath at his feet did. He was tall with long, straight, shapely legs and broad shoulders. He was strong enough to carry her halfway back to the castle, likely up the stairs and to his bed.

She tried to ignore the warm frisson trickling down her spine and watched him disappear into the privy. She waited, comfortable in his bed, trusting that he'd return and bring her no shame in it.

"So you don't remain here in winter months?" she asked when he reappeared adjusting the laces of his breeches, his belt discarded.

"I've spent last winter here," he told her, moving toward the door. He opened it, pulled off his léine, and set it in front of the doorway. "Before that," he said, shutting the door once again and turning to her, "I was away."

She remembered to breathe. That is, she thought she did until she grew light-headed. She realized she was staring at him. She commanded her eyes to look away, but they lingered, absorbing the stunning view of his long, tight torso and the powerful interplay of muscles in his shoulders and arms.

When he grinned at her blatant admiration, she blinked out of the spell he cast and cleared her throat. "What made you stay this last winter?"

He laughed a little, further turning her insides to tree sap and making her heart race when he padded nearer. "Ye ask the right questions." He studied her with careful eyes. "Ye dinna ask where I went, but what kept me here."

"Well, what did?" She had to keep her focus on something other than the sight of him, all darkness and light, strength, and what she hoped was sensitivity.

"'Twas the cold nights," he admitted on a low, masculine laugh that made her belly feel warm. "I found that I liked the gatherin's. There's much laughter, and many tales are shared, new and old. I've been wonderin' of late," he said, looking off to the side and smiling, "if 'twas the brew or the company that warmed the blood on those coldest of nights."

"You make it sound rather nice." She began to smile but then drew in a short little gasp and pulled up her knees when he threw himself across the bottom of the bed.

"Shall we lie in bed all day?" He smiled, looking up at her, proving he liked the idea.

"Of course not," she told him, snapping off the blanket and swinging her legs over the side.

"Good," he said, rising up and following her to her feet, "because I thought we could breakfast in the heather, and then mayhap go fer a swim."

She turned on her way to the wardrobe for a fresh gown. "A swim?"

He nodded. "In the bay."

"If 'tis as chilly as yesterday—"

"'Tisn't." He looked toward the window. "The heather is still."

"I don't know how to swim."

He crooked his mouth at her. "The tide will be oot fer the next few hours. 'Tis shallow fer a long way oot. Ye dinna need to swim, just take pleasure in the day."

Take pleasure in the day by wading into a freezing bay before the sun had time to warm it? She would prefer a carriage ride in the park or afternoon tea with her friends Poppy and Eloise.

Eating outside in the heather sounded pleasant enough though, so she agreed—to eating, not to swimming.

"Thank ye, lass."

She wasn't sure why pleasing him made her go a little soft. Perhaps it was his wide, handsome smile and the spark of surprise in his inviting gaze. It worried her to think about which other of his wishes she would eventually give in to. How long would it take her heart to respond the way her body was? It was already beginning! Not only was Adam MacGregor the most magnificent man she'd ever laid eyes on—and there were plenty coming and going at court—but he grew more enchanting every time he opened his mouth— whether it was to tell her tales about honor, to apologize for reacting a certain way, or to get her riled up, which, disturbingly, she had enjoyed a little and so did he.

"I'll go pack our food," he said, slipping into a fresh léine but not bothering with his boots. "Bare feet." His grin was wide, playful, stirring all sorts of temptations within her. "Dress light and dinna bring yer arisaid."

He snatched his plaid from where it hung, and left the room with Goliath.

Alone, Sina wondered if she'd gone completely mad.

Surely that was the reason she was smiling. It wasn't because for the first time since she'd arrived—no, for the first time *in years*—she was looking forward to the day...to being with him. It wasn't that.

She reached into her wardrobe and pulled at her skirts.

Breakfast in the heather with Adam. It sounded fanciful and romantic. It made her catch her breath and her traitorous heart skip a beat as she dressed and hurried out to meet him.

Chapter Fifteen

Sina climbed the misty heather-lined hill with Adam beside her and Goliath cantering ahead.

She drew in a deep breath and let the sweet scent of Camlochlin wash through her. After almost a sennight of being here, the fragrance was growing familiar. She closed her eyes, trying to define the many subtle parts that made it so unique: heather and other flora, clean mountain mist, and fresh, briny air from the sea beyond the cliffs.

She opened her eyes and spread her gaze over the mist-covered landscape. She'd thought it brutal and lonely the first time she'd climbed up to the crest. But now it appeared more magnificent than terrifying. A hundred different shades of green burst forth beneath the drifting clouds while pink and purple heather moors draped the braes in the distance.

"I don't even know where we are," she said, overcome by the stunning grandeur of it.

Adam stopped and stretched out his plaid in the lush stalks. "Skye."

"Skye," she echoed, looking up. "It feels close."

"'Tis."

Her gaze fell to his and they exchanged a smile before he invited her to sit.

He'd prepared a full basket of black bread, different jams, cheeses, and fruit. He remembered to bring wine and cups and even napkins. Had he done this before? She didn't want to think on it or why she cared.

While they ate, he told her about the land, pointing out the Black Cuillins in the distance and the smaller Sgurr na Stri rearing up behind the castle. Some of the women, awake with the dawn and with children in tow, carried their soiled linens and clothes to the river Camas Fhionnairigh for washing, while others swept the entryways of their homes. A few men were also awake, leaving their home to gather water from the wells. Cattle and sheep grazed in the shadows of another mountain called Bla Bheinn, where, according to Adam, many a lass had been kissed since Camlochlin was built. The castle was guarded from raiders by men Sina could not see. Other men patrolling the battlements of the castle, visible to all, guarded everyone else.

It was quiet, save for the waves rolling in from the bay, an occasional dog barking, or a child's laughter.

"'Tis very peaceful and beautiful here."

Adam nodded, biting into his bread and looking out over the vale. "Sometimes too much so. Sometimes yer blood needs stirrin'."

She shifted her gaze to him and marveled that his profile, half-shrouded in the mist, was even more breathtaking than the land. Who was he? A man of honor, or a man of barely veiled indifference? "Peace and beauty do not stir you?"

He cast her a side-glance, then settled his gaze on the distant sea.

"My life hasna been entirely peaceful," he told her, "due to my own defiance."

"Oh?" she asked, curious to know more about him. She hadn't shared moments of intimacy like this with William in years. She knew it was foolish to share them with Adam. Foolish and dangerous, but he'd already begun, and if she were going to remain here, it was best to know him better. "What were you defiant against?"

He turned to offer her the full force of his doubtful grin. "D'ye truly want to know the dull details?"

"Aye," she said softly, watching his gaze dip to her dimple, her lips. His grin softened and then faded to uncertainty.

She loved looking at him, watching his many expressions. She loved this moment of just sitting here with him, listening.

He turned back to the sea while a breeze blew his raven hair off his shoulders. Sina waited while he decided how much of himself he wanted to share with her.

"I was defiant against becomin' chief," he began. "My trainin' started early. I knew how to read when I was five."

"My," she whispered, stricken by how wrong she had been about him and his kin.

"I was taught aboot the past and the present—much more knowledge than I ever wanted—or hoped I needed. This king. That king. This duty and that." He smiled and rolled his eyes as if it was a minor annoyance, when in truth, it was much more. He continued after another moment. "I was strictly trained in both defense and offense. I know how to sow and harvest, how to repair rooftops, doors, and walls, and how to settle arguments fairly. The list is endless and I endured every lesson."

"And you hated it."

He turned to her fully and nodded. "I wanted to be oot of doors with my cousins, playin' in the sun or the snow—but there was never enough time. The more I learned, the more—" He dipped his chin to his chest and laughed a little. "I dinna know why I'm speakin' of this with ye."

She didn't want him to stop. She liked that he was sharing this intimate part of himself with her. It helped her understand a part of who he was.

"Who else can you speak of it with?" Her dimple deepened. "Goliath?"

His smile widened into a low chuckle that fired a spark in her belly. "Goliath knows all my secrets."

She watched the hound move closer and rest his head on Adam's leg.

She understood the bond between them in a new way.

"Tell them to me." Was that her voice, her request whispered on the morning mist?

His steady, searching stare unsettled her. He too doubted the good of his ears. Finally, his eyes flicked back to the sea. "I grew defiant to the responsibility of havin' so many lives in my hands. Lives of people I hardly knew because, oot of everything I'd been taught as a child, I'd never learned how to care fer many. My life was protected behind Camlochlin's walls. When the Menzies attacked and my cousins, children like me, fought, I watched everything from a window."

"Until you broke free of the weight of it."

"Aye," he said, his smile deep and curious.

"I finally traded my lessons fer provin' I'd never become the man they thought I would be. I learned how to do it well."

"It sounds very lonely."

"Ye grow accustomed to it," he said quietly. "But it robbed me of my peace because my faither wouldna make a choice aboot who would be chief. 'Twas as if he had more faith in me than I did and he was just waitin' fer me to catch up." He paused and let his gaze sweep toward the castle. His smile, though it wasn't aimed at her, made her want to draw closer to him, to his body, and deeper. It was as if he was just now coming to the conclusion that his father had been correct to wait.

Sina felt privileged to witness Adam realizing his destiny and accepting it.

He finished his wine, then turned to her. "I'll be chief. Weddin' ye sealed my faither's choice. There's nothin' to fight anymore."

She lowered her gaze. He hadn't accepted his destiny willingly. He'd been forced because of her. "I'm sorry."

He reached out his fingertips to her chin and lifted her head until she looked at him. "Dinna be," he said gently while a breeze fragranced with heather lifted his black hair across his eyes. "In truth, it feels rather good. Fer the last few days, peace..." His gaze on her went soft, intimate. "...and beauty, *do* stir my blood. I have ye to thank fer that."

She felt a little breathless and terribly warm from the sun—or from his smile—or his touch. What kind of spell was he weaving over her, stirring something deep inside her that she was sure she'd never felt before? When she was with him, her belly ached with unfamiliar things.

His eyes skipped over her features. His smile coaxed one from her. "Now tell me something aboot ye that no one else knows."

William knew many things about her life—up until three

years ago. She'd written him during his tour but never about anything vexing or that would cause him to return to England.

"When I left Hanover two years ago to serve the queen, a distant cousin of mine, Frederick von Kampen, began to pursue me. He knew I was betrothed, but that didn't stop him from trying to lay his hands on me."

Adam's eyes darkened like the pale sky before a storm. Goliath lifted his furry head, as if sensing it.

"What did he do?" He growled, or perhaps it was Goliath.

"Nothing that harmed me," she reassured with a tender pat on his knee. The moment she became aware of where her hand was, she moved it away, stretching her fingers as they left him. "I did far more damage to him," she confessed with a sly smile.

His gaze strayed to her lips. "What did ye do, lass?"

"You must promise never to speak of it again. Do you vow it, Adam?"

"Aye, I vow it."

"I went to the gardens and gathered a beehive in a burlap sack. I brought the hive to Frederick's room after the maids were done with it, and left the sack on his bed. I knew he would open it. And he did. He was stung very badly, much worse than I'd imagined—foolish in my anger. He was sick abed for half a dozen months. He nearly died."

Adam stared at her for a moment, looking quite shocked and amused.

She was relieved. What she had done to Frederick was terrible—though, truthfully, she didn't feel repentant after he'd groped her and forced a kiss on her the night before. She'd hoped for this reaction from Adam instead of one of judgment—especially after she'd accused *him* of being the savage.

"I have thought about apologizing," she went on, trying to be sincere, "but then he'll know 'twas I who left the hive. I don't think he will forgive me."

As if he'd been trying to hold it in, a short burst of laughter erupted from his lips.

Sina nearly forgot what they'd been talking about. God help her, she'd never been so beguiled by the very sight, the very sound of a man in all her life.

What if no one came for her? What if Camlochlin and Adam MacGregor were her future? Would it truly be so terrible? Everyone was happy here, and kind to her and to one another. Her husband was the most handsome man in Scotland, England, and Germany. He was loyal and honest, and he made her laugh. Could he be trusted with her heart?

"I once put fire ants in Braigh's bed and, when we were younger, frogs in Abby's," he admitted, his shapely, succulent lips pressing together before separating into a grin.

"Why did you do it?" she asked, not really surprised that he had a mischievous side.

He shrugged his broad shoulders. "No reason, really."

They both laughed, and Sina thought she might have let go of a piece of herself in that moment. A piece layered with lofty airs she wouldn't need here in Camlochlin.

"You're more trouble than I first thought," she told him, but it wasn't true. She knew how much trouble he was the instant she set eyes on him.

He leaned in—just a hairbreadth closer but enough for Sina to slip into the depths of his silvery-blue eyes. "And ye are hellfire covered by a golden shield of eloquence and innocence."

Oh, but he was the eloquent one, wooing her with pretty

words any lady would like to hear. Was he trying to woo her? Did he like her, then?

She was beginning to think he was the man she used to dream about when she was a little girl. Patient, playful, and romantic. So she didn't resist or deny him when he rose to his feet and offered her his hand. "Come."

He pulled her to her feet. For a moment, his close proximity overwhelmed her. She looked up at his mouth, into his eyes—and then at his other hand holding a sprig of heather between them. Her heart boomed in her ears, and her kneecaps tingled. He'd told her he'd never picked heather for anyone.

No one had ever picked a flower for her.

She smiled, accepting his offering. He leaned in, as if he meant to kiss her mouth. She wasn't sure she would stop him if he did. He brushed his lips over the side of her jaw, softly, sweetly, making her toes curl in his spread-out plaid. She wouldn't stop him, she told herself as his hair fell across her face like scattering wings.

He didn't kiss her but withdrew with a sensual crook of his mouth. "Careful aboot lettin' me have my way, lass," he said on a husky whisper. "I might begin to think ye like me."

She flashed her dimple at him. "Heaven forbid you think that."

He laughed and then pulled her toward the bay.

She went, running barefoot with him and his dog down the hill. He didn't stop when he reached the frothy edge of the bay but ran headlong into the water, still holding her hand.

She screeched when the cold waves covered her ankles and water splashed around her. She tugged her hand away from his and turned to run the other way.

He caught her by the wrist and pulled her into his arms. "I'll keep ye safe, lass," he promised on a husky whisper.

She looked up into his heated gaze. She could barely think straight. The air grew warm and charged between them. She closed her eyes when he dipped his lips to hers, and then went weak against him.

He'd barely begun to kiss her when someone called out his name. Adam lifted his mouth from hers, his eyes painted with regret. They both turned to see his cousin Violet hurrying toward them with Ettarre at her side.

"Amelia is aboot to give birth! There's goin' to be a new MacGregor in Camlochlin! Come, Sina, we need all the help we can get!"

Help? What kind of help could she offer? She knew nothing about giving birth. She turned to Adam for help, but she recieved nothing more than a smile.

"And of course there will be a celebration tonight," Violet added with a bright smile, as if they weren't heading off to *help* a woman push a child out into the world.

"Are you coming?" Sina turned to ask Adam when, after walking them inland, he released her hand.

"That's no place fer a man, lass. Besides, I have to bring the sheep in. Ye'll do fine," he said with more confidence than she felt.

She watched him head back up the hill to retrieve his léine and plaid and wished she were staying with him. She thought about his lips on hers, so brief, so tantalizing. Her blood warmed as she thought about being held in his arms, against all his hard plains, feeling his heartbeat quicken.

She couldn't be falling in love with him. Oh, but she was pitiful! He made it so damned easy!

"D'ye like him now?" Violet asked her as they walked

back to one of the manor houses on the far right of the vale.

"Yes," Sina confessed, "I do."

His cousin squealed with joy, much to Sina's delight. She should feel guilty about betraying William, but at the moment, she could think only about Adam and kissing him.

Chapter Sixteen

Sina stepped into chaos precisely controlled by over a dozen women. Four of them stood over Amelia, dabbing her brow with a cool cloth, holding her hands, encouraging her. Abby sat on her knees on the bed, between Amelia's feet.

The deep wail that burst from Amelia's throat shook Sina to her bones.

"Sina, fetch more water," someone called out.

After that there was too much to do to worry about the screaming and the blood. The ladies, all except Abby, rotated duties after an hour, and Sina found herself mopping Amelia's forehead and speaking softly above her.

The birth of little Laurel MacGregor three hours later was difficult to watch but also thrilling and emotional. The babe's mother worked hard but she wasn't alone. Her family was there for her, urging her on, helping her through the worst pains. Despite the urgency and bustle of every woman at work there was a sense of warmth and love here that Sina had never felt before.

They made her a part of it. They trusted her to help,

taking her in as one of their own. She accepted, helpless against the longing for a family. She had hoped to have a family with William, but this...this was bigger than anything she'd ever desired. Here were sisters, aunts, mothers, even grandmothers. She struggled to keep her tears back. What were paved streets and shops compared to candlelit gatherings and a Highlander who picked heather for her?

"D'ye want to hold the babe?" Davina smiled and held the tiny bundle out to her.

Sina accepted her and drew the babe to her chest. Her throat burned and she finally let her tears flow. "She's beautiful." She smiled at Amelia and prayed a blessing over Laurel. The gesture drew Davina's hand across her back, pulling her a bit closer.

"Ye'll go now and get ready fer the celebration," Davina said. Her eyes sparked with excitement and anticipation. "There will be dancing."

Dancing. Sina smiled at the thought of a night of merriment and dancing. What was it like celebrating with Highlanders? She bid the ladies farewell and left with some of the others.

She looked for Adam in the halls. Should she let him take her, make love to her in his bed? Possibly carry his child and give up any hope of ever leaving? Was her mettle so weak that she would toss away her future because of one morning in the heather? Because he'd carried her to his bed more than once—and left her there, honoring her unfair request? Because she wanted his family?

She found their chambers and hoped he was inside. He wasn't, but he had been there, evidenced by the sprig of heather on her pillow.

Everything inside her grew warm as she went to it and

lifted it in her fingers. She held it up to examine the tiny, bell-shaped flowers dangling from the tender stalk, each blossom perfectly intact. It wasn't simply romantic that Adam had picked heather for her. It meant more to him and to the people who lived here. Adam had told her it was a symbol of love and that the MacGregors took it very seriously, even making an art of picking it without losing any blossoms.

Would she deny everything else because he gave her a flower? Because the brush of his lips against her jaw carried her away to another place, where she was free to offer him anything? Or for his deep, lilting voice when he told her about Sir Gawain and honor? She wasn't a child to entertain such fanciful notions as romance. She'd never had "romantic" encounters with William. They were friends, and their deeper feelings for each other had grown out of it. She'd been perfectly happy with that.

Until now.

She heard music coming from the great hall, fiddles and pipes. She hurried to wash up and change clothes. She chose the lavender gown Davina had given her. It fell over her like mist covering the mountains. It fit perfectly with a thin gold cord around her waist and bell sleeves. There were no petticoats or stays. Just her shift and the gown separated her skin from...

She blushed while she pinned up her hair. In the middle of pinning it though, she changed her mind and pulled out all of the pins, letting her waves fall over her shoulders. She pinned up the sides and left the rest loose.

She hurried into her heels, enjoying the freedom of movement in her gown and the freedom to wear what she liked instead of what everyone else liked.

As she hastened out of the room and to the great hall,

she remembered William. Poor William. What would he do without her?

She shook her head. She didn't want to think on things she couldn't change. Not tonight. Tonight she wanted to dance. Hopefully, with her husband.

The doors to the great hall were open, spilling music and laughter into the corridors.

Sina's heart thundered in her ears as she stood at the entrance and looked inside. The cavernous hall looked even bigger with many of its long trestle tables moved aside to make room for the lively dancing. The steps were very different from the dances at court, with people bouncing up and down, kicking their pointed feet. She couldn't remember a time when she was this excited about a night of celebration. Perhaps when she was younger with William...no, never like this.

She spotted Adam across the hall sharing words with a few of the men. It was he who stirred her blood and made her heart thrash. He was tall, lean, and broad in hide boots and a léine beneath his plaid. She sized him up from his bare knees to his chiseled face. He laughed at something one of them said. He laughed often, giving the impression that he was careless when in fact he was carefree.

She saw the difference. His relaxed, easy nature beguiled her. How could she have thought him a savage when he didn't seem to care about enough things to provoke his wrath?

But he cared about his clan—enough to marry her. And perhaps he was beginning to care for her too.

He turned, as if sensing her there by the door. His eyes cut through the crowd and settled on her. He broke away from his companions and made his way toward her with Goliath leading him.

Sina wished she had a fan to fan herself. Her belly knotted and her kneecaps ached from holding her up.

She shouldn't feel this way about him. She had to stop. Her heart belonged to someone else.

She watched him as his gaze roved over her gown, taking his time to enjoy her natural curves.

She blushed and lifted her hand to her scandalous loose locks. His gaze immediately followed, taking her in like a starving man at a lavish dinner table.

"Ye enchant me," he confirmed, moving in to take her hand. "Ye helped deliver Amelia's babe. Many of the women are restin', but here ye stand as fresh as the mornin'."

She smiled and looked down to offer Goliath a gentle pat on the head, thankful that he didn't bite off a finger. "The dress was your mother's and my hair is—"

"Perfect, lass. Yer hair is perfect." His voice seeped through her like liquid fire burning her blood.

She let the heat wash over her and then smiled as it settled. "I was...carefree with it."

"Carefree suits ye," he said, his grin wide, rattling her senses. "Are ye hungry?"

Would he try to kiss her tonight? She wouldn't stop him if he did. She nodded and he led her to his family's table.

Braigh was the only one sitting at it, a huge plate of food set before him.

"Third?" Adam asked his brother, pointing to the plate while he took his seat.

"When ye train as hard as I do," Braigh said, barely looking up, "ye work up an appetite."

"When ye eat as much as *ye* do," Adam corrected with a

smirk, "ye *have* to train hard or we would have to roll ye to the table."

Sina laughed softly beneath her hand. When Braigh cast her a wounded look, she returned it with a repentant one.

"Have you both seen Laurel?" she asked them while she and Adam waited for their food. "I think she resembles her father."

"I saw her," Braigh informed them. "She's bonny."

"I was waitin' so I could see her with ye," Adam told her.

She thanked him. It seemed she thanked him often. He was thoughtful and considerate to wait so they could see the newest MacGregor together. It was what couples did. Though he'd been forced into something he didn't want, he was resigned to it, had accepted it, and appeared quite happy about it.

It made her go soft inside to think he could come to truly care for her, that he was the one who tempted her to let go of it all, the shame of her parents' denial, the "correct" way to behave, dress, eat, speak—the list was endless—and be free.

He was showing her how. For though he'd been forced into marriage same as her, and though he believed he would soon be forced to be chief, he hadn't let the weight of it tie him down.

"How was it today?" he asked her, setting his spoon into his roasted mutton with stewed mushrooms and parsnips.

"Oh, Adam." She forgot her food and turned to face him, then blushed at his intimate smile. "'Twas thrilling. I never thought to witness such a miracle. Everyone was a part of it. I was a part of it. 'Twas a day I shall never forget."

His eyes glittered in the light, sparking fire in her blood.

She moved closer, overcome with the desire to be consumed.

"I'm glad, wife."

His voice enveloped her like smoke. She smiled at his claim on her and felt his breath on her cheek as she turned away.

He wanted her. She could feel it in his gaze. She'd denied him long enough. A thread of heat coursed through her at the thought of lying naked in bed with him, touching him with curiosity and awe, kissing him, letting everything and everyone go. William. She could never return to him if she was bound to another man. Other than William and Poppy, what was she giving up? Living at the palace while her father ruled? Whether he claimed her publicly or not, her life would change. London would become much smaller. A family? If she had Adam's children, she'd be surrounded by family.

Davina and the chief returned from dancing and fell into their chairs, laughing. Sina watched them. Anyone could see their love for each other, feel the chief's utter devotion to his wife. It was lovely to witness, and heart wrenching because it was everything she ever wanted.

She'd always believed the only way to have it was with her best friend. How could she betray that because of a man she'd known for a handful of days?

Thankfully their conversation turned to the babe Laurel and her birth, which soon led to the men inviting them to dance in the hopes of avoiding any details.

The women laughed and teased that they could see blood fly in a fight but the thought of birth frightened them.

Sina's heart clattered as Adam led her to the floor, then turned and bowed to her when they reached the center. She curtsied, not sure what the dance would be or if she would know the steps. Not caring. She smiled into Adam's beaming face. Oh, but he was so effortless to be with. He made it so easy to forget everything…everyone else.

When the music picked up, he stepped forward and bowed. The other couples standing in her row did the same.

She did her best to keep up with Adam's leaps and turns. After a little while, she matched each one, pointing the correct foot and lifting the correct arm. The dance was vigorous and challenging, and when it was over, she fell against him, exhausted and laughing.

It took her only an instant to realize his arms had closed around her. The music had stopped. The other dancers were leaving the floor, but Sina and Adam remained, lost in each other's eyes. With her palms pressed to his chest, she could feel his heart beating hard beneath his léine. His breath came heavy, but not from exertion. He ran his fingertips along her jaw, over her lips, dipping his gaze there, wanting to kiss her.

The music started up again and someone pushed into them as the couples lined up once more. They separated and laughed at some of the light teasing coming their way.

They were pulled into the next dance, and the next, dancing and laughing as if they hadn't a single care in the world.

Later, Edmund brought Laurel to the hall for all to see and coddle. The babe was swaddled in a striped wool shawl and passed around to loving arms. The women all discussed what to make for the babe and agreed to meet the next day to begin sewing.

"What will ye be makin' her?" Maggie asked Sina while they sat at the table drinking ale and whisky.

Sina's heart warmed at the unspoken invitation for her to join them. Should she grow attached to them all? Was that it, then? Was she resigned to staying?

"I'll make her a gown and a matching bonnet."

Maggie's blue eyes narrowed. "I'll be interested to see it."

"She's hard on everyone's sewin'," Nichola assured Sina. "Dinna let her intimidate ye."

"I'm only hard on them who need it," Maggie said, turning to her great-niece. "Mayhap if ye practiced yer stitches more, yer skill would improve."

Nichola smiled and patted her thick golden locks. "I'm in pursuit of Ennis MacKinnon's nephew, Roderick. I can sew anytime, but Roderick is only here fer another fortnight."

"I dinna like him," Maggie muttered.

"Ye hardly know him!"

"He should be pursuin' ye, not the other way roond," Maggie told her. "I'll speak to yer father aboot it later."

"Nae!" Nichola protested, her smile vanishing. "Aunt Maggie, ye know he'll listen to ye and ferbid me to see him!"

"I shall reconsider if ye come and sew with us tomorrow."

Sina smiled behind her fingers and turned to Adam sitting beside her. "She's adorable and ruthless."

He nodded, setting down his cup. "And an extra mother to us all."

"Two mothers," she sighed, and rested her elbow on the table and her chin in her hand. She closed her eyes. She'd had too much to drink. "I barely had one." Until she met Anne. And then she betrayed— She sat up straight and looked at Adam. Had she ever been here? If she'd been here...if she knew them, it might explain why she sent Sina to live among them.

Of course Anne hadn't been here. She would have told her. Besides, she could barely walk when Sina met her.

"Dinna worry, love," Adam said, bending to her. He took

her hand and held it between them before he kissed it. "Ye'll have plenty of mothers here."

She watched him lift his lips from her knuckles, and she knew he was stealing her heart from William . . . stealing her from everything she knew.

Chapter Seventeen

*A*dam carried Sina to bed. He'd lost count of how many times he'd done it already. He didn't mind. In fact, he'd be happy to do it every night. He'd like it better if she were awake though.

He didn't blame her for passing out. They'd danced and drunk well into the night. By the time everyone had left, Adam could barely make it up the stairs, but he'd managed, carrying his wife in his arms and smiling proudly at Goliath when he made it to the top without wavering.

He wasn't as drunk as his wife. Poor wee lass couldn't hold her whisky. She would learn to.

He pushed the door open with his shoulder and shushed Sina when she let out a little snore in his arms.

Hell, he was falling in love with her. He knew it was love because he'd never felt anything like it before. He'd admit it was a bit disturbing how happy it made him feel to look at her, but everything else he could get used to.

He knew he was a fool. She would never truly be his. But what could he do, ride to England to rid her of William once and for all? The thought had crossed his mind, but he wasn't a damned savage.

He laid her in bed and leaned down to plant a brief kiss on her lips. "What have ye done to me, lass?"

She changed everything, set his life on a course for which he was destined. He wanted her there at his side for the journey.

All his life he'd sought freedom from duty, from his destiny. When he walked out on his lessons, he thought he was finally free, but he'd worked just as hard to be someone he wasn't.

Only when he met Sina had everything changed. His duty, the most important duty of them all, had been forced upon him. When he faced it in the church and took a wife to keep the clan safe, it frightened him, but it also made him realize he was prepared to be chief. He still hadn't wanted the burdensome title, but it was done, and he could finally stop hiding. But it left him vulnerable, open to her and to others.

He thought visiting with his kin and stopping to speak to the villagers was for her benefit, but it helped free him of the weight of caring for many and changed it to a desire to keep Camlochlin the way it was.

He left her dressed and climbed into bed next to her, too drunk and too tired to care about his clothes.

He lay awake for a while, watching her sleep, thinking about waking her. He wouldn't. He'd wait for her.

But while he waited...

He closed his arms around her. She snuggled closer, fitting her knee between his thighs. He smiled at the feel of her, the scent of her, the rhythm of her breath.

He fell asleep holding her, wanting her and denying himself, knowing that if anyone tried to take her, he would kill them.

* * *

Sina came awake, aware of Adam's heavy arm across her waist, his sleeping face so close to hers. She didn't move. She remained still in his arms, their bodies close but not touching. She could feel his heat, his breath. She wanted to move closer, but she didn't want to wake him. They were both dressed. She even wore her shoes. They'd been drunk and had been having such fun at the table with everyone they ended up staying until she didn't remember leaving.

Had he carried her to bed again? Fallen into it beside her? She smiled at him. How was it possible that a man could make her feel the same way she did when she read her favorite poems? Warm and hopeful and breathless?

How was it possible that, despite what she felt for William, she'd had the best day of her life with Adam?

But in the light of a new day, she realized what she was doing. Whom she would be hurting.

If she stayed, she had to find a way to see William and bid him farewell the way he deserved.

Oh, how could she bid farewell to William?

She suddenly felt as if she couldn't breathe.

She looked toward the windows and was surprised to find that the sun hadn't yet come up. She hadn't slept long. It must be why she felt a little ill.

She moved away from Adam slowly, reluctantly. But she needed air. She needed to consider what she was thinking of doing.

Adam didn't stir as she slipped out of the room with Goliath at her heels.

"You don't have to come with me," she told the hound as she made her way quietly down the stairs. "I think 'tis safe enough here."

He remained with her as she approached the castle doors. She was stopped by a guard who thankfully recognized Goliath and let her out after he sent word to the patrols that she'd be outside.

The first thing that hit her when she stepped out was the vast sky painted in streaks of indigo and crimson on the brink of dawn. It stopped her breath and urged her further along, wanting to climb higher, closer to it.

Illuminated beneath the soft purple glow, the small kingdom of Camlochlin was quiet. Thin plumes of smoke rose up from various chimneys in ribbon swirls. An eagle flew across the jagged line of mountain ranges cutting through the mist.

The stillness of the world perched on waking was so complete that she could hear the soft wind like music to her ears.

Sina's heart soared in the midst of it all.

"Oh, Goliath," she whispered on a shaky breath, "do I dare let it all go?"

The hound took off running.

Sina smiled, lifted her skirts, and followed. She hadn't realized the castle was built on a slight incline until she picked up speed running past manor houses and cottages.

The sky grew lighter, and she could see Goliath already making his way up the vale toward the crest.

She kicked off her shoes and let her laughter ride the wind. Somewhere, a dog who wasn't Goliath barked. She held her hands over her mouth and ran faster, not wanting to wake everyone.

By the time she reached the heather, her breath came in pants. Holding her side, she took a moment to rest and fell into the lavender sprigs.

When she felt Goliath's cold nose against her neck, she laughed and rolled away, then sat up. The hound sat beside her, facing Camlochlin.

She turned to it as the sky burst into splashes of bronze and yellow. Golden rays of light filled the mist descending on the castle.

"Camelot," she said, catching her breath. "Who knew outlaws and savages could build such a place? Is this what I've always dreamed of? Is Adam...What about William? Oh, I'm so confused!" She dropped her head into her hands, but before she had time to think, Goliath barked and took off running again, this time back toward the vale.

Sina watched him find Adam, who was exiting the castle. She thought about what she would say to him. Why she was out here alone at the break of dawn. Should she tell him she was falling in love with him and it was killing her? No matter how much she ran, the truth remained. How could she be free—be with Adam when part of her heart was still in England?

She kept her eyes on her beautiful husband as he grew closer. She was certain she couldn't hide the unrest in her eyes, but he smiled, calming her as he sat next to her.

"This is the best time of day," he said, spreading his blue-gray gaze over the vale. "Before everyone awakens, which will likely give us five or six more hours after last eve."

She smiled, agreeing with him. He could make her smile, even when she felt so torn.

He pushed his shoulder into hers a little. "What keeps ye awake, lass?"

"My heart is troubled," she couldn't help but tell him. She had to tell someone. "Staying here means staying hidden in the Highlands with your clan, most likely never seeing anyone from my past again. Is that not true?"

He looked into her eyes, and she had the feeling that he wanted to say so much more than he did. "Aye, 'tis."

She wanted him to understand it was about more than William.

"Even though my parents weren't in my life as much as I would have liked, I will miss them. 'Twill be as though they died if I can never see them again."

His gaze softened on her. "No one would stop yer parents from visitin'."

She looked away from him—from Camlochlin. "I cannot imagine my father ever traveling here."

"I know kin who have done it."

Did he say *king* or *kin*? She turned back to him and he smiled again. Damn him for making this so much more difficult!

"What about the others? What about William and Poppy?"

His smile faded and it made her angry. "Adam, William was...is a big part of my life whether you like it or not. You cannot expect me to simply forget someone I've known since I was eight because you are jealous."

He snorted. Goliath whined and lay down in the heather. "I'm not jealous!"

"Of course you are," she insisted, lowering her voice. "You sulk every time I mention him."

"Sina, I dinna know who ye've been livin' with since ye got here, but it hasna been me if ye think—"

"I see," she cut him off and folded her arms across her chest. "You don't care about me. I was wrong, then."

"Ye werena wrong," he corrected on a low, thick voice and severed their gaze. "I care aboot ye. Ye're my wife."

"And if I weren't your wife?"

"The question is no' if ye werena my wife." He met her

gaze again. "The question is what if ye didna love another man?"

She felt the sting of tears in her eyes. Indeed, that was the question. She didn't have the answer. There were so many unresolved things with William. She hadn't seen him in three years. Did he still love her? Need her? He said he did when he'd returned, but she hardly knew him anymore. Did she still love him? Was it enough?

Did Adam love her? He'd told her he had never been in love before. Was she just his duty now?

"How did you keep from loving any of the women you've known?"

He pushed himself off the ground and stood to his feet over her. "I never got to know any of them."

Sina looked up at him, her heart hammering in her chest. He'd defied being chief by becoming a careless rake. But he was so much more than that.

She held up her hand and he pulled her to her feet. "You're getting to know me," she pointed out, stepping closer to him.

"Aye." His voice sounded like distant thunder as he closed his arms around her waist and dragged her closer.

"How is your armor holding up?" she asked softly, tilting her face to his and smiling at the closeness of his mouth.

"No' too well, I fear."

She closed her eyes as he dipped his face to hers. "Don't be afraid."

She caught her breath as her nipples hardened beneath her gown and his hungry mouth covered hers.

His tongue inside her was nothing she'd ever experienced before. Every intimate stroke made her weaker against him until she had to coil her arms around his neck.

He was hard everywhere, and growing harder.

His mouth took hers like a consuming fire, engulfing her in sweet, scintillating pleasure. His large hands slid down her backside and caressed her so intimately that she gasped into his mouth.

She felt her cheeks flush at her inexperience and turned her face away, breaking their kiss and pressing her palms against his chest. "I didn't mean to...I'm not adept at..." Not knowing what else to say without sounding like a fool, she smiled.

"Fergive me, love," he whispered, bending his lips to her neck. "But now that I know, it makes ye all the more beautiful." He kissed her throat, her chin, her smiling mouth.

Locked in passion's maddening embrace, they didn't take notice of Goliath leaping up and taking off toward a small mountain pass opposite the crest.

Only when the dog began to bark did Adam break free and look toward the sound.

A large carved wooden carriage, pulled by two horses and driven by a Highlander carrying a flag of scarlet and black, rolled toward the castle. A single rider cantering beside the carriage had veered off when he saw them.

"Leave it to him," Adam said, smiling while he watched the man come closer, "to make Patrick drive the carriage while *he* protected *them*. He's really quite arrogant."

Sina backed away as a horn sounded from the castle. No! The man riding toward her couldn't be Callum MacGregor, his wife, Kate, most likely in the carriage.

Not now! They couldn't have returned on the day she was barefoot and tangled up in their grandson's arms in the middle of the heather.

Adam called something out to Callum and took her hand to pull her along. Her legs didn't want to go. She patted her hair and almost turned and ran the other way when heather blossoms fell out.

"Welcome home, Grandfather," Adam greeted as he neared. "We werena expectin' ye fer another month or two."

"Yer grandmother didna want to travel in the cooler months."

If Camlochlin were a kingdom, then this was its king. He still had the look of a warrior in his long, belted plaid, kidskin boots, and a long claymore strapped to his back. He looked down at her from his mount. Sina thought she should bow.

His face was weathered with age, but his rich blue-green eyes still held within them power and authority. He was beautiful, likely even more handsome than Adam when he was a young man. He sat tall in his saddle. His shoulders were once strong enough to carry his sister out of a massacre.

"Grandfaither," Adam said, breaking Sina's reverence, "let me present my wife, Sina."

His grandfather narrowed his eyes and dismounted. "Did ye say yer wife?"

"Aye." Adam smiled. "'Twill all be explained to ye later."

The chief lowered his gaze to their entwined hands, then lifted it back to her.

Sina was glad Adam hadn't let her go.

"Welcome to Camlochlin, granddaughter."

She curtsied and released a long, relieved breath. "Thank you, Laird."

He turned his cerulean gaze back to his grandson. "Is it well with the clan?"

"Aye," Adam assured as they began to walk back. "Amelia gave Edmund a daughter yesterday. She is called

Laurel MacGregor. We celebrated long into the night, and I'm afraid everyone is likely sleeping."

"Another MacGregor," his grandfather remarked, "'tis a good reason to celebrate." He slowed his pace, leading his horse by the bridle. "Since they're most likely going to want to continue sleeping, I wish to hear from my new grand-daughter how she finally captured yer heart."

But she hadn't captured it. Not yet. "I am the daughter of George, the prince elector of Hanover." She paused while he shared a brief look with Adam. "I arrived from Kensington Palace with a letter from the queen. She ordered that your grandson and I be wed."

"And ye both agreed to it?" He cast Adam a doubtful look.

"I did," Adam replied, surprising him.

"I did not," Sina said, pulling his attention back to her. "But your grandson is working at changing my mind—for the good of the clan."

Chapter Eighteen

Adam watched Sina flit around their bedchamber, rifling through her clothes to find the right thing to wear.

"What's wrong with what ye're already wearin'?"

She turned to aim a surprised look at him. "I slept in this gown and then rolled around in the heather with Goliath in it!"

He raised his brows and turned a stunned expression to his resting dog. "Ye did?"

"I need pins for my hair! Where are my pins?"

"Lass"—he rose from his chair and went to her to stop her from moving—"no one cares what ye're wearin'. Why d'ye fret so over it?"

She shook her head at him. "You don't understand. I have made a terrible first impression on everyone. Everyone." She bit her plump lips, drawing his gaze there. "And now your grandparents too."

He closed his arms around her. "Ye worry over nothin'. My grandfaither doesna care if we were kissin' on the hill. He—"

She broke free and heaved him out of the way. "You are no help."

He laughed and threw up his hands. "What would ye have me do?"

"Leave."

"Verra well, but if the night goes long again," he said over his shoulder as he left the room, "I'll meet ye in the heather at sunrise."

He smiled at the sound of her laughter following him out. It pleased him that she cared about the impression she made on his kin. Though she seemed to care too much what others thought. "Palace life," he muttered under his breath. *Polite society.* From what she had described to him so far, it sounded nightmarish. She should be rejoicing at being away from it.

Instead, her heart was troubled.

She'd called him jealous, but was it so wrong not to want his wife pining over another man?

He tried to convince her that he couldn't love her while she loved William, but she looked deeper, listened to more than just his words, and knew he was lying. He'd come to know her, and he wanted to know more.

He smiled, remembering her telling his grandfather that he was changing her mind about marrying him "for the good of the clan."

She wanted him to tell her that he loved her. What was the sense in waiting? It seemed he loved her whether she loved William or not.

Damn it.

He heard the laughter coming from the solar, where his kin were gathering to welcome his grandparents home. Tonight would be just for Callum and Kate's children and grandchildren. Tomorrow night, if his mother had anything to do with it, they'd have another celebration in the great hall with everyone.

Adam smiled, glad that his grandparents were home, then turned the other way, hurried down the stairs, and left the castle.

Sina watched Adam move through the solar, quiet in the midst of the revelry. He reminded her of a lone wolf on the prowl for a mate or food. Or her. His pewter-blue eyes found her in the crowd. He made her blood go warm. He made her forget propriety and run into his arms.

He was late in arriving. She'd been here for at least an hour with no sign of him until now.

She sat with Davina and Maggie and some of the other ladies, save for Abby, who sat with the laird, around the hearth. They all listened while Kate MacGregor told them about helping bring her great-grandson Cameron, Patrick and Charlie's second bairn, into the world.

Sina thought the laird's wife was just as lovely as she must have been the day she slew her Highlander's heart. What must it have been like for her to be kidnapped and brought here with no one but her enemies? What did she see in the Devil that made her fight for him and win?

She turned back to Adam, but lost him in the crowd.

She'd been hard on him earlier, impatient while she was running to live according to the standards of a different place... another world, when Adam had been correct after all. No one cared. Everyone was too busy laughing and drinking to worry over what anyone else was wearing.

Still, Sina was glad she'd chosen the sapphire-blue gown Maggie had made for Davina years ago. Sina loved the snug fit and the feel of the soft wool against her flesh, the thin silver embroidery at the neckline and cuffs; and, she had to admit, she loved that Davina and Maggie both noticed it and were pleased.

There was a bit of a commotion, and Sina turned to see Edmund carrying Laurel to his grandfather, who was already covered in children.

With a cup in one hand and the babe tucked into the crook of his other elbow, the laird stood. In the process, he lost some of the other children, save for three who clung to his shoulders, laughing while everyone else grew quiet.

Abby pulled them away and hushed them while she sat them in their seats.

When the solar was quiet, he began. "I remember the night Brodie and Nessa had their son, Will. He was the first MacGregor born in Camlochlin. Remember that night, Katie, my love?"

"Aye, Callum, I remember it well," his wife answered warmly.

"I could never have imagined that night how many sons and daughters would come after him," the laird continued. "Those who built Camlochlin are truly blessed to see what it has become. May God bless Laurel and the babes before her and the ones after, and may the name MacGregor flourish forever!"

Everyone cheered. Laurel cried, and Adam leaned over Sina's chair and whispered in her ear, "Ye are a goddess among queens."

Inclining her cheek to his breath, she curled her lips into a smile. Having him here, close, completed the second best day of her life. He smelled like heather. "Where have you been, rake?" she whispered back while the laird took up speaking again.

"I also lift my cup to my grandson Adam. I'm verra

proud of what ye've done, but after spendin' time with yer bride, I realize 'twas no sacrifice at all."

"Nae, 'twasn't," Adam agreed behind her. She turned and laughed softly, knowing how difficult it had been for him. Her laughter faded when she thought about how patient he had been in their bed. She would make it up to him. She would be his wife and worry about William later.

"Sina," the laird said with a smile, fixing his warm gaze on her, "I welcome ye to the clan. Ye are kin now. I pray ye'll make Adam a proud faither soon enough."

Sina felt her face go hot, but when everyone cheered and demanded Adam kiss her, she let him lead her around her chair and into his arms.

His kiss was brief, though tender and intimate. When he withdrew, he pressed his forehead against hers and whispered so that only she could hear, "We begin tonight, aye?"

"Aye," she promised, wanting more of him. Wanting *all* of him.

She stepped back, but he held her close to his side.

"Adam," his grandfather continued as the crowd grew silent again. "I've spoken with yer faither and with Abigail, as well. This is no discredit to her, for I think had she been unmarried and in yer position, she would have done the same. She has already proven she would do whatever was needed fer the clan when she went to England in yer mother's stead."

Sina stopped breathing for a moment. What did she just hear? Abby had gone to England...and in Davina's stead? Why? To see whom, the queen? Why hadn't Adam told her?

She turned to him, but he was staring at his grandfather and looking rather ill.

"...and yer faither and sister agree," the laird continued. "Ye are firstborn. The title of chief is yers unless ye refuse it."

He looked as if he might refuse it. It was what he'd expected, and what he'd run from his whole life.

"Grandfaither, I—"

"Chief!" one of Camlochlin's guardsmen called out from the entrance, bringing everyone's eyes to him. "I just intercepted a messenger. He carried this and requested it be delivered to ye."

Rob MacGregor went to him and took the sealed letter from his outstretched hand. "Thank ye, Hamish."

"'Tis from London," Rob said and shot his gaze to his wife and then to Adam and Sina.

Sina's heart battered wildly in her chest. A letter from London? The queen? Had she changed her mind?

"Something urgent, my love?" Davina came up beside him when his expression turned dark as he read.

"'Tis the queen," he said. His voice was quiet as he set his somber gaze on her. "She is dead and has been buried."

His arm was quick to catch his wife when her legs grew too weak to stand.

Sina closed her eyes to stop her tears. Anne was gone. She knew the queen was very ill. She'd even considered that her hell here might end when her father took the throne. But Camlochlin wasn't hell, and the queen was her friend.

"There's more." The chief's heavy voice broke through her guilty thoughts. "George of Hanover has been declared king and has ordered the immediate return of his daughter. His carriage was dispatched at the penning of this letter five days ago. They could be here as soon as tomorrow."

Chapter Nineteen

"We're all fond of the lass," someone close by said, "but surely she doesna want us to go to war over her!"

"Aye," another voice to her left said softly. "It has only been six or seven days since they met. I'm no' sure they even like each other."

Sina felt as if someone shot her in the chest with a pistol as she listened to the conversations around her. They thought she didn't like him. She'd given them no reason to believe otherwise.

"Nae," another voice disagreed. "When they visited us, they appeared quite taken with each other."

She tried to be strong as she stood there, feeling more alone than she ever had in her life. She'd never gotten along with her uncle and aunt. She loved Anne and now she was gone. She never had anything close to a real family. But for the past few days, she felt as if she were part of something she'd wanted her whole life. And it was being taken away.

She was going home. It was what she had been praying for, to have her old life back. She was going back to her fa-

vorite streets and shops in London, to her friends. She was
going back to William, her marriage to Adam annulled.

As if it had never taken place.

But it had—and she had a sense from somewhere deep
that nothing in her life would ever be the same.

Where was he? After the message was read, Adam had
argued with his grandfather for a few moments and then
read the letter again. After that, he left the solar and still
hadn't returned.

She didn't consider that Adam or anyone here would
defy the king. To a proscribed clan it could mean their end.
But would he just send her off without a fight? Is that what
she wanted?

She hadn't been sure her father would save her. She
should be rejoicing that he truly cared for her, that he
wanted her back, but she felt too heavy to leap with joy.

Sensing Adam, she turned to the doorway to find him
returning with General Marlow. They appeared equally
solemn as they entered. The general and Anne had been the
closest of friends. The sorrow in his eyes revealed his love
for her.

Adam's eyes revealed something altogether different.
They glinted in the firelight like lightning flashing through
a stormy sky. The usual hint of a smirk was gone from his
lips. Was he troubled about her leaving? Angry? Had he
hoped she'd changed her mind about wanting to leave? Dear
God, she had. She didn't want to go.

"This must be good news fer ye."

Sina choked on her tears and turned to Abby, stepping toward her.

"Going home, I mean," Adam's sister clarified with a
tender smile—much like her mother's. "No' about the
queen being dead. We are all sorry over that."

Yes, especially Adam's mother, who left immediately after the reading of the letter, held close and led away by her husband.

"To be perfectly truthful," Sina told her with as much of a smile as she could muster, "I...I thought I would be happier." She wouldn't weep. Not again. Not in front of a woman these men had considered to be their next chief. "Your fam—kin have been so kind and welcoming, so unlike the people at home. Camlochlin is a truly remarkable place." Her eyes misted over and she bit her lip. "I will think of it often and with fondness."

"And my brother?" Abby asked her candidly. "Will ye think of him the same way?"

"The same way as what?"

Both women turned at the sound of Adam's voice to find him standing close by, his gaze cast in shadows of uncertainty.

"As I will fondly remember Camlochlin," Sina told him without looking up. She knew what he had to do. Send her back. Avoid a war.

"Ye're eager to go, then."

"It has already been decided. Has it not?" She looked up at him, hoping, praying... What? That he would defy them all and refuse the king?

"'Tis no one's decision but ours," Adam told her. His expression went from uncertain to cool and aloof so quickly that Sina wasn't sure which was real. It was as if a mask had just fallen from his face. "Neither one of us wanted this. Now that there's a way oot, let's take it, aye?"

Sina nodded, aware of Abby stepping away.

Sina knew that if she blinked, her tears would fall. She worried about them stopping. He was correct. Neither one of

them had wanted this. But that was before she was willing
to give up everything for him.

He spared her his most radiant smile, filled with whimsy
and charm…and the cool undercurrents of a heart that
wasn't touched by her at all.

"We dinna need to pretend anymore."

"Good," she said, trying to sound as detached as he. The
truth was, she felt as if her skin were shattering, falling away
to expose something raw. He should have been the darkest
part of this journey—but he was the light. She'd allowed
herself to fall in love with him. She thought him kind and
thoughtful and romantic until the moment he could toss her
back like an unwanted fish. "Now you will have what you
wanted."

His eyes pierced through hers, unsettling her deep within.
She clung to her good sense. He'd admitted to never falling
in love before. Why should she have been any different?

"As will ye," he said and turned away.

Sina clutched one hand into a fist at her belly and reached
the other hand out to stop him when he moved to brush past
her.

"Adam, I—"

"Tell yer faither I agree to whatever ye want."

She swallowed. She was free. He let her go without the
bat of his lush black lashes.

"Thank you for being kind and patient with me," she
whispered, ignoring her stinging eyes, the lump in her throat
she thought was her heart wanting to leap out of her and
cling to him.

He plucked her hand from his wrist, folded it over his,
and brought her knuckles to his lips. His kiss lingered for
the briefest of moments, halting her breath—her heart.

"No man should be anything less to ye," he replied on a

faltering breath as he straightened. "I hope ye're happy with William."

Happy with William. How could she be now that she'd felt the passion of Adam's kiss? How could she be happy with anyone but him?

Sina watched him walk away and leave the solar. She wished she were leaving Camlochlin now. She didn't want to be here, around Adam, knowing that he couldn't wait to be rid of her. Oh, she'd been a fool to think she'd touched the rake's heart. To think she'd found a man even better than William.

Something furry moved beneath her palm, lifting it. Sina dipped her head to smile at Ula.

She found Goliath there instead.

He stayed with her for a moment before he leaped forward at the sound of the castle doors opening and ran off to be with Adam.

Sina swiped at the tear falling down her cheek and hurried out of the solar as the rest of them fell.

Adam's smile vanished as he turned away from Sina and left the solar. It was over. He should be happy, relieved, but instead he wanted to hurt something.

The new king had deceived Anne. He'd gone back on his word. He'd never regain the MacGregors' trust after this. Especially not Adam's.

If Adam became chief now, he would keep his clan out of English affairs. Anne was dead. The ties to the throne were cut.

Just like his tie to Sina de Arenburg. It was for the best, he thought, tightening his fist around a letter in the pocket of his breeches.

He'd found it on the floor when he'd returned to his room

earlier. It must have fallen from a pocket or other hiding place when she had all her gowns out on the bed before. He'd picked it up and, thinking it was something he'd written, put it in his pocket. He remembered it while he was insisting to his grandfather that he wasn't sending her back.

He'd read it, there in the solar, angry with himself for feeling jealous, possessive.

It had been difficult keeping his calm, careless expression intact when he'd returned and all she could speak about was going home—to *him*.

Adam ripped the letter free from his pocket and read it on his way to the stables.

My dearest William,

Her salutation was enough to make him swear an oath at the setting sun.

Her complaints that she found little to admire in her new husband and her calling Goliath a hound from the piths of hell angered him, but it was her vehement promise never to love him that hooked him in the guts the hardest.

She'd told Adam the truth the first night in his bed. She loved someone else. She'd told him her heart was troubled. Troubled over William. She loved him. Here it was! He held up the blasted letter and cursed it to the heavens. Things would never have worked between them. He shouldn't have allowed himself to try.

But hell, he'd let down his guard. He'd let her in. What the hell was he going to do now? Just let her go and wait for someone to make him feel how he felt with her? He'd be old and gray by then.

He thought loving many would be difficult, but loving one was so much harder.

I vow to you, my dear William, that I will never love him. If I am not released from this marriage and must stay here for the remainder of my days, I will never let him have my heart, for it belongs only to you…

He reached the stable, groaning about what a fool he'd been, and saddled his horse. When he leaped up, he noticed his aunt Maggie standing in the hay, watching him.

"How did ye get here so fast?" he asked her, looking around as if that might somehow answer the question.

"Are ye runnin' away, Adam?" she asked, not bothering to answer him. "What d'ye mean by leavin' yer wife when she's clearly heartbroken?"

"She isna heartbroken and she willna be my wife in a few days," he muttered from his saddle.

"She's yer wife today!" Maggie argued. "She'll be yer wife tomorrow! 'Tis yer duty to see to her! Go with her to England. Speak to the new king and make amends on our behalf, then—"

"Amends fer what?" he demanded from his saddle. "We were obeyin' the queen's order."

She shrugged her frail shoulders. "Ye'll go and make friends with him."

He laughed, though he felt like bursting out of the stables and getting as far away as he could.

"Let Abby do it. She can accompany her husband and speak fer the clan. I never wanted any of this."

"I'm sorry ye think I give a damn aboot what ye want, Adam. We willna insult the king by having him think we wed his daughter to a man who sends his sister to do his work. 'Tis time to start behavin' like the son of Callum and Robert MacGregor."

So this was what filling those boots required? That he

go to England and grovel at King George's feet? That he personally hand Sina over to her beloved William? Beg everyone's forgiveness for something neither he nor his kin had any control over?

"Nae, I willna go," he said quietly.

"Ye care fer the gel," she continued, changing the topic, much to Adam's relief. This topic, though, was worse. "We all see it, but she must go back."

He turned to look down at her. Was it that obvious that he didn't want to let her go? What did it matter? He knew he had to.

"Was the marriage consummated?"

"If it was, I wouldna be sendin' her back, king's orders or no'."

"Ye musn't say that, nephew," she warned him, pointing a bony finger at him. "Would ye defy his command and possibly bring war to Camlochlin?"

No. He didn't want to. He hated the new king for doing this. "Since when do I care what anyone in England thinks?"

"Since we're no longer related to anyone on the throne."

He waved his hand to discount her concerns. "MacGregors did just fine after King James died and William of Orange became king."

"William fully imposed the proscription against us once again, Adam. Ye ferget so quickly because ye have no reason to remember. But I remember all too well the *real* terror and punishment fer bearin' our name."

"I know, Aunt," Adam said, dismounting to go to her. She rarely spoke of her childhood. He knew of her travails from his grandsire, her brother, who had carried her into freedom from bondage. He was sorry he'd made her think of it.

"Nae, ye dinna know," she told him in a softer tone when

he reached her. "Ye've never known—and I'm thankful fer it." She lifted her fingers to his face. "Ye look so much like Callum." Her smile on him faded. "But ye've never lifted yer blade in defense of yer life, or the life of another."

"D'ye think I canna do it, Aunt Maggie?"

"I hope ye never have to, my dear," she told him tenderly.

He drew her in to kiss the top of her head. He loved her dearly. He would do anything he could for her. But he couldn't do this. What if he hurt William? What if he laughed at the king?

"Then fer everyone's sake," he said into her gray hair, "'tis best I dinna go to London."

Chapter Twenty

Adam climbed the stairs to his chambers. He hoped it was far enough into the night that Sina would be asleep.

He'd left the castle and his aunt hours ago. He'd had a drink at Will's, fought off Mary, and climbed Bla Bheinn for some peace and quiet.

It hadn't helped.

He didn't need Maggie to tell him that Sina had to go back to London. He knew it. But he wasn't doing it for the king. He didn't give a damn about the throne. George was getting his daughter back. Let him be happy with that.

It was his wife's love for William that pricked him in the heart.

He didn't need to read the letter again; he'd read it enough to remember her words. How could he ever forget them?

He clenched his jaw, refusing to care. So she was beautiful. He knew plenty of beautiful women. He'd never tried to win any of them or suffered the weight of having to make them happy—as he had for his wife. He could have stayed away every night and continued to live the way he had before her. But the weight had become light at the first sound of her laughter.

Damn her for making him try...and for making him like it.

He opened the door, ready to fall into his damned chair and get some sleep. The aroma hit him right away. He'd forgotten.

The candles by the bed and the window were lit. Sina sat propped up in his bed in her nightdress, surrounded by all the heather he'd picked for her earlier tonight and laid on their bed.

"Where have you been, Adam?"

Why did she have to look so appealing with her golden hair splashing down her shoulders like liquid sunshine, her cheeks slightly flushed, and her eyes a bit puffy?

"That's nae longer any concern of yers," he replied.

She looked around at the heather. "I...I don't understand this."

He laughed, pulling his léine over his head. "What dinna ye understand, lass? That I'm a damned fool?"

Her eyes raked over his bare chest and belly. She looked angry for some ridiculous reason. He considered taking off his breeches to truly infuriate her.

"D'ye want to see more?" he asked on a throaty whisper, his smile going dark.

Her lips parted and her face went pale. "I've...I've already seen too much to..."

"Too much to what?" he asked when her voice faded off.

"To forget," she confessed softly—like silk across his ears.

He stopped in the middle of kicking off his boots and stared at her. What was she saying? Why was she bothering to say it?

"You are formidable," she breathed, lifting her fingers to her throat. Her anger was gone. Now she appeared shy and untried. She looked away, presenting him with the silhouette of her delicate profile in the candlelight.

Like one caught in the frenzy of a storm, he fought to keep from going to her and taking her up in his arms. How had she succeeded in doing what no other woman could?

"You already know that," she murmured, keeping her gaze on Goliath, "which is why you undressed."

He knew he probably shouldn't, but he laughed. "Ye think I wish to tempt ye?"

She looked up from beneath her lashes. "Do you?"

A muscle in his arm twitched. No. He shook his head and stared at her, defying desires born from being in bed with her, fighting with her, dancing with her...carrying her.

"I willna tempt ye to betray yer heart."

When she didn't deny that that was what she'd be doing, he fell into his chair and reached down to pet Goliath. "Or me to betray mine."

His faithful hound wasn't there but curled up on the floor beside Sina's side of the bed.

"Yes, yours." Her gaze and her tone hardened. "You disguised your aversion to me very well. I commend your effort."

"*My* aversion?" He nearly bounded back to his feet. "'Tis ye who has made it perfectly clear where her heart belongs." He glared at his dog. "Goliath, come here."

His dog rose slowly and skulked toward him.

"You cannot wait to be rid of me!" she flung at him.

He looked up from Goliath's large repentant eyes. "Ye have fergotten that 'twas ye who had spoke of leavin' first. And after findin' this"—he leaned forward and pulled her letter from his pocket—"I didna see any more point in ye stayin'."

Her eyes widened on the wrinkled parchment and then blazed on his. "Where did you get that?"

"I found it on the floor."

"And you read it?" Before he answered, she flung her legs over the side of the bed and came to stand before him. "Give it to me."

He handed it to her, glad to see it go.

Snatching it from his hand, she stepped around the bed. Her long hair bouncing down her back tempted him to go after her. "You had no right to read it."

"I had every right as yer husband to read a letter penned in yer hand that begins 'My dearest William.'"

Trying to remain even tempered was difficult enough without spotting Goliath creeping back to her side.

"What the hell have ye done to my dog?"

Her hair swirled around her face as she spun around, glaring at him. "Your dog?" She glanced at Goliath at her feet and appeared as perplexed to see him there as Adam was.

"Is this your attempt to distract me from what you have done, Adam?"

He scowled at her and rose slowly from the chair. "No' at all, Sina. I found yer letter to William and I read it," he said, moving toward her. "I'm no' tryin' to hide or dismiss it."

She took a step back, holding the letter to her chest.

"'Tis something a man should know aboot his wife"— he said, coming to a stop at arm's length; he didn't trust himself to move any closer—"that she will never love him as long as she lives. He has a right to step away before 'tis too late."

His gaze dipped to the quick rise and fall of her chest, the candlelight splashing over the golden waves resting on her flushed skin.

"Why would I want to be a servant of endless, unappreciated duty?"

"Is that what our marriage would be?" she asked, sounding oddly dismayed. "Endless duty?"

She looked so offended—and a bit defeated that, for a moment, he didn't know what to say.

"Every husband in Camlochlin considers it his duty to keep his marriage a happy one," he defended, not really knowing why.

"I see," she said, almost too quietly for him to hear. "So that's why you are so against being wed. You think it a duty, a task—something from which you're good at running."

"I dinna run from duty," he corrected without hesitancy. "Remember, I stood before a priest with ye. Aye, 'twas a duty, but I might no' have minded spendin' my days makin' ye happy if I thought I could truly do it. But yer heart belongs to someone else."

"And if it didn't?" she asked on a still, soft breath. "Would you defy my father?"

Och, hell, he feared he'd do more than that. Before he could stop himself, he stepped forward and pulled her into his arms. She didn't resist but went utterly soft against him and stared up into his eyes, her head tilted slightly back.

"If yer heart were free," he whispered across her lips, trying not to sound like a lost, pitiful fool, "I would do whatever it took to win it."

When she closed her eyes and parted her lips, his muscles went tight. She tempted him to claim her as his, to defy her heart, the king's command.

Slipping one hand down her back and the other behind

her nape, he pressed his lips to hers. He wouldn't take more than this. Just a kiss...to help her remember him.

But he knew he'd be the one haunted by the sweet taste of her, the feel of her fingers clutching his shoulders and then, as their kiss deepened, his hair.

He wanted to carry her to bed. Would she hate him for it later?

Just a kiss, he reminded himself, moving his mouth and his tongue over hers, devouring her softness. He didn't want to let her go, and it scared the hell out of him.

But madly enough, it was his aunt Maggie's warning sounding in his head that made him withdraw and step out of his wife's embrace. Could he truly take a chance of bringing war to Camlochlin by not sending her back? The thought of English soldiers here made his blood run cold.

So did the thought of handing Sina back to her father as if she were some prize cattle being traded back and forth.

"Sina." He tore her name from his lips and forced himself to look at her, though when he did, the rest of what he had to say was even more difficult. "I canna bring war to my home. I willna be responsible...remembered fer that. If I stay here with ye tonight, I willna be able to send ye away in the mornin'. Yer faither wants ye back. I have nae choice, once again, but to obey."

She closed her eyes, covering her lips with her fingertips while tears spilled down her cheeks. She nodded and drew in a breath. "I understand. I will make certain my father holds no contempt for you or your clan."

He nodded and stepped away. "Farewell, lass."

He turned back for the bed, grabbed one of the blankets, and headed for the door.

"Goliath, move yer arse!" he commanded when his hound tried to stay behind.

Adam looked down the dimly lit corridor. There were plenty of empty rooms in the castle, but he didn't want to be here in the morning.

"So ye decide to like her the night before she leaves?" he scolded his friend as they left the castle together and headed for the hills. "Ye're supposed to be smarter than that. Ye're a dog."

Goliath muffled a bark and pushed his snout into Adam's hand.

"I know," Adam said, scratching him between the ears. "I love her too."

How had he let this happen? Never before had he let his heart rule him when it came to lasses. Sina was correct about him. So was his aunt. He ran. He'd run his whole life, and now, when he finally came to accept his duties and was trying to see to them, they changed once again.

He'd been forced to take a wife, and now he had to let her go.

He never thought anything could feel this bad.

Chapter Twenty-One

The king's carriage arrived early the next morning.

Sina did not leave Camlochlin the way she came. Now she knew these faces coming to bid her farewell outside the castle. They had all been kind to her, inviting her into their homes and their hearts, despite how she'd insulted them. They loved with passion, honor, and, best of all, romance. It sprang from every shoot of heather decorating the corners of every house, including her—Adam's room. It slowed her steps on the way to the carriage and tempted her to turn back.

She spread her gaze over the dozens of faces waiting outside the castle to bid her farewell. Adam was not among them. She looked over the hills beyond, but she didn't find him there either.

She'd barely slept last night. She prayed for God to send Adam back to her and prayed for him to stay away. She'd been afraid to sleep and dream of his kiss, his touch. Even now, fully awake, she wasn't sure if any of this was real. How could the caress of a man's mouth make her feel wanton and innocent at the same time? How could being in his arms tempt her to defy her father, forget William? She'd never felt anything like it before. Being near him sparked desires in her that she didn't know she possessed. Kissing him was like lightning striking through her, making her feel more alive.

She'd wept into her pillow as the night wore on, unable to understand how the reason for his resistance both broke her heart and gave her strength. She had thought he wanted to be rid of her, but he'd been hurt by her letter to William. She wished she had thrown it into the fire the night she wrote it. She kept it with her now, so Adam would never be tempted to read it again. None of it was true. Not anymore. He had to protect his clan. She wanted that as well. If she told him she loved him, he might try to defy her father and hell would come to this heavenly place. So she hadn't told him. And he hadn't told her.

Each step forward was more difficult than the last, and she was glad General Marlow held her arm.

"Do you know where he is?" she turned to his friend and asked. "Is he with someone?"

The general set his gaze toward Bla Bheinn. "Just Goliath, I'd wager."

It gave her relief and tore at her heart at the same time. "Keep an eye on him, will you?"

"Of course, my lady," he said quietly, looking at his feet.

They stopped when they came to Davina.

Sina looked into her large, bloodshot eyes. In whatever way the queen's death had affected her, the chief's wife didn't let it stop her from seeing Sina off.

"I'm sorry to lose ye as my daughter," she said without reserve and dabbed at her eye. Behind her, her mountain of a husband placed his hand on her shoulder.

Anne was gone. Her mother had denied her. Sina would

have liked to look at this warm, welcoming woman as her mother. But it wasn't to be.

"We have loaded the carriage with enough food to last until ye come to the end of yer journey."

What if this was the end? What if the end of the world was where she should be? No, she wasn't thinking right. She was tired. She missed London, her friends, her handservant Katie, whom Sina appreciated more after having to dress and undress herself every day.

"I will tell my father of your kindness and care for me," Sina choked out, wringing her skirts in her hands. In just a few short days the MacGregors had won her over—the people and their hounds.

"I hope," the chief offered, finally speaking, "that ye will fergive my son's absence."

"There is nothing to forgive, my lord. Adam left me to keep all of you safe. 'Twas a difficult choice for him, but he made the correct one. He should be chief"—she managed to smile at him—"though he may resist."

"Aye," Rob MacGregor said, making one word sound more meaningful than a hundred. He glanced toward the hills, his expression going as somber as his wife's.

"Farewell, daughter." Davina threw her arms around her and held her close. "I wish ye were not leaving."

Sina squeezed her eyes shut and whispered back, "As do I."

When she straightened, she looked into Davina's eyes and hoped that all Sina felt for her son, for all of them, was clear.

No one had a choice in this. Again. And this time, she feared it might be worse than the first.

There were a few more tearful goodbyes between her and Maggie, Kate, Abby, everyone. They were all there to see her off, even dear Ula.

Everyone but Adam.

She was led to the carriage by Callum MacGregor. She stopped before getting in and looked around the hills and rugged mountaintops, the dark castle rising up against the mountain behind it.

"What you've built here," she told the laird and swiped a tear from her cheek, "is magical."

He smiled, and Sina saw Adam in his eyes. "Camlochlin is simply stone. 'Tis love that makes it magical."

She smiled and bit her tongue to keep from crying all over him and stepped up into the carriage. His hand on her arm stopped her.

"I'll see ye again, lass."

"What?" she asked, level with his gaze. "How?"

He smiled. "MacGregors fight fer what they love. They dinna give up."

What was he saying? Were these the ramblings of a grandfather? Did Adam love her?

"Have a safe journey, lass."

She stepped into the empty carriage and let him shut the door.

The instant it closed, she pulled aside the curtain and leaned out the window. Tears blurred her vision as they rode away.

Adam had done the right thing by staying away. If he defied her father, she didn't know what the consequences would be. Camlochlin, even hidden in the mountains, couldn't hold off the Royal Army for long.

They did the right thing. The only thing.

Was she going to think of him all the way to England? She looked toward the mountains and shook her head.

It was over.

She smiled, telling herself she was happy to finally be

going back to civilized life. Soon her marriage to Adam would be annulled, and things would go back to how they were. For Adam as well. What would he do with his freedom? Marry someone else? Never marry at all and remain the king fish, sought by tavern wenches and farmers' daughters? Who among them could take Davina's place as lady of the castle if Adam became chief? Who could help him become the man he was born to be, a man in full glory? He certainly had the necessary ingredients to be a dream come to life. Who would finally win his guarded heart?

She hated thinking of it. She didn't want anyone to win his heart. She didn't want anyone to kiss him...ever again. She wanted to be the one in his bed. She had made up her mind to offer herself to him.

Oh, how could she be so disappointed about going back to the palace when it was all she'd thought about for days?

She looked out the window many times on the way home, wanting to remember the brutal magnificence of the landscape and the terrifying isolation of it.

But somewhere deep within those mist-covered mountains was a village, tiny in the grand scheme of everything around it, where families lived in peace, laughing, loving, and taken care of by their chief.

She would miss the intimacy of Camlochlin, the way the women got along without gossiping about one another, the way they helped and comforted one another, the warm camaraderie between the men...Adam.

Yes, she was going to miss his face, his scent, his voice...There was nothing to be done about it. She wouldn't bring her father's army down on the MacGregors. Now she didn't have to break William's heart.

That didn't mean she wasn't going to. She loved Adam. She should have told him. Now it was too late. She could never be with him—unless she could convince her father to let her go back.

God help her, how long would she be consumed with thoughts of her Highland husband? How would she get through this trip alone, thinking of him?

She wiped her tears. She hadn't realized she was crying. She closed her eyes and was soon asleep. For the next three days, she slept, wept, and ate. On the fourth day, she finally stopped crying and let a heavy numbness cover her.

When she arrived in London two days later, Camlochlin felt a thousand years away. Unfortunately, Adam felt as close as her breath.

Chapter Twenty-Two

Melusina de Arenburg stood at the entrance of one of Kensington Palace's grand staterooms, her gaze fixed and steady on her parents sitting at the farthest end of a long, polished table surrounded by servants.

So, then, their affair was finally in the open, Sina thought. Did this mean the king would publicly recognize her as his illegitimate daughter?

"Miss de Arenburg." Her father acknowledged her with a warm smile. "Come in."

She didn't know what to do. Should she hurry into their arms? Would their arms even open when she reached them? Servants were watching. Would her mother continue to deny her in public?

Much had changed in the short time she'd been gone. Her father was the king. Worse, she didn't care. Whether recognized or not didn't matter the way it used to.

Instead of being overjoyed at the thought of seeing William again, she was anxious, afraid of how he was going to take what she told him. Then again, what if she saw William and forgot Adam?

She took a step forward, and then another. Her mother rose from her seat and dismissed the servants with a wave of her hand. When they were gone, the king's mistress held out her arms.

Madly, Sina thought of Davina and felt her eyes burn.

"Were you married?" her mother asked softly after a brief embrace.

"Yes."

"Was it consummated?"

Sina looked down at her muddy boots. Should she tell them the truth? What would happen if she answered yes? For Camlochlin's sake, she wasn't ready to find out. "No."

"Ah, good."

Sina's hand on her arm stopped her mother when she moved to return to her chair. "So we are to live here together, as a family?"

"Eventually, dear," her mother assured offhandedly and moved in closer. "Now, enough talk of that. Come greet the king."

She was still an object of shame, then. Sina remained quiet and curtsied low before her father. "Your Majesty."

She was angry, hurt, insulted. His mistress had been acknowledged, but not his child. "Father."

"I'm glad to see you safe," he said, his voice marked with sincerity. It had been two years since he'd seen her. He'd visited her as a child and had never denied his love for her, but it hadn't been enough to trust him to rescue her. He'd done it after all, and she was glad she meant something to him. But everything she cared about had changed.

"I was never in any danger," she vowed. "I was treated

very well. The MacGregors were kind to me. They did their best to make me feel welcome, but I felt too abandoned and betrayed to see their effort. They persisted until I no longer felt the need to weep all day long."

She slipped her gaze to her mother. She didn't know why she hoped to see some kind of regret or pity staining her mother's face. There wasn't any.

Sina looked away. "Why did you give your consent to let me go?"

"Anne wanted it done," her father answered. "She told me the throne needed their alliance, that they were a powerful force in the Highlands. She had agreed with their request when General Marlow married one of them that she would keep their existence quiet. No one was to know where you were sent. But William found out."

"William?" she asked, surprised.

"Yes, and he helped me see the truth. Anne had assured me the MacGregors were civilized and well-bred despite where they live."

"She spoke true," Sina agreed. "They—"

"She did not tell me that a band of MacGregors once kidnapped Lady Amelia Bell, the Duke of Queensberry's niece. According to some, she has never been returned."

Amelia had been kidnapped? Adam hadn't told her.

"I have met her," Sina interjected before her father's deep scowl had time to set. *I helped deliver her daughter.* "She is quite happy and very much in love with her husband, to whom she has just given their third child."

Sina felt a pang of regret that she would not see Laurel grow into a woman.

"I see," her father muttered, nodding his head and slipping his gaze to his mistress. "Is it also true that there is a Stuart among them?"

"Yes," Sina told him. "Lady Huntley, Claire Stuart, Anne's distant cousin. I was told."

"Do you think she has interest in the throne?"

She smiled, remembering Claire. "I think it would take an army to get her here, and she'd likely kill them all before they got out of Scotland."

His eyes narrowed on her. "They are indeed fierce, then?"

"They are indeed."

He thought about it for a moment and then waved his hand. "The fact remains, Anne deceived me. I did the right thing bringing you back."

"You have my eternal gratitude, Father," she remarked numbly. "But the queen, God rest her soul, did not deceive you." Sina may have been brought up to be polite, but that didn't mean she had nothing to say. "The MacGregors cared well for me. Their son accepted me as his wife though I had been forced upon him."

"I'm certain it wasn't a difficult duty to accept." The king granted her a tender smile.

"It was difficult!" she insisted. "He had other plans for his life, as did I. The queen...and you had no right to put two people before God *in secret*." She paused on a strangled breath. "Is that what my life will always be, a secret?"

"No, daughter," he promised, rushing toward her and taking her hands in his. "I will make amends."

"Mend ties with the MacGregors," she said. "They have been allies since Charles was king. Many have served the throne, including General Marlow, General Colin MacGregor, and Captain Connor Grant. Anne knew they were loyal to her because she protected them from the law against them."

"And because her cousin lives among them," her father tried to interject.

"'Twas loyalty she valued, Father. Loyalty they do not give to many, yet were willing to give to you because of me. Now you have broken your word."

The king didn't argue. He rarely did with either her or her mother. Still, he always did what he wanted.

"What would you have me do?" her father asked.

"Perhaps consider sending me back."

He stared at her for a moment and then laughed. Sina closed her eyes and bit her tongue.

"Are you so concerned for my protection that you would sacrifice your life for it?"

It wasn't that much of a sacrifice, Sina wanted to tell him. But she wasn't sure how he would take the news that she loved her Highland husband. She had to tread lightly and not give away her heart. "Yes. You're my father...and they are not what you think. They read and write and play chess. They—"

"They are outlaws and pirates."

"They are more than that," she insisted softly.

"Sina, tell me, is your heart still set on marrying William Standish?"

How could she betray William? He meant everything to her. He'd been there for her when few others had. What must he have gone through to get this information about the MacGregors to her father? He loved her, but he'd left her for three years. "I—I don't know."

He cast her mother a worried look. Sina wrung her hands. She was too obvious. What would he do if she threw herself at his feet and begged him to send her back to Adam?

Had she gone mad on the long carriage ride? She was home. Where she wanted to be. Her father wasn't going to send her back. The less he knew about Camlochlin...about Adam, the better.

"Perhaps," she corrected. "But I need time to recover."

"Of course," he agreed tenderly.

Sina breathed deeply as she stepped into Kensington's beautiful gardens the next afternoon, her palms pressed to her silk stomacher.

He was waiting in the alcove—where they had met. She was eight when he'd found her sitting on the bench, weeping into her hands. It had been her first day here. She arrived with her grandmother and was introduced as the daughter of a dear friend. She was left in the care of a young handservant who ran off with a gardener twenty minutes later.

"What's the matter with you?" he'd asked, skidding to a halt when he almost passed her by.

He was eleven at the time and small for his age. His hair clung to his forehead in dark, damp streaks from his exertion. His cheeks were flushed, and his eyes were wide and glassy when he darted his gaze to the path from which he'd come.

She hadn't wanted to talk to him, but she was lonely and he was curious. If he was playing with the other children, she might want to play too.

A moment or two later, she realized what was happening when three bigger boys broke through the citrus trees and shouted, "Get him!"

He ran. Sina ran with him. They'd been friends ever since. He knew all her secrets, and she knew his. Their bond had grown from loneliness and into love. No one had meant more to her than William.

She walked the path lined with lemon and lime trees, bordered with a sweetly scented array of flowers. She thought about Camlochlin bursting with wild heather. The queen would have liked it.

Sina did her best not to think of Anne and how much she missed her. There weren't many people in her life whom she loved. Anne had been one of them.

She also did her best not to think of Adam and the heather he had picked for her and laid out on their bed. She'd kept that first sprig he'd given her and had taken it with her to England.

She missed his carefree smile and the way his eyes softened on her, ached with desire for her.

She fought to get Adam out of her head. She was about to see William! She needed to know what she still felt for him.

She saw him sitting alone on the bench beneath the stone archway. With his head bowed and bare of wig, or hat, his dark auburn locks fell over his brow, shielding the rest of his face.

William. Her dear William.

He lifted his head as if hearing her. His gaze found her instantly. He rushed to his feet and, without waiting another instant, reached her and gathered her in his arms.

"My dearest," he groaned into her ear. "I feared I would never see you again."

"I feared it as well," she whispered into his shoulder.

He withdrew and regained his composure.

"Are you unwell in any way?"

She shook her head and looked away. No, save that she was more aware now of the *un*familiar. William had aged much in three years. His skin was tanned from the sun and weathered by taking in the whole world in so short a time. Where had he been? What had he seen, and done, and learned? He hadn't been home long enough for her to find out before she was taken. There was so much she didn't know about him anymore. He smelled of tobacco and sandalwood. He'd never smoked before. When did he begin? Where?

His voice sounded the same, concerned, yet clipped. "I've been utterly distraught."

"I'm perfectly well," she assured him and rolled her arm through his. "'Tis a lovely day. Let's walk."

"Were you wed, love? Did your father and the queen truly do it?"

She nodded. "Yes, I was wed."

He paused and turned to her. "Did he . . . ?"

She shook her head and rested it on his shoulder.

"Thank heavens." He breathed out a heavy sigh and turned to kiss the top of her head. "I would have had to kill him."

Just the thought of William and Adam fighting stilled Sina's breath. William wouldn't stand a chance against him. He would lose, but that wouldn't stop him from trying. She knew William's temper made it possible for him to do the unthinkable. She'd had to talk him out of killing three boys who killed his cat when he was thirteen.

"Don't say such things," she gently admonished. "I'm safe and home now."

"Yes, and soon to be my wife." He pulled her closer.

"I'm still married until the bishop says otherwise." She pulled back. "My darling, everything has been so overwhelming. You'll forgive me for wanting to slow things down a bit, won't you?"

"Of course," he said, sounding hurt and shielding his eyes beneath his long lashes. "I want you to know I did everything I could to see you set free."

Yes, it was William who had told her father about

Amelia's abduction and about Claire... and the pirates. She should feel grateful that he'd gone to such lengths to see her returned. But what might it cost the MacGregors? Her father didn't know them. He barely knew General Marlow. He'd always thought poorly of Highlanders, and thanks to William, his opinion was validated.

The MacGregors would most likely lose the king's support in anything, thanks to her.

What could she do to fix it?

"How did you know I was with them?"

He smiled. "The queen." He told her of his visit to Anne's bedside before she died, and how she'd repeated the name MacGregor so many times that it convinced him she understood what she was saying—what he was asking. "Your father didn't deny it when I brought it up."

"You're clever." She patted his arm. He'd found a way to find her. "But how did you know she wasn't speaking of General Marlow being with the MacGregors?"

"I didn't," he confessed. "I didn't understand most of what she was saying. But she spoke about the MacGregors, her sister, and an abbey—or Abby, as in a person, I don't know—"

Abby? Sina thought as they walked. Why would Anne call for Abigail on her deathbed? The laird had mentioned something about Abby visiting England. What was it? It had to be about Abby. It made more sense than an abbey. Where had she heard something about an abbey recently? Davina. Davina was raised in an abbey. Did it mean anything? What did it have to do with Anne's deceased sister Mary?

"I think the three are interwoven," he said. "I don't know how, but I will find out."

Was there something to find out? This felt dangerous

deep down in Sina's bones. She'd felt from the beginning that the MacGregors were hiding something from her, something about them and the queen. Whatever it was, they didn't want it known. "No, William. Let it go, please. Let me put this behind me. Forget the MacGregors, as I have."

Chapter Twenty-Three

𝒶 dam dropped his head into his hands and raked his fingers through his hair.

A pair of weeks.

Sina had been gone for a pair of weeks now. Each day that passed was harder to bear than the one before it. He was weary from denying what was going on inside him. His ears ached to hear the sound of her again. His eyes longed to bask in the sight of her unguarded smile.

Ah, God help him, he was tired of thinking about her, questioning his decision to let her go, not going with her, allowing himself to be bound to her in the first place.

He looked out over Camlochlin and the vale from a deep crevice high atop Bla Bheinn, his feet dangling over the edge.

"I miss her, Goliath. I'm goin' mad with it."

His faithful hound rested at his side on the wide ledge. The only sign that he was awake was his wagging tail at the sound of Adam's voice.

Adam liked the returning silence. He didn't want advice. He knew what it would be. He'd refuse it and no doubt have the offer of chief stripped. What else could he do? He had to go get her. Whatever it brought to Camlochlin would be his fault.

So he had to make certain it brought only good things. He'd get her and keep his clan safe. He just didn't know how yet.

His gaze roved over his home nestled in mountains and mist. Safe, peaceful, and quiet. He often came here to see it from this view when he needed to ponder things.

He realized several nights ago that it was familiar—pondering...alone in a high window, looking down on his home.

No matter where he went, or what he did, he couldn't escape his past. But now, the things he'd been taught in the room of that high window had life. It was Sina who reminded him of who he'd been raised to be.

Adam found that Sina's disdain for his name, his clan, and his character was something he'd never experienced before. Defending them sparked his pride in what they stood for. He liked how it felt. He liked spending time with everyone at the celebration, with people he was born to protect.

But the cost was high...it was too high. He wanted her back. He wanted to ride into Kensington Palace and kill anyone who got in his way. But he couldn't do that.

There were days though, moments when he didn't give a damn about any consequences.

Later, he made his way with Goliath back to his room for much-needed sleep.

The heather was gone, cleaned up weeks ago and thrown into the fire by Teresa. But the scent was still here, lingering like Sina's smile—

"Adam."

He looked at the back of his chair and his aunt Maggie's head craning around it.

"Come sit. I wish to speak with ye."

He did as she asked and sat on the edge of his bed. "I should ask ye what ye're doin' in my room in the middle of the night, but I'm too tired to care."

She crinkled her nose at him in a display of affection or annoyance; he'd never been able to tell which. She, the smallest of all the MacGregors, the one most affected by the hatred of their enemies, was sometimes the hardest to read.

"I'll get straight to it, then. What are ye going to do about yer wife? You've been moping around here fer weeks, going off on yer own often. What are ye planning to do?"

Was he that transparent that she could tell he was planning something? Why couldn't he control his damned emotions? Worse, he couldn't even mask them! He'd never found it difficult to hide his feelings in the past. He didn't hide them to be deceitful but to spare the feelings of others—his father's when it came to his firstborn son not wanting to follow in his footsteps, those of the lasses he'd left behind, who wanted more from him than he wanted to give.

But now, he felt as if his skin were too tight to hold the strong passions building up within. His bones felt too heavy to move.

"Aunt Maggie, I—"

"Yer wife isna dead."

"What?"

"When I lost my dear Jamie, I thought I would go mad with grief. Even the dungeon wasna as bad as losing him. I would have done anything to have him back, anything. But alas, there was nothing to be done but wait until I too leave this earth." She leaned forward in his chair with a gleam in her eyes that promised she wasn't leaving anytime soon. "But yer wife isna dead."

"What are ye gettin' at, Aunt Maggie?" he asked, patient with her. She tended to veer off.

"I understand what ye're going through, my dearest nephew," she told him gently. "I understand what's been on yer mind." She smiled as if he should know what she was talking about.

He did.

Why was she smiling?

"Ye must do it, Adam. Go get her."

He laughed. "What? Ye're the one who told me I must give her up—"

"I said she must go back to England. I also said ye should go with her and make friends with the king. Ye never let me finish the rest!"

He held up his hands in surrender when she bounded from his chair.

"Ye love the gel," she said, satisfied that he was finally considering her words. "'Tis plain to see."

He shook his head. He'd made his choices. If he looked hard enough, he was sure he'd find other paths he could have taken. He could have refused to marry her, not given a damn if she was forlorn and afraid. He could have abandoned the codes he'd been taught, refused to try to make her happy, ignored her vigor and vibrancy. But he hadn't. He let her in, believing it was his duty to share his life with her.

He'd let her go without a fight because he didn't know if he could win.

He shook his head, then rubbed his tired eyes. "What aboot the clan, Aunt Maggie? Are ye tellin' me to ferget the consequences? Because I canna do it. I've thought aboot it. Och, believe me I have. But I need a plan."

"Good." She took him by the hand and gave him her widest smile. "Get some sleep, and tomorrow I'll teach ye all about the Duke of Hamilton and how ye can sound more like a Lowlander."

"Who?" he asked.

She waved over her shoulder as she went for the door. "Hopefully the man who will help ye get back Sina without a war."

Sina closed her eyes and counted to ten while her friends Ladies Poppy Berkham and Eloise Warwick argued over who was more handsome, Lord Roderick Newton, Viscount of Nottingham, or Lord Henry Fitzsimmons, Viscount of Ipswich.

It was Sina's fifteenth day home, the twenty-first day since she'd left Camlochlin, and her third ball. The first two were hosted by Poppy's and Eloise's families to celebrate their birthdays, which were four days apart.

Tonight's grand ball was a celebration of her betrothal to William. They should be hearing from the bishop any day now about the annulment, but William didn't want to wait to make the announcement.

Why should they? Her life with Adam was over.

None had been told of her marriage to a Highlander, or that she'd been sent to the Highlands. Residents of the palace were told that the queen had sent her off to visit friends. Only William and Poppy knew the truth.

Tables had been elegantly arranged throughout the vast hall for anyone who preferred dining over dancing. Large, ornately carved chairs were set in two rows, facing each other with the dance floor in the center. Master musicians played various instruments while stately lords and ladies moved with graceful precision to the latest dance. Everything was subdued, so unlike Camlochlin.

It was everything Sina had missed during her first few days with the MacGregors. Now, tired of smiling, exhausted from dancing, and unable to sit because the hoops in her gown were wider than some of the staircases, with her hair pinned up and stuffed tightly under a lace cap, she questioned what was so wonderful about it.

"Did you both see that?" Eloise perked up. "Lord Ipswich just smiled at me."

"Oh no, I missed it?" Poppy asked, setting down her glass, then rolled her eyes at Sina.

"Stop it, Poppy," Eloise huffed. "Can I help it if he prefers me over you?"

Poppy slashed her painted lips and slanted her glittering green eyes behind her fan. "I already turned him down yesterday."

Eloise narrowed her eyes and tightened her lips. "But you think him handsome."

"So? That doesn't mean I want him in my bed." Poppy's smile faded when Eloise stormed away.

"I'll have to coddle her for days now," Poppy sighed, then snapped her fan shut and leaned in to speak close to Sina's ear.

"Tell me, is your Adam as handsome as those two?" She pointed her fan at the viscounts.

Sina blushed and rounded on her. "You promised never to bring it up."

"In public," Poppy pointed out. "I'm whispering."

"William will be here any minute."

"But he isn't here now. So, darling"—Poppy gave Sina's sleeve a little tug—"is he? More handsome than those two?"

In the old library, Sina had told Poppy everything about Adam, and the MacGregors, and Camlochlin. She'd wept with her when she realized, after more than three weeks without a word from him or the MacGregors, that she'd been forgotten yet again.

She understood why he let her go, but still felt hurt and angry over it.

She closed her eyes now to see Adam's face in her mind. "Yes. He is more handsome than ten viscounts."

"Poor little bird." Poppy took her hand and squeezed it. "What will you do?"

"There is nothing to be done. Even if Adam wanted me back, my father is dead-set against any alliance with the MacGregors." Sina mourned and looked into her trusted friend's eyes. "He let me go. I am letting him go, as well. 'Tis getting easier. I am betrothed again to William. He has been doting and wonderful, and he has even been trying to be more passionate since I mentioned it. Now, I do not wish to speak of Adam anymore."

Her gaze swung to the entrance where William had just appeared, fashionably late. He entered the hall dressed in a wide-skirted coat of red with heels to match. A wide-brimmed hat above his periwig shadowed his steady gaze as he took in every face until he found hers.

When he reached her, he greeted Poppy before she ran off, then dipped his head to kiss Sina's hand. She wished he wouldn't wear that overly scented wig. Her nose tickled and she tried to swallow the sneeze threatening to erupt. It was coming. She had no kerchief or napkin to cover herself—

bad enough she was sneezing in public. Her body involuntarily drew in a short breath.

She remembered the lace cap on her head. She reached up, tore it from her head at the last moment, and sneezed into it. William looked slightly amused and equally mortified.

In her effort to cover her sneeze, she'd torn away two pins, releasing a long curl down her temple. His gaze was fixed on it.

"You are beguiling, my dear," he said softly and reached down to pick her hairpins off the floor. "But I would rather you beguile only me." He handed her the pins and waited for her to make herself presentable again.

She didn't.

He constantly did his best to reach some enormously high standard he wanted her to live by as well. She'd always been satisfied to do it to make him happy. She took her lessons with more seriousness until she knew every rule of etiquette. Every ridiculously useless rule. She was tired of following them all. "I was thinking of wearing my hair loose on occasion."

He visibly paled but then managed a smile. "Whatever you want, my love."

She smiled at his effort to please her. "You are a good man, William."

"It means everything to me that you should think so, Sina. You saved me from myself and became my reason to never give up. I regret that I wasn't here to save you from being bound to a barbarian."

"What could you have done?" she asked on a breath. "'Twas the queen's order. There was nothing to be done without risk of the noose."

"Yes," he said, finally smiling. Sina liked seeing it.

"You're right, but it still plagues me. You know I would do anything, risk anything, for you."

Whatever she had with Adam was over. She had to move on. Take what she was offered by the man she'd loved all her life.

His eyes blinked away from her for a moment. "If you will excuse me, my love, I need a word with my cousin Roderick. I will return to you shortly."

"Of course," she said, letting him go.

She looked around for Poppy. It was going to be a long night—since William had just now arrived.

She spotted her friends huddled in a corner with the Desmond twins, Lords Henry and Freddy. What would they say if they ever saw Braigh and Tam MacGregor? Or if Braigh and Tam ever saw Poppy? What if Adam ever saw her?

She waved the ladies over when she caught their attention. They disengaged immediately and hurried over on their heeled feet.

Her friends made it halfway to her when they stopped in their tracks, their wide eyes on the entrance.

Sina's gaze followed. Her lips fell open and her heart threatened to leap from her mouth.

Adam.

Was it Adam? The massive hellhound at his side proved that it was.

He didn't wear his plaid but a black coat with buttons from neck to hem. None of them were fastened. But then, he didn't look like the kind of man who would be restrained by buttons. The coat's deep cuffs were pushed back from his wrists to expose his frilled shirt falling over long fingers. Instead of hose and garters, he wore black breeches and high boots. Around his neck, a white cravat was elegantly knotted and tied. His raven-black hair was tied away from his face into a slick tail, secured at his nape with a black ribbon.

His beauty was otherworldly, elegant, and dark as he stepped forward with Goliath at his side.

Chapter Twenty-Four

He'd come.

Sina's heart thundered in her ears. Could others hear it? Dear God, everything...everything she'd tried to forget, to deny, came washing over her like a wave.

She hadn't dreamed him. He was real, dripping with more virility than any man in the palace—any man she'd ever known.

His diamond-cut gaze was already on her, only her, stripping her of everything, all her layers down to her most hidden, secret parts. She couldn't move. She couldn't breathe.

Had he come for her? What should she do? She was torn between running to him and running away.

She looked at Goliath, understanding the horror on many of her guests' faces. He wasn't so bad. In fact, he was a good dog, a loyal friend to Adam. She lifted her lips in the slightest of smiles. Goliath responded with a step forward, his long tail wagging slowly behind him.

A word from Adam stopped the hound from going to her.

"Sina!" Eloise rushed to her side, while Poppy hung back a bit. "Who is he? Do you know him?"

"I…" When he began to move toward her, she closed her eyes, wishing that everyone in the hall would disappear, save him. She didn't want to miss him, but she did. Damn him, why had he come? It couldn't be for her. What about the safety of the clan? What if he'd toss that all aside and was here to bring her back? Could anyone stop him? Did she want them to?

"He's magnificent!" Eloise breathed, yanking her from her plaguing thoughts. "Oh, we simply must find out who he is." She pulled on Sina's sleeve. "Do you think he's a viscount? A baron? Look! He's coming over here!"

Sina cast a panic-stricken glance at Poppy, who caught on immediately and hurried to intercept him.

When the red-haired beauty stepped in front of him, Adam smiled.

Sina forgot what Eloise was talking about and cursed herself for sending Poppy to save her.

But soon enough, his gaze settled on her again even while Poppy shared words with him. What was her friend telling him? He smiled at her. She popped open her fan.

"Who is that, and what in God's name is that creature next to him?"

Sina turned to William coming to stand at her side. He closed his arm around her waist and she nearly passed out when Adam took a step forward like death coming for her cherished friend.

Poppy grasped his arm and looped hers through it, ignoring Goliath's growls.

"I don't recall ever seeing him before," William said

curiously, oblivious to the threat. "Did my mother invite him?"

Sina bit her lip.

What was he doing here? If William found out this was a MacGregor, he'd run straight to her father before either one of them could.

"Ehm, sir?" William called out, not waiting for any answers from her.

Poppy said something to Adam that tore his gaze from Sina. He nodded and put on a smile.

"Lord Standish," Adam greeted coolly, moving forward.

Sina's insides grew warmer with each step that brought him closer. She hadn't forgotten how big he was, but having him close again was like being caught in the warm shelter of a mountain in the middle of a storm.

"We finally meet."

Or perhaps he was the storm.

"Lord Adam Hamilton," he introduced himself, "grandson of the Duke of Hamilton."

What was this? Sina stared at him. Why was he pretending to be someone else?

"A Scot." William's smile was a bit stiff. "I don't recall seeing your name on the guest list," he said, dragging Adam's attention away from Sina and onto him.

"An oversight." Adam's husky voice rang through her, overriding William's lofty one. "As I assured my grand-faither."

"He was at my birthday celebration, William," Poppy said, sounding bored with the introductions. "If you had been there, you would have met him then." She turned her exquisite face up to Adam. "You attended the Duke of Sussex's wedding last year, did you not?"

"I did," he replied, playing along.

"I don't remember him," Eloise told her.

Poppy smiled indulgently at her. "You were engaged in someone else's company, my dearest."

William finally relented, not wanting to cause the duke's grandson any more insult. The Standishes were all about appearance and opinion. A duke's favor was well won. "I'll be certain to let my mother know. In the meantime, you're welcome to anything here."

Sina drew in a tight little gasp and looked away when Adam's gaze boldly stole to hers.

"Miss Warwick," Eloise purred at him. "Are you married, Lord Hamilton?"

Sina's hands tightened into fists at the bottom of her stomacher. Was she breathing? Why did she suddenly feel like weeping for him and for herself for a terrible circumstance they had no choice in making? She darted her gaze back to him and caught his eyes on her.

"Aye," he told Eloise. "Recently married. But I lost her."

Oh, why had he come to court? Why was he pretending to be Lord Hamilton? Why did every muscle in her body ache to fall into his arms...or run and hide until he left?

"Come, Lord Hamilton." Poppy pulled on his arm. "Let me introduce you to anyone you don't already know."

A few salutations were exchanged, but Sina didn't know what anyone said. Adam had gone back to looking at her, his gaze piercing through all her logic.

What was going to happen now? What was he planning to do? What would William do if he found out who Adam really was? She wasn't going to be able to keep this from him for long. Just looking at Adam, remembering his patience and laughter, his storytelling voice, was enough to tempt her to seek him out. No! It was too dangerous, for his clan and for William.

Adam looked over his shoulder at Sina while her best friend, Miss Berkham, pulled him toward another group of people he had no interest in meeting. He wasn't here to kiss English arses. He was here for her.

He wanted her back. He wanted to be chief with her at his side. He wanted to see her in his bed every night and wake up with her every morning, sore and swollen, ready for more.

He nodded and smiled when Miss Berkham introduced him to some other stately, stuffy, powdered faces and engaged in conversation with them.

Adam found Sina through the crowd Miss Berkham had put between them.

It was hard to look at her in her tight bun and rogue waves spilling around her face and not stride forward, gather her up in his arms, and kiss the hell out of her.

Somehow, he'd lost his heart to her. Mayhap it happened while he carried her to bed, or home from Will's after a night of laughing and drinking. Mayhap it was her soft voice and the fire hidden beneath her cool control that made him burn to strip her bare. It didn't matter when she'd taken his heart. She made him doubt every conviction. She made everything appear pale and dull in comparison to a few moments with her. Because of her, he'd come someplace he swore he'd never set foot. To England.

He wanted her heart, the one she'd given to *him*.

William Standish.

His frame was slight, his shoulders narrow beneath his

flared, red coat. He had a cool gaze and a mouth carved in cynicism.

Adam didn't know him, but he'd been right about him. Sina's beloved was pitifully dull. Though he possessed haughty airs, he surrendered easily to the weight of propriety.

Adam eyed him, frowning when Standish reached out to touch the curls falling over Sina's shoulder. Adam didn't like him touching her. In fact, he suffered a fleeting thought of ripping Standish's arm from his shoulder.

He resisted. He couldn't be a fool about this. He couldn't defy the king, for the sake of his clan. He wanted to find out why her father had called her back. What was the king's position on the MacGregors? And if it was poor, Adam wanted to change his mind and win his daughter's heart.

But if he wanted a chance to speak to the king, make friends with him as his aunt Maggie had put it when she helped him plan everything, he wouldn't get the chance in his plaid and muddy boots. He didn't mind the confines of his English clothes, though the high cravat did tempt him to tear it loose and celebrate the ability to swallow again.

He resisted that too.

He stopped when Miss Berkham pulled him further along.

"Fergive me, Miss Berkham, but tell me again why ye're doing this. Ye said ye were Miss de Arenburg's friend and I should do as ye say. So I did. Now tell me what this is about."

"Please," she said, stepping closer, "call me Poppy."

Adam shook his head and smiled. Flirtations were nothing he wasn't used to. He often found that being blunt worked best at warding off unwanted attention. "'Tis more intimate than I want to be, lass."

He spread his gaze over her shoulder and spotted Sina sitting with her friend Miss Warwick.

"Oh, I'm not interested in you, my lord," Sina's friend told him, dragging his gaze to her dazzling smile and dimpled chin. "That's not why I'm here with you."

"Then why are ye here?"

She looked up at him with a challenge in her twinkling green eyes. "I will put the same question to you, *Mr. MacGregor.*"

Adam kept his smile intact. How much had Sina told her?

"You're the one who let her go," she continued, addling him further.

Now he gave her his full attention. She took a step back, unprepared for it. "She told ye that?"

"She told me much," she said with a satisfied sigh as her eyes took him in from foot to crown. "She did not embellish." She flapped open her fan and waved it in front of her face.

"I'm not going to tell anyone who you are, my lord. You have my word."

She perplexed him, but he believed her.

"I must ask. Do you know what we're celebrating tonight?"

"Nae, 'tis only by good fertune that I came during a celebration and was able to enter the palace with the other guests."

She smiled, but it looked strained. "Good fortune. Yes. Come, Lord Hamilton. Let's walk together." She took him by the arm and let him lead.

"There's no easy way to say this," she said on a sigh, "so I'm going to just say it. We are celebrating Sina's betrothal to Lord Standish."

He stopped and took a step to go back. Nae! She hadn't agreed to wed the proud peacock again, had she? "She gave up on me so soon, then," he muttered on a pained growl.

"How was she to know you would ever come? Have you even come for *her*? Would you prefer she grew old waiting for you?"

"That wouldna have happened," he said, lowering his brow over his eyes. "It has been exactly twenty-one days since I last saw her. I know it felt longer but—"

"I'm going to ask you some questions," she interrupted without breaking stride. "If your answers satisfy my desire to protect my closest friend, I will let you ask me anything about her."

"And if they dinna please ye?"

"Then I will ask you to leave her alone—or I *will* go to the king."

"Let's no' waste our time," he said, pausing to turn to her and letting his Highland burr flow naturally. "I'm certain I willna measure up to yer fine standards."

She smiled as though the sound of him delighted her. She tugged on his arm and pulled him forward. "You don't know what my standards are. First question, what did you think the first time you saw her?"

Interesting first question, Adam thought. Lady Berkham was clever, and she seemed to genuinely care about Sina. "She was like a sparrow caught in a net. Her tears made me feel like the monster who'd captured her."

"Hmm," Miss Berkham murmured, staring up at him without blinking. "Good answer. Next, is she safe where you live? Would anyone there seek to harm her?"

"There is no place safer on this earth than my home," he told her, vowing to himself at the same time that he would

keep it that way. "We are kin and would never hurt one another."

"Kin?"

"Family."

Her eyes glistened beneath the sun as she repeated his
reply.

"Last one," she said, fanning herself. "Why did you wait
so long to come? You broke her heart."

This question wasn't so easy to answer. When he heard
that he broke her heart, his own heart broke as well. Was
it too late? Had he waited too long? "I couldna just come
and take her withoot possibly bringin' an end to my clan. I
need to do this the clever, peaceful way. Fer that, I needed
a wee bit of time to prepare."

She smiled and snapped her fan shut and tapped him on
the shoulder with it. "Your answers were better than I would
have expected from the best men I know. So, well done.
Now 'tis your turn."

He smiled, being found worthy. Miss Berkham was perceptive. If anyone knew Sina, it was this lass.

"I willna ask ye fer her secrets," he told her.

She smiled at him again. "I won't tell any of them to you,
but I can tell you this, she has wanted nothing more in her
life than a family. 'Tis her dream, not her secret."

He could give her that. She'd been accepted by his kin,
the same way Kate Campbell had once been when she first
stepped into Camlochlin.

"And," Sina's friend continued, "because I was so
pleased by your answers, I will also tell you that her heart
inclines toward the romantic."

Hell, the romantic? Adam brooded.

Miss Berkham tugged his cuff, pulling back his attention.
"She wants a man who cannot live without her, who would

travel hundreds of miles to see her again, or fill her bed with heather. As much as I love William, he is not that man. He packed up and left her for *years* for some grand adventure. Where was he today? He returned home. He only comes here when he must. They are finally reunited after more than three years. Why aren't they off making love until neither one can walk straight?"

A thought Adam would prefer not to have was planted in his head. "Is there no passion between them?" he asked, wanting to know now.

"None. He promised to try though." She paused to let him ponder how ridiculous it was. "He is comfortable, like a blanket she has grown used to. But he is devoted to her and takes great pride in the fact that she loves him. He will not take losing her without a fight, and she does not want to hurt him."

Adam didn't know why Miss Berkham was telling him these things. But he was thankful for the insight.

"Thank ye," he said, turning to shine his smile on her. "I'll consider it all while I win her from him."

"Oh, Lord Hamilton," she teased. "Stop before you make me swoon. Tell me, do you have any brothers?"

"Two, but I fear they are no match fer ye."

She smiled at him. "Whatever I can do to help, you just let me know."

He was about to thank her when he spotted a drunken man arguing with Standish. The much bigger man took a swing at William and hit Sina, who was standing with Standish, in the shoulder.

Adam pushed Miss Berkham out of the way and leaped over a table, shattering plates as he trampled them.

He reached the intoxicated nobleman, grabbed him by the throat, and smashed his face into the wall.

When the drunken man's drunken friends attacked him, Adam had no choice but to fight.

When it was over, which wasn't too long after it began, he turned to Sina, wanting to make certain she wasn't hurt, and was promptly taken into custody by the king's guards.

Chapter Twenty-Five

*A*dam had wanted an audience with the king. But not like this. Not standing before him bound at the wrists, clenching his bloody hands behind his back. Not when he was ready to kill if someone didn't tell him where Goliath was.

Adam knew what was at stake if he spoke too harshly to the king. All his plans and good intentions would be for naught. He would lose Sina unless he kidnapped her and started a war.

Still, it was his dog.

"I ask again, Yer Majesty." He kept his voice at an even, nonthreatening pitch. "Where is my dog?"

"You're in no position to ask any questions, Lord Hamilton. You came into my home and saw fit to beat a dozen men senseless."

"They attacked me."

"Yes, after you broke Lord Geoffrey Markham's nose!"

"He struck Miss de Arenburg," Adam cut him off mildly. "He is fortunate I did not kill him."

The king bounded from his chair, his face red with fury.

Obviously, he had not been given the full tale. "Have Lord Markham taken to Newgate prison after his wounds are seen to," he barked at a guard standing behind Adam. "And bring Lady de Arenburg to me immediately."

He set his hard, dark eyes on Adam again. "As for you, you should have left the matter to my guards. I won't have my guests fighting in the halls, no matter whom they fight for. Do you understand?"

"Not if ye're telling me to do nothing if I see a man strike a woman in yer palace."

King George narrowed his eyes at him. For a moment Adam feared the king suspected him of being a MacGregor.

He slowed his breathing. There was no reason for the king to suspect Adam wasn't who he claimed to be. George spent most of his time in Hanover. According to Aunt Maggie, he wouldn't know many of the noblemen in England and especially in Scotland.

"Release him," the king ordered his guards.

The instant he was freed from his bonds, Adam strode toward the door.

"Lord Hamilton," the king called out. "I'm assured your dog remains exactly where you left it and is safe. Return and have a seat. I wish to ask you some questions."

This was what Adam wanted. He could charm the crown off the king if he put his mind to it.

"I would have him returned to me first," Adam told him, trying to sound as respectful as he could. He turned for the doors just as they opened and William Standish plunged inside.

"Your Majesty. 'Tis your—" His gaze slipped to Adam and the king's guards. "'Tis Miss de Arenburg. I fear she is about to get herself shot."

Adam was the first one out.

Rushing to the hall, he saw that a crowd was gathered around where he'd left Goliath. The music had stopped. Where was Sina?

With his heart thundering in his chest, he pushed his way through the onlookers.

He saw her standing in front of his dog, her deadly glare locked on a man in front of the crowd to Adam's right.

Her crackling voice rang out. "Put that pistol down, Captain, or I'll see you flogged!"

The bastard's pistol was pointed at her and Goliath.

Without a moment of hesitation, Adam reached him and plucked the pistol from his hand. The man was so stunned that he barely had time to react as Adam stepped around him, pointing the pistol at him and at anyone else thinking to make a move.

"Enough!" The king's voice boomed through the hall. "Pistols aimed at Miss de Arenburg?" His dark eyes settled on his daughter, concern and anger vying for dominance. "Are you all right? I heard you were struck by Lord Markham." When she nodded, his gaze burned on the man whose pistol Adam finally lowered. "Guards, take him away! Lord Hamilton, get your dog and then get yourself back to my chamber!"

Adam would go, thankful for the chance, but first he turned to Sina. He would never forget what she'd done for Goliath. "Thank ye, lass."

She looked up at him with eyes he wanted to gaze into forever, and offered him a slight, guarded smile. "We're friends."

Her and Goliath, or her and him? Adam wanted more. He wanted to speak with her, smile freely at her, tell her how sorry he was for letting her go, for breaking her heart. But Standish and the crowd were watching. He wouldn't mortify her, and he didn't need any more trouble right now, so he nodded and remained silent except to call Goliath.

He returned to the king's chambers, but his thoughts remained in the hall.

She cared for Goliath, and that alone set his heart to pounding.

He rested his hand on his dog's back as they went. Faithful boy, Adam thought, thankful that his friend had obeyed him and hadn't tried to attack the king's guards.

"Was she no' fierce and bonny when she protected ye?"

Goliath wagged his tail and circled him, then licked his hand.

"I know," Adam told him, not looking up when Eloise giggled past him. "Me too."

Adam didn't tell the king who he was, and when George asked him about his home, Adam used descriptions of burghs he'd visited in Perth during his visits to his cousin Malcolm Grant.

The more he lied about his life, the harder it was to tell the king the truth. He'd made a poor impression tonight swinging his fists *and* a pistol. No matter what he'd done or why he did it, he would be seen as a savage—just as Sina was raised to believe all Highlanders were. He might even be arrested for being a MacGregor. Anne was dead. His clan's protection was over. Hell, it was up to him to fix it.

He possessed no doubts of his prowess. He could be tactful and wily. But if he confessed the truth of his identity now, he'd never win the king's favor.

Still, it meant his staying in England longer. He didn't

like it here. He was more convinced than ever before that he wasn't born for stone streets and strangers' faces at every turn.

"That dog of yours is quite a sight," the king said, looking at Goliath lying beside Adam's chair. "One could understand the fear he strikes in a man...or a woman. I was quite stunned to find Miss de Arenburg standing guard over him. I'm told she has a terrible fear of dogs since she was bitten as a child. But this...this was almost as if she had no fear of the beast."

Adam looked toward the door. "She's very brave," he said on a low breath.

The king nodded, then eyed him over his cup. "Did you rush out to save her—or the dog?"

The king wasn't a fool, and Standish hadn't mentioned Goliath when he'd burst into the chamber.

"Both, Sire," Adam admitted.

Adam noted the slightest trace of gratitude softening the king's expression. "I see." He spread his gaze over him and then swished his hand in front of his face. "You may go. And stay out of trouble!"

The moment Adam returned to the hall and saw Sina sitting with Standish, he knew obeying the king would be difficult.

"I don't understand why you would put yourself in harm's way for a *dog*," William said, sitting beside Sina. "'Twas reckless of you. You know I was against it."

She nodded with her chin in her hand and looked around. She was not in the frame of mind to have to help William understand why she wouldn't let Goliath be shot.

She hadn't thought about it when she stepped in front of the hound. She knew what he meant to Adam.

"Yes, I know," she insisted in a soft voice, "but as I've already told you, the dog hadn't harmed anyone who wasn't fighting. Besides, after what Lord Hamilton did for you, I thought it the least we could do not to kill his dog."

"Yes," William agreed with a slow nod. "Although one must wonder if 'twas you he was defending."

Yes, Sina thought wistfully. Lord Markham had barely touched her. He could hardly stand. But his hand had made contact with her shoulder and sent her off balance. She'd spotted Adam atop a table, coming at him like a dark plague.

She shook her head. William wasn't the man in her dreams. The one she loved with more of her heart every day. *That* man had ridden all the way to England on a horse. He'd leaped to her rescue when he thought she was in danger. And the way he looked at her, even in Poppy's presence, proved that whatever had been happening between them in Camlochlin wasn't over.

But she was betrothed to William...again! When it had sunk in that Adam was gone, she tried to find what was missing with William. She couldn't break his heart again.

"My darling." William smiled at her and slipped his hand in hers. "You are right about the dog. It's your compassionate heart that compels you, and it is one of the things I love most about you."

Poor William, Sina thought with guilt plaguing her gaze. She lowered it, careful to keep him from seeing what she tried so hard to conceal. Here they were, supposed to be celebrating their lives together, and she was pining over someone else.

She must stop! She couldn't be with Adam. She didn't

even know if he came back for her. William hadn't left her side, so she hadn't had a chance to speak with Poppy. No matter what she felt for Adam, she couldn't hurt William again, and Adam couldn't bring danger to his clan. There was nothing left to consider.

Chapter Twenty-Six

Sina looked out over the terrace at the moonlit gardens below. Music and laughter from the celebration still going on behind her wafted through her veins like sour wine. How could she be so miserable on a night when everyone was dancing? She was going to have a respectable marriage with a man whom she'd known her whole life. Her mother and father were living publicly, and soon, she hoped, they would declare her as their own.

But she'd pled illness to William and claimed she needed air when she saw Adam enter the hall. Why did she want to be away from the guests and the resumed merriment and come away to weep for herself?

How could she miss a man who, when he wasn't infuriating her, was beguiling her heart with his blue eyes, wide smile, and understanding ear? She closed her eyes and saw him naked in their bed for the first time, his hand reaching down to his arse to verify her panicked claim.

He'd slept in bed with her and obeyed her command not to touch her. She knew not many men would respect their wives' wishes when it came to such things. Did he not find her appealing? She hadn't thought of it before. Yes, he'd kissed her, but he'd let her go.

Wasn't that what she'd wanted? Wasn't that for the best?

Something wet spread over her fingers. She looked down to see Goliath staring back at her. She smiled and then remembered that the hound rarely left Adam's presence.

He was here, likely behind her. She started to turn but... she didn't want to see him. She didn't want to be reminded of what she couldn't have.

"You shouldn't be here," she said on a quiet voice.

"Nor should ye."

Her eyes closed and she bit her tongue at the sound of his rich baritone. Memories of it and things he said bombarded her thoughts.

Ye are hellfire covered by a golden shield of eloquence and innocence.

Ye agreed to take me as yer husband in the sight of God. Shall we lie in bed all day?

She sensed him moving closer until he came to stand beside her, blocking out the moonlight and bringing the scent of heather to her nostrils. Was she imagining the sweet fragrance? How could he still carry it on him?

What was he doing here? He obviously hadn't told her father who he was, or she was sure he wouldn't be standing here right now. She had a horrible feeling this wasn't going to end well for Camlochlin.

She should demand that he throw himself at her father's mercy or leave London. But she didn't want to be away from him again.

She slipped her gaze to him and then couldn't look away. He'd turned the opposite way and was facing her, leaning his hips on the terrace railing so that she had a full-on view of him.

She felt light-headed and was tempted to smile. She didn't. "I thought I would never see you again."

"A grievous error on my part," he said, his moonlit eyes glittering on her beneath his dark brow.

A grievous error? No. No, he couldn't be here for her. Their marriage would be dissolved any day now, if it wasn't already.

"You should leave England."

"I will, after I have what I came fer."

She felt as if her blood were leaving her body. Had her heart stopped beating, or was it beating so fast that each thump blended into the next? "And what is that?" she asked on a whispered breath.

"Yer faither's favor toward the MacGregors."

Relief and regret battled for dominance over her features.

"And fer ye."

She reached out for the railing and clung to it until her knuckles grew white.

"Why have you changed your mind?"

"I miss seein' ye in my bed." He quirked his playful mouth, validating that he knew it was the most ridiculous of reasons to come all the way to England. He didn't care, and melted whatever else he'd already set aflame in her.

He'd come for her. Every part of her wanted to rejoice and swoon at his bold, romantic gesture—every part but her heart. This couldn't be. *They* couldn't be.

"What about your family?" she asked.

"They urged me to come."

She wanted to smile. Of course they would. They probably piled him with heather before he left.

"What about my father?" she asked with hopelessness

tainting her voice. "I've tried to speak on the MacGregors' behalf a dozen times, and he rejects everything. I'm afraid his heart has been turned against you."

"Aye, by William Standish, the man ye claim as yer beloved."

She met his gaze head-on. "You would have done the same to get me back."

His smile faded. He pressed his lips together, not denying her claim.

"Our marriage is over, Adam."

His unblinking gaze set her nerves to burning. He looked as if he was about to push off the railing and drag her into his arms. She prayed he didn't. Not here. Not when William could come looking for her.

He didn't move, save to reach down for Goliath's ear to tug it. When he spoke, his voice was low, deep, meaningful. "I told ye if yer heart were free, I would do whatever it took to win it. Are ye tellin' me it belongs completely to Standish?"

She severed their gaze and wrung her hands together. Should she tell him the truth? That she loved him, couldn't stop thinking of him? No. He would believe there was a chance for them when there wasn't. This could start a war, and she wouldn't let that happen.

"Yes. That is what I'm telling you."

Before she sensed him moving, he swept her up in his arms and pressed her to his hard body.

She didn't try to break free. Her mind told her to escape him. Her heart didn't listen.

"Ye're a terrible liar, lass," he whispered, dragging his mouth over hers.

His breath scalded her skin as he moved to speak against her ear. "I'm goin' to prove it, and then I'm takin' ye home."

His thundering heart against her set hers to flying.

He released her without a kiss, bowed before her like a proper gentleman, and then left the terrace with his dog, leaving Sina grasping for the rail and burying her face in her hands.

Sina woke early the next morning with red, swollen eyes. She'd wept into her pillow most of the night thinking about why she hadn't told Adam she loved him before she came back—the night Laurel was born. Now she didn't dare. She thought of his mouth so close, so eager for her—of his eyes and the way they danced over her features, the passion and excitement he invoked in her.

She didn't feel them with William, and it made her want to weep all over again. She had tried, but there was no romance with her friend. She had to tell him.

She lay in bed thinking about Adam until Katie, her handservant, arrived to help her dress. She declined her wide hoops for something more slender.

In Camlochlin, no one cared what anyone else wore. One wasn't frowned upon if she wasn't up on the latest fashions. No one cared if she wore her hair twisted atop her head or flowing down her back.

She missed Ula.

"Are you unwell, m'lady?" Katie asked behind her while she pulled the laces of her stay. "You're looking very sad since you returned."

"I'll be fine, Katie." Sina wiped her eyes with her small flowered handkerchief and smiled when her handservant stepped in front of her.

"Forgive me for asking, but is it Lord Standish, m'lady?" Katie's large sable eyes darted to the bed. "Has he...harmed you?"

"Harmed me?" Sina asked, touching her arm to draw her attention back. "Whatever do you mean?"

"I didn't mean anything," Katie assured and moved on to lace Sina's shoes. "You just seem so sad all the time. This morning especially."

"Well, I'm not. You see? I'm smiling," Sina said, showing her. "But I still don't understand why you would think Lord Standish had harmed me."

"Men are known for such things," her handservant muttered, helping Sina into her footwear.

"Not William."

"Forgive me."

"Of course." Sina smiled and let her help with her petticoats and mantua of sapphire blue.

Sina lived in one of the smaller apartments in the queen's quarters, so it wasn't a surprise when she met her mother on the stairs. Still, it was a rare occurrence since they'd lived apart for so many years, and one that Sina wasn't certain she would grow accustomed to.

"Have you been crying, Sina?" Her mother came closer to examine her with concern filling her eyes.

Sina moved back. "No. I've been sneezing. I think I'm coming down with something."

Now her mother moved back as well. "No, you cannot come down with an illness now. You're to serve as mistress of robes to Princess Caroline beginning next month. We must get her apartments in order. After that we'll begin preparing for your wedding and the coronation." The lines in her mother's face softened, along with her smile. "'Tis nice having you here."

Was she telling the truth?

"But you chose to send me away," Sina reminded her softly, wanting to say it for years. "Off to live with my uncle."

She expected to see anger in her mother's eyes. She didn't know Sina enough to know of her daughter's quiet boldness. Her mother spoke with crisp authority no one defied. Not even Sina's father. She wouldn't take kindly to being reminded of her offenses.

But there was no anger, only a mist rising in her mother's eyes. She stopped them from descending any more stairs with her hand on Sina's arm.

"The king's wife had the heart of Hanover. You were a babe when George had her put away in the castle of Ahlden. There were threats made against your father's life. Threats to me. We sent you away to keep you safe. 'Twas not an easy decision, if that's what you believe. But now, the need is over. I want you here."

Did she now want to be a mother? Did Sina want her to be? "As your daughter? Publicly?"

"Yes. The king will make the announcement soon."

Sina couldn't help but smile. It was what she'd always desired—to be acknowledged.

"But you must keep this knowledge from your father. He wishes to tell you himself."

"I won't say a word," Sina promised with a lighter feeling in her heart. If things could be mended between them, then let them be. The shame was going to be lifted.

"Now," her mother said, moving once again, "I want you to rest today so that you're well tomorrow."

"Yes," Sina promised as they reached the bottom step.

"One last thing." Her mother stopped her with a hand to her wrist when Sina moved in the direction of the dining hall. "I saw you leave the terrace shortly after Lord Hamilton last night. Did you speak to him outside?"

Sina's heart battered hard against her ribs. Had her mother seen her in his arms, ready and willing to be kissed?

No, Sina told herself, steadying her breath. She'd only seen them leaving.

"Yes, he thanked me for protecting his hound."

Did her voice just crack? Was it noted?

"Nothing else?"

Sina shook her head.

"He's quite handsome," her mother said. "Three earls have already come forward showing interest in his bloodline and the possibility of him becoming their son-in-law."

Sina did her best not to react, though it was difficult. What if her father promised him to one of them? What if it were Eloise or Poppy? What if they had the wedding here and she had to watch it?

No. She balled her hands into fists. She'd rip someone's eyes out first.

Chapter Twenty-Seven

Adam cursed the high cravat around his neck and glared up at the sun over the brim of his tricorn hat. Why the hell did the English wear so much clothing? Something was pinching him under the arm, tempting him to tear his clothes away.

He took another look around the garden and at the people strolling in the early morning. Peacocks—and in his long coat, hose, and heels he fit in perfectly.

He scowled at how low he was willing to go for...*her*.

He spotted her walking up the path between the orange trees. He'd been waiting for her, hoping to find her here in the gardens. She was looking at her hands, twisting them together at her waist. When she raised her head and saw him, she stopped—as did his heart.

"Oh!" Sina brought her hands up to her chest. "Adam—Lord Hamilton."

Would he ever get used to looking at her? Her face had been emblazoned on his soul. He remembered every one of her compelling expressions, her large, luminous eyes where all her truths lay hidden. She'd been up all night weeping, from the look of her. He'd seen that same small nose, red and sore from wiping the morning after their wedding.

He watched her lids flutter as she turned her gaze away, and then brought it back.

"I didn't think I would see you here so early," she said.

"There is no reason to stay in my bed."

She pursed her mouth as if she'd just tasted a sour apple. He smiled, aching to kiss her.

"You're staying at the palace, then," she deduced, trying to keep the topic from swerving.

"Aye, in one of the guest apartments."

She shook her head and appeared so downhearted he almost considered leaving England to save her from any more distress. She'd been through much in a short period of time. She'd told him last night that her heart belonged completely to William Standish. He didn't believe her. Her love for William was different. Thanks to Miss Berkham, he understood that now. It was something born from childhood, a bond no one could break. Adam didn't want to break it. It went deep. William was her friend, the only love she knew—but not the only love there was—and Adam was asking her to betray him.

She was going to be harder to win than he'd first realized. He loved her more because of her stalwart heart. She wasn't a fickle lass. She loved deeply. It made him want to be the one she loved most. But he didn't want to hurt her.

He took a step closer. "Was I the source of yer tears last eve, lass?"

She moved away, her eyes darting around the garden, pausing everywhere except on him. "Don't be ridiculous. I'm coming down with something. It has nothing to do with you."

"Hmm." He lifted his brow at her, though she still hadn't looked up. "Is it marrying Standish that makes ye so gloomy, then?"

A spark of fire lit her eyes as she lifted them slowly to his. "No, Adam. 'Tis not that. 'Tis you, in truth." She drew in a short gasp, as if she were just now remembering to breathe. "You cannot keep appearing in my life and turning everything upside down. Why are you here? Why have you come as Lord Hamilton?"

"I told ye, Sina. I'm goin' to win the king's favor, let him get to know me withoot my name gettin' in the way. I canna have ye withoot his blessin'"—he took a moment to tug on the torturous amount of damned lace around his neck—"so I must get it. But first, I would mend yer heart."

"I cannot let you," she told him. Her nose and her eyes grew redder. "I promised William...I cannot...I don't know what is best for me anymore."

He knew he shouldn't, but he couldn't help but smile at her beautiful teary face. "Ye do know what's best fer ye, lass," he argued gently. "Ye want to make yer own choices, same as me, but yer fiercely loyal heart keeps ye here, trapped in propriety."

"No—"

"Are ye happy here, then?" he put to her sincerely. "Livin' under the scrutiny of everyone, tryin' to look like everyone else?"

"As opposed to living in some isolated vale in the mountains?" she countered.

"Aye. With me."

She faltered—just a bit, but he saw it. For one blissful, perfect moment, she let herself imagine it, let herself go to it. He saw it in her eyes and in the mist that filled them. She could be happy with him.

"Where have you been?" she asked with tears filling her eyes to the brim.

"I couldna rush in, lass. I wanted to come—"

"Miss de Arenburg." A man's voice rang out from behind Adam, halting the rest of his words.

Adam controlled his desire to strangle him as he turned to see the Viscount of Nottingham strutting forward in his elegant suit with full skirts pinned at his sides, colored garters, and frilled gloves. Dangling from one of his buttons by a blue ribbon was a cane with an amber head. No doubt this was the height of fashion, since all the men here looked the same. Like peacocks.

The ladies here seemed to like it, judging from the beautiful young woman daintily attached to Nottingham's arm. They were all too frail and fragile looking to Adam's way of thinking—like porcelain statues easily shattered.

"Lord Hamilton," Nottingham greeted, bobbing his scented periwig. "Are we interrupting?"

"Not at all," Sina answered, snapping open her fan and lowering her misty gaze. "Lord Hamilton was just apologizing for striking Lord Markham at the celebration."

"No need to apologize, Hamilton." The viscount waved his hands before his face, sending lace cuffs flying. "He had it coming. 'Twas very brave of you." He smiled, flashing dimples that made him appear too pretty to be a man. "Imagine him accusing my cousin, Lord Standish, of beating his servant." He looked at Sina, waiting for her agreement.

She appeared a bit taken back. "I hadn't heard any accusation. Markham was swearing and making threats."

"'Tis a heinous accusation to spread about an upstanding gentleman," Nottingham said. "My family is in your debt for putting an end to his tirade, Hamilton."

Adam nodded, but what he did to Markham had nothing

to do with Standish. If he'd known the accusation at the time, he would have hurled a fist into William as well.

"Have you met my sister, Lady Catherine Newton? I thought you might escort her to dinner this evening."

Adam heard Sina's tight intake of breath and flicked his gaze to her. Her lips were puckered and plump, tempting him to pull her close and kiss them. But he knew that look. He'd seen it just before she flung his father's chess piece at him.

"Miss Newton," he said quickly. "My apologies, but I've already asked Miss de Arenburg if I may escort her."

"Oh?" Nottingham lifted a golden brow at Sina. "And her reply?"

Adam watched her while she thought about her reply. She darted her gaze to Miss Newton's large ebony eyes and bit her lip, knowing that if she refused, Nottingham would insist on Adam escorting his sister.

"I consented," she told him with a tilt to her chin that she turned on Adam.

"My lady," Nottingham told her. "You are betrothed—to my cousin, in fact. Why is he not escorting you to dinner?"

"Because he has left and will return tomorrow," she told him.

"Nottingham." Adam stopped him before he insulted Sina further. "I'm not carrying her off to my bed. I'm simply escorting her to her chair. Same as ye asked me to do fer yer sister."

The viscount stared at him for a moment, fear and uncertainty shadowing his hazel eyes. "Of course. I didn't mean to suggest…"

His voice trailed off in Adam's ears, replaced by Sina catching his gaze while the viscount stared at the grass. She looked stunned and pleased that he'd turned Nottingham's suspicions into an apology. When he smiled openly at her, she averted her gaze.

"Are you escorting her back to the palace this morn, as well?" the viscount asked more politely, pulling Sina's gaze from his.

"No," she answered before Adam could reply.

"Good," Nottingham said, "then he can bring Catherine back now."

He handed his sister over without waiting for a response. Miss Newton reached for Adam's arm with one hand and for Goliath with the other.

When Goliath licked her fingers instead of biting them off, Adam looked at her and smiled.

"Well, let's be back now," Sina said, turning to reach for the viscount. She stumbled and cried out before she fell to her knees.

Adam rushed to her and, crouching beside her, looped her arm around his shoulder.

"Here!" Nottingham reached for her. "Let me help her."

"Oh, 'tis twisted," Sina lamented, dangling from Adam's shoulder. "I think I may be ill!"

She covered her mouth with her hand, and the viscount leaped backward and tossed Adam a panicked look. "You take her back." He pulled his sister away. "I'll check on her later."

Adam nodded and bent to curl his arm around her knees and lifted her in his arms.

"You don't have to carry me," she said when they were alone.

He stared down at her face, so close that all he had to do was lean down to press his mouth to hers. "I dinna mind carryin' ye, lass." It was all he thought about.

"I feel better," she insisted. Her cheeks were painted with a natural blush he found enchanting.

"What do ye mean, ye feel better?" he asked, his smile turning into a curious smirk. "Has the pain left ye?"

"Yes."

"Miraculous."

She frowned up at him. "Put me down."

"I dinna trust yer judgment. Ye were swoonin' a moment ago."

"I was not swooning," she defended with a forced chuckle. "I was protecting you from Miss Newton's company. She's manipulative and will have herself betrothed to you in a sennight."

It took every ounce of strength Adam possessed not to grin at her like a fool. She was jealous.

"She seems quite pleasant to me," he countered. "Even Goliath likes her."

Sina frowned even harder and aimed it at his dog walking beside him. "I noticed."

She noticed. She hadn't twisted her ankle. She'd stopped him from being alone with another woman who liked his dog. He wanted to toss back his head and shout with victory, but he'd likely shatter the statues.

"Adam, everyone is looking. Please, put me down."

"Twisted ankle!" he called out, giving the onlookers a reason why she was in his arms.

She sighed at him. "You don't have to carry me."

"I dinna mind." Hell, he loved carrying her. She made him feel strong, and bound to duty—and for the first time in his life, he ached to perform it, to do his best at it.

"What do ye make of the accusation toward Standish?" he asked, growing serious.

"I've never known him to strike anyone," she told him.

"Oh, my lady, what happened?" A young handservant appeared in front of them.

"Nothing, Katie, I—"

"Twisted ankle," Adam informed her.

"'Tis not twisted," Sina hissed at him.

"Then why would ye say 'twas?"

She didn't answer and closed her eyes when Katie led him through the doors and up the stairs to her rooms.

"Fetch a physician," Adam told the handservant when she stepped aside to let him in.

"What am I going to tell a physician?" Sina demanded when they were alone.

He carried her through her sitting room, a small but impressive library, to her bedchamber and set her down, gently, reluctantly, onto her bed. He stared into her eyes. He didn't want to leave her. Not even for a few hours. But he had to use caution. He couldn't bring shame to her.

"Tell him ye have found the man who makes ye happy." He leaned in as she pressed her head to her pillow. She didn't recoil. "And ye would go to any lengths to protect him from the wiles of a manipulative woman."

"You're a pigheaded fool," she said without a trace of anger.

He wanted to stay. He wanted to take her in his arms and tell her he loved her, and it was nothing like he'd imagined. It set him free and gave him courage and confidence to do anything. Even resist her for now.

He brushed his lips over her cheek, then her temple, and then he straightened. "I'll see ye this evenin', my lady."

He followed Goliath down the stairs and went in search of the king.

Chapter Twenty-Eight

Adam stood outside the doors to the king's quarters and waited. He'd been waiting over an hour. He'd wait all day if he had to. When he'd asked for an audience, he was denied. The king was resting this morning in preparation for a busy afternoon and did not wish to be disturbed.

Adam figured George had to leave his quarters sometime today. He'd be here to speak with him when he did.

He smiled at the staff as they came and went with trays of fruit and silver flagons of wine. He spoke to no one, save in greeting, and thought about what he would say to Sina's father.

He wanted to try to spend some time with him. He needed to if he was ever going to gain his trust.

Finally, after another quarter of an hour, the door opened and a servant ushered him inside. "The king wishes a word."

Adam pushed off the wall he was leaning against, pulled off his hat, and followed her in. The king's quarters were a lavish display of overindulgence. There were a dozen rooms, many of which were decorated in polished wood and gold and red fabrics.

Adam was led to a small private chamber where George sat waiting for him before a large hearth. He wore a silken robe stitched with gold thread and the finest lace. His gray head was absent of any wig.

"My staff tells me you refuse to leave my door," he said, lifting a fig to his mouth.

"I was not asked to leave, Yer Majesty."

George humphed and then looked around. "Where's your dog?"

"He awaits me in the hall."

"Bring him," the king ordered, shooing Adam away. "And then you'll tell me what makes you stand at my door all morning."

Adam retrieved Goliath and returned to the king. He sat in a chair almost as big as the chairs in Camlochlin and took the drink the king offered him.

"Now, what is this about?"

"'Tis about Miss de Arenburg, Sire." Adam stopped and drew in a breath to help him begin. "I'm not one to listen to gossip, but I heard she was recently given in marriage to a MacGregor but you ordered her return."

George's scowl wasn't a good sign. "You use good judgment not listening to gossip, Hamilton. But why does it concern you?"

"I would be interested in courting her." It wasn't untrue. "I do not want there to be any complications." Again, not untrue.

"Well, there *are* complications," George told him. "She is betrothed."

Adam set down his cup on the small table between them. "That can be broken."

The king chuckled. "There are plenty of other offers for your company. I can arrange—"

"Give them my regrets."

The king studied him with narrowed eyes and then asked, "Why her? You met her only last night."

Adam knew this was his chance to speak to her father from his heart. He hoped when George heard him, he would be better willing to accept Adam as a MacGregor.

"She is brave and bold, Sire. I spoke to her earlier and found her to be refreshing and filled with grace. Her beauty drives away every other thought, every consequence."

"What consequence do you mean?" the king put to him. "The MacGregors?" he asked, taking a guess. "The marriage is being annulled as we speak."

"What if 'tis not what she wants? Not what *he* wants and he comes to plead for her return?"

"A MacGregor plead?" the king laughed. "I've never heard of it happening. I've been digging a bit into their history, and I cannot recall a single story of them pleading for anything."

Adam struggled to keep his shoulders from straightening with pride. Hearing that the king was digging around into his clan's history helped keep him focused.

"He will not come," the king continued. "He was as happy to be rid of Sina as she was of him. But if he does show his face here, I will have him thrown in Newgate."

Adam's heart pounded so hard that it made him feel ill. Protection would no longer come from the throne. If George knew who he was, he would never give Adam a chance to prove him wrong about him and his kin. He couldn't reveal who he was yet. He was here representing more than himself, and he didn't want the prejudice of his name interfering.

"Then may I proceed in trying to win her favor?" he asked in a controlled voice. At his feet, Goliath whined, sensing the fire coursing through Adam's veins.

"You won't win it from Lord Standish," her father assured him. "Though I don't believe he is the right choice for her."

"Because he left her? Her friend told me," Adam added to explain how he knew.

The king shook his head and sipped his wine. "Because of what he did during his time away. 'Twould bring her shame if she knew."

He'd been unfaithful. The son of a—

"I will have a letter sent to your grandfather asking for your details," the king granted. "Until then—"

"Ye have my gratitude, Sire."

George smiled at him over the rim of his cup. "You're an eager lad."

Adam returned the gesture and shook his head at himself. "As Solomon once said, 'I have found the one whom my soul loves.' Why waste any more time?"

"That sounds very serious," the king remarked.

"'Tis."

"Very well," her father said after thinking it over for another moment. "I will allow you to try, and hope you succeed."

"I'll do my best," Adam promised him. And somehow, Adam would win him, as well. He spotted a chess set on a nearby table and smiled. "Do ye play?"

"Do you?" the king challenged with an arched brow.

"Aye," Adam told him. "Verra well, I might add."

"We'll see about that," George laughed, rising from his chair. "Set up the game while I send for more refreshments." He went toward the door and then stopped to look at Goliath. "And a meaty bone for you."

Adam smiled at his dog. The king seemed to like him. It was a start.

They spent the rest of the morning playing chess and discussing politics, while Goliath chewed his bone.

"I confess," Adam told him, capturing the king's knight, "I know little about the Whigs and Tories, save that one opposes Catholic succession to the throne, and one supports it."

"Where do you stand on it?"

If it were somehow proven that Adam's Catholic mother was the true heir of James II—and the Tories had their way, his parents' lives would be forever changed, destroyed. And so would his as next in line.

"I stand with the Whigs. Opposed."

George sighed and moved a pawn. "Last year Anne created twelve new Tory peers to take over the majority in the House of Lords."

Adam's stomach flipped. The Tories, who fought for Davina's younger half brother James to take the throne, held the majority? Hell, this was something his kin should have been following more closely, but no one in Camlochlin believed Davina would ever be queen. There were too many obstacles in the way, not to mention lack of proof. But having a Tory parliament could tear away one of those obstacles. And who knew what secrets would be revealed once a Catholic monarch was once again possible?

"I have much to do to bring the Whigs back into power," the king said, watching Adam's next move. "I might consider breaking a betrothal in exchange for your help."

Adam abandoned his piece. How far would he go to ensure his kin's safety, to win Sina's heart? If not for the royal blood in his veins, he would consider himself a Tory...but there *was* royal blood in his veins. "Ye have it. What do ye need me to do?"

"Get to know the people here. I've spent most of my time in Hanover, so I don't know many of the lords. Find out who is a Whig and who is a Tory. Be my ears."

"A spy," Adam said. He wouldn't be the first one in his family.

"Just for a few months, until after my coronation. I'll be making some announcements and, if things go well for you and Miss de Arenburg, I think you may want to be here for one of them."

A marriage announcement? The king's blessing on their union? It meant spending a few more months in England. And damn it, he might need them to convince the king not to hang him when he found out who Adam was.

"Verra well," Adam agreed. "I'll do as ye wish, and at the end, when I leave, if I wish to take Miss de Arenburg with me as my wife, I will have yer blessing."

"If 'tis what she wishes as well."

Adam nodded and checked. "Of course."

The king smiled at the board and then at him. "You actually might beat me."

"The chances of it are good," Adam pointed out with a grin.

"I haven't been beaten in twenty years," the king told him, sounding more pleased and surprised than angry.

"I've never lost."

"Were you taught the game at a young age, then?" George asked, studying the pieces. There was nowhere for him to move.

"Aye. I was taught many things. Checkmate."

The game forgotten, the king proceeded. "Can you read and write?"

"Aye."

"Are you a skilled swordsman?"

"Better than any man in yer service."

"Why haven't you been granted titles yet?" the king asked, narrowing his eyes at him.

"They will be granted when I marry."

George cast him a knowing smirk. "So, then, you wish to—"

"I could have a wife ready at the altar tomorrow morning if titles were all I was after."

Sina's father nodded, agreeing with him. When he stood from his seat, Adam rose with him.

"We shall play again," the king said, walking him to the door.

Adam slanted his smile. "You'll likely lose again."

Adam left with the sound of the king's laughter ringing in his ears.

So far, the day was going extraordinarily well. The king didn't hate him or Goliath. Of course George didn't know he was the MacGregor who had married his daughter, but Adam hoped that soon he wouldn't care. He had a few months to gain the king's trust and, more, his friendship. Time he would also spend with Sina, proving to her that she loved him as he loved her, with passion fueled by every moment they spent together, and making certain she didn't marry her childhood friend.

Chapter Twenty-Nine

S ina sat in her father's private sitting room and stared into her cup. She thought he'd called her in here to tell her he was ready to declare her, not to discuss her betrothal to William.

"When I agreed to let Standish have you a second time," her father said, standing by the window, dressed in his finest flowing silk and lace suit and polished red heels, "things were different. I no longer need the Earl of Chesterfield's alliance."

Sina shifted in her chair. What was he saying? What was this about? "We just celebrated the betrothal last night. You're not suggesting…Father, that's no reason to—you cannot go back on your word."

But she had already decided it was over with William. Poor thing. Not only had she deceived him, but so had the king.

"I'm the king. I can do whatever I want," he reminded her.

"Yes, I suppose you can," she said in a soft voice, remembering that he'd gone back on his word to the Mac-Gregors. "I must confess I…"

Her father wasn't listening but staring out the window, down into the practice fields. "He's incredible."

Sina frowned, dipping her brows at him. "Who?"

She rose from her chair when her father motioned her over.

"Lord Hamilton."

She looked out, and then, like her father, she couldn't stop looking. He'd removed his coat and hat and untied his cravat. He moved too quickly for her eyes to catch every detail of his perfectly laid-out defense. He fought off three men with his sword, blocking and swinging and pushing them back. Locks of his raven hair had come loose from his queue and danced around his face as he moved.

"He was telling the truth," her father murmured beside her. "He fights better than any of my men. I need him on my side."

Sina severed her gaze from Adam and looked at the king. "On your side for what?"

"I'm going to replace Parliament. Lord Hamilton has already agreed to stay for a few months and help me. But after seeing him fight, I'd prefer for him to serve as captain of my personal guard."

Her mouth went dry. She reached her hand toward the edge of the window to steady herself. No, no, no. Adam couldn't stay that long! What was he planning on offering himself to the king's aid? Whatever it was, given a few months, he would succeed.

"I'm having rooms set up for him in the east wing."

"Father . . ." Oh, what could she tell him? That Adam was deceiving him, and so had she by going along with it? That a secret part of her was happy Adam had come for her? She stepped away from the window and wrung her hands together. Unfair judgments, along with fear of another Stuart so close in line, had caused the king to dislike the MacGregors. She didn't want to ruin the only chance Adam had to win her father's favor—for the MacGregors' sake or, God help her, hers. She couldn't bring herself to do it. "You know nothing about him."

"Leave that to me," her father said, waving away her concerns. "He seems quite taken with you, Sina."

She blinked and fought for control to breathe without fluctuation as her father continued. "He's asked me to allow him to court you."

Sina returned to her chair and sat in it, her spine stiff as everything began to make sense. "Lord Hamilton is the reason you wish to dissolve my betrothal to William."

"Not dissolve it, dearest. Postpone it for now."

She nodded. And what would happen when he found out the truth? Lord Hamilton was Adam MacGregor, the Highlander he'd forced her to marry. Whatever Adam had promised him and asked for in return would be forgotten. He might even have Adam arrested and thrown into prison.

She rose again from her seat and stood before him. Her hands shook and her heart raced. She had to make a choice—here and now. Tell her father the truth and save William's heart or agree to her father's new decision and save Adam's life... for now.

"I will tell William," she forced herself to say calmly. "No announcements will be made until I speak with him. Do you agree?"

He nodded. "Lord Hamilton asks to court you, not marry you, Sina. The choice will ultimately be yours if his request changes. But for now, I will grant what he asks."

"Is that all?" she asked, waiting to go, needing to get away and fully consider what Adam had done in a day.

The king nodded, but called her back before she reached

the door. "There is one other thing. It has come to my attention that Lord Standish was indiscreet on his tour, behaving shamefully with questionable women."

Sina stared at him until he looked away, hopefully repentant of the depths to which he would sink in order to have his way.

Finally, and without another word, she left him. Angry with him for lying about William. There wasn't any need to lie. She didn't wish to marry William. Not because of lies, even though she had to pause and consider that this was the second accusation about a man she hardly knew anymore.

She stopped on the last step as Adam entered the palace, laughing with some of her father's guardsmen who'd practiced with him.

Adam stood out among them, as was confirmed by the dozens of female eyes settling on him throughout the large foyer. He was taller, broader, and darker than the rest. He looked less tame now with inky locks falling loose from his messy queue, his coat slung over his shoulder, and his damp shirt clinging to his sculpted physique. His silvery-blue eyes, more piercing as they swept over the faces of his admirers, settled on her.

As if drawn by an unseen tether, he stepped toward her, away from the others. At his side, Goliath followed.

Sina couldn't move. She didn't know what she would have done if she could. Run? Which way? Faint? It was possible. As he approached her, she wondered how he made her feel as if she were the only woman in the world, the only one who mattered, and he didn't give a damn who knew it.

"My lady," he greeted with a slight bow and slant of his mouth when he came back up. "How is yer ankle?"

"Just fine, thank you," she said, flashing her dimple before it disappeared again. "I understand you'll be staying for a while."

"Ye've spoken to the king," he guessed, his smile fading.

"As have you," she countered. "And now he is going back on his word to William once again. He is postponing my betrothal because of you." She didn't tell him she had no intention of marrying William. If Adam knew she loved him, he'd never give up this mad scheme.

"I owe him much."

She nodded, offering him a stiff smile. "The truth is a good place to begin." She stepped around him and walked toward the doors. She needed to get out of the palace, away from all the scheming and deceit.

"I will tell him the truth, lass," he said, catching up with her and leaning in to her ear.

He was too close. Too warm. She fought not to let his masculine scent go straight to her head. He was clever and confident. She liked it.

Oh, why had she ever met Adam MacGregor? Why had Anne sent her away to a man who was so—she paused to look up at him tugging at his loose cravat—right for her? It was as if the queen had somehow known that Adam, despite his aversion to propriety and power, or perhaps because of it, would make her happy.

She shook her head at herself. Anne hadn't known. She couldn't have.

"This is all useless," she said on a shallow breath, forcing herself to move away from him. "Until you tell him who you are, there really is no reason to court me. He will revoke whatever promise he makes the instant he knows you're a MacGregor. He will be angry and will never agree to our being together. All you've succeeded in doing today was hurt William—and for nothing."

"Fer everything," he corrected, reaching for her. "And I dinna want to hurt him. I know what he means to ye. He's yer closest friend. But I dinna want ye to marry him." He bent to her hand and brought it to his lips. A stray lock of his hair fell across her fingers. "I want ye to marry me, Sina."

His eyes closed and he kissed her knuckles. Her heart rammed against her ribs until she felt light-headed and unsteady on her feet. She drew her free hand to her chest.

"Why?" she breathed, unsure how she managed it. "Barely a fortnight ago you were as miserable as I."

He straightened and let his hand slip slowly from hers. His eyes swept over her features, taking her in. He swallowed and began, then stopped and began again.

"Only fer a moment or two," he told her with a catch in his breath. "The days after ye left were far more miserable fer me. I dinna want any more days to pass withoot ye in my life. I want to make ye happy, lass."

Sina felt her knees buckle. No man had ever spoken to her with such passion in his gaze, tangled in the rich cadence of his voice. He came here to win her, and it frightened her that he would fail.

"Though our time together was brief," he continued, "ye have affected me in a way that would take more time to explain than we presently have. But I suspect ye already understand."

Because she'd been miserable after she left him? Because she loved him too? He told her he'd prove it. But there was too much at stake.

She shook her head and looked down at Goliath nuzzling her hand. Oh, she wanted a life with him and his dog. "My father will never allow it, especially after we deceived him."

"And if he did?" He put her to the test. "Would ye leave William and come home with me?"

"No," she said without thinking about it long enough to tell him anything else. He was mad. This would never work.

He smiled, seeing the truth in her eyes. He was kind enough not to mock her with it. "Ye're no' goin' to be easily won. 'Tis one of the things I love aboot ye, lass."

She watched him turn and leave with Goliath at his side. He loved something about her. What else did he love about her? She blinked and turned for the garden.

Chapter Thirty

Adam looked down the long hall, its cherry-paneled walls illuminated by dozens of candle stands and littered with more paintings. His eyes settled on the double doors, painted white at the end of the hall. He wasn't sure how one escorted a lass to dinner, but he didn't imagine it involved letting her walk down the grand stairs alone. Standing in front of the doors when she opened them would seem too forceful. Waiting at the stairs gave her time to decide whether she would accept his arm or refuse it.

He pulled on the wide lapels of his coat and tugged on his high cravat. Truly, he hated the things and cursed the man who invented them. Cravats and heels. Damn it, but his feet were killing him.

It didn't take long for the doors to open. Thanks to Katie, Sina's handservant, he knew approximately when to expect Sina to leave her room. He owed Katie much for helping him. He wondered why she had.

Every other thought vanished when Sina stepped into the

hall. He tried not to think about how easily he'd fallen for her...what he would give up for her.

She wore a silk brocade mantua of emerald green over her stays. The overskirt was drawn back over her hips to expose her floral petticoats. Most of her glorious golden hair was tucked inside a lace cap, with several curls dangling about her ears. Pearls adorned her perfect lobes, her elegant throat.

At his side, Goliath whined and wagged his tail.

"Go on," Adam told him in a low voice, glad that his friend had finally come to his senses and accepted her.

Adam smiled at her as she approached, realizing in that moment how limitless love can make a man. Who could bother with pride or selfishness when the heart was consumed by love?

She didn't look unhappy to see him and even smiled back at him before she dipped her chin.

"My lady," he gently greeted, offering his elbow when she reached him. "Ye look beautiful."

She briefly looked up as she looped her arm around his, blushed, and then looked away again.

"But," he said, leaning down closer to her ear, "I would prefer to see ye wrapped in an arisaid with yer hair loose and flowin' aroond yer shoulders."

"That will be all, Katie," she said softly, dismissing her handservant.

Adam smiled at the gel before she left.

"You look very handsome," Sina said, returning his compliment, continuing slowly to the stairs. "But I prefer to see you against a backdrop of hills and heather."

"Well," he laughed softly while every nerve ending burned to touch her, every muscle ached to hold her. "I can arrange that."

"The king and William will stop you."

"What can William do?" His laughter faded into a smirk.

"He can find things out about your family. He already told my father about Claire and Amelia. He will be persistent, Adam. He went to the queen on her deathbed, trying to find me, and certain words she repeated piqued his interest. 'MacGregor,' 'sister,' and 'abbey.' One of them led him to me. Where might the other two lead him?"

To his grave, Adam thought. He didn't want to have to kill Sina's best friend. But what would happen if Standish discovered Anne had another sister besides Mary, and she was alive and well in Camlochlin?

"I dinna know where 'twill lead him," he told her, doing his best to sound unaffected by those words. "But if he makes trouble fer my kin, it willna go well fer him."

He felt her arm tighten around his. He didn't want to worry her. He would handle William Standish—without killing him.

"Dinna fret," he reassured her. "There is nothin' else to find oot." He shoved his finger under his cravat and pulled at it. "Is it always so formal here?"

"Yes, it always is," she replied vaguely. "Do you know what puzzles me?"

He looked at her and smiled. "What?"

"That in her last moments, Anne spoke of an abbey, or your sister. Either way, it can tie in with your family. Your grandfather mentioned that Abby had visited the queen, though you never mentioned it. But why would Anne call for your sister on her deathbed? And unless Anne also knew your mother, why would she give importance to an abbey?"

Adam continued leading her down the stairs, trying to maintain his composure. How many people knew about his mother? Could Standish put Anne's cryptic words together? "Did ye discuss any of this with William?"

In the light, her eyes sparkled with challenge. "No. Will you continue to deceive me?"

"No," he exhaled. He didn't want to deceive her...or tell her the truth. If she had stayed at Camlochlin, she would have been told. But she hadn't stayed.

"Why did the queen send me to you, Adam? Did you know her?"

Could he trust her with the biggest secret of his life? If he wanted to win her, he needed to win her trust first.

"Adam, did you know her?" she asked again as they reached the bottom of the stairs.

What difference did it make if he told her now or later?

"Aye," he said quietly, with hesitancy. "I knew her."

She slipped her arm from his and stopped to turn to him. Looking into her eyes was difficult. He could see everything in their luminous sea-green depths. Anxiousness, dread, curiosity, and a glint of anger.

"Why didn't you tell me?"

Her first question surprised him. It proved this was more about him than about how he knew Anne. He'd kept this from her. His entire family had. He felt like hell for it. He wanted to mend what he'd broken.

"Let's take a walk in the garden."

She looked down the hall at the dining room.

"Unless ye're hungry. We can always—"

She shook her head. "'Tisn't that. We will be missed. Lord Nottingham and his sister know you were to escort me to dinner."

"Aye, if ye're worried aboot what they'll think, we could speak aboot it another time." He turned to lead her to the dining hall, eager to postpone the inevitable. She pulled back, tightening her arm around his.

"You won't get out of it that easily."

He ground his teeth and switched direction. She let go of his arm, and they made small talk about Laurel MacGregor and Ula until they came to the entrance of the garden.

Goliath seemed restless, as if he could hear Adam's racing heart.

"If what I tell ye gets oot, it could mean the end of my mother's life, and mine, as well."

Her skin grew pale beneath the moonlight. "'Twill never get out," she vowed.

"I hope ye'll understand the gravity of it and why I kept it from ye."

She nodded while they strolled toward the alcove. They passed a handful of others heading toward the palace and nodded in greeting.

Finally alone, they reached the bench, and she waited while Adam drew his hands down his face and exhaled a long breath.

"My mother was hidden away in an abbey from birth until it was attacked by Dutch soldiers sent there to kill her. They burned it to the ground, but my faither saved her."

"Why were they sent to kill her?" she asked on a breathless whisper.

He looked at her and sighed again. "Because she is the firstborn daughter of James II."

Her expression went blank for a moment, and then broke on a short laugh. "You're telling me there is a royal heir whom no one knows about and she is your mother?"

"Aye, lass," he told her. "She has lived in secret her whole life."

She sank to the bench as things became clear to her.

"Oh. Anne's last words. They make sense now." She brought her hands up to her chest. She spoke so softly that he could hardly hear her. "Oh, Adam." Her eyes opened wider, drawing him to sit beside her. "You are the prince," she breathed, "your mother, the true queen."

"We denounce those titles," he told her. "We will denounce them in writing. If marryin' the prince holds any influence over yer final decision, let it go."

Her eyes narrowed at him. "My final decision has been made."

"Aye, so stop denyin' me, and agree to marry me withoot any royal title."

"I should slap your face for thinking me so empty-headed as to be swayed by titles. That is my parents' task." She turned her face from him, shielding herself in moonlight and shadows.

He wouldn't argue by reminding her that she thought him a savage without knowing him. "Fergive me, lass." He touched his fingers to her hand in her lap. Her body stiffened as if lightning had struck her. "So, then, we agree? Ye'll return with me to Camlochlin as soon—"

She leaped from the bench and spun around to face him. "You're infuriating, Adam! How many times must I tell you I don't love you?"

"Until yer lips say what's in yer eyes."

She shook her head. "Don't ask that of me, I beg you. Especially now. If the king ever found out who you are, who you *truly* are, he would try to have you killed—your mother—"

He stood up before her and reached out to move his fingers over her jaw. "Should I go, then, lass?"

She closed her eyes and turned her face toward his hand. He leaned in close enough to feel her breath across his mouth. "I'll save myself from the king's wrath and then spend the rest of my life makin' ye happy." He spread his fingers over her soft cheek, behind her ear, into her hair. "I'll give ye everything ye need, everything ye desire."

She didn't deny or resist him when he covered her mouth with his. He slipped his other hand around her waist and drew her closer. Never had a woman felt so perfect in his arms.

He parted her lips with his tongue, and she drew in a little breath before giving him entry. He smiled. She'd missed him. Everything in him went soft and then hot and hard.

He pulled her closer, spreading his hands along her back, molding her to him, breathing her, tasting her.

She lifted her arms around his neck and buried her fingers in his hair as he deepened their kiss. Her firm, yielding body tempted him to madness. He never wanted to let her go. He wished they were home so he could carry her up to bed. He would keep her there for days, making love to her day and night, in every way.

The thought of her naked and wild in his bed made him stiff against his breeches. He swiped his tongue over hers and bit down on her lower lip as she withdrew, wide-eyed and breathless.

She took a moment to compose herself and then drew back her hand and slapped him across the face. "You must not do that again. Do you not care what's at stake?"

She hurried away, leaving him smiling after her. She wasn't worried about William. She was worried about Camlochlin. So was he.

He headed back with Goliath, talking to his friend on the way.

Chapter Thirty-One

Sina swept inside the palace and stopped inside the cavernous foyer. She looked around and began to tremble, not knowing what to do. Her nerves were already raw from having Adam back, but this knowledge of Davina, graceful, kind Davina... it was too much. And then, after all that, to be kissed as though he meant to devour her, it was all too much!

She was in love with him. She wanted to go back to Camlochlin with him, but if Claire was such a threat to her father, Davina would surely cause a war. Adam needed to leave before William discovered anything else! And he needed to leave without her.

"Ah, Miss de Arenburg!"

She turned at the sound of Lord Nottingham.

"How is your ankle?"

She'd almost forgotten... "Much better."

"Are you alone?" he asked, his eyes wide with confusion. "I thought Lord Hamilton was escorting you to dinner."

She held up her hands and smiled. "I thought so too." She

looked toward the doors. He'd be coming soon, tempting her to cast away the weight of her worries—no matter how monumental they had just become, just by smiling at her.

"Will you escort me, my lord?"

"Of course." He offered her his elbow. She took it, needing help to keep going.

Adam's kiss had drained her, robbed her of her strength and logic. She wasn't sure she would ever recover. She knew for certain that William would never kiss her like that—his body, a living flame, consuming every part of her.

She needed to think clearly so that she could absorb all that Adam had told her.

Davina was Anne's sister. Her older sister. Was it possible? The chief's wife looked twenty years younger. They'd lived very different lives.

If not for the Act of Settlement prohibiting Catholics from taking the throne, Davina MacGregor would be the true queen of Great Britain. With a Tory parliament, that act could be repealed.

Sina felt ill with the knowledge of it. She'd wanted the truth, and Adam had given it to her.

"You look lovely with your hair a bit disheveled," Nottingham paused and pointed out. "But we can take a moment for you to repair it if you like."

God help her, her hair was disheveled? As if someone had been kissing her? Did Lord Nottingham know? "Thank you." She managed a smile while she tucked some loose strands back under her cap.

"Do you think Lord Hamilton is a poor fit for Catherine?" he asked, offering his arm again.

"Yes, yes, I do think he's a poor fit," she replied as they approached the dining hall. "She can do better, and as her brother, 'tis your duty to see to it."

"I'm afraid she has her heart set on him."

Sina turned to face him, her hands balled into fists at her sides. "And what about what Lord Hamilton wants?"

"What does he want?" Nottingham asked. "Do you know?"

"No. How would I?" She saw her chair and Eloise sitting beside it. She'd had enough of this conversation. She didn't want to think about Adam with Catherine. She uncurled her arm from Nottingham's and offered him a pleasant smile. "Thank you."

"Let me bring you to your chair at least," he insisted.

"'Tis just a few steps away. I won't keep you any longer." She moved away before he had a chance to stop her and stormed toward her chair.

When she fell into it, Eloise put down her cup and gaped at her. "What's the matter with you, and where have you been?"

"Nothing is the matter." Sina spotted Catherine Newton and brooded. Her heart was set on Adam, was it? Oh, Sina could have marched over there and tore out her hair.

"You haven't been the same since you came back," Eloise told her, turning in her chair to look at her. "What happened to you while you were away? Why do you always seem so melancholy?"

Was her pining over Adam so transparent? "Oh, Eloise, forgive me. I keep thinking of Anne and how I wasn't here for her." It wasn't untrue, but it wasn't the only thing weighing heavy on her heart. Sadly though, Eloise wasn't one to share secrets with. Where was Poppy? She looked around.

"I know, dear," Eloise repented. "Forgive me for being insensitive."

Sina began to smile, but her eye caught Adam entering

the hall with Goliath and she forgot everything else. How could the very sight of him make her belly tighten and ache with a need that felt more primitive than anything she'd ever called him? How could his kiss make the ache even more painful?

He saw her and kept moving. Was he angry with her for slapping him? She was the one who should be angry with him for kissing her as if he had every right to and to hell with the consequences. She wasn't angry with him for not telling her about his being a prince. She understood the magnitude of that secret.

Nottingham rose from his chair and called Adam over to the other end of the table, where he was sitting with his sister.

Sina bristled and then forced a smile when she felt Eloise's eyes on her. She wanted to leave. Was she supposed to sit here and watch him flirt with Catherine? She could do it. In fact, she told herself, it was better this way.

She ignored the plate set before her and rubbed her knotted belly. She did her best not to look in his direction, but she found her defiant gaze on him more than once. He was smiling! Enjoying himself while Catherine batted her long lashes at him.

The night wasn't going to go well. Thankfully, Poppy arrived and slipped into the seat next to her.

"I see Catherine got her claws into Lord Hamilton."

"He doesn't seem to mind them," Sina muttered sourly and sipped from her cup of warm wine.

"Would you have him treat her poorly?" Poppy asked her.

Sina rolled her eyes. Poppy knew her too well to ask her such a question. "In truth," she told her friend, "I really don't care. They are no concern of mine."

Poppy quirked her lips at her. Her eyes shone with amusement. "Very well, love, if that's where you're keeping this…"

"Eloise." Sina turned to her. "I believe Lord Somerset just tipped his drink to you."

Eloise immediately primped her curls and waited for him to look at her again so she could smile back.

Sina knew it would keep her attention off her and Poppy.

"'Tis the truth," she whispered leaning in. "He means nothing to me anymore."

"What are you so afraid of?" Poppy challenged. "Your father might rant and rave a little, but he'll accept things in time."

Tears burned Sina's eyes. "How do you know that, Poppy? What if he throws Adam in Newgate? What if—"

"Let's go for a stroll, shall we?" her friend offered, setting down her drink. "Before Catherine sees a glimmer of moisture in your eyes and thinks she caused it."

"What about Eloise?" Sina asked in a hushed tone. She didn't have to. Eloise was already on her way to Lord Somerset's side of the table.

"Come, then, love," Poppy prodded. "He won't let Catherine beguile him."

Sina hesitated, not wanting to go somewhere and open up the floodgates. What if she let Adam's secret slip? *He's the prince! His mother, the queen!* If the Jacobites ever found out…

"Come." Poppy took her hand and pulled her out of the dining hall. "I know this is very difficult for you, my darling," Poppy told her, looping her arm through Sina's. "But the truth is in your face when you see him, when he sees you." Her friend tossed back her head and fanned herself.

"'Tis all I can do to keep from swooning at the sparks between the two of you."

Sina felt sick to her stomach. How hadn't William seen it if it was so obvious? She fought back her tears and bit her lip. She was going to shatter her friend's heart.

"He's offered his service to my father, thinking to win him *before* he tells him who he truly is. In return, he asked that my betrothal to William be postponed so that he can court me." Sina pressed her palms to her cheeks and shook her head. Hearing the words coming from her mouth shocked her. This was really happening.

"Even if my father doesn't do the worst when he discovers the truth, I...I can't leave William completely and go live in the mountains somewhere, never to see him again, knowing I broke his heart."

"Sina," her friend said as they walked the long, wall-papered corridors. "You aren't his nursemaid, or his protector. If you have a chance at happiness with your Highlander, take it. William will find someone in time."

"This will be the second time he's lost me. I fear he may do something drastic."

"I agree," Poppy sympathized, "'tis cruel, but better a quick kick to the guts than a lifetime of misery and regret for *you*. Don't you agree?"

"I don't know what I think anymore," Sina lamented.

"Are you in love with William?" Poppy asked her. "Do you want to spend the rest of your life with him?"

"No," Sina said without hesitation. She didn't know him anymore, and what she remembered lacked the passion she wanted in a husband. "But I don't want to do this to him. He's always needed me—"

"Oh, for heaven's sake, Sina!" Poppy threw up her hands and fell into one of the many settees and chairs lining the grand corridor. "We used to talk about this all the time. William is not your responsibility. He did fine on his own for three years."

Sina slumped beside her on the settee. Poppy was right. But there was more...so much more.

"And your father," Poppy said, sensing her distress. "Perhaps Adam has a point in gaining his trust first. I don't think there is any other way for him to accomplish what he came here to do."

"Oh, I don't deny 'tis the only way," Sina cried, "but my fear is that it doesn't go well."

Poppy rested her head on Sina's shoulder and sighed. "Did I tell you he called you a sparrow?"

Sina smiled. Poppy often referred to her as little bird. "No."

"Has he kissed you since he returned?"

Sina blushed and smiled, then looked away. "Yes. Tonight as a matter of fact."

"And?" her friend prodded.

"I slapped him when 'twas over." Sina sighed. "But every part of me felt alive and on fire. 'Twas thrilling and frightening to know someone else could hold such power over me."

"Imagine what the rest of him will make you feel."

Sina blushed even darker and felt a rush of warmth course through her.

They heard footsteps approaching and giggled into their hands at almost being caught talking about bedchamber things.

They stood from the settee just as Adam turned the corridor with Goliath and faced them.

What right did he have to look so damned good either put together in a tight cravat or wild and untamed in a flowing plaid?

"Ah, Lord Hamilton, we were just discussing you," Poppy greeted, ignoring the pinch to her side from Sina.

His silvery-blue gaze dipped to Sina. "I'm pleased to see whatever 'twas made ye smile."

Sina felt extremely warm and pinched her friend again when she giggled behind her fan.

"Well, I'm off to bed!" Poppy barely spared them a smile before running off, leaving both Sina and Adam looking after her.

"Ye're no' still angry with me fer kissin' ye, then?" he asked softly.

Her mind immediately went to their kiss. It was ecstasy, passion, and oblivion. Her body craved it. Her heart desired it. Her mind fought a valiant battle.

"No." She shook her head. "Not for kissing me."

"Then what?"

How could she tell him without sounding like a jealous fool? Which was exactly what she was. "You sat with Lady Newton."

"And her brother the viscount, who is a Whig, by the way." He shifted his shoulders in his coat, and Sina thought he might have shivered. "And disturbingly preoccupied with his sister."

Sina covered her smile with her fingers, and then remembered what her father had told her. "You're doing this for him."

"Fer ye and the clan," he corrected.

Sina wanted to resist and deny him. It was safest if he went back to Camlochlin and they forgot each other. Her father would forget him, and the MacGregors and their lives would remain unchanged.

But she didn't want to resist him. "I'm sorry for slapping you."

"Good," he said on a husky growl as he stepped closer, close enough to smell sweet wine on his breath. "Because I'm goin' to kiss ye again."

He took her face in his palms and tilted her mouth to his. She didn't stop him. She wondered if he could feel her heart thrashing in her chest. He took her mouth with slow, sensuous seduction. His full, succulent lips caressed her, molded her to him. His tongue swept inside her mouth as he closed his arms around her and drew her in.

She coiled her arms around his neck, careless and reckless with desire, and held on while he laid waste to her senses.

She knew she wanted to live and die in his arms. But she didn't want him to die in hers.

So, with great reluctance, she moved away and broke their kiss.

"Good night, Adam." She smiled, probably brighter than she meant to, touched her fingers to her lips, and left him alone.

Chapter Thirty-Two

The sun peeked meekly through the clouds as the viscount's carriage rolled across London's cobblestone streets.

Sina peered out the window at the men and women hurrying from one shop to another before the sky opened up. This outing was William's idea. He'd arrived at Kensington early in the morn but hadn't sought her out until they were ready to leave—further proving to her that there was much missing from their relationship. Still, telling him wouldn't be easy, which was why she hadn't done it yet.

She'd also thought they'd be going alone, but when she saw that they were traveling in Viscount Nottingham's carriage, with Catherine Newton sitting across from her, she'd almost backed out of accompanying them. But Adam was here…outside…somewhere on his horse, choosing his mount when Nottingham invited him to share his carriage with his sister, William, and herself.

A wise decision. She hoped it didn't rain.

"My darling," William said, sitting next to her. He entwined his fingers in hers and brought them to his lips. "You look as if you haven't slept in days. You should rest when we get back to the palace."

She didn't want to rest, but perhaps staying locked inside her room for the remainder of the day was a good idea. She didn't want to tell William how she felt and that her father was postponing the betrothal. But he needed to be told, and she had demanded to be the one who told him. She didn't want to run into Adam and fling her arms around him like some hapless trollop, unable to control herself.

"You do look a bit pale, Sina."

Sina turned her blazing gaze on Catherine Newton. Normally, she wouldn't bother replying. She didn't have a short temper, but her nerves were already frazzled, her heart out of sorts, so she retorted, albeit in a gentle tone, "I don't think any of us looks our best today, Catherine."

It didn't take much more than that to bring Catherine's hand to her hair, the other to her dark mantua. Her expression crumbled with worry until her brother assured her that she looked perfect.

"That was harsh, Sina," William whispered close, giving her a disapproving look.

She wondered what he would call the look she was giving him now. "What was I thinking?" she muttered as droplets of rain started hitting the roof. If he was expecting her to apologize, they would all be waiting long.

She turned from him and looked out the window again. She saw a rider pass her carriage at a slow trot. Her eyes fixed on him. It was Adam, tall and strong in his saddle, his eyes shadowed beneath the rim of his tricorn. Goliath kept stride alongside Adam's mount. For a moment, she wished she had the courage to call a halt to the carriage, jump out, and run to him.

She watched him slow his horse to a steady pace across the wide street, presenting her with the glory and masculinity of his profile while he kept his eyes on the road.

She didn't mind if he pretended disinterest. She preferred it for William's sake—even if he didn't presently deserve it.

She looked away—to the only two things facing her—Nottingham and his sister. She closed her eyes.

"Sina, what are you doing?" William tugged on her sleeve. "I didn't mean for you to rest now."

"I am weary now," she told him, angry but keeping her voice evenly pitched. "Do you care more about what they will think than you care for me?"

"No," he said regretfully.

She offered him a stiff smile and turned toward the window again. This time, she caught Adam as he was turning away from watching her with rain splashing off his hat and shoulders.

She understood now the haste in seeing her wed to Davina's son. The queen was protecting her family. A family she could never tell anyone about. Poor Anne. Sina wished she'd told her.

She closed her eyes and blocked out the voices and sounds around her. She may have been about to fall asleep, when a memory of Anne flashed into her thoughts.

It had been over a year ago. They were enjoying an afternoon in the garden when the queen asked Sina a peculiar question.

"What do you think of a prince who does not want to be king? Is he a fool or is he wise?"

Sina had thought it over before she answered. She'd been raised among royalty and nobility. Her grandmother had been the direct heir to the throne after Anne lost her eleventh child. Sina's father was next in line after that.

George, whom she saw once a month when he visited her uncle, couldn't wait to be king. He spoke of it all the time. When she went to live at the palace, she learned through Anne the weight such a title brought with it.

"I think he is both a fool for rejecting an opportunity of such great power and wise for the very same reason."

"Hmmm." The queen had nodded and slanted her gaze at her. "And were you married to such a prince, what would you advise him to do?"

Sina had laughed. "I would tell him to remain a prince."

"Why?"

"He would have more time for me and our children. You said yourself that your dear, departed husband *Prince* George was very thoughtful and doting and kind. That is what I want in my husband."

Anne was so pleased with her answer that Sina had sworn she heard the queen murmur, "Perfect." They'd never spoken of it again.

Sina opened her eyes now and sat up with a start as the truth finally dawned on her.

He was *the* prince! Anne had been speaking of Adam MacGregor, her nephew. Having Sina marry him hadn't been a hasty decision but a careful one, designed in the best interest of everyone, including the country. She had been happy that Sina didn't want the prince to be king. A wife, in some instances, could have powerful control over her husband's desires. Anne didn't want Adam's wife to convince him he should be king. A proscribed MacGregor on the throne would cause more than one war.

"Perhaps we should summon the physician," she heard William say. She shook her head to clear it.

"No," she insisted, "'twas just a fond memory of Anne that came to mind. It felt as if she were right here." She smiled at the idea of it, feeling better than she had in weeks. Her three companions stared at her as though she'd gone daft. She didn't care. She'd thought Anne had betrayed and forgotten her, but she hadn't.

Anne had known him. She had known what he was like, kind and raised in an environment of love and romance. Sina had been so angry with Anne for doing this *to* her she didn't see that her friend had done it *for* her.

"She did it for me," Sina whispered to herself, looking out the window again. The weight of anger and sorrow over being betrayed fell from her shoulders, and she smiled.

He was there. Her Highland prince with lightning streaking across his eyes, guarding her carriage. If only there was a way to keep Camlochlin safe and guard William's heart from this.

Thank you, Anne, she said silently. *Now tell me what to do.*

If Sina thought the carriage ride home was torturous, dinner was excruciating. Adam was the perfect gentleman, sitting at the table, surrounded by a dozen ladies. He was polite and well-mannered, doing his best not to be charming... and failing. Even Catherine was brooding over all the attention he was getting.

Sina knew when she'd first laid eyes on him in Camlochlin's chapel that he was the most strikingly beautiful man she'd ever seen. She wasn't the only one who thought so, but the majority of the women in Camlochlin were his relatives. It was nothing like this, with every available lady in the palace vying for his attention.

"Lord Hamilton has become quite popular very quickly," William remarked, sitting beside Sina at the table.

"It appears," she replied, looking away from Adam and his admirers and sipping her wine.

"Didn't he say he was recently wed?"

Sina closed her eyes and remembered to breathe. "He said…he'd lost her."

"Ah, yes," William said, casting Adam a pondering look. "I wonder if she left him for another, or if she died. Did he say?"

She looked at her plate. "No. William, there is something—"

"I understand he played chess with the king yesterday."

They had played chess? She didn't know how Adam had gotten an audience with the king, let alone played chess with him.

"I don't know what Lord Hamilton does all day, William."

"Oh?" he asked. "You weren't aware of him practicing with the garrison yesterday and beating half of them on his own? The tale is on everyone's lips."

"I too heard about it," she said and yawned.

"Let's invite him to sit with us."

"What?" She snapped to attention. "No. He's perfectly fine where he is. There is a matter I wish to discuss with you."

"Lord Hamilton!" William stood up and called out down the long table.

Sina looked around for a place to hide while William motioned for him to sit with them.

"William, I was hoping for a few moments with you."

He glanced at her and smiled. "Darling, we have our entire lives together. Can't it wait?"

She nodded. "Of course."

"Ah, Lord Hamilton, join us for some wine."

Sina wanted to throw her cup at William's head. Adam had stayed away from her all day to avoid hurting him. How were they going to sit together without exposing to William what they truly felt? Blast it all, he was going to find out anyway.

To her dismay, Adam accepted and took a seat.

Was she being hopeful to think he appeared relieved to be away from his admirers? She wanted to smile at him. She smiled at Goliath instead.

"You already know my future wife," William mercilessly continued, motioning to Sina, who had no choice but to look at Adam now.

He wasn't smiling.

"Lord Hamilton," she greeted softly.

He nodded, giving her the same amount of attention he gave the other women.

"I see you're enjoying London so far," William said, sneering at the dispersed crowd of women.

"In truth," Adam replied smoothly, "I don't care fer it much. I prefer country living."

"An uncommon sentiment in English courts," William pointed out.

"What do I care about courtly sentiments when I live far from it?" Adam picked up the cup set before him and held it to his lips. His gaze fell to hers for the briefest of moments, soaking her in as if she were one of God's most perfect designs.

He casually looked away and set down his cup without taking a sip. "A man wastes his life caring about such things."

"Should a man not always strive to be better?" William countered.

"Aye," Adam told him in his patient sorcerer's voice. "Better than himself, not everyone else."

Sina's heart melted, warming the rest of her. She smiled. She loved him. She loved every part of him. He was a prince who chose to live as a commoner. But there was nothing common about Adam MacGregor. He shone like a brilliant star among the highest nobles.

"Of course," William replied.

He said something else after that, but Sina didn't hear. Her eyes were locked on Catherine Newton making her way to the empty chair beside Adam. She almost reached it, when Poppy appeared in a whoosh of linen, lace, and russet curls and slid into it.

"Just in time," she said with a slight flush to her cheeks and a wink aimed at Sina.

Sina would hug her later.

"The king arrives," Poppy said, looking over Sina's shoulder.

Sina's blood froze. She hadn't told William about their betrothal yet. She didn't want him to learn of it from the king, in public.

She bolted from her chair and begged William to follow her. After making apologies for her to Adam and Poppy, he did.

"Are you no better even after your rest?" he asked, catching up to her.

"I'm fine," she assured him, and led him into an alcove lit by a single torch. "William, I wanted to tell you first."

"Tell me what?"

"Oh, my dearest William, so much has changed." She tried to sound soothing, but her voice was quaking. She was about to tear out her best friend's heart. "You know how much I care about you. But—"

"But?" he demanded in a hushed tone.

There was no way to say it gently. Why had she put it off

all day? Now she had to hurry lest her father look for her, which he was sure to do.

"Things have changed," she cried and reached for his hand. "I'm so sorry. I'm...I'm not in love with you. I want to be your friend, not your wife." She closed her eyes as if that would somehow block out the pain she caused him.

His silence was louder than a scream. She knew what she was doing to him. She wouldn't blame Adam. She was glad her father was postponing the betrothal. But it needed to be broken. As mad as Adam was to think he could win her father's favor, she knew she had to help him. She couldn't let him go to Newgate, or to Camlochlin without her.

"Why does he take pleasure in torturing me?" William spat angrily. "He uses you to do it. You are his power over me." His eyes gleamed in the torchlight as he reached out and swept his hands over her throat. "Who has he promised you to this time?" He pulled her closer by the neck. Tears spilled over his lids while he studied her.

"What are you doing?" She clawed at his hands, beginning to panic. "You're hurting me, William."

"All my life they had the power." He squeezed his fingers tighter around her and closed his eyes. "But I've taken it back. Forgive me, my darling."

She couldn't breathe. She couldn't fight. No. She couldn't die this way! Instead of trying to get him off her, she touched his face and then watched his fury fade.

He loosened his grip suddenly. "No. No. I cannot cause you—"

Adam's brawny body colliding into his cut off the remainder of his words. Before their bodies hit the ground, Adam hauled William to his feet, dragged him to the nearest wall, and smashed his head into it, knocking him out.

Sina wept in Adam's arms over her unconscious friend and everything he'd just destroyed, and then looked up to see her father and his guards.

Chapter Thirty-Three

$\mathcal{H}$e let me go," Sina mildly defended.

Adam frowned at her. How long would she go on championing William? "After he left yer neck bruised," he growled.

She didn't argue.

"Miss de Arenburg—"

"Oh, stop it, Father. Lord Hamilton knows who you are to me. I told him."

The king looked from one to the other, his expression frustratingly unreadable. "I see."

"Yer Majesty," Adam said, shifting in his chair. "I do not care who ye are as long as ye do not let Lord Standish anywhere near her again."

Adam was thankful that, again, Sina made no objection.

"Lord Standish has been taken to Newgate prison, where he awaits word from me."

"Let him go home to his father," Sina implored. "Ban him from the palace, from London, but don't bring such shame upon him by keeping him in prison. His heart is broken, Father. Because of me. Show him mercy."

Adam wanted to interject. Mercy? He'd show him the tip of a blade if Standish returned.

"I've sent a letter to notify his father," the king told her. "I will let you know what I decide. You may go, Sina. Let the physician see you. I wish to have a word with Lord Hamilton."

She looked so defeated that Adam wanted to rush to her and hold her in his arms. He watched her leave, anxious to go with her. Couldn't whatever the king wanted wait?

"Hamilton," the king said, "pour us some wine. Face me while you do it."

Adam breathed slowly. He wanted to leave, not drink. He did as the king asked, but poured only one glass and handed it to George.

"You're not drinking?" the king asked, looking up at him from his chair.

"Sire, yer daughter is in pain. I want to go to her."

"How do I know you won't tell everyone who I am to her?"

Adam flicked his gaze to the door. "Because 'twould mean more to her if *ye* told everyone."

The king dropped his eyes and nodded. "I plan on it." He studied Adam fidgeting and then smiled. "You know her well already."

"Aye, and right now she could use a shoulder."

"You saved her."

Adam's anxious gaze settled on him. "I would give my life fer her. But right now—"

"All right." The king swooshed his hand in front of him and laughed. "Go. And, Hamilton…"

Adam stopped at the door and turned to face him again.

"Do you hunt?"

"Aye, Sire."

"Good. We're hunting tomorrow. Bring Goliath."

Adam nodded and hurried out of the room.

Sina had nothing more to say to her father and Adam on the matter. How could she continue to defend William after what he'd done? He'd gone too far. He was in her father's hands now.

She wept on her way to her apartments. She felt as if her best friend just died. In a way, he had. Their friendship would never be the same—if it survived.

When she reached her doors, she hurried inside before anyone could stop her and bolted it behind her. She fell into the nearest chair and wept. She had feared that William might try to do something rash but she never dreamed...She lifted her fingers to her neck and ran them over where his fingers had been, tight, suffocating. His eyes had been so empty, so dark, looking at her and seeing someone he hated.

She wept because she loved William, she loved Anne, and she lost them both. It didn't matter how. William was as lost to her as the queen. She would likely never see him again. She hoped she never did. She never wanted to look into his eyes again, eyes that were once more familiar than her own.

And it broke her heart.

Adam caught up with her before she entered her apartments. But he stayed back in the shadows, hearing her sobs. It tore at his guts, and he brought his hand to his belly. Her best friend had tried to kill her. He couldn't imagine what she was going through, and he didn't know how to comfort her.

When she closed her door behind her, Adam went to it and pressed his forehead against the cool wood. He listened to her sobs and closed his eyes.

He didn't know how long he waited there, his body, his heart, every part of him aching to go to her. When Goliath scratched at the door, Adam finally knocked. "Sina," he said softly through the barrier. "Let me in, lass."

Silence answered. At least she'd stopped crying.

"I'm grieving, Adam," she finally responded from the other side. "Grieving for *him*."

"I know," he reassured her. He didn't care if she mourned her friend. "I want to comfort ye, love. I want to wipe yer tears and offer ye my shoulders to do with as ye will. I've made ye smile and laugh a time or two...toss chess pieces and shoes at me. I think I even made ye love me, though ye swore ye never would. But the one thing I canna seem to do is comfort ye. Open the door, please, lass."

He heard the bolt moving. His heart accelerated as the door slowly opened. She stood before him, small and alone. Her eyes were swollen and red, as was her nose. Flaxen curls spilled down her temples to the fingerprints around her neck.

His muscles tightened under his coat. He wished he had killed him. Sina might have hated him for doing it, but he'd know she was safe.

She was safe with him. Only him. He wouldn't leave her. He stepped inside and waited while she bolted the doors again.

"You got what you wanted, Adam," she said, coming to face him. "William is gone."

"I didna want this," he told her. "'Twould be like some-one takin' Goliath from me."

She stepped back. "You're comparing William to a pet?"

He shook his head. "Goliath is my friend."

She finally smiled, though her tears still fell. He reached out to wipe one away with his thumb. "I'm no' here to tell ye how to feel. I just want to be here with ye."

She moved toward him and fell into his arms, weeping again. This time he was able to hold her. He closed his arms around her, covering her in his strength. He held her until she finally looked up without sobbing. "I'm so thankful you're here, Adam. If you hadn't come to London, I would have married him. If you hadn't come, you would have haunted me my entire life."

"I willna leave ye again, lass," he promised, picking her up and carrying her to her bed.

He set her down and straightened to remove his coat and tear away his damned cravat. "Ah," he groaned. "'Tis good to breathe again."

He was glad to see her smile and climbed in after her. Propping up her pillows, he sat up with his back against the headboard and pulled her across his lap. He held her close against him with one hand pressing her cheek to his chest.

He listened for over an hour while she recounted stories of her childhood with William. She wept at first, remembering happier times with him, and grieving the loss of them. But finally she began to smile again.

Cradling her in his arms, Adam watched her while she shared her life with him. He memorized every expression, everything that brought life to her eyes, like when she spoke about her friendship with Poppy and helping to deliver Amelia's babe. He wanted to make her passionate about many more things. He reveled in the slopes and valleys of her lips and had to stop himself from leaning down and kissing them several times. He traced her dimple with his fingers and vowed to himself to always make her happy—

not because it was his duty, but because she made him so damned happy. Even sitting in her room helping her through the loss of a man she loved, he felt thankful to be with her.

He finally understood why his father took on the king of England for his mother, why his uncle Colin abandoned the throne for his wife, why love was so valued and honored at Camlochlin.

He told her about Grendel, Goliath's father, who, like his namesake, hated music, which had made life at Camlochlin a little torturous for the poor hound.

He told her about meeting his grandfather, King James, when he was a young lad, and later Anne.

"He came to Camlochlin a few times to see my mother and once when I was old enough to remember him. His visit is one of the saddest memories I have. He smiled often and played with me and Abby, but I caught him wipin' tears from his eyes when he looked at the daughter he'd given up to nuns. He had sacrificed much and fer what? His own son-in-law took his throne from him.

"Anne's life was no better," he told her. "The weight of her family's power crippled her, and in the end her closest lady friend betrayed her." He paused for a moment, rubbing his cheek over the top of her head and realizing things about himself he never thought to consider before. "I think my aversion to power stems from them. They made me afraid of it, and in the background I was being molded into the next chief of the most powerful clan in the Highlands."

Sina lifted her head and smiled at him. "She told me about you once, but I didn't know 'twas you until this morning."

"What did she say?" he asked with a playful smile. "Something pleasing, I hope."

"She told me about a prince who didn't want to be king and asked if I thought him a fool or wise."

He laughed. "And yer reply?"

She told him what she'd told the queen and added, "Now I understand why you don't want that kind of power."

"Aye," he agreed, loving that she tore away his layers. She made him feel ready and confident about his future because she would be at his side. Her steadfast heart would always be his. He rubbed the pad of his thumb over her chin. Hell, if he didn't kiss her, he'd go mad.

"So," he said, lowering his voice and his head, "Anne wanted us together."

"I believe so," she whispered back, watching him descend.

"She was a wise queen." He closed his eyes and captured her stalled breath with a kiss.

He didn't want to push her. Not tonight. But she cupped her hands around his face and plunged her tongue into his mouth.

His guts were on fire, set ablaze by his quickened heart. He tightened his arms around her, drawing her flush against him, kissing her, cherishing her. How long had he ached to hold her like this, lost in passion's embrace? He deepened his kiss and slid his hand down to her soft rump. She gasped into his mouth. He smiled against her teeth, knowing that her passionless years with William had left her innocent.

He withdrew and looked deep into her eyes. "I want to ravish ye, but I dinna want to frighten ye."

"Ravish me." She closed her eyes and tossed back her head.

He couldn't help but smile first at her sweet display. But his gaze darkened on her neck. He ran his lips over her discolored skin, kissing her softly. The overwhelming desires to possess her, protect her, and kill for her coursed through him. He'd never loved anyone like this. He felt weak, yet stronger than ever before. He couldn't think straight, but it was clear to him that she had claimed his heart.

She moaned when he stretched his palm over her tightly encased bosom.

He ran his tongue over her collarbone while he pulled at the laces of her stays. Every inch of her shift that he exposed brought a slight gasp or languid sigh from her lips, compelling him further.

He freed her from her stays and pulled her hairpins loose, sending her hair tumbling down over his hands.

"Hell, lass," he ground out on a throaty whisper when he stopped to gaze at her. "Ye're beautiful."

She lowered her gaze, blushing in her shift. The thin linen barely concealed her tight, upturned nipples. He felt himself growing harder beneath her rump. He slowed his breath. Slowed for her.

"Take off your léine," she requested on a quavering whisper.

He felt a charge through his body, the way it felt to be out in the vale in a lightning storm. He wanted her, to finally make her his. "Lass, if we make love, there's no goin' back."

She smiled. "That's always been the issue, has it not? Sometimes I wish you hadn't been so noble." She tugged at his shirt, emboldening him to help her.

"The first time I saw you take off your léine..." She ran her palms over his bare chest and the trembling muscles along his arms. "I thought, how will I ever be able to fight him off? But I never had to. You didn't force yourself on me when so many other men might have."

She wriggled atop him and pulled at her shift. "You won my heart without putting a finger on me. I was just too guilty over William to admit it. Now," she said, pulling her shift over her head, "I give you my consent."

Adam gazed at her shrouded in her golden mantle. Her hair covered her breasts, but she closed her arms around herself anyway.

"I've never done this before with William," she said shyly.

Adam knew. "Good," he said with a smile and pulled her into his arms for a kiss.

Chapter Thirty-Four

Sina closed her eyes as Adam's mouth covered hers. His flesh against hers felt like steel armor, but it was warm and malleable beneath her fingers when she coiled her arms around his neck.

She loved kissing him. She felt cherished and desirable in his arms. It was more than anyone had ever made her feel.

When he moved his mouth down her neck, and lower, her body tightened. She might be a virgin, but thanks to Poppy's and Eloise's tales, she knew of some of the things men and women did to each other in bed. She was nervous and excited to do them with Adam.

She closed her eyes and sucked in a short gasp when he dipped his mouth to her breasts. His lips and teeth gently played with her sensitive buds, sucking each in turn. He drank from her until she squirmed in his lap.

Holding her in his arms, he lifted her from his lap and laid her on the bed.

Hovering over her, he unbuckled his belt and unlaced his pants. Her heart stopped beating while she stared up at him.

Gazing at him was like looking at some mythical being who was about to have his way with her. She wanted to tear off her petticoats and offer herself up to him. Give him all he asked, all he had so patiently waited for.

Seeming to read her thoughts, he turned her gently over on her belly and untied the laces of her skirts. He pulled them down around her thighs, kissing the soft mounds of her buttocks and making her heart bang madly in her chest.

After worshipping the back of her, he turned her again and reveled in the sight of her body, clothed only in her woolen stockings.

She tried to cover up but he kissed everything she sought to hide. Soon, his mouth and his tongue on her made her forget everything else. She let him sweep her away on pure bliss and excitement that titillated her senses and made her ache between her legs.

She pulled on the ribbon at his nape, freeing his inky hair around his broad shoulders. He rose up on his knees, giving her a full view of his rippled abdomen and the dark line of hair disappearing beneath the loose laces of his breeches. He took her ankle in his hand and lifted it to his lips.

Exposed to his hungry gaze, she blushed and looked away, holding her breath.

"There is no one more beautiful than ye on this earth, Sina," he whispered along her stockinged calf. "I finally understand what Finn has been singin' aboot all these years."

He eased her apprehensions and emboldened her to move her leg along his neck. He leaned in and traced her inner thigh with his fingers, and then slipped his fingers between her legs.

Sina bit her lip and rolled back her head. His touch was so intimate that she felt as if she belonged to him, only him. She would never want any other man.

She wanted more of him now. She moved in his hand as he rubbed her crux and made her groan. Everything in her tightened and burned with an uncontainable fire. She never felt anything like it before. She relaxed her other leg and opened it wider, inviting him where no other man had been before.

He tugged at his breeches, slipping them down his hips.

Sina watched, entranced and terrified, as his heavy lance sprang upward and at the ready. She couldn't look away...until he pushed his breeches over his long, muscular thighs and bent and pulled to get them over his knees. The interplay of powerful muscles made her catch her breath and say a quick prayer.

He was ready, eager for her.

He moved over her like a shadow, his breath warm above her flesh. She closed her eyes and fought not to tremble. She didn't want to think about how much that thing was going to hurt. Eloise had described her first time as "stabbing and excruciating."

"Lass," he whispered, his mouth hovering above hers. "I'll listen to yer body and do only what it tells me."

She smiled, relieved to be in control of what was going to happen. She didn't know how he would do what he promised, but she trusted he would do it.

She curled her arms around his neck and pulled his mouth to hers. Slowly he settled his big body atop hers, letting her take in the feel of his weight, the shape of his desire.

Running his fingers over her jaw, her neck, he promised to protect and take care of her. To fill her days with heather and happiness...and him.

He kissed her chin, her neck, her mouth. His tongue searched longingly, deeply, while he moved his hands over her body. He flooded her senses with his size, his strength, his scent until she became aware of nothing but him.

When he pressed his hips against hers, she caressed his heat and ground out a satisfied sigh at his pleasured moan.

She thought she'd be more shocked at the feel of his aroused, naked body against hers, but he fit so perfectly—as if he were made to be with her.

Boldly, she ran her fingers down his back, over his hips and the corded sinew of his arms. He kissed her neck, licking a path downward to her breasts.

Oh, nothing in her life was ever like this—so…explosive, so earth-shattering. It had always been different with Adam. Even before she lost her heart to him, she'd thought about losing her virginity to him. He'd lit a spark of sexual desire in her she hadn't known existed.

Now he was going to make them one in the eyes of God, and she was going to let him. She didn't care about her father, or anything else. She felt invincible in Adam's arms.

Driven by some primal instinct, she lifted her legs around his hips, spreading herself beneath him.

With a deep moan of pure sexual pleasure, he drove the length of his cock over her crux, sending scintillating tremors throughout her body. He did it again, slowly, staring into her eyes.

"Ye're mine, Sina."

She remembered his refusal to seek out the beds of other women when she'd denied him. He'd waited, letting her move at her own pace. "And you are mine."

She buried her face in his hair and dripped around his long shaft.

She felt the tip of him push gently at her entrance—and then she felt his hands cupping her face, his lips covering hers. He pressed a series of short, slow, hungry kisses to her mouth, and she was lost to the desire in his hooded gaze.

She barely felt him push again as he dipped his mouth to her nipple and caught it in his teeth.

Pain subsided and she moved her hips beneath him, inviting him deeper.

Slowly, and with great patience, evidenced in his clenched jaw, he broke through her barrier and caught her cries in his mouth.

He stayed close, pressing himself against her core as he drove himself deeper, their bodies locked in passion's sweet dance.

"Ye drive me wild," he breathed on a husky groan.

She liked driving him wild. He didn't give himself up to many things—love, titles, duty. But from the beginning, he'd given himself up to her. He not only accepted his unwanted bride, he did his best to make her transition easier. She was glad he gave himself up to her.

He sank deep, gyrating his hips, creating delicious friction between their sweating bodies until all pain and fear left her and Sina felt her world begin to tilt.

They were one, joined together, her thighs stretched tight around his waist, her fingers clutching his shoulders.

She never thought such pleasure was real. She'd learned well the art of self-control. But there was no way to contain the fire rising up in her like a deluge. Every tender stroke that pulled her wider fanned the flames until she succumbed to the rhythm of his thrusts and let passion free her.

Everything went red before her as she climbed to the precipice with him, unencumbered and unafraid. She pushed and pulled beneath his body and arched her back, lost in ecstasy.

His mouth around her nipple cast her over the edge.

She cried out as her body writhed and pulsed with pleasure of release she'd never known. She clung to him as she let go, knowing she was safe in his arms.

Her eyes fluttered open in time to see him grind his jaw and pull himself out.

She watched, light-headed and breathless, while he rose up on one hand and took hold of himself with the other. She felt his seed spilling onto her belly and closed her eyes when his mouth sank to her neck.

He didn't collapse on her but rose up off the bed and trudged to the basin of water atop an ornate table.

Sina watched him, admiring the back view. He dipped a cloth in the basin and returned to the bed.

She looked away from the front of him, but when he stood over her to clean her, she lost the desire to resist, and let her eyes take their fill.

He looked to have been carved from stone. His chest was dusted with dark hair. Shadows danced over his sleek curves. His belly was as tight as a bowstring. And below...

He was still hard enough to arouse her. She closed her eyes to sever her gaze, and let him cleanse her in silence. She wanted to rest with him for just a little while longer, take time to consider that this truly just happened—and she wanted it to happen again. But there wasn't time now. He couldn't stay.

Were they mad? What would her father do when he found out? How long could they keep it from him?

She began to shiver thinking about it all, and from being wet. He hurried and dried her with a cloth and then climbed into bed next to her and pulled the blankets up around them.

"Come closer, lass. I'll keep ye warm."

His voice played like deep, sensual music to her ears. She

moved closer, pressing her ear to his chest and winding her limbs around him. She listened to the sound of his heart, his breath.

"This is very nice, but you cannot stay."

"I know. A few moments before I go." He held her close and spoke into her hair. "If I have things to do in my life, I want to do them with ye by my side. Will ye come home with me, Sina? Back to Camlochlin? I know 'tis no' the life ye're used to. Ye're as oot of place there as I am here. I'm no' askin' ye to sacrifice alone. We'll live in Camlochlin fer half the year and London, God help me, the other half."

She wiggled closer in his embrace and looked up into his eyes.

"I dinna know where yer heart is with Standish," he continued, while she contemplated her words, "but I know he willna be allowed near ye again. There is nothin' ye can do fer him."

"Though, I will not lie, the end of him pains me, my heart is no longer his."

"I know 'tis painful," he said. "I dinna know what I would do if Goliath ever turned on me."

At the mention of his name, Goliath lifted his front paws onto the bed and stared at them, ears perked to attention.

"He would never turn on you." Sina smiled warmly at the dog and thought about how fortunate Adam was to have such a loyal friend.

"Or on ye," Adam told her. "He was jealous at first, but he's come to love ye."

She laughed. "He told you that, did he?"

"Aye, he did." He smiled with her. "Words are no' the only way to communicate."

She agreed after what they had just done. There were

few words spoken between them, and yet, they were both changed.

She reached her hand out to pet Goliath's big head. Her heart still accelerated, but she wasn't afraid of him anymore.

"I think," she said, watching Goliath close his eyes while she scratched his head, "nine months there and three here would be better."

She looked at him and grew serious. "But only if my father approves. I will not bring an army to Camlochlin."

"Then I will make certain he approves," he whispered, leaning in to kiss her. "Because I willna leave withoot ye. I love ye, lass. I want to take ye as my wife again, with ye happy this time."

"So, then," she whispered, biting his succulent lower lip, "I'm the first woman you've ever loved."

"And ye'll be the last."

He took her mouth with sublime possession, tangling his fingers through her hair, then down her back.

"No, you have to leave!" She giggled and pushed him out of her bed before she couldn't walk for the rest of the day.

She clutched him by the wrist just before his feet hit the ground.

"Adam."

"Aye, lass?"

"I love you too."

Chapter Thirty-Five

G entlemen," the king announced early the next morning as he reached his horse. "This is Lord Hamilton, grandson of the Duke of Hamilton. He'll be joining the hunt today."

Adam greeted the others and leaped into his saddle with Goliath at his side. He'd rather return to the palace, to Sina's bed—but spending time with her father was part of getting her back.

"You're a bit unconventional," remarked Lord Somerset, coming up on his flank and glancing at Adam's bare neck and kid breeches.

Adam set his pale eyes on him. "Are we going to hunt or dance?"

"He's Scottish," the king reminded Somerset with a chuckle.

"Where's your pistol?" asked another stately noble, his back stiff in the saddle, his nose tilted upward.

"I do not hunt with a pistol," Adam told him and pulled a short blade from his belt. "I hunt with this."

The men around him looked equally horrified. Adam smiled, understanding more clearly now how savage his kin must have appeared to Sina the first time she saw them. He remembered how she'd wept and prayed and challenged him at every turn. She was braver than most of these men. She faced her fears about him, his kin, and Goliath and overcame them all.

"Yer Majesty," he said, catching up to the king and cantering beside him. "What of Lord Standish?"

"He's being released into his father's care later today. If he's seen anywhere near Sina, he will be caught and hanged."

"Do ye think he'll give her up that easily?" Adam asked him. He already knew the answer—and so did her father.

"The Earl of Chesterfield is an ally I cannot afford to lose presently. Showing mercy to his son is a favor he will not forget."

"Unless his son is hanged," Adam murmured.

"You question my decisions," the king pointed out, slipping his gaze to him.

"With Sina's safety in mind, Sire. He tried to strangle your daughter, whom he loves. She needs someone to guard her."

The king tossed him a knowing half smile. "Hmm, yes. I was going to speak to you about your prowess the other day. Impressive."

"I had the finest teachers in all of Great Britain. I can protect her."

The king nodded. "I don't doubt it. How are you and she getting along?"

"Verra well. In fact, I would have ye know that I'm falling deeply in love with her."

The king's face was unreadable. Adam knew the king

loved his mistress. He'd never given her up and divorced his wife for her. Maybe love meant a little to him.

"And she'll have you," the king countered, "now that Lord Standish is out of the way."

"She would have had me whether he was here or not. He used her to find his happiness. I will spend my days helping her find her own."

George said nothing for a few moments while they rode, then said, "She won't believe it, but I've always wanted her to be happy."

"She wasn't, Sire. She hasn't been fer a long time. I can change that too."

"I would like a chance to change it as well," the king said quietly. "Do you think we can?"

Adam was glad her father wanted to try, but it meant staying long enough to give him time to do it. "Aye, I do."

"Good." The king took a breath of relief and slowed his horse. "You seem to know much about her. She's opened up to you already."

"She does not cloak what she's feeling. One only has to look and listen."

"You'll tell me what she likes and dis—"

"Nae." Adam shook his head and glanced at the others riding over the hillside and into a small forest. "Ask her yerself. Spend time with her. Get to know her. That's how ye will make her happy. 'Tis what I am doing."

George wanted to be angry with him for refusing. Adam could see it in his eyes, but at last they softened on him. He knew Adam was correct, and was not so proud that he wouldn't concede. It was a good sign.

"In the meantime," Adam told him, "I will speak favorably of ye in her presence."

It occurred to Adam more in that moment than any other

that he might not be able to continue this façade with Sina's father. He'd always sworn to himself that he'd never kiss the arse of any king, and here he was doing just that, even sounding like a Lowlander to do it. Prostrating himself before a man who had gone back on his consent, who didn't care how many times he went back on his word or if he started a war with the MacGregors.

But he wasn't here to harbor ill will toward the king. If he had to kiss arse a little to have Sina or to save his clan, he would gladly do it.

They headed into the sparse forest and listened for any sign of the others.

"They have the dogs," the king complained.

Adam pointed to his dog, heading deeper into the woods. "We have Goliath." He kicked his horse forward to follow his hound.

He thought the king was just behind him a few moments later when he spotted the others beyond the brush. They were about to shoot a buck, so he remained still.

The shot rang out. The buck raced away, as did Goliath. The hound swung his head around, ears perked, and then took off in the direction they'd come.

Where the hell was the king?

Why had Goliath gone back?

Adam turned his horse around and flicked his reins.

He saw something moving in the bramble ahead of his dog. The flash of its overgrown teeth and the massive size of its shoulders proved what it was. A wild boar. A big male. The direction it was heading turned Adam's heart cold.

The king was up ahead, going the wrong way.

Adam kicked his mount's flanks to go faster and yanked his blade free. He wasn't going to make it in time.

The boar reached the king's horse and ploughed its large

head into the mount's leg. The horse went down, bringing the king with it.

The boar ran in a half circle and headed back for the king. It tipped its chin, pointing its sharp canines upward.

Goliath reached the beast on lightning-fast legs and, with a snarl that silenced the birds, sank his fangs into the boar's neck.

The thick-skinned beast fought and kicked its hooves at Goliath's belly. Its high-pitched, piercing cries echoed through the trees. Adam knew his dog couldn't hold on to the boar's thick neck too much longer.

He leaped from his saddle a few inches away from the roiling bodies, and without hesitation fell upon the boar and drove his blade deep into its neck.

When movement ended, Adam sat up and checked on Goliath. When he saw that his friend was unharmed, he drew him in for a kiss on his furry head, and then stood up, bringing the boar with him.

The king was standing beside his lame horse. The other nobles were watching Adam from a short distance away, too stunned to move.

"You and your dog saved my life."

Adam came toward him. "'Twas nothing anyone else would not have done. Are ye hurt?"

"Only because I must shoot my favorite horse." The king sighed and wiped his brow. "But tell me, do you truly think any one of those behind us would have leaped from their horse and killed that boar with their hands? I tell you not a one. You and Goliath have my gratitude. We will speak more of this later. Now, if you will wait with the others, I will take care of my horse."

Adam did as he was asked, tied the boar to his horse, and then offered the king his mount to ride home. The others rode on ahead while the king kept pace with Adam and Goliath on their feet.

"Tell me, Hamilton, why did Goliath attack the boar when it turned on me? Did the order come from you?"

"There was no order given, Sire," Adam told him truthfully. "Goliath and I came upon the men shooting at a deer, and the next thing I knew Goliath was racing back here. The shot must have startled the boar and sent it running in yer direction. Goliath knew where 'twas heading. He's intelligent."

"He's incredible."

"Aye, I know," Adam agreed, looking down to wink at his dog. "I tell people all the time, but most have a hard time seeing it."

"Would you consider selling him?"

"Nae. Never."

The king smiled. "I didn't think so."

"Sit at my table tonight at dinner, Hamilton. We'll discuss things."

They saw the king's staff hurrying toward them, alerted, no doubt, by the noblemen who'd raced back to tell the rest.

Adam watched the king dismount and reach out to pet Goliath on the head. "You're invited too, of course."

He ordered one of his servants to bring the boar to the kitchens and to bring to Lord Hamilton anything he requested.

Adam requested Sina.

Adam waited for her in a small library outside the palace. She'd sent Katie back with a note, asking him to meet her here. According to Sina, it was the least visited place on the grounds.

Light spilled in from the high windows to illuminate

benches and bookshelves. There weren't many books—not compared to Camlochlin's library, and not enough candle-light by which to read them once the sun went down. Judging by the layers of dust on the books, Sina was correct. No one would come upon them here.

He liked the silence of it, the stillness that quieted his anxious thoughts.

He and Goliath had saved the king's life. He couldn't have hoped for any better way to gain George's favor. Mayhap it was a good time to tell him the truth. Mayhap the king would gladly give his daughter's hand to Adam now. They could be wed again here in London. Adam didn't care where.

He shook his head. He was getting ahead of himself. He couldn't be too hasty. He had one chance to save his clan from the king. He had to be certain his deception would be forgiven before he confessed.

But he wanted her. His body craved her, and not just his body, but also every chamber of his heart. She lurked in the corner of his every thought, pulling his attention back to her pert breasts in his mouth, her legs coiled around him, her body writhing beneath him. He'd fought himself all morning not to be distracted by the memory of her. He'd kept her at bay.

But now...she was coming to him and he couldn't wait to hold her in his arms again. He loved her madly, hope-lessly, and after last night, more than he ever thought possi-ble. He'd let her in because he thought he had to. Now she filled every chasm of his heart. The only thing stopping him from having her was his name.

Goliath sprang from where he'd been sitting at Adam's side and galloped to the front doors.

They opened and she entered on a summer breeze. Adam

watched her lift her delicate fingers to push back her hood. She saw him as sunlight touched her face, and her smile nearly buckled his knees. She was happy to see him, happy to be here with him...and with Goliath. She actually bent her face to his black muzzle and planted a kiss on his furry head.

"Thank you," Adam heard her whisper.

She had already heard of what happened on the hunt. Her gratefulness told Adam much about how she felt about the king.

"I have your promise, then?" she asked Goliath next.

He responded by lowering his shoulders and dipping his tail between his legs.

Adam laughed, loving that she talked to his dog. "What have ye made him promise?"

"Goliath is never going to allow Catherine Newton to touch him again."

"I see," he said, unable to stop himself from moving toward her. "And what if she touches me?"

"Then I will tear out her throat myself."

"Hmm"—he smiled, slipping his hand behind her nape— "this is a side of ye I've never seen before."

She tilted her head back to receive him and whispered across his lips, "You've set my passions free."

He descended, taking her mouth with tender possession. He breathed her, knowing her scent was growing more vital to his lungs than air. He closed his arms around her, knowing no one, not even a king, could take her from him.

She broke away, her cheeks and her lips red from kissing him. Her eyes danced with mischief. "Come with me."

She took him by the hand, locked the doors, and then led him up the stairs.

Chapter Thirty-Six

Sina led Adam to the second-floor landing and to a giant, arched window made of glass, cut and soldered to extend overhead—the stroke of a master designer. Sunlight burst over brightly sewn pillows and coverings strewn about the cozy nook. She looked at her stack of books and parchments and she smiled.

"Ye've spent much time here." Adam stepped beneath the grand window and looked out over the manmade landscape of rooftops and beyond.

"I discovered early that I needed a place to come to clear my head in peace and quiet."

"Aye," he agreed, looking out. "I often went to Bla Bheinn fer the same reason." He turned from the window to gaze at her.

She had thought that once they were together again, he would cease to haunt her thoughts. She was wrong. He filled her every waking thought *and* her dreams. She was glad now that he'd gone hunting with her father, but she woke this morning missing him. If they were in Camlochlin, they wouldn't have left their bed. She wanted him. She wanted to feel the size of him atop her, inside her.

When had she become so wanton? She didn't know this bold side of herself. She felt awakened and exhilarated, and it was because of him.

"You are the first male I have ever invited here." It was true. She'd kept things from William...secrets, like this place, and her love of the romantic. He had never been romantic, and the one time she brought it up to him, he laughed, amused.

Her blood burned and made her nerves itch when Adam curled his mouth and bowed to her. "Thank ye, lass. I'll return the gesture when we go home."

She tipped her head and laughed a little. "You expect me to climb a mountain?"

"'Tis more like a tall hill," he told her, his gaze searing over her throat. "But 'twill make ye stronger and more resilient."

"Stronger and more resilient for what?" she purred against him when he pulled her into his arms.

"No' what, love." The sensual cadence of his voice flowed through her like molten lava. "Whom."

His lips touched hers and sent quivers down her spine, the backs of her knees. She fell, weak in his strong embrace, lost in his intoxicating kiss.

They undressed each other with urgent fingers and fell into the pillows in a tangle of limbs and laughter.

"I dreamed of you last night."

"Nae, lass," he whispered across her ear, "that was real."

"Oh?" She rolled over on top of him and smiled. "Because I don't remember doing *this* to you before."

She straddled him but quickly lost her nerve to impale

herself on him. He laughed softly and pulled her down for a kiss.

His body was warm and hard beneath her, his mouth masterful and teasing.

Soon, she found her hips gyrating over the steely length of him. She knew in his arms there was nothing to fear. Trusting him allowed her to marvel at the masterpiece beneath her fingertips and compelled her to take her time enjoying him.

They ran their hands over each other, curious, learning shapes and sensitive hollows. They kissed, sharing breath and quiet whispers of love.

"Are ye ready fer me, my love?" he asked, spreading his hands down her back to her buttocks.

"Yes, I'm ready," she cried out, needing him closer, aching for more.

His deft hands cupped her and spread her for him. He pushed against her opening and ground his jaw. At first, Sina wondered how she would do it again. He felt even bigger than last night. She'd been too bold to mount him. But the more he pushed, the deeper she drew him in.

When he pushed his back up off the pillows, taking her with him, it felt as if he were going to burst through her.

He moved, slow and deep, grinding his sinewy abdomen against her. With his hands cupped around her buttocks, he guided her over his thick shaft, impaling her deeper with each thrust.

She cried out, holding on to him as waves of pleasure cascaded over her, sent her over the edge of oblivion. Her body tightened and pulsed around him. She trembled in his arms, riding him up and down until he tossed back his head and shot himself deep into her.

They both collapsed into the pillows, with Sina spread out atop his chest.

"You saved my father's life," she whispered after a little while. "He's now in your debt. Do you think that is enough to keep you safe from his wrath?"

"Nae, love," he told her, pressing his mouth to the top of her head. "I think *ye* are enough."

She pushed up off him. "Me? What do you mean?"

"I mean, he loves ye. He wants a chance to make ye happy."

"He told you that?"

"He did."

Sina climbed off him and pulled one of the blankets over them. She rested beside him, pressing her cheek to his chest and tossing her leg over his.

She'd shared many of her secrets up here with Poppy. But there were some things that even Poppy didn't know.

"He was not a terrible father," she began, her voice husky with the weight of the telling. "I didn't even know he *was* my father until I was ten years old. He visited me several times and even stayed here for a month every summer that I was here. He provided everything I needed to become a reputable lady-in-waiting. Everything but his name. I was not his daughter. I was his secret—and the shame it brought me has been one of my greatest burdens."

Adam gathered her closer, offering his strength and comfort.

"My mother told me he is finally going to announce me."

"I'm glad, my love," he whispered against her temple. "Ye will have what ye have always wanted."

But was it? Perhaps years ago, even months...weeks. But was it all she ever wanted still? To be known by all as the king's bastard? Or to be loved by Adam MacGregor?

"Yes," she said against the soft dusting of dark hair on his chest.

"He knows my heart is lost to ye," Adam told her, stroking her back. "He knows I can protect ye, and I *will* protect him."

"He thinks you are someone else."

He grew quiet for a moment. Sina listened to his breathing, as close as her own.

"When the time comes," he told her. "Ye must let him know ye love me, lass. That I make ye happy."

When the time comes... She didn't want to think on it now. "I do love you, and you do make me happy." She tilted her chin to kiss him. "I will tell him tonight if you wish it, but for right now, let's enjoy this and each other. Tell me, who was your closest friend growing up? You told me a little about your childhood. Tell me more."

She loved listening to the musical lilt of his voice. The deep timbre of it covered her like an intimate caress.

"I didna have time to form deeper friendships with any of my kin. There were always lessons to be learned. By the end of the day, I was too weary to play."

"It sounds very lonely," she said, running her fingers over his chest.

"'Twas. Until I ran into Goliath in the hall seven years ago. He was six weeks old. Edmund had taken him and his sisters for a walk through the castle. A few weeks after that, he wouldna leave my side. We became friends, partners in trooble, and he hasna left my side yet."

"He is a good boy," she cooed at the black mound on the other side of the alcove.

"He doesn't respond to coaxing—" Adam stopped when his dog rose up and lumbered over to them.

"Oh yes, he is! So good!" she said in a high-pitched, excited voice that excited Goliath, as well. He climbed over them with long, bony legs, causing them both to cry out at his weight. When he threw his furry body down on the blanket between them, belly up, they laughed and kissed his furry cheeks.

Sina knew the new future she wanted with Adam. She wanted a family with him. She wanted to bear his children in Camlochlin and wake up to them jumping into her and Adam's bed.

She didn't want her father or anyone else to get in the way.

This time, she wouldn't let anyone stop the plans she made for herself. She wouldn't let her father or anyone else take her from Adam.

Lady Catherine Newton peered around the corner to make certain no one saw her, and then slipped into Sina's rooms. She wasn't sure what she was looking for, but it was the best time to search, as she'd seen Sina leave the palace a short while ago. She didn't know how long Sina would be gone, so she needed to be quick.

She looked around. Roderick would be angry if he knew she was doing something so nefarious as snooping around someone else's apartment. Especially Melusina de Arenburg's. William worshipped her.

Her poor cousin William, in prison because of her.

Catherine had spent a good part of the morning with him at the prison—a horrible place, filled with miscreants and thieves. No place for a Standish. She'd waited with him until his father had arrived and William was released—banned from ever stepping foot in Kensington Palace again.

Catherine had never seen her cousin so desolate. Yes, he choked the precious Miss de Arenburg. He was sorry. He'd wept over it while they waited. Of course he'd been angry when he learned his betrothed no longer loved him. He'd been blind with rage.

Catherine thought about telling him what was going on while he was absent. How his dearest Sina flirted with Lord Hamilton, and how she was often caught staring at him since the day he carried her home and escorted her to dinner. But why discredit poor Lord Hamilton for falling for Melusina's charms? She was clearly jealous of his affections toward Catherine and sought to keep him away. Well, Catherine would have him.

Just the thought of being swept up in his arms, kissed by his perfectly carved lips, made her warm all over.

After Catherine found a way to publicly disgrace the trollop, Lord Hamilton would want nothing to do with Sina and would be free to pursue the true gem.

What was she looking for? There had to be something here she or William could use against Melusina. But where should she begin?

She started at Sina's writing table and prayed the proof wasn't here, since her reading skills were basic at best, particularly bad when it came to someone's personal writing. She found nothing that appeared important. She checked under cushions, behind paintings, on shelves, and inside Sina's chest of drawers. She found a dried-up weed of some sort placed delicately beside Sina's folded stockings. She shoved it into her pocket and hurried on to Sina's wardrobe.

She stopped when she saw an odd-looking striped shawl and thick petticoats. There were other gowns sewn in outdated fashion. She ran her fingers over a fold of lavender wool as fine as satin. She touched something stiff. It was a pocket. She put her hand inside and pulled forth a folded parchment. It was wrinkled and worn and had the form of a letter. Catherine studied it for a moment, trying to read the first few words.

She thought she could make out William's name and a few other words but nothing more. Why had Sina hidden it in her pocket? Catherine would let William decide when she met with him tonight.

She heard a sound outside and quickly hurried from the rooms.

Chapter Thirty-Seven

Adam stepped into the grand dining hall and spotted Sina standing with Miss Warwick and the Viscount of Nottingham beside the king's grand table. No one sat until the king arrived and sat first.

How was it possible that every time he saw her, she grew more beautiful to him? She dressed for dinner in a gold-and-black brocade gown with small hoops and yellow petticoats. Her golden locks were swept up high off her face in soft plaits pinned in pearls.

Adam watched her, barely breathing as she smiled at something Miss Warwick said, flashing her dimple and enchanting the man standing next to her.

Adam didn't mind if Nottingham felt something for Sina. Any man would be a fool not to. As long as no one put a finger to her, there wouldn't be a problem.

"She seems happy despite everything that has happened."

Adam looked at Miss Berkham and returned her smile. "I think she is, though last eve was verra difficult fer her."

"If I wasn't there, I would never have believed William

could do such a thing to her," she said, looping her arm through his. He noted Sina's attention turning to them. Her smiled deepened as he escorted her friend into the hall.

"I'm glad you were there to help her through it." Miss Berkham grinned like a cat, slanting her eyes at him.

"Aye." He nodded, his eyes dancing off to the side. "So am I. But she is strong and brave. She will get over the loss of William in her own time."

"And with you at her side, I hope."

"Yer approval means much, my lady."

"Based on what you've proven so far," she told him while she smiled at Sina coming toward them, "you have earned it."

"Lord Hamilton," Sina greeted him and then kissed Miss Berkham's cheek.

"How are you feeling, dearest?" her friend asked, frowning at the bruise on Sina's neck. "If I ever see that scoundrel again, I'll rip out his eyes."

"If he shows up here," Adam said, "ye willna have time to get to him before I do."

"I'm fine, you two," she assured them. Her gaze flickered to Adam's. "Better now."

He did his absolute best not to drag her into his arms. She filled his senses and made him want to carry her away from the crowd.

"Poppy, Adam was specifically invited to dinner by the king."

"Ah, yes," Miss Berkham said. "You're a hero. I'm not surprised."

"'Tis Goliath who is the hero, no' I," he said as Miss Warwick and Nottingham approached. "Goliath gave me time to reach the boar by getting to it first. He was in much more danger than I. His belly was exposed to the boar's kickin' hooves, and the boar's neck is tough to break."

"He's quite a fascinating dog," Nottingham remarked.

"Aye." Adam smiled proudly, happy that Goliath was finally getting the admiration he deserved. "He is."

The king finally arrived with his mistress, and his guests took their seats. Dinner was roasted boar and stuffed pheasant. Wine was sipped and toasts were made.

After a little while, King George stood from his chair and raised his cup. He waited until everyone quieted down, which they did quickly.

"Today, as most of you already know, while hunting deer, I was attacked by this fierce creature." He pointed his cup at their dinner. "Fierce enough to take down my favored horse. It turned on me next, grunting and snorting, ready to ram its head and sharp teeth into me."

The king was telling it right. Adam smiled at Goliath, and then at Sina, who was watching him.

"My horse was down," the king continued. "I couldn't outrun a wild boar. I watched it run toward me and fumbled for my pistol. Something big and black sped past my vision on long, powerful legs. It hit the boar with such force the creature went down. Thank God 'twas Lord Hamilton's dog, Goliath. But even Goliath couldn't kill the beast."

By now the sound of people's breathing was the only thing to be heard in the hall. Everyone listened, fascinated by the tale.

"I still don't know whether Lord Hamilton was trying to save me or his dog, but I'm grateful he arrived and leaped right into the fray, killing the boar with a paltry knife."

The guests let out a collective sigh and began clapping. Sina smiled at him, but it faded when she saw that every woman at the long table was smiling at him too.

"Tonight," George shouted, "I honor Lord Hamilton and Goliath for saving the life of their king!"

Cheering and toasts ensued until Adam rose from his seat and raised his cup to the king.

"Fer as long as His Majesty holds true to his words, my loyalty and the fealty of my kin shall be his."

Adam knew he was taking a risk giving the king of Great Britain a condition to his loyalty. But he'd been bold from the beginning. He wouldn't stop now when he had the king's ear. He made promises for his kin as the chief's heir. He would stand by them if George stood by his.

He turned from the king to the faces sitting at the table. "I've heard many whispers about 'savage Scots.' They are all true. That's why"—he turned back to George—"'tis wise to have them on yer side. They will win ye many battles."

"You bring up interesting points, Hamilton," the king said, returning to his seat. "Let's talk about this more over a game of chess later this eve."

Adam would rather spend his time with Sina, but this was a decisive moment in his relationship with the king. He might even tell him that he was a MacGregor tonight.

Sina spoke up beside him. "I would also like a few moments of your time, Your Majesty."

"Of course, Miss de Arenburg," the king granted. "Would one hour from now suit you?"

She nodded and smiled to show her gratitude.

Adam knew there was love between Sina and her father. He wanted it to flourish for Sina's sake. Fathers were important. He'd grown up in a completely different environment, where fathers played a vital role in their children's lives. Sina hadn't had that. But it wasn't too late. He could put aside that her father had ordered her back, and that he hated the MacGregors without ever meeting one, and be grateful that this father wanted to make his daughter happy.

"My lord?" Sina's soft voice drew him away from his thoughts.

He blinked and smiled openly at her. "Aye, lass?"

She motioned toward Goliath with her delicate chin. Adam thought about kissing it before he turned to see his dog sitting near his chair, his eyes fastened on the king.

"Come, Goliath!" The king tempted him with the full, roasted leg of the boar. Goliath wanted it, but he didn't move.

"Go on and get it," Adam said and then called out when the dog took off, "Easily!"

The king and others around the table marveled at such obedience. Adam couldn't help but wonder when the king would leave the table so he could escape with Sina for a little while.

When the king and his hostess finally did leave, Adam wasn't the first one out of his seat.

"Lord Hamilton!" A woman of mature years stood before his chair. She wore a black and dark blue mantua with matching skirts. Her silver hair was piled atop her head and pinned with pearls. Attached to her chubby fingers was a bonny lass of marriageable age with pale yellow curls falling over her temples.

"I'm Lady Mordaunt," the older woman said, "wife of Viscount Mordaunt, and this fair lady is my granddaughter, Miss Pratt."

Adam stood from his seat and bowed politely. He could almost feel the icy stillness of Sina's gaze behind him. He smiled, thinking about her being possessive of him.

"A pleasure, ladies. What can I do fer ye?"

Lady Mordaunt snapped open her fan and smiled behind

it. Her granddaughter peeked up from beneath her lashes and turned three shades darker.

"We enjoyed hearing about how you saved the king," Lady Mordaunt continued. "My husband and I would be honored to have you call on our granddaughter."

Adam looked at the poor gel behind her. Like Miss Newton, she remained silent to the decisions being made for her. It helped him understand even more what it took for Sina, being raised this way, to fight back.

He turned to set his gaze on her. She'd looked away, but the slight tilt of her neck revealed that she was still listening.

"That will be impossible, Lady Mordaunt," he said with a polite smile. "I currently have my heart set on winning Miss de Arenburg's affections."

"Oh." Lady Mordaunt stared up at him with surprise and disappointment marring her features. She slipped her gaze to Sina, and it went cold. "Perhaps Miss de Arenburg should take a little time to remember that she was betrothed to another just days ago."

Adam stepped aside when Sina rose from the chair. Her spine was straight, her shoulders set, her chin lifted slightly up.

"Lady Mordaunt." Her voice snapped across the air as she moved closer. "I remember his hands around my throat, squeezing until he cut off my air. I remember looking into his eyes and seeing a merciless stranger. Should I mourn that?"

"But you had a past with him," Lady Mordaunt defended.

Sina laughed softly, mesmerizing Adam. "What good is a past when he tried to take my life from me? I should be celebrating that I am free of him."

Adam agreed with her and nodded his head. He didn't interrupt. She didn't need him to.

"As you would be doing if I were your granddaughter."

Lady Mordaunt tossed her a nervous half smile, then dragged her granddaughter away.

"This is going to happen often," Sina sighed, looking up at him. "Especially now that the king made you a hero."

As much as it satisfied him that she was jealous, he didn't want her to be. "It willna last once word spreads that my heart is set on ye."

"Is it, Highlander?" Her anxious heart melted before his eyes with a bewitching crinkle of her nose and the flash of her dimple.

"Take a walk with me so I can show ye, lass." He offered her his elbow and she accepted without hesitation.

He'd won her. He was grateful she let him. He wasn't leaving England without her.

"Goliath," he called, and waited a moment while his dog came, carrying his bone, then left the dining hall with Sina.

They stepped out into the queen's garden as it began to rain. There were still people strolling about, so they walked beyond the citrus trees and came to the alcove. No one was there.

He pulled her into the shadows and dragged her into his arms, unable to wait another instant for her.

He took her face in his hands and stared into her eyes knowing she saw his heart there. He leaned in and tilted her face to his. His gaze dipped to her lips, parted and ready to receive him.

"Ye have my heart, lass," he whispered and kissed her reply from her mouth. Ah, but he loved kissing her. He loved the taste of her and the feel of her in his arms.

His tongue stole across hers in a beguiling reminder of their passion. He pressed her closer—not close enough.

He deepened their kiss, wanting more of her. Sensing she wanted the same thing.

Lightning flashed outside the alcove as waves of rain fell. They watched for a moment, both realizing what it meant.

No one was coming.

Chapter Thirty-Eight

Sina was late. She'd asked her father for a word and agreed to meet him in an hour—an hour and a half ago.

After making love to Adam in the alcove, they'd waited until the rain abated before they hurried back to the palace. She was wet and had to change her clothes.

Finally, she stood at the door to her father's private chambers and knocked.

One of his servants opened the door and allowed her entry. She waited a moment until the king and her mother appeared from another doorway. Her father looked sullen and angry. At first Sina thought she was the cause. But he carried a letter with him and shook it in the air.

"Sit down, Sina," he said solemnly. "I have news from the Bishop Robinson."

Her heart skipped. The bishop? Did she dare hope? "What is it, Father?" she asked, taking a seat in a red brocade cushioned chair.

He waited until Sina's mother sat facing her daughter.

"'Tis terrible news, my dear," he told her, still standing.

"The bishop has refused to annul your marriage to Mac-Gregor."

Sina thought she might faint where she sat. He was still her husband! She, his wife! Oh...She caught her breath and wilted into her chair, pretending now to almost faint at this terrible news.

"He has been informed that the MacGregors have in their possession a letter written and signed by Queen Anne giving your hand in marriage. He will not annul it until he speaks to you himself. He will be here in three days."

"There *was* a letter from the queen," Sina said, doing her best to sound numb. "She said you consented."

"She deceived me about what kind of people they were."

Sina shook her head. "No, she didn't. She told you the truth. You know one side of the story."

"Sina," her mother asked, astonished. "Are you defending them?"

"Of course I am. I have been from the beginning. They are kind and loving, and they were following the queen's orders. They did nothing wrong."

Another thought occurred to her and her mouth went dry. "Did the bishop say how he received news of the letter?" Were the MacGregors in London? What if they came here? Chances were, they would. Her hands began to shake.

"He did not," her father said. "I'm afraid I must deny Lord Hamilton your hand until this is resolved."

Sina felt terrible about not telling him the truth. It was worse now than before. She'd let it go on, let Adam make a fool of him. He would never forgive them and would hate the MacGregors even more.

"He's never going to forgive or trust me." Her father finally sank into his chair. "He saved my life, and now I must refuse him the one thing he wants."

It made her eyes misty that her father was worried about Adam forgiving him. "He will forgive you, Father. He is kind and understanding."

"I know, daughter," he said, reaching out to take her hands. "You've opened up much to him and he's helped me to understand where I have failed you."

"You haven't failed me—"

He held up his hand to stop her. "I'm going to declare you publicly. I will even legitimize you so that one day you may be queen."

"No," she told him. "I don't want to be queen, only your daughter."

"That, you are," he said, smiling. "And soon all of Great Britain will know it."

Her heart swelled. This is what she wanted her whole life. To have a family, to be one—openly.

But, it didn't seem as important as it used to be.

"Thank you, Father."

"Now, don't worry about the bishop," he said, patting her hands and moving back in his chair. "The union wasn't consummated, and you were wed against your will. Once I declare you, the bishop will not agree to a union between the king's daughter and an outlaw."

Sina's head spun. The marriage was consummated, and often. She might even be carrying Adam's babe right now. The thought of it filled her with images of being surrounded by sisters, mothers, aunts, and cousins.

Dear God, what were they going to do?

"Now, what was it you wanted to speak to me about?" he asked gently.

He had to be told the truth. But she didn't have the courage to do it alone. "'Tis about…Lord Hamilton. I love him, Father. 'Tis a different kind of love than what I felt for

William. It consumes me and doesn't let me think of anything but him. I will never be happy with anyone else. I want to be his wife."

"I will do everything I can to make it happen, Sina," her father promised. "I like the lad. He's brave and he loves you. Of that I'm certain."

Sina wanted to rejoice but couldn't. It was all a lie.

She left her parents, feeling worse than she did before.

"We must tell him the truth, Adam." Sina wept in his arms. They sat together on a settee in her apartment. She found him and brought him here to tell him what happened. They were both happy to still be husband and wife, but they agreed their deceit was growing—and soon there would be no turning back. It might already be too late.

"I'm meeting him for a game of chess before bed," Adam soothed. "I'll tell him."

"No"—she looked up from his chest—"*we* will tell him. I'm coming with you. We both deceived him."

He shook his head. "Ye wouldna have—"

She halted the remainder of his argument with a kiss. She didn't want to think about tonight or tomorrow. She wanted to continue kissing his warm, plump mouth, safe and happy in his arms.

But they had to see the king and confess. "I'm afraid," she whispered, breaking their kiss.

"Everything will be all right, lass."

"How do you know?"

He met her teary gaze with a confident smile. "Because I willna give up. But fer now, let's leave Goliath here."

They left her room and went directly to the northwest side and made their way up the marble staircase to her father's rooms.

"Yer hand is tremblin'," Adam said, stopping and turning to her. "Why dinna ye wait fer me dounstairs?"

"No, I'm fine." She straightened her shoulders and pulled him along. "We're doing this together."

She reached the doors and rapped on them soundly.

"Ye're a brave lass," Adam said beside her, smiling at her while they waited. "Any man would be proud to have ye at his side."

"You are the brave one," she whispered back. "You are the one smiling. You never seem concerned with things, and yet, I know you are."

"I'm glad ye know. 'Tis one of the things I love so—"

The door opened and the king's private butler offered them entry with a swish of his arm.

Adam was wrong. She wasn't brave. Her knees were shaking. Her head was pounding as hard as her heart. What would her father do? Did Adam have a plan? Why did he seem so confident? Why did he *always* seem so confident?

Never mind why, it calmed her fears.

They were led through the sitting rooms to the inner chamber, where her father sat at his chess table, waiting.

When he saw her enter with Adam, he rose from his seat to greet them.

"Hamilton, I'm sure Melusina has told you about her annulment to the MacGregor. I assure you, I had no idea."

"I know, Sire," Adam told him. "We've come to have a word with ye."

"Of course. Sit," her father ordered softly. "Drink?"

Sina shook her head, as did Adam.

A knock came at the door before it opened and the butler entered with a folded parchment in his hand. He handed it to the king and spoke softly toward the king's ear.

Sina watched her father's expression go from curious to angry, then back to curious.

Dismissing his servant, he unfolded the letter and looked up from it briefly to address them.

"'Twas delivered by Miss Newton on behalf of Standish."

Sina looked at Adam. What in blazes was William trying to do?

Her father began to read and then looked up again.

"'Tis a letter to him...from you."

No! It couldn't be! How had he gotten it? What did it say? What did she write him? She couldn't remember. Her thoughts raced and collided. She heard Adam's voice in the clamor.

"Sire, allow me—"

The king held up his palm and continued reading.

"'To help you understand the barbarian I've been sworn to, his closest friend is a black hound from the piths of hell he calls...Goliath.'"

Sina's heart stopped.

Everything stopped. For a moment, the world went completely dead.

Then her father spoke. His voice quavered with rage and stunned disbelief. "You are MacGregor."

"Sire, my intention was—"

"—not to deceive me?" the king finished for him. "You think me a fool?" He continued before Adam could answer. "You almost tricked me into giving my daughter's hand to you, yet again."

"Nae, I would no' have gone before a priest with her until ye knew the truth," Adam defended. "I simply wanted—"

"There is nothing simple about this!" her father roared. "You made a fool of me!"

Sina closed her eyes to halt her tears, but they still came.

"I saved yer life," Adam reminded him stiffly. "Even after ye betrayed my kin by takin' her back."

"Yes, you saved my life, which is why I won't have you hanged. Bernard!" He shouted for his servant. "Have my guards brought in immediately."

"Father, no!" Sina bolted from her chair. "Please hear what we have to say!"

He turned to her. The rims of his eyes were red. His mouth was drawn tight over his teeth. "You love this man. You went along with all this."

"There was no other choice."

His expression hardened. "I'll inform your mother that you'll be leaving for Hanover in the morning."

"Sire, let me—"

"MacGregor!" the king shouted at him. "You will not speak another word!"

"This is precisely why I couldna tell ye," Adam told him, shaking his head at him. "How will ye be a good king when ye dinna listen or know how to control yer temper?"

For an instant, her father paused in his tirade and stared at him as if he were remembering their quick friendship.

"I trusted you," he told Adam solemnly. "'Tis hard for a king to find someone he can trust."

"'Tis hard fer any man," Adam replied as the guards filed into the room.

"Pistols," the king advised them. "No one tries to fight this man. You will lose."

"Father!" Sina grasped his robe. Two of his guards turned to look at her. "Please, I beg you. Don't put him in Newgate. I have never asked you for anything. Never! Do this one thing for me."

But he was too angry to listen. "He betrayed me," he replied coolly.

"Only in my name," Adam told him, rising from his chair and preparing to go quietly. "Only that."

"If you do this," Sina shouted at her father, "I will never forgive you!" Let them arrest her too! She ran to Adam and clung to him. "He is my husband," she said looking into his eyes, "and not just in name."

Adam smiled at her and kissed her hand, then held it between them. "Give him time to take it all in," he said quietly. "Go back to yer rooms and take care of Goliath. I dinna want ye near the prison. He'll release me. Dinna fear."

He looked over her head at the king. "Lord Standish was obviously here when he stole that letter. He's a danger to her. Keep Goliath with her."

Her father nodded, then looked away as the guards led Adam out.

Chapter Thirty-Nine

S ina followed them out into the moonlit night and waited in Adam's arms for the carriage that would take him to Newgate. Her heart broke into pieces at the thought of him in that horrible, filthy place when he hadn't done anything but be a MacGregor. Everything he had feared for his kin was happening to him.

"I'm proud to still carry your name, husband," she breathed into his neck when he lifted her in a consuming embrace.

The carriage had arrived.

"Dinna be too hard on him, lass," he asked of her. "Be strong. I'll return to ye."

She tried to be strong and only wept instead of doing what she really wanted to do, which was yank on the carriage door and try to get him out.

It began to rain as they drove him away. Sina stayed where she was, watching the carriage disappear. She wanted to pull out her hair and scream. How could this happen? She couldn't lose him.

Finally, she returned to her rooms to take care of Goliath. She wouldn't speak to her father tonight. She might never speak to him again. She hadn't yet decided.

Her heart went cold when she opened her doors and Goliath wasn't there waiting. She called him and began searching her rooms. Did he get out? How did he close the door behind him? "Goliath!"

She saw a sheet of parchment laid out on her bed with her dried-up sprig of heather atop it.

She picked it up and read it. *Come to the library. Come alone if you want the mongrel to live.*

She ran out of the room, out of her apartment, and back out into the night.

It couldn't be William! He didn't know about her alcove in the library. But he'd gotten her letter, her heather. He'd been in her room. But how the hell did he get Goliath out of her rooms without a fight? Had he hurt the dog?

She ran, lifting her skirts and letting the letter and her bun fall away. When she reached the library, she ripped open the doors the way she'd wanted to do earlier. She knew she should have taken a weapon, but it was too late for that now. She plunged inside.

"William!"

He appeared at the top of the stairs. "Hello, my dearest."

"Where's Goliath?" She couldn't bear to look at him after all he'd done. But she climbed the stairs two by two to get to the top. "Goliath!"

"You have no words of greeting for me?" He tried to stop her from passing him.

"You tried to kill me," she seethed and slapped his hand away. "Goliath!"

"Stop your bellowing. The creature is over there." He pointed to her alcove and she ran to it.

When she saw Goliath lying on her blankets, still and quiet, his snout tied shut with rope, her knees nearly buckled. She went to him and, kneeling beside him, listened for his breath. He was alive. "What did you do to him?"

"It attacked me when I went into your apartment. It had me down on the ground, like so many others..." His voice faded into the past for a moment. "I hit it in the skull with the handle of my pistol. Twice, as a matter of fact. The beast wouldn't go down. I brought it here because I knew you would come for it. You've protected it from the beginning, and now I know why."

Sina squeezed her eyes shut and buried her face in Goliath's fur. "Wake up," she whispered.

"Don't untie him, or I'll have to shoot him, Sina," William warned when she moved to pull the rope off his face.

"You better pray he wakes up."

He came closer and knelt beside her.

"I read your letter. You said you would never love him. I know you're angry with me, but don't discard our years together."

She stared at him. She knew every inch of his face, every expression. She'd watched it go from small, round, and a bit cherubic, to hard and cynical over the years. She'd felt so guilty about betraying him that she couldn't see the truth: she loved him like a brother. It was never anything more than that, not to say her love hadn't been immeasurably strong. She hated losing him, but it was too late. She would never forget his face while he was choking her.

"You stole my letter and gave it to the king. Adam is in prison because of you."

His eyes shone in the moonlight coming in from the window overhead. "You lied to me, Sina. We promised we would never do that to each other."

"Oh?" She lifted her brow at him. "Did you spend time in the beds of other women while on the tour?"

He didn't answer right away, which was answer enough.

"I didn't love any of them," he finally said, weakly.

She turned away in disgust. When she thought of keeping herself from Adam out of loyalty to her betrothed, it sickened her. "Don't speak to me about deceit."

"You mean everything to me, and that is the truth," he told her.

She shook her head. "It's too late."

"Because you love a MacGregor?" he spat.

"Because you tried to take everything from me, William, including my life!"

"I didn't mean to—"

She held up her palm. "Enough. Help me carry Goliath back to my rooms so I can fetch the physician."

He shook his head. "I can't get out of Kensington alive with you. I won't let you belong to anyone else, especially a savage. I just want a little more time with you."

"What . . . ?" She looked at him and the pistol peeking out from behind his coat. "What are you talking about?"

"How can you think I could live without you, Sina? I need you. You know that. You are everything to me. I can't let you go. Not ever."

She tried to run, but he grabbed her wrist, yanked her back down, and swung at her, knocking her out. She landed in Goliath's soft fur.

King George paced his bedchamber as his sleepless night wore on.

He wished he'd insisted on his beloved staying in the king's quarters tonight. He could tread his way to the queen's side of the palace to see and speak to her, but he felt an urgency to speak to someone else.

He still had a hard time believing MacGregor had come here, convincingly disguised as someone else. It made sense now that, as Hamilton, he'd claimed to love Sina so quickly. And Sina loved him. George would have thought his daughter brainwashed, but then, so had he been. He liked the lad. Hamilton—MacGregor was witty and clever, and he didn't kiss George's arse. Of course, there were savage subtleties in his demeanor, now that George thought about it, like when his dog was in danger after MacGregor broke a man's nose and knocked out four teeth for striking Sina, or the way his expression turned ruthless and cold when he spoke of William Standish.

Other than that, he carried himself like a prince, sure and confident. He was well-versed and well-mannered, excellent at chess and at fighting. It had been easy to believe he was the grandson of a duke. How could he be the grandson of the Devil MacGregor?

George had found out some things about this particular clan on Skye. This Devil had killed an entire garrison of men on his own and then took on the rest of the Campbells in a personal war.

In truth, the more George had learned about him, the more curious he became about the rest of them. He was able to find out little about the Devil's children, save that one of his sons had been a personal friend to King James and a general in his army.

They were fighters, for certain. And mighty, if the rest of them were as big as Hamilton.

Oh, how had he been so deceived? He should have

known the lad was the MacGregor. Here to make a fool of the new king, or here because he had fallen in love with his daughter?

MacGregor's concern, even while being taken away, was her safety. His interest had been in her and no one else from the beginning.

What father didn't want a man for his daughter who would travel on horseback for days to find her? Who could protect her? William Standish was a worm, led by whichever way the wind was blowing. It was Sina who'd always protected *him*!

George scowled. He never liked Standish, as a boy, or as a man. Rumors of his exploits on the tour were disturbing, so when Hamilton, a man who put his daughter's happiness first, swooped in, George had been relieved.

Now what was he to do? How was he supposed to feel?

George decided to speak to him. He had things to say, things to learn before he made any final decisions. In return, he would listen to MacGregor's defense. For Sina, he had to at least listen.

His little girl had grown into a bold, beautiful lady. She had done so without him. He wanted to make that up to her. She seemed happy, and MacGregor was the one responsible.

But could he, in good conscience, hand over his only child born from love to an outlawed Highland clan?

He called for his servants. He wanted to be dressed and on his way out as soon as possible.

He thought about stopping to speak to Sina first, but the sun was barely up. He'd let her sleep.

"Newgate prison," he told the carriage driver and stepped inside.

On the way there, he wondered what the rest of the Mac-

Gregors were like. Anne had trusted them. Was it simply because there was a Stuart among them? Or was it something more? General Marlow left his service to the queen and became one of them! His daughter defended them, calling them kind and loving.

As his carriage rolled into the front courtyard of Newgate, he wondered why the queen had never told him about Claire Stuart. As far as he could find out, she was married to a Grant—not a MacGregor.

The prison was filthier than his stomach could bear at first, but at least MacGregor hadn't been taken below stairs where the stench was worse.

A guard led him to a shadowy cell at the end of a long, dark corridor.

"Let me inside," the king commanded. The guard took out his keys without question, but cast the king a curious look.

"Do you want me to come inside with you?" the guard asked.

George looked him over and almost laughed out loud. The scrawny, grimy guard was no match for MacGregor if the Highlander sought to hurt them.

"No. Stay here," George ordered and waited while the guard pulled open the door. He looked inside the cell, dimly lit with a small torch and a single candle. When MacGregor saw him, he stood up from a small stool where he'd been sitting.

The door shut behind George with a resonating clang that made his heart thump harder.

The Highlander appeared even bigger in such a small space. "MacGregor."

"Aye," he answered with a tilt to his chin.

He looked more like a Highlander now, with his raven

hair coming loose from his ribbon and his cravat tossed to the floor.

"You deceived me."

"Nae," MacGregor argued and then offered him the stool. "I wanted ye to know me withoot the preconceptions that come with my name."

The king refused the stool and eyed him. "You're telling me the man I came to know is the real you?"

"Aye."

"Then tell me the truth," the king said. "Why did you come to London? Are you here on behalf of Claire Stuart?"

"Claire...," MacGregor repeated with a confused look. "I came fer Sina. She stole my heart before I even knew it was happening. She was forced to marry me by the queen's order, and she fought back." He smiled, as if remembering. "I accepted her into my life to save my clan but she ended up saving me."

George listened. He liked what he was hearing, so far. "You must understand, I've heard some stories."

"Ye havena heard them all," MacGregor replied with the torchlight shining in his gaze like lightning-tipped arrows.

"I would like to," the king admitted. "But for now, let's discuss your family's ties to Anne."

"Is there a purpose to all this?" MacGregor asked him, not flinching when a rodent scurried past.

"Yes, there is."

"Then can we do it somewhere else?"

George knew the prison wasn't properly tended to, but he had no idea it was this bad. He didn't want to remain another second, but he didn't want to release MacGregor just yet.

"Where is the king?" he heard a woman shout in the corridor. "I have urgent news! Bring me to the king at once!"

Poppy Berkham, Sina's spirited friend. Sina!

The king pulled open the door and called to her, forgetting MacGregor behind him.

"Your Majesty!" she said, rushing to him. "I went to check on Sina. She was not in her apartment. When I questioned the palace guards if they'd seen her, they hadn't, but a few of them claim to have seen William Standish last night."

"I'll have them quartered for not bringing this to my attention last night!" George roared, moving to leave the cell.

"Release me," MacGregor said, stopping him. "I'll find her. I'll bring her back."

The king stared at him for a moment and then nodded and tried to keep up with him.

Chapter Forty

Sina opened her eyes. It took her a moment to realize where she was, whom she was with.

He'd struck her. She would never forgive him. Never.

She sat up and rubbed her sore jaw. She felt something cold and wet touch her cheek and threw her arms around Goliath. His mouth was still tied shut and there was another rope tied around his neck, securing him to the wall.

Waves of memories flooded her thoughts. Adam...Adam was in prison, arrested by her father for being a MacGregor.

William had nearly killed Goliath and—

"Ah, just in time to eat," William said, smiling as he came closer carrying two bowls in his hands.

Goliath leaped forward, growling from deep within. He clawed at his nose when he tried to open his mouth to bite. William laughed and stepped closer. When the valiant dog moved in front of her, she pushed him back, unsure of what William was capable of.

"When did you become what you hated most, William? You lord yourself over a dog that is helpless to fight back."

William's laughter faded to a smirk. "Tying its muzzle was a wise decision, dear one. Not a foolish one."

"Well, it needs to come off so he can eat," she demanded.

William pouted and shook his head. "There's only enough for you."

"He can have mine. I'm untying him." She reached around his head, but William drawing his pistol stopped her.

"All right." His sinuous smile returned. "If you want the dog to have the food, then you may loosen the rope enough to squeeze your fingers between its fangs and feed it."

Bastard, Sina cursed him. He knew of her terrible fear of dogs. He wanted to enjoy this. But he didn't know she had changed. And he didn't know Goliath.

She continued to loosen the thick knots beneath his furry chin, giving him room to open his mouth to eat.

"That's enough, Sina," William commanded, waving his pistol around. "Feed it. You're trying my patience."

"If you want to see me possibly get bitten"—Sina boldly defied him and continued loosening the ropes—"his mouth needs to open a little more."

"You think very low of me if you think that's what I want." His smile belied his cold gaze.

She snatched the small bowl from his hand. Inside were a few slices of venison, some turnips, and bread. "Where did you get it?" she asked. "You didn't get inside the palace again, did you?"

"No. Catherine, my dear cousin, just delivered it. She is also the one who found your letter and that stem of heather. Did he pick it for you? Was it before or after your letter to me?"

"Ah, Catherine, of course," she muttered, ignoring his questions. Helping to kidnap the king's daughter wasn't going to go over well with *her* father.

She broke up small pieces of meat and held her fingers up to Goliath's mouth. For a moment, her heart thrashed wildly in her chest, but Adam's faithful hound would never hurt her. He pushed out his tongue to lick her fingers and then gently ate from them.

Sina watched him while her heart swelled with love. Goliath had been a difficult adversary, but he was worth the fight.

"I've indulged you long enough, Sina."

Everything she felt for the dog faded from her expression when she turned to look at William. "And I've indulged you by not ripping out your eyes for doing this."

"You always were so spirited," he said, admiring her with a soft smile.

"How long do you think you can keep us here?"

"Not much longer, I'm afraid." He looked at the pistol in his hand. "There are some things I wish to tell you first. You are my best friend. I must confess, and you are the only one I trust."

He told her about the things he'd learned abroad, depraved, sexual things that men paid to do to women.

"I found that I enjoyed inflicting pain on women during sex." She would never forget him saying it. "It opened up a whole new world to me. One of power. For the first time in my life, I was in control."

"You feel in control when you're hurting a woman?" she asked with seething disgust. How could she have loved this creature?

"'Tis temporary pain and many of them enjoy it."

"And the rest?"

"The rest were paid well," he said woodenly, boosting her disgust.

"And I denied a man I promised myself to before God because of you."

"I didn't give my heart to any of them, Sina. It belongs to you and you alone."

"I don't want it!" she shouted at him. "You are the one who should be in prison!"

"I am not the one who deceived the king," he retorted. "How can you defend a MacGregor? They are the scourge of Scotland, the lowest form of human being there is."

Goliath growled. Sina looked up to find that he had scratched off the loosened rope from his muzzle and was showing William his long, glistening white fangs.

She heard the click of William's pistol being locked. She looked at him. The pistol was pointed at Goliath.

"There is no more need for the hellhound."

"No!" Sina screamed and threw herself on Goliath.

She heard the rush of feet and looked up in time to see Adam running toward her. Was she dreaming? Had William shot her?

She watched, horrified, as William turned the pistol on him. He fired and missed. Adam never stopped coming at him. Goliath was going wild trying to get loose as Adam reached William and smacked the pistol out of his hand, punched him in the mouth, and tossed Sina a dagger in one fluid motion.

"Cut Goliath loose," he said.

"Don't kill him," she whispered to Goliath and cut him loose. He bounded forward and clamped his teeth around William's leg at the same time Adam reached her and took her in his arms.

"What are you doing here?" she asked, still unable to believe he was here. Had he escaped?

"I'll explain everything later. Are ye hurt, lass?"

"No," she told him and then went still as her mother,

the king, and his guards arrived. Would they arrest Adam again?

She let out a breath she'd been holding and relaxed as her father's men bypassed him and went to William.

Adam told Goliath to let go of William's bloody leg and waited while the guards dragged William to his knees.

"He was aboot to shoot her," Adam told her father while her mother drew her in for a tight, tearful embrace.

"Bring him straight to Newgate!" her father commanded.

"His cousin Catherine helped him," Sina informed them. "She is the one who stole my letter."

"Find and arrest Miss Newton," the king ordered.

He took her in his arms next. "Your mother and I are thankful for your life, daughter."

"Adam saved me."

"I know," he whispered into her hair. "I made the correct decision to release him, then."

Sina pulled back from their embrace and stared at him first, and then at Adam. When he smiled and nodded, she threw her arms around her father again and kissed his cheek. "Thank you. You have made me very happy."

"We still have things to discuss, MacGregor," her father said as she broke free and ran into Adam's arms. "Freshen up, the both of you. I will see you in my quarters in an hour."

"Two," Adam called over his shoulder as the king and her mother set off for the stairs.

Her father didn't answer, but she thought she heard him grumble something. She smiled and looked up into her husband's silvery-blue gaze, eclipsed by strands of ebony hair. "He released you."

He quirked one side of his mouth. "I told ye he would."

She loved his confidence. It shone like a radiant light

in him and drew others like moths to a flame. It had drawn her out of her anger, her loneliness, and into the marvelous light of living her life with passion. "You'll tell me how you did it."

"Aye."

"But first—"

His smile went soft and warm. "Aye, first..."

Sina lay naked, sprawled out over Adam's hard, glistening planes. Their breathing came shallow and fast after separating. He ran his hand down the column of her back while she kissed his chest.

"I never thought anything could feel so good," she purred against him.

"I'm glad you like it." His voice came from deep in his chest, a rumble that set her blood to sizzling.

She leaned up on her palms and gazed down at him, heavy-lidded and slightly disheveled. How was it possible to love someone as much as she loved him? She asked him, but he had no answer, for her or for himself.

"When I saw him pointin' that pistol at ye and Goliath, I think I went a bit mad," he told her, running his fingers over a golden curl falling to her cheek. "I wanted to kill him, but I couldn't do it in front of ye. I know what he was to ye."

He was correct. No matter what William had done, she wouldn't want to see that. "You are kind and thoughtful, Adam." She kissed his chin, his lower lip. "You are honorable and brave. And so very romantic."

He smiled slyly and pulled her on top of him. "I'm no' well practiced in romance, lass."

"Even better," she whispered, straddling him. "What you do is genuine, and that makes it even more romantic."

He laughed softly, filling her with warmth. She rubbed herself against him. He was hard enough to take her.

Pressing her breasts to his chest, she snaked up his body and kissed his neck.

When he cupped her buttocks in his hands, she let him guide her over him. She sank down on him, pushing him deeper inside of her. When she took him to the hilt, she sat up and gazed down at the man beneath her. She moved her hips, gyrating over him, and lifted her arms over her head.

He sat up, bending to her, and closed his arms around her waist, holding her close as they moved to passion's ancient song.

"I want to marry ye again, lass," he whispered across her throat as she arched her back and he leaned forward. "The right way this time."

She clutched his shoulders and rode him, up and down, faster, deeper.

"I want to make all yer days happy—and if they are no' always happy, they willna be dull."

They laughed together, finding their cherished freedom in each other's arms.

Epilogue

Sina held her baby daughter, Anne, after eleven hours of birthing pains. She admired her babe, swaddled in a striped wool cloth. Her tuft of raven hair and her tiny lips moving slightly as she slept made Sina smile.

She lifted her face to the women around her, to the ones who had helped her through it, who wiped her brow, held her hand and her legs apart. They were her sisters, and her mothers. Her kin. She loved them all.

She leaned her head back into the crook of her husband's shoulder and trembled a little at the memory of him being here throughout. He'd burst into the chamber after a loud cry from Sina and refused to leave. Even when Aunt Maggie complained that it wasn't a place for men, he strode past the gaping women and planted himself behind Sina's head and encouraged her.

She loved him most of all.

"She looks like ye," he said at her ear, sounding as awestruck as she felt.

"No, she looks like you." She closed her eyes and pressed her cheek to his jaw.

"May we hold her now, Sina?" Violet asked impatiently.

Sina didn't want to hand Anne over to anyone, but she remembered Laurel being passed around after her birth. Holding her bonded the women to the babe.

She offered her daughter to them, glad that Anne would have so many loving women in her life. She caught her mother's eye and smiled, thankful that her parents had traveled here from London to see her. And it wasn't the first time. In the past nine months, they'd been here three times. The MacGregors had the king's favor.

"Chief, d'ye want to hold yer daughter?" someone asked.

Adam came around the side of the bed and sat at the edge and waited for them to hand her to him. His large hands, so deft at everything else, seemed awkward, but only for a moment. With a quick adjustment to his wrist, he looked more at ease.

"Ye will always have my love and devotion," he promised his daughter on a soft, shaking voice. "And I will always love and adore yer mother and strive to make her happy."

"You do." Sina touched her fingers over his hair when he leaned in to press a kiss to their daughter's head.

He looked up, catching her hand in his and bringing it to his lips. "Let this be the first of many."

"Perhaps this isn't the best time to bring up having more," she told him, smiling.

He laughed and held up their daughter. "Aye, she is enough. Fer now." He grew serious again. "Ye've made me a faither, Sina. I'm proud that my name will live on through our love."

They kissed and barely noticed Maggie lingering about them until she spoke up, grinning as she passed them. "We're MacGregors, despite them."

Temperance Menzie is starting to fall for the mysterious, wounded Highlander she's been nursing back to health. But Cailean Grant has a dark secret, and only a Christmas miracle can keep them together.

See the next page for an excerpt from *A Highlander's Christmas Kiss*.

GLEN LYON, SCOTLAND

WINTER 1711

Chapter One

"Need a room fer the night, sir? A bed?"

"Nae."

"A warm bath then, mayhap, to shed ye of the dust of travelin'?"

Cailean Grant looked down from his horse and cast a scathing glance at the lad about to reach for his reins. "I said nae."

The boy swallowed and jumped out of the way of the three riders following him. Cailean didn't look back at the child and he didn't seek forgiveness for not caring. It didn't matter what the circumstances were. He kept people out. For his own good, not theirs.

"Ye should take the bath," Patrick MacGregor said, catching up. "It might do ye some good to have the cockles of yer heart warmed."

Cailean didn't acknowledge his cousin's good-natured suggestion but kept his eyes on the icy road before them. He liked his cockles the way they were. Cold. Empty. Safe.

"I think the boy shite his breeches," Erik Mac-

Cormack laughed from his saddle behind them, then kicked another lad out of his way.

"What?" He chuckled again when Patrick glowered at him. "The waifs will likely rob us the moment we remove our purses."

"They'd be disappointed by yours, Erik," said Erik's brother, Dougal, riding at his left.

Patrick moved his horse closer to Cailean's. "These are the men ye chose over yer kin?" He shook his head at him. "Men who kick children oot of their way?"

Cailean glanced over his shoulder at the brothers, who had arrived at Lyon's Ridge a fortnight ago to join Lord Murdoch's band of mercenaries, the Black Riders. "They've been hardened by their pasts," Cailean told him, turning back to the road. "What d'ye expect from them, courtly manners?"

"Ye dinna belong with them, Cailean. Let's go back home."

It was a conversation they'd had often. Cailean didn't want to go home and Patrick wouldn't leave without him. "I do belong with them, Patrick," he said, and turned away to spread his gaze over the packhorses ambling through the market, laden with grain and other wares and led by peasants from the local farms.

He'd come to Kenmore to purchase some fresh vegetables in the hopes of eating something other than the shite served by the cook at Lyon's Ridge Castle. If he had to consume another moldy carrot he was going to kill someone. He missed eating at Camlochlin. He missed home. But he couldn't go back. After Sage...and Alison, he had changed too much to go back.

He didn't mind Patrick's traveling with him to the marketplace. Patrick's easy nature and constant reassuring smiles had a way of making everything seem trivial, save for Cailean's decision to join Lord Edward Murdoch's Riders. Patrick didn't approve of thugs for hire, but Cailean was where he needed to be—with men who didn't care about love or dancing around with their words—or anything else. They left him alone for the most part, save for when Patrick was around. Patrick was well liked by everyone who knew him.

Cailean had been like him once, smiling at life and wreaking havoc on village lasses. But that part was gone.

Living at Lyon's Ridge helped him forget the crushing weight of what he'd lost—what his cousins back home had: bonny wives in their arms and loyal hounds at their feet. He'd wanted the same. He'd lost it, and with it his confidence that no cataclysmic tragedy would ever befall him or his family. Nothing was certain. In fact, it seemed the cards were stacked against him. It had changed him into something harder, emptier, and determined to stop feeling.

He'd been surprised when he saw his reflection in a basin this morning. His physical appearance had changed since Alison died. His hair had grown long and fell down both sides of his face. It created shadows along the gaunt planes and dips of his features. He appeared as dark and hollow as he felt.

"How much do you think *she* costs?" Dougal asked, eyeing a merchant's daughter while she beat a blanket outside a cutlery shop with a painted sign depicting crisscrossed knives.

"To hell with the lass," said Erik, called the Red by the other Riders, due to his red hair and Viking heritage. "My belly grumbles. I want to eat!"

Erik and Dougal MacCormack were two of the twenty Black Riders in Lord Murdoch's employ. Both of them combined couldn't muster up the compassion or courtesy of an angry ogre.

But Cailean didn't mind them, since he was the ogre.

They came to a shop with a barrel on a pole and stopped for a cup of ale.

"Go on inside," Cailean told them, dismounting. "I want to purchase a few things. I'll catch up with ye all later."

He left them to wet their tongues and headed off toward the tightly packed vendors selling everything from onions to surgical procedures.

Pulling his fur cloak tighter around him, he looked up from beneath his hood at the useless sun caught between billowing dark clouds, and grumbled. The sun offered him no warmth, the clouds reminding him of his life, gray and ominous.

He spotted a vendor selling apples and went to have a look. It wasn't unusual that a lass caught his eye. He was still a man, after all, even though he hadn't partaken of the pleasures offered to him by any of the gels at the castle.

This lass, though...this lass parted the clouds.

She strolled out of a nearby fabric shop, dressed in pale layers of soft cream-colored wool. Her face was half-hidden beneath a matching hood, her wrist was looped through the handle of a basket, and a sweetly content smile was on her lips.

What was she so happy about out here in the cold mud and the reeking stench of sewage on the wind? And why did she draw him like a moth to a flame? He moved behind the vendor's tent, his curious eyes fixed on her while she pushed back her hood and bent to feed a piece of bread to a stray dog.

Something in Cailean's chest softened just a little at her gesture.

Eyes painted in vivid hues of blue and wreathed in lush, inky lashes danced across the faces of the folks she greeted when she lifted her head. Hell, the sight of her and the way the sun illuminated a hundred different shades in her flowing mahogany hair buckled his knees a little.

"She's bonny."

Cailean turned to Patrick biting into an apple, his cousin's glimmering green eyes on her. "Let's go greet her."

Cailean stopped him from leaving with a hand on his arm. "Nae, I'm no'—"

"—As devilishly attractive as I am?" Patrick's grin was wide and playful. "Dinna let it get ye doun, Cousin. Few men are."

Cailean cast him a cool glance. "Why are ye no' drownin' yerself in ale with the others?"

He paid for Patrick's apple and bought a bag for himself.

"And listen to their God-awful conversations aboot their lack of basic hygiene? I can only find so much humor in mindless chatter. I'm no' a saint, ye know."

"Farthest thing from it," Cailean agreed, then fastened his eyes on the lass again.

"Who is she?"

Cailean closed his eyes when he heard Dougal's voice behind him next. "Now's there's a rump I'd like to shove my—"

Cailean's fist, crashing against Dougal's jaw, silenced him. He collapsed to his knees but not before Patrick had swiped the drink Dougal carried with him and saved it from falling to the ground with its original owner.

Patrick held up the cup to his cousin. "'Tis good to know ye still possess some decency." He guzzled what remained and then tossed the cup over his shoulder.

Cailean ignored him and the man knocked out cold at his

feet, and his frown deepened when he noticed the lass had gone.

After they revived Dougal with a bucket of water, they purchased more winter supplies and then met up with Erik for a few hours of drinking before heading back to the castle.

They reached the mountain pass above the River Lyon with Patrick's off-key singing to break the wintry silence. Cailean almost didn't hear the thump of the arrow piercing his cousin's chest.

This isn't happening, Cailean told himself as he kicked open the doors of Lyon's Ridge Castle. This wasn't real. Patrick hadn't just been shot by an unseen assailant. Cailean hadn't pulled him unconscious and barely breathing off his horse and onto his own.

Stepping out of the cloud of snow he'd loosened from the stones above the door, he entered and stood with his cousin and best friend hanging limp across his fur-clad shoulders.

Cailean could scarcely see through his misty eyes. "Come quickly!" he shouted through the halls, his call reaching the rest of the Black Riders in the great hall. "Quickly!" he commanded with his heart battering against his chest. He felt sick with horror, filled to the brim with sorrow. *Not him. Dinna take him!* "We must help him!"

They would. They had to. These men fought for a living. They were familiar with wounds and patching them up. They would know what to do.

"What happened?" John Gunns, a mercenary from Caithness, asked, reaching him first. Two more men appeared and carefully removed Patrick from his shoulders.

Briefly free of his cousin's dead weight, Cailean inhaled

a breath that stretched his cloak across his chest. Still his heart refused to slow its frantic pace.

He raised his trembling hands to his hood and pushed it back. Dark hair fell over his forehead and hollowed cheeks. He swiped it away from his eyes. "We were returnin' from the market in Kenmore..."

His mournful gaze fell to the arrow that rose from Patrick's chest while the men carried him to the great hall. Cailean looked away, almost overcome with the basic need to scream, to run...to fall to his knees. *God, please, don't have me watch someone else I love die. I will perish altogether. Is it not enough that hardly any part of who I was still remains?*

"Does he still breathe?" His own breath still came hard, freezing in the chilled castle air and floating before him. He hadn't wanted to ask because he wasn't sure he could accept the answer. But he had to know.

This was his fault. If he'd left his new profession as a mercenary and returned home to Camlochlin as Patrick had wanted him to do, none of this would be happening.

"He breathes," said Cutty Ross of Orkney before he swept his massive arm across the table in the center of the cavernous hall.

They laid Patrick out and began to remove his clothes. The lasses who worked at the castle helped bring the men what they needed to soak up the blood.

Cailean looked at all the blood. He felt it, still warm at the back of his neck.

He stepped back, away from the work of saving Patrick's life. His breath faltered and his hands shook at his sides. He vowed that whoever had done this would die. He would ride through every villiage like a plague no one would ever forget until he found who was responsible.

"Hell," Brodie Garrow of Ayr swore. "It'll be hard to get out."

Cailean's muscles twisted into knots. Part of him was afraid of what he would become if he lost his cousin. Patrick was more than that. He was Cailean's closest and dearest friend, the only one who'd managed to bring a little light back to his life, and with it a wee bit of his old self. He raked his fingers through his hair as that same feeling of helplessness he'd experienced twice before coursed through him. What would he tell Patrick's parents, Tristan and Isobel?

His blood sizzled in his veins. He wanted vengeance now. He flicked his gaze to the only man who had not risen from his chair to help. Duncan Murdoch, son to Lord Edward Murdoch of Glen Lyon.

"Ye know this land and the people on it. Who could have done this?"

Duncan grinned. Cailean wanted to punch his teeth out. The lord's son was a jealous, squeaking twit who'd hated Cailean a day after he'd come here, when his father, Edward, first began praising the Highlander for battle skills superior to his son's. Their dislike for one another had grown after Cailean began visiting the lord's solar for long, quiet games of chess. His son, Murdoch had told him, had never been able to learn the game. Despite Cailean's brooding nature, the lord of Glen Lyon was fond of him. Still, he wouldn't take kindly to Cailean's killing Duncan. Presently Cailean didn't give a damn.

"If ye dinna answer me," he warned, his voice deep and taut, his eyes glimmering behind strands of dark chestnut, "I'll be standin' over yer chair before anyone can stop me, includin' ye, and I'll see to it that ye never speak again."

Cutty may have heard him because he stopped working

and turned to look at him, as did Tavish Innes of Roxburgh. What would the other mercenaries do? Cailean wondered. Would Cutty try to kill him if he went after Duncan? Cailean had given his allegiance to Edward Murdoch, not his son. He'd come here to escape the memory of a life filled with expectations. He was paid to fight and protect Murdoch's land. Not to give a damn about the men who fought with him. But today he needed them to help Patrick.

"Where did the shooting occur?" Duncan asked him with an irritated sigh.

"The arrow was fired from the direction of Fortingall. That's all I know."

"The Menzies," Lord Murdoch's son told him, his smile returning, this time with a curl more sinister than mocking.

The Menzies. The lord's tenants in Linavar. Decades-long enemies of the MacGregors and Grants. The closest villagers to the mountain pass.

Immediately Cailean's heart turned hard toward them. "Why would they try to kill innocent men?"

"Because, Grant"—Duncan sneered as if Cailean were too dense to figure it out—"all they know in these parts is us, the Black Riders. They hate us."

"They dinna know who we are," Cailean argued. He wanted to be sure before he took his vengeance. "We were no' wearin' our coverin'. Why would they think we were Black Riders?"

"Do you want to conduct an investigation or do you want justice, Grant?"

Cailean didn't like him. At all.

"I want justice."

Murdoch's smile widened. He liked trouble. He also liked wine and women—one in particular. Cailean had never asked her name. He didn't care what it was. He felt pity for her to have such an admirer. Nothing more.

"When do you want to leave?" Duncan asked.

"As soon as Patrick is stable."

Murdoch laughed at him. "Your sentiments make you weak."

Cailean dipped his head and glared at Duncan from beneath the shadows of his raven lashes. "Come with me to the practice field and let me prove ye incorrect." One corner of his mouth curled in a cold sneer. "Yer faither will likely thank me."

"I'll kill you for that, Grant," Duncan promised. "But not tonight. It'll be dark out soon thanks to these damn short days and I'm drunk," he added, as if his slurred words weren't proof enough. "Tomorrow perhaps."

Cailean shrugged, finished with the useless conversation. Duncan would never touch him. As much as he envied Cailean, he knew his father's admiration was fairly given. Cailean could fight with weapons or without, a dangerous man created in the misty northern mountains.

He went to stand near the table where the men worked on Patrick, but closed his eyes, still unable and unwilling to watch the outcome.

Three times he'd felt life leaving people and a dog that he loved. Two had died in his arms. He prayed Patrick would not be the third.

Sage first, a scrappy hound who had chosen him from among many better men at Camlochlin. Had she known his life would need saving one day, and that she would die for saving it?

Alison. The first lass he'd ever cared for, the one who'd stolen his heart in a brothel. He could still remember her rich russet waves tumbling over her breasts while they made love, he for the first time. Memories of her haunted him. So many things did. It was why he'd given up his passions for cooking and writing, and left Camlochlin five months ago. Why Patrick, who was perfectly content to bed wenches in the Highlands, had followed him all the way to Glen Lyon with the hopes of talking some sense into him about strong-arming defenseless people for pay.

Patrick couldn't die. How could Cailean do anything but live out the rest of his days in dreaded anticipation of the next catastrophe if he did?

"Ye look like ye'd do well to take some comfort in these."

Cailean opened his eyes and looked down at the giant, milky mounds jiggling beneath him. He lifted his gaze to the woman's equally round cheeks dabbed in crimson powder. Madam Maeve herself. The woman in charge of the lasses hired by the widowed Lord Murdoch to serve meals to and satisfy other appetites of his private guard of twenty men, including Cailean and Duncan.

"Ye look tired. Come with me to my bed. I'll help ye forget all this blood."

Forget? How could he ever forget it? "Not now, Maeve," he practically growled at her.

She pouted her ruby-red lips at him. "Beautiful Cailean," she purred, and moved closer to him. "Whatever 'tis that makes yer eyes smolder like smelted iron and yer jaw tighten like 'tis taking everything in ye not to take yer sword to all of us—whatever that is and wherever it comes from, hold on to it. Share it with me tonight."

"Another time mayhap." His voice was low, as deep as the shadows that plagued his days and nights. He hadn't taken any of her girls before. Why did she think he'd take her now when his cousin was possibly dying ten feet away?

A better question was, why did he expect anything more from the people in this damned castle? They were soulless and void of compassion. The kind of people he'd chosen to be with. That kind of man he'd become.

"Have ye met Marion?" Maeve asked, and motioned to a lass who was standing on the other side of the hall, watching what was going on and wringing her hands together.

"She's *new*...and free fer ye."

He gave Marion a slow looking-over. She had rich, russet hair like Alison's. That was likely why he decided to help her.

"Is she untouched?" he asked Maeve discreetly. When the madam nodded, Cailean reached into his cloak and pulled out a small pouch. "Let's keep her that way, aye?"

Not knowing that the smile he offered her while he looked into her eyes was as well practiced as his sword arm, Maeve agreed to anything he wanted. Of course the leather pouch filled with coin that he tossed into her hand didn't hurt.

"Dinna offer her to anyone else. In fact, bring her to Perth, to Ravenglade Castle, and after I put m'sword through my cousin's attacker, I'll see to the remainder of yer payment. Now leave me."

The madam curtsied, showing off her ample cleavage once more. "If ye change yer mind about what ye need sooner—"

He wouldn't. He didn't want comfort. He wanted blood.

Looking for more historical romance? Forever brings the heat with these sexy rogues.

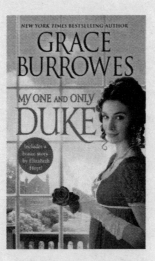

MY ONE AND ONLY DUKE
By Grace Burrowes

When London banker Quinn Wentworth is saved from execution by the news he's the long-lost heir to a dukedom, there's just one problem: He's promised to marry Jane Winston, the widowed, pregnant daughter of a prison preacher.

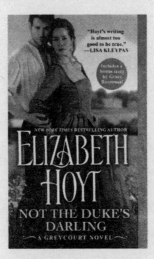

THE HIGHLAND RENEGADE
By Amy Jarecki

Famed for his fierceness, Laird Robert Grant is above all a loyal
Highland clan chief. But when redcoats capture his rival's daughter, he
sets aside their feud and races to her rescue. Aye, Janet Cameron is
beautiful, cunning, and so very tempting, but a Cameron lass is the last
woman he should ever desire.

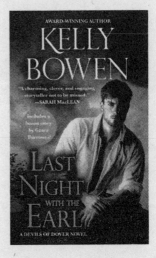

CEN

C.1